Savo

Savoy Dreams is the Second Volume in a Trilogy of Anthologies

The Savoy Book
Savoy Dreams
Savoy Swords & Sorcery

Adolf Hitler, nahezu die Verkörperung des heroischen Sturm-und-Drang, Zauber-und-Schwert-Archetypen, 1934 auf dem Bückeburger Erntedankfest, unmittelbar vor seinem an Herrn Chamberlain gerichteten berühmten Ausspruch, "Das Leben kehrt sich einen Rattenschwanz darum, wer es lebt". Bei Hitler überschneiden sich Kunst und Leben genau an den Traumpolen unserer Einbildungskraft.

SAVOY DREAMS

Edited by

David
Britton

Michael
Butterworth

Savoy

Michael Moorcock

Samuel Delany

Harlan Ellison

Henry Treece

James Cawthorn

Jack Trevor Story

John Warren

Mike Harding

Ishmael Reed

Ken Reid

Gerald Scarfe

Langdon Jones

Charles Platt

M. John Harrison

Published by Savoy, 279 Deansgate, Manchester M3 4EW, England

ISBN 0 86130 068 8 (s/c)
ISBN 0 86130 069 6 (h/c)

Design: Stuart Watson
Setting: Bryan Williamson, Todmorden, Lancashire

Printed and bound in Great Britain by The Arc & Throstle Press,
Todmorden, Lancashire

Acknowledgements

The editors would like to extend their special thanks to the
following newspapers, periodicals and television programmes
for permission to quote from articles and reviews:
Sunday Times, Observer, Daily Express,
The New York Review of Books, Die Welt, Spectator, The Sun,
Los Angeles Times, Fantasy Media, Le Mond, Locus,
Rolling Stone, Creem, London Review of Books,
San Francisco Chronicle, NASA Activities, Ludd's Mill,
Video World, Spare Rib, TV Times, Fantasy Newsletter,
Time Out, New Scientist, New Musical Express, Autocar,
Crawdaddy, The Next Big Thing, Lancashire Life,
Corriere Della Sera, Manchester Evening News,
The Comics Journal, Something Else, Chicago Tribune,
The Anarchist Review, Newsweek, HOBbIE MNPbl,
Lovebirds, The Patchin Review, 'Steranko's' Preview,
People Weekly, Stubb's Gazette, The South Bank Show,
The Bookseller, Body Politic, Record Collector.

This book is respectfully dedicated to:

Anthony Burgess, Martin Amis, Derek Jewel, Auberon Waugh,
Clive James, Peter Blake, John Fowles.

But most of all, and for always *being* Savoy

to

P. J. Proby

P.J. Proby pictured by Savoy, summer 1983, Alderley Edge, Cheshire, England.

"Every tribe thinks the other tribes are the ninnies and the twits. So you could have 12 tribes all separated by walls so they weren't able to see each other, watching the band. And each one of them would think, 'yeah, eliminate the ninnies and the twits', and the ninnies and the twits are right next door.

*"Those people (politicians) are powerless to deal with the situation because they're using outmoded techniques. We're creative people, politicians are parasitic people. They obviously deal with the **control** and **suppression** of the imagination. That is just not the arena for people of our temperament. Rock music **is** an important arena, because it is theatre and fashion and ideas and music and lifestyle and media, media of the most mass nature, the most eclectic nature. It is really wide open and anyone with the imagination can walk in and really use it."*

— **Devo...The Truth About Devo,** Savoy Editions, 1984

"'You don't read, do you, Albert?' Alice said from the pages of her book. 'I've never seen you pick up a book.'
"There are times in any marriage when the partners take secret looks at each other.
"'You can never take flight if you don't read books,' Alice said. And a moment later, unbidden: 'You never leave your perch, you never see over the roofs. The person who doesn't read has no horizons except the one under his nose'."

— Jack Trevor Story, **The Urban District Lover,** Savoy Books, 1980

"In the cool, misty hours of early morning, life in Hollywood, as in many other places, assumes a weird but enticing perspective. When the flattening glare of the sun has left, night shadows give strange and intriguing form to life, moulding it into an unreal thing, a compelling thing. The world becomes a place where lonely and frightened souls can be free and secure, having shut out the terrifying life of daytime, having left behind the fearful time when they must fit in and keep up. It is a place where misery is understood, but forgotten; where sorrow is inherent, but so commonly shared that it is accepted. It is an easier place to live, if you are afraid, or if you do not belong."

— William Bast, **Biography of James Dean,** Savoy Editions, 1984

"The writer is probably fighting a losing battle all his life, for his perception is perhaps always one jump ahead of his technique, his ability to set down the inner turmoil and its resolution."

— Henry Treece, **Notes on Vision and Perception (The Dark Island,** Savoy Books, 1980)

"As children, gaping at the Sunday 'Tarzan' page we cherished that primitive prerogative. But the six other days of institutional brainwashing ultimately prevailed. We collaborated in the shrinkage of our sweet polymorphous perversities; indeed, we even stopped gaping. As disillusioned adults, we — like (Burne) Hogarth himself around 1970 — can refresh ourselves by reminding ourselves what every child knows. Twice in our lifetime Hogarth has served us. Twice he has served himself by serving his art."

— Walter James Miller, Introduction to **Jungle Tales of Tarzan,** Watson-Guptill Publications, 1976

"It was the slightly gamy residue of the super-elegant and exotic pictures of Aubrey Beardsley. I have always considered the 1900 period as the psycho-analytical end-product of the Greco-Roman Decadence. I said to myself: Since these people will not hear of esthetics and are capable of becoming excited only over 'vital agitations', I shall show them how in the tiniest ornamental detail of an object of 1900 there is more mystery, more poetry, more eroticism, more madness, perversity, torment, pathos, grandeur, and biological depth than in their innumerable stock of truculently ugly fetishes, possessing bodies and souls of a stupidity that is simply and uniquely savage!"

— Salvador Dali

"I have life **dicked.***"*

— Ted Nugent, **The Legendary Ted Nugent,** Savoy Editions, 1982

"For the most part heroic fantasy, 'Sword & Sorcery', as it is often called, is the most degenerate kind of fantasy fiction. An indiscriminate mix of elements from ancient literature and legend, distilled from an ever more dilute epic tradition, it is imitative, crude, and rarely more than a reiteration of conventions. Predominantly adolescent in appeal, it offers escape to a world where individual will is the most important principle, and no problem is too complicated to be solved with a sword."

— Colin Greenland, **The Entropy Exhibition,** 1983

SAVOY

contents

DREAMS

contents

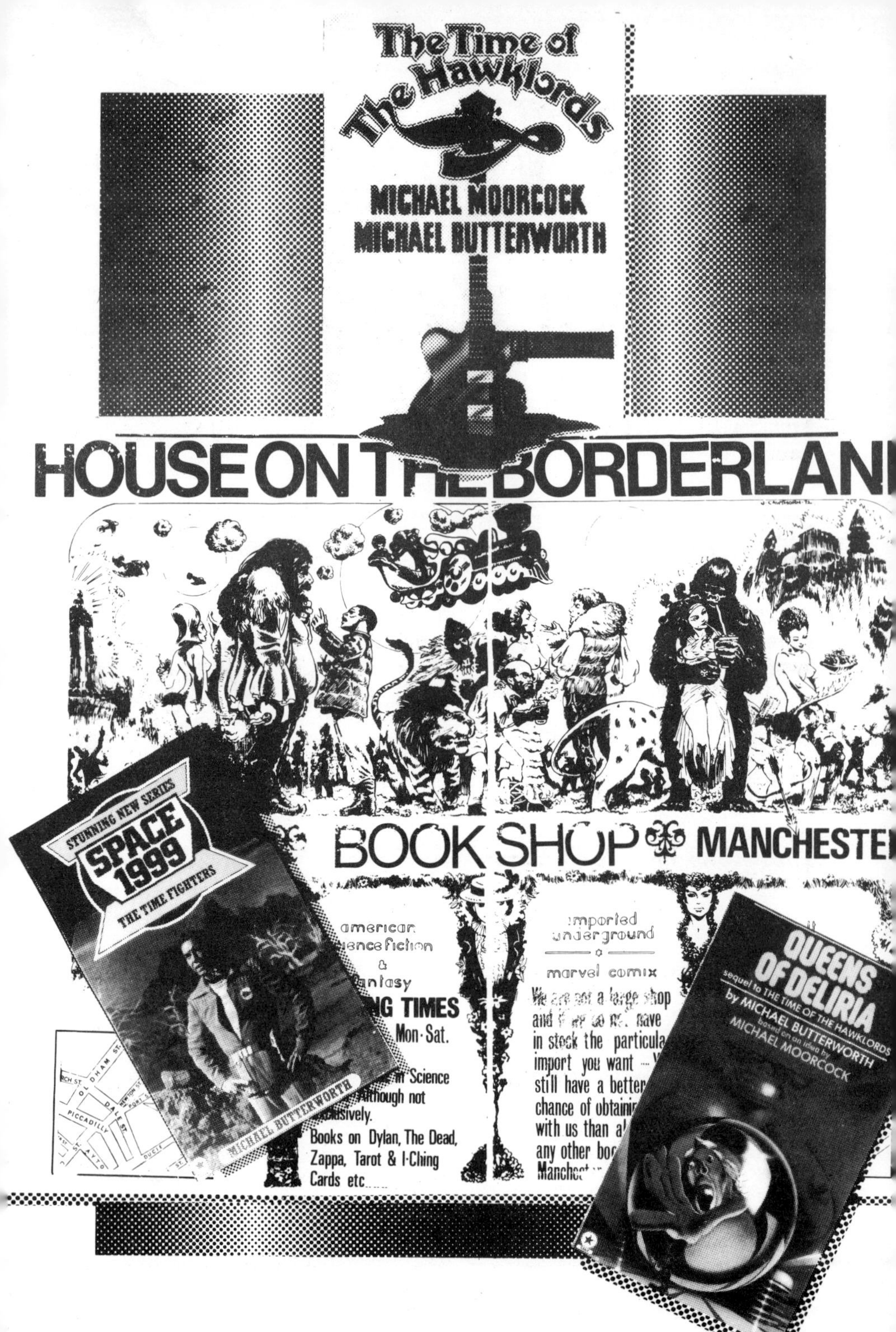
The Time of The Hawklords
MICHAEL MOORCOCK
MICHAEL BUTTERWORTH
HOUSE ON THE BORDERLAN
BOOK SHOP
MANCHESTE
STUNNING NEW SERIES
SPACE 1999
THE TIME FIGHTERS
MICHAEL BUTTERWORTH
american
science fiction
&
fantasy
NG TIMES
Mon-Sat.
Science
Although not
exclusively.
Books on Dylan, The Dead, Zappa, Tarot & I-Ching Cards etc.
imported
underground
marvel comix
We are not a large shop and if we do not have in stock the particula import you want — still have a better chance of obtaini with us than a any other bo Manchest
QUEENS OF DELIRIA
sequel to THE TIME OF THE HAWKLORDS
by MICHAEL BUTTERWORTH
based on an idea by
MICHAEL MOORCOCK
OLDHAM ST.
DALE ST.
PICCADILLY

ANDREW DARLINGTON

Ooin' that savoy shuffle

"LAUNCHED ON A SEA of sperm?" from Britton, fin de siècle fantasy-flow from each gesture.

"Too involved" from Butterworth, birther of Hawklords. "You'd have to know the connections. The sale of shrink-wrapped soft-porn that finances the project. The ratio of ejaculations necessary to finance each new title. The masturbatory fantasies that..." Manic image of Bookchain, Manchester. Britton uncoils, leaps across a detritus of badges, D.I.Y. records, magazines, paperbacks. A predatory yell riding above endless tapes pressured up high to limits of aural tolerance ("We want blood to ooze from eardrums, subliminal 4/4 rhythm staccato etched direct on cerebral vortex inducing Pavlovian twitch, impulse to consume product"). And he grabs at a customer lucked out in the act, shredding shrink-wrap for furtive despoilation of inner erotica/slipping copies of Peaches inside raincoat − tension stood out in runnels across forehead ("apprehension seen as a question of survival...").

Again, slogan for Savoy Books (you've seen their *The Golden Barge*, Michael Moorcock memorabilia package in its exquisite vid-back jacket). Direct − in *Stiff's* tradition. So far we got 'SAVOY BOOKS STOMP YOUR MIND − EFFETELY', inlain on letterheads. Add a Savoy Books logo (script raped from the cover of Lovebirds). Add product, Samuel Delany's most salaciously profound odyssey *The Tides of Lust*; Charles Platt's *The Gas*, an uncontrollable nightmare of perversion, violence and insanity; Heathcote Williams on a breathless ganja-fuelled ride to the palace of excess; Brion Gysin; Harlan Ellison's teats...

Quest dissolves, adjourns to Chinese round windy Manchester corners ("so far out to lunch he's having breakfast" − Britton). I'm walking hunched between Mike Butterworth, tall, stick-insect angular and precise, and Dave Britton, assumed air of chaotic disorganisation and free-association spiel, belied by lurking haunted artist of clean lines, exact monochrome gradations, and controlled sensual grotesquerie. The Man-

13

chester streets squirm with unclaimed noise, a patina of tactile sound, while beneath us is the Bookchain cave where M. John Harrison word-weaves fantasy novels between customers and amid reefs of It back-numbers, antique Eagles', Friendz', New Worlds and Styng. A basement that reverberates with indecent exposures of stolen sound, bootlegs sucked from hidden mikes, stacked in neat piles. Perhaps you've heard tales? The busts splurged across smug tabloids, Savoy got burned by Operation Moonbeam. Legal fingers probing the Bookchain basement gloom, sinking into viscous mounds of round black sounds – R-E-C-O-I-L-S in legislative horror, detecting oral disease that must be flushed into orderly matrix catalogues.

"It's annoying (Britton) that one gets notoriety for something as essentially trivial as selling bootlegs and gets nothing for doing Savoy, which is a hundred times more important on a creative level – still, the raid provided much amusement in the shop. Quite a few media people, Pete Shelly (Buzzcocks), Tony Wilson (Factory Records), etc, have been in to commiserate. The appearance we made in High Court – the performance of it all – was pure sinister farce." A landscape not entirely uncharted in my head. Was thirteen, trapped for shoplifting an Eddie Cochran 45, hypnotic it adhered to my fingers. Later came the Genesis P. Orridge and Styng obscenity busts.

"We were charged £7,250 costs (Butterworth)."

So is bootlegging evil? Vile? Pernicious? A bootleg can be as valuable as the published letters of Franz Kafka, as Dylan fragments, as Beefheart improvisations otherwise dissolved in air and lost. Charlie 'Bird' Parker's mythology rests to a large extent on Dean Benedetti's bootleg tapes; just as bootlegs provide credibility-index (Patti Smith allegedly producing her own as self-image fabrication components, others re-mixing live tapes for bootleggers as a product quality control exercise).

"We're basically Rock'n'Roll publishers (Britton). Most of the books we're doing are in essence nearer to Rock'n'Roll than to literature. It's a stance – Mike Moorcock is Rock'n'Roll. M. John Harrison is Rock'n'Roll. Jack Trevor Story, despite his age, is Rock'n'Roll. He stands outside the establishment, and I think we do the same." I know the symptoms. Of all the copious gifts of Western culture the only things to touch my adolescence were cheap Science Fiction and loud Rock'n'Roll. Memorising matrix numbers and chart positions instead of doing homework. The pulse of base lines that coil and snare unsuspecting feet. So now the kids sniff around Bookchain with the same hypnotic hunger. Roll over Dean Benedetti and tell Dave Britton the news.

"We were two days late making the first payment of £1000 (Butterworth). They sent the cheque back and instructed the bailiffs to move in straight away and stuck further costs on top." "Two police raids in one fortnight (Britton). They took the keys from our shop, turfed us out, and said we had until Monday lunchtime to raise the money, but we raised the money and are now back in possession of our premises and goods."

MOONBEAMED

Record companies smash big 'bootleg' syndicate

By MAUREEN KNIGHT

...AIN'S recording industry cracked a bootlegging ...dicate.

...ndercover agents working on an ...estigation code-named Operation ...onbeam have carried out raids in ...ndon, Manchester, Newcastle and ... Helens.

As a result, five men and a woman who appeared in the High Court in London yesterday gave undertakings not to deal in bootleg recordings until a full trial can be heard.

The action was taken by British Phonographic Industries Ltd., representing the record companies and artists including Bob Dylan, David Bowie and Elton John.

Bootlegging is the unauthorised recording of live performances or broadcasts—and it will cost the British record industry an estimated £20 million this year.

The artists whose works are being copied receive nothing.

Operation Moonbeam began in April with a tele-phone tip-off.

BOOTLEGGED: Bob Dylan, David Bowie, and Elton John

Inquiries led to Manchester where stocks of bootleg records were being imported from America.

One investigator posed as a manufacturer to infiltrate the network.

Suspects were trailed all over the country by BPI investigators with long-range cameras and last week they had enough evidence to get

" search and seize " orders from a court to authorise the raids.

The searches were carried out on Monday.

In the High Court yesterday were a representative of Rough Trade Records, of Notting Hill, London; Mr. Michael Jones, of Clegg Street, Manchester; Mr. John Miller, of Mu...

Avenue, Eccleston, St. Helens; Mr. David Daniels, of Beatson Walk, Ancoats, Manchester; Mr. David Edward Britton, trading as Bookchain, of Peter Street, Manchester; and Ann Bentley, of Selby Street, Beswick, Manchester. They all gave Mr Justice Vinelott undertakings not to make, sell or offer for

sale any "bootleg" recordings.

Mr Britton agreed to submit to a permanent injunction and said he would pay BPI £7,250 for damages and costs.

A further undertaking was given by Mr Michael Corrie, of Oak Road, Withington, Manchester, who promised not to infringe EMI's copyright by pirating.

The judge continued anti-bootlegging injunctions against Mr David Grant, of Gainsborough Terrace, Newcastle, and Mr David Hattam, of Whorlton Grange, Westerhope, New-castle.

None of the defendants made any admission of bootlegging or piracy or copying an existing record and duplicating it for sale.

HIGH COURT   QUEENS BENCH DIVISION
David Robert Jones and Susan Ballion and Others -v- David Edward Britton (trading as Bookchain).

A JUDGEMENT HAS BEEN GIVEN AGAINST YOU AND THE SUM OF £ 8086·01 SHOULD BE PAID TO ME FORTHWITH OR YOUR GOODS WILL BE LIABLE TO SEIZURE WITHOUT FURTHER NOTICE.

Kodachrome SLIDE

Kodak

PROCESSED BY KODAK

Though I think I know what to make of *Socialist Worker*, I have no idea at all what to think about *Crucified Toad*. No, I kid you not. It really is called that. It is edited by, the contents are the copyright of, and its pages are largely filled by the drawings of, one David Britton. The copy I have contains an article on Mervyn Peake's fascinating novel *Titus Groan*, which I could understand (although I wonder why the author didn't mention anywhere that *Titus* is part of a trilogy. Perhaps he hadn't read the other two). It also contained several more articles that I couldn't. The typography is the sort to make you ring up your optician at once, and Mr. Britton's drawings are the sort to make you ring up your psychiatrist. He draws in a sub-Beardsley style and is fond of ladies with their heads wrenched off, while those who have retained their heads are keen on wearing breathing apparatus. And in such an atmosphere, who can blame them? The titles of Mr. Britton's pictures are intriguing: *Golden Showers*, *Low Napalm Novena*, *The Particular Baptist Church*, *Jockamo's Dilemma Part One*, *Wreck a Pum Pum*, *Three Kinds of Air*.

This last is, of course, made up of two pictures, not three. Well, I don't blame Mr. Britton. He had to call them something. The subtitle of *Crucified Toad*, by the way, is "The Journal of Adult Fantasy; Incorporating *Rubber News*."

I do not know what *Spare Rib* would make of all those ladies with their heads torn off while other parts of their bodies are being dealt with in most extraordinary ways. *Spare Rib*, I had ...ly Women's Lib monthly, so stro...

Text: Bill Grundy,
Punch, January 8 1975

"It's all in a day's work." In fact Bookchain has also been raided thirteen times in the last two years resulting in seizure and destruction of 'obscene literature' of the kind freely available from W.H. Smith. "If there's enough determination, and if there's enough skin left on your body for another flaying, we will survive" — from Britton.

Savoy Books lineage traces back to Concentrate, a magazine-venture that crawled out from under the legendary New Worlds journal of experimental writing (circa mid-'60's). Directed by Butterworth — impatient for change and literary revolution — it ran three issues of great shovelfulls of manic prose. It was followed by the potently consciousness-expanding Corridor/Wordworks, a seven issue Manchester magazine, an object lesson in what could be achieved with limited finance, but unlimited energy, and editorial inventiveness. Britton, fresh out of producing Crucified Toad, infiltrating its pages with intricate drawings. Elements of Beardsley's euphoric pornographic art colliding with Magritte-complex mind-game landscapes of ludicrous and bizarre juxtaposition, all enacted across in-the-head Victorian drawing rooms.

"Dave alone is responsible for Savoy's tremendous visual packaging (Butterworth)." Britton claiming "no unifying structure" beyond the fact that most of those published by the financially precarious Savoy "were heroes of our formative years. The whole enterprise is very indulgent at core. Its saving is that possibly a number of neglected artists/authors will have the chance to reach a new and hopefully responsive audience." Henry Treece books, raunchy novels exploring Celtic/Arthurian myth like no historical fiction before or since. Much of Moorcock's Elric stuff has Treece ancestry. And the timeless Ken Reid 'Fudge' books originally run in the Manchester Evening News, as early as the '30's, charming pre-Tolkien fantasies now distributed for Savoy by Big O; plus ground-breaking works by newer iconoclastic writers of the S.F. 'New Wave' school, Ellison, Moorcock, Philip José Farmer, plus a possible William Burroughs, all stylishly packaged (style is important). Integrity? "Something you can do without getting your balls cut off" from Butterworth.

Manchester bus terminal, beneath a mile of concrete, air trapped into eddies of stale exhalation. Me and Butterworth slide between patterned vinyl tables like staggered oblique chessboards. In this cathedral of stressed ferro-crete labyrinths people wait for buses that never come. Like conventional wisdoms of creative wastelands, experimental impasses, economic impossibilities, and the drying up of ineptly pathetic media-hyped abilities, this place is shot full of one-way streets and no-exit signs. Could this be where it all leads, with no way out? Oh Mama can this really be the end? First came across Butterworth in New Worlds, a brilliant cut-up piece called *"Disintegration"*. Later he was in Ambit, d'Fontaine for the soft-core Blade. He wrote the Hawklord novels with Moorcock (now fattened into a trilogy and sold to the Japs), and fleshed the dire Space 1999 scripts into the TV-series novel-length merchandising spin-offs. He can write. Try his *Treaty of Light* in the recently

LOCUS

THE NEWSPAPER OF THE SCIENCE FICTION FIELD

Issue #243 Vol. 14,

Ar

Savoy Bankruptcy

Savoy Books Ltd., British publishers of *science* *serie* and fringe science fiction, has gone into liquidation with debts totalling at least £250,000. Savoy was originally formed with the aim of perpetuating the radical spirit of *New Worlds* magazine, and published authors such as Michael Moorcock, Edward Bryant, Samuel R. Delany, Charles Platt, M. John Harrison, and Langdon Jones. Initial capital was raised by running bookstores and other retail businesses in Manchester, England. Subsequently a deal was made with New English Library, which agreed to distribute all the Savoy titles and provided additional funding. Savoy's co-founders and directors,

Michael Butterworth and David Britton, had no prior experience of book publishing and suffered production problems from the start. Many titles appeared months late, or did not appear at all. However, advances paid to authors were generous by British standards.

The end came when it became obvious that New English Library simply was not selling the books. Some titles sold fewer than 500 copies. Already plagued by other financial problems, Savoy became unable to pay authors and printers, came unable to pay authors and printers, Bankruptcy was declared early in 1981. Several books have been left in limbo. About 2,000 copies of WHO WRITES SCIENCE FICTION? by Charles Platt (titled DREAM MAKERS in the U.S.) were distributed by New English Library before Savoy ceased operations.

There is equal uncertainty about Delany's THE TIDES OF LUST and Platt's THE GAS. Savoy reissued these two sexually explicit Essex House titles in 1980. But British distributors and retailers almost unanimously refused to handle such "pornographic" material, and the Savoy offices were raided by Manchester police who seized about 2,000 copies of each title, apparently under an order from the Director of Public Prosecutions. There has been no legal follow-up to this seizure, however. Presumably the remaining stocks of each book still exist, but Britton and Butterworth refuse to comment.

Despite the bankruptcy of Savoy Books, Butterworth and Britton are undaunted. They have formed a new company, Savoy Editions, and will operate for the time being as book packagers and designers. They plan to start an American operation and have been reported as naming Charles Platt as their US representative. Platt, however, says he has not made any such agreement with them and does not plan to do so, now or in the future. "*The writing must be sincere with no at-*

Paperback Collecting E

Science fiction paperbacks are among those most wanted by collectors, according to Kevin Hancer in the PAPERBACK PRICE GU_ (Harmony, 1980). Jack Vance's THE DYI___ _ (Hillman #41) is worth up to ___ ___ TARZAN IN THE FORBIDDEN CITY __ ___roughs (Bantam #23) __ ___NCING SANDWICHES (De___ __ ___tte by sf au___ ___ for $50. Th___ ___ is r___

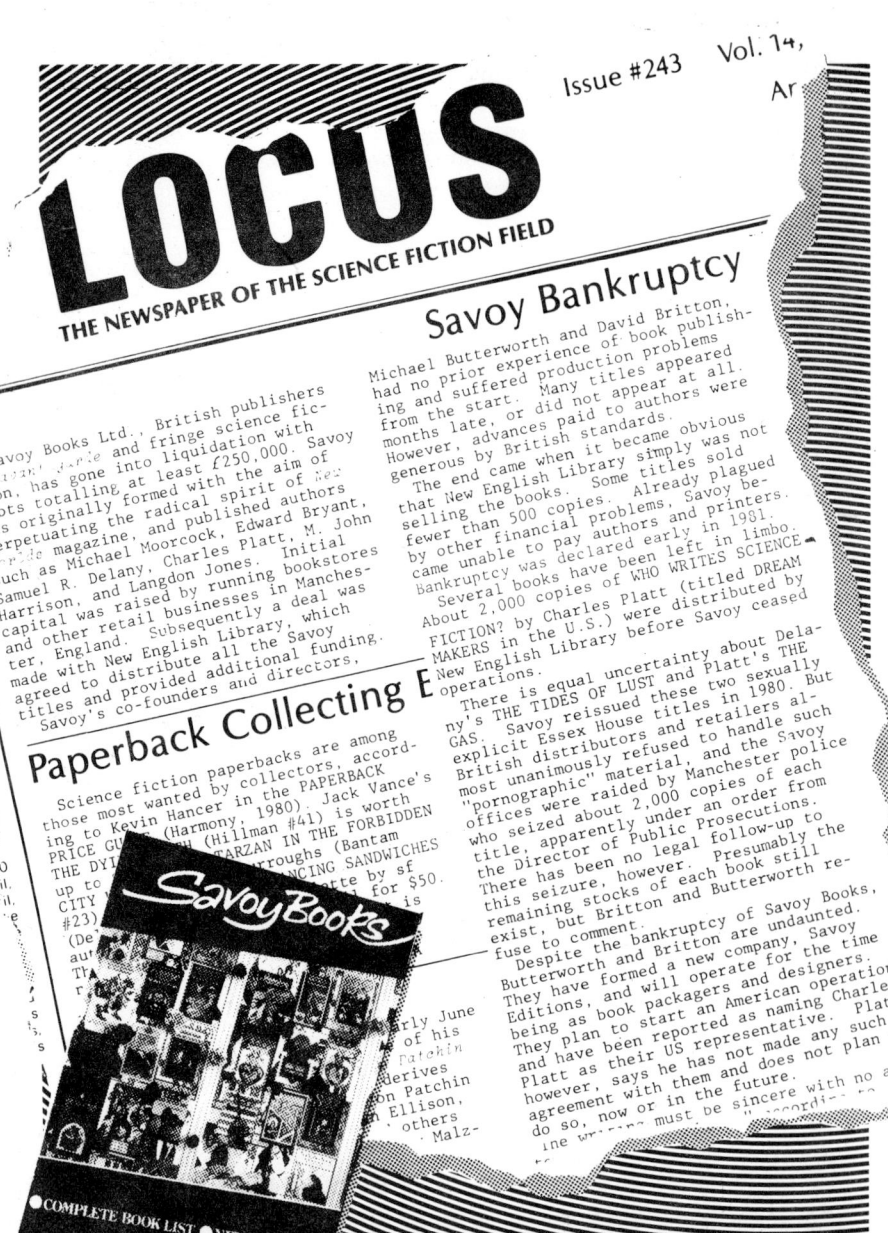

Savoy Books

● COMPLETE BOOK LIST ● NEW RELEASES

1980

rly June
of his
Patchin
derives
on Patchin
n Ellison,
others
Malz-

Specialty Publishers and Magazines

Savoy Books continue to try and bring overlooked books to the public against all odds. As co-director Michael Butterworth recently commented, "We are having to do a lot of rubbish in 1981 in order to keep the money coming in to support the good books; the 'rubbish' includes romance, cookery books and soft porn, so collectors of Savoy books B E W A R E !!"

Their offices were raided by the Manchester Police on October 17th. 2,000 copies of Charles Platt's *The Gas* and 3,000 of Samuel Delany's *The Tides of Lust* were seized (the latter title had also been seized from John Menzies bookstore in Bristol earlier this month).

It seems ironic therefore that the same publishers should issue two children's annuals for Christmas *Fudge and the Dragon* and *Fudge in Bubbleville*, both written and illustrated by Ken Reid. These are reprints of the annuals originally published in 1948 and 1949

and previously serialised in the *Manchester Evening News* a few years earlier. What will interest the collector far more than the younger readers are the new items at the end of each volume. The first includes an interview with Ken Reid by David Britton, and the second carries a complete bibliography of the many Fudge comic-strip and annuals, compiled by David Britton and David McCulloch.

New books lined up for 1981 include *Who Writes Science Fiction?* (Jan:£1.75) a series of thirty interviews by Charles Platt, *The Committed Man* by M. John Harrison (Feb) and *Sweet Evil* by Charles Platt (Mar). Moorcock's *The Brothel on Rosenstrasse* is currently scheduled for June along with the study of Moorcock's works *The Cruel World and Its Pierrot* by John Clute.

The following release from Virgin Books gives notice of a market or material for a forthcoming anthology of all-original

Virgin — Josephine Saxton's publisher — is a new publishing house: the latest offshoot f... usiness con-

---

GORDON LARKIN'S LONDON REPORT

SAVOY BOOKS RAIDED BY POLICE

Savoy Books of Manchester were raided in mid-November by police who seized 2,000 copies of Charles Platt's *The Gas* and 2,000 copies of Samuel Delany's *The Tides of Lust*. No mention or production yet. Savoy are continuing what they call their "over-the-top" series with Charles Platt's *Sweet Evil*, and in mid-1981, Michael Fleisher's *Chasing Hairy*.

New releases from Savoy include *Who Writes Science Fiction?* by Charles Platt. This edition is larger than the Berkley one and includes an additional interview with Ben Bova). M. John Harrison has delivered the manuscript of *Inviolcnium* (the third in the series that began with *The Pastel City* and *A Storm of Wings*) and Savoy will publish it in late 1981. Harrison's *The Committed Men* is due shortly. Newly published are two large format, comic strip books by Ken Reid, *Fudge in Bubbleville* and *Fudge and the Dragon*. These strips originally ran in the *Manchester Evening News* in the forties and fifties and were never syndicated, remaining largely unknown to the fantasy audience in general. According to Savoy "The strips predate Tolkien's *Rings* and, to our knowledge are the only original fantasy works involving elves, dragons and the like, comparable in scope and consistent creative excellency to Tolkien."

Savoy have bought—for a five figure sum—William Burroughs' new book *Cities of the Red Night*. They will not be publishing it until mid-1982 in order to give Calder and Rinehart are publishing their hardcover sold. Burroughs collaboration entitled *Planet R1OT*. It will contain a selection of rare, unpublished texts and photographs and, as well as interview material, it contains passages from the film script of *The Naked Lunch* and showing many photos never published before showing Burroughs and Co. in their earliest, formative years. This is due late 1981.

In the spring Savoy Books are planning to set up an office in New York for the purpose of publishing their titles in the USA. The office will come under the aegis and purpose control of Charles Platt. The first titles will, in all probability, be the four Henry Treece titles but repackaged. Garry Kilworth's fourth science fiction novel, *Gemini God*, is due from Faber &

Faber next summer.

Douglas Adams' cult masterpiece first put it onto vinyl as a double LP in 1979 by Original Records (ORA42), available in the UK only through mail-order. At that time the *Hitch-Hiker* cult was just gaining momentum and the album sold increasingly well throughout the year and into 1980. It is now being distributed nationally along with *Part Two*, *The Restaurant at the End of the Universe* (ORA54) a tie-in with the Pan paperback original and the forthcoming television series. These records are essential items for galactic hitch-hikers in the USA being dramatic presentations of the first order and zany, Monty Python science fiction to boot. Currently there is no American distribution although they are available through certain specialist shops, e.g. Gandalf's Den in Los Angeles, OR. and A Change of Hobbit in Eugene.

Richard Cowper's follow-up novel to *The Road to Corlay*, is titled *A Dream of Kinship* and will appear from Gollancz in the spring and from Pocket Books later. The novel carries on from where *Corlay* left off and follows the fortunes of Jane and her son Tom up to the year AD 3037 when the Cult of Kinship is becoming established in the western world.

Arena SF magazine has been awarded an Arts Council grant for the second year running. Its eleventh issue was published at the end of January and included John Brunner's convention address delivered last year in Krakow, plus an interview with Kate Wilhelm's Guest of Honour speech at "Noreascon"; an article by Ian Watson entitled "UFOs, Science and the Inexplicable"; plus book reviews and letters. *Arena SF* costs $1.50 and is available from Geoff Rippington, 6 Rutland Gardens, Birchington, Kent, U.K.

Keith Roberts recently sold two short stories to *F.&S.F.* "The Checkout" is his first story in ten years to deal with "Anita"—a centres around some bizarre happenings in a large supermarket and a beautiful, young checkout girl with whom Anita becomes emotionally involved. "Kaeti's Nights" is Roberts' first attempt at a vampire tale and constitutes "a radical reappraisal of the vampire legend."

reincarnated anarchist fragmentation-device New Worlds.

He and Britton produced *The Savoy Book*, "a catalyst which hung around in printed form for about a year before it saw publication, because of distribution problems". In the book Heathcote Williams wrote that 'the sky begins on the ground', and in accordance with this philosophy Savoy Books has sky-shooting artistic ambitions grounded in sound hardnosed business machinery. It lays ghosts. It provides a slap in the mind for boring tedium by the very vibrancy of its existence, it exorcises conventional myths of cultural apathy. Writ large SAVOY BOOKS ARE AS GOOD AND BETTER THAN ANYTHING CONCEIVED BY THE SHALLOW DAYGLO '60s. It's happening now. In the '80s.

"The main thing is we are having fun with Savoy, it's the sort of enterprise we've always wanted to have. And if we go broke, well, fuck it. We did some good books just the way we wanted." Buy them or lose out. The sky begins on the ground. Savoy is shooting that sky into fragments with or without you.

A slogan?

Savoy Books – like the Dormouse said – feed your head.

Orgasms for your mind.

ʊp ɔɑte

Andy Darlington caught us on the bottom step of a rapid upward-curving excalator of publication dates long before most of Savoy's 'first phase' of production reached the book stands. After what seemed like an eternity of floundering through trade restraints, entropic impedimentation and official circumscription the escalator suddenly shot up and, by the time Andy's article appeared in International Times in the summer of 1980, a sickly Savoy flower had burst and cast its succulent pollen of Michael Moorcocks, Harlan Ellisons and Henry Treeces everywhere! Too late for the authorities from Mancunia's lobotoland to stem the flow, though the deployed drones rushed around seizing what they could – for starters 2,000 copies of Samuel Delany's **The Tides of Lust,** *3,000 copies of Charles Platt's* **The Gas** *and one copy of Jack Trevor Story's* **The Screwtape Lettuce** *– impounding files and correspondence, swabbing here and dabbing there in an attempt to plug the outpour and clean up.*

This first full flower aberrantly shooting from the side of the main stem wilted almost as soon as it had bloomed and by the time **Doin' That Savoy Shuffle** *appeared in print had all but withered and fallen away. In reality, it wasn't Savoy that bothered the police but the Savoy shops which – with their ambience of "tapes pressured up high to limits of aural tolerance" – Andy had*

Secret of a sex book shop

WHEN police searched the basement of a city-centre bookshop they found obscene books and magazines behind a secret wall.

The 2,500 books were taken from Bookchain Ltd, in Peter Street, and at Manchester city magistrates' court stipendiary Mr John Coffey ordered that they be forfeited.

Three men who were working in the shop at the time of the police raid, Mr David Britton, of Cooper Lane, Blackley, Mr Thomas Sheridan, of Walmer Street, Rusholme, and Mr John Mottershead, of Winfield Drive, Gorton, had been summoned to show cause why the books and magazines, should not be forfeited.

None of them appeared at court and the stipendiary made the order after saying he was satisfied the books and magazines were obscene.

Mr Gordon Smith, prosecuting, said it was in October last year that officers raided the shop and took 2,999 books and magazines from the shop. In the basement the officers found 1,853, the large majority of which were hidden behind a secret wall in the basement," he said.

SavoyBooks

ORBIT BOOKS

BOOK LIST ● NEW RELEASES

1980

noticed were the true focal points of official attention. The shops, where the vital conversions of shrink-wrap 'fun' packs into monetary units takes place, had been repeatedly, blindly, systematically raided throughout our period of operation, their stocks of 'soft' so-called 'pornography' seized and destroyed at a rate almost but not quite exceeding the spending powers of our clients.

Mostly the raids were of a trivial nature, designed to harass, because Manchester, peculiarly out of step with the cultural norms of the rest of the country, cannot act as heavily as it would like, and we grew accustomed to absorbing the large financial holes each raid made in our side. Then, one day, we learned of a further escalation in the war that has been mounted against us — the war of one mad impossible dream fighting another in this culturally shrunken dockland of Victorian warehouses, endless Blackleys and skyscraper banks.

In the conditions brought on us by Savoy we scarcely noticed the thirtieth or so raid — we were too busy hanging on! But as we go to press,* in the calm determination of a 'second phase', we have learned that raids conducted simultaneously on three Savoy shops in October, not long after Andy's article appeared, have resulted in prosecution as well as stock seizure. The charges being brought against us are not for the Platt, Delany or Story books, but, ludicrously, for a series of 10-year-old Grove Press paperback readers which have gone past their day and which were bought many years ago at 'remainder' prices. The charges are for the storage and sale-for-gain of titles that have been erotically equalled by the contents of ordinary mass market best sellers.

We've struck back, of course. We've had to, or else face the possibility of closure due to not being able to sell, in Manchester, even the commonest material. We've elected to go for trial by jury. The efforts of our solicitors and barristers to insist on a fair hearing, have resulted in the trial officially being declared a 'test case' for Manchester.

As a further strategy we've opened three new retail outlets in the city. While we await the outcome of the new moves against us we thought it necessary to write about the events that have occurred, and to show that although in the first great shaking the Savoy edification itself was brought down, it now escalates horizontally, and with a lot less clatter. Now it spreads like a creeper on the ground.

Manchester, September 1981

* Publication of Savoy Dreams was originally scheduled for December 1981 but had to be re-listed because of police raids and ensuing prosecution.

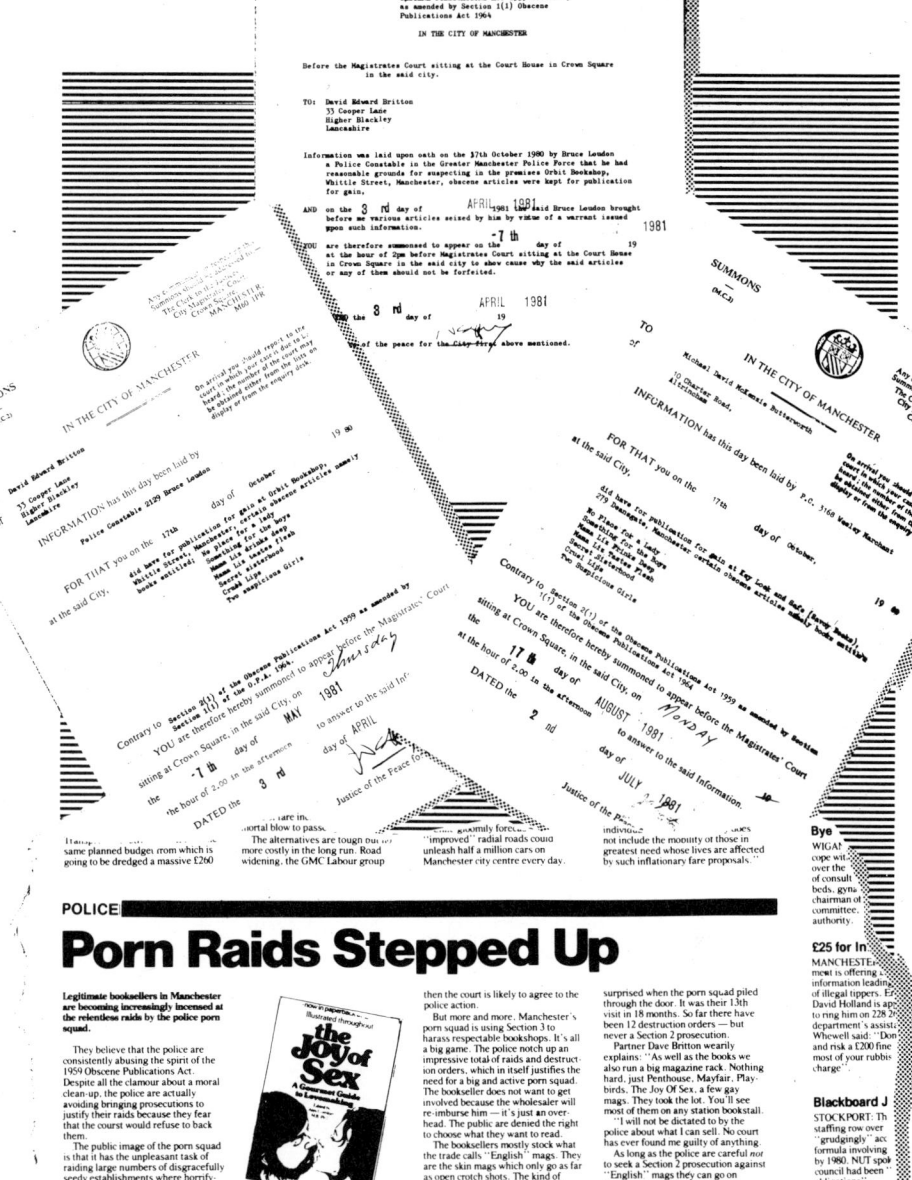

POLICE

Porn Raids Stepped Up

Legitimate booksellers in Manchester are becoming increasingly incensed at the relentless raids by the police porn squad.

They believe that the police are consistently abusing the spirit of the 1959 Obscene Publications Act. Despite all the clamour about a moral clean-up, the police are actually avoiding bringing prosecutions to justify their raids because they fear that the courst would refuse to back them.

The public image of the porn squad is that it has the unpleasant task of raiding large numbers of disgracefully seedy establishments where horrifyingly sordid porn is concealed in back rooms; where vile literature portraying the abuse of children is "peddled".

This theme, pushed out to a simple minded popular press makes great reading. The reality, in most cases, is very different.

Under the 1959 Act the police may take action under two key sections. Under Section 2 they can bring a prosecution and seek both fines and what in the trade is known as "Swedish" literature.

New Manchester Review

This is NOT illegal but Mr Anderton says you must not look

then the court is likely to agree to the police action.

But more and more, Manchester's porn squad is using Section 3 to harass respectable bookshops. It's all a big game. The police notch up an impressive total of raids and destruction orders, which in itself justifies the need for a big and active porn squad. The bookseller does not want to get involved because the wholesaler will re-imburse him — it's just an overhead. The public are denied the right to choose what they want to read.

The booksellers mostly stock what the trade calls "English" mags. As well as the skin mags which only go as far as open crotch shots. The kind of publication that few courts would ever rule obscene.

A TYPICAL RAID was the one three weeks ago on Bookchain, in Peter 'Street. A short walk from Bootle Street. Bookchain is highly regarded in Manchester: As well as stocking a wide range of paperbacks, the owners also publish a range of fiction through their company Savoy Books which is the North West's only independent small publisher.

The counter staff were hardly

surprised when the porn squad piled through the door. It was their 13th visit in 18 months. So far there have been 12 destruction orders — but never a Section 2 prosecution.

Partner Dave Britton wearily explains: "As well as the books we also run a big magazine rack. Nothing hard, just Penthouse, Mayfair, Playbirds. The Joy Of Sex, a few gay mags. They took the lot. You'll see most of them on any station bookstall.

"I will not be dictated to by the police about what I can sell. No court has ever found me guilty of anything. As long as the police are careful nor to seek a Section 2 prosecution against "English" mags they can go on harassing respectable book and magazine shops for ever.

For it is widely believed that Manchester's Stipendiary Magistrate Mr John Coffey is not an illiberal man. And if he were to dismiss a Section 2 case than the police would have to send the easy job of lifting "soft" skin books.

It seems that Chief Constable James Anderton is more frightened of the law than are the boot ↔ ters. An↔

Bye
WIGAN ↔
cope wit ↔
over the ↔
of consult ↔
beds, gyna ↔
chairman of ↔
committee, ↔
authority.

£25 for In↔
MANCHESTE↔
ment is offering ↔
information leadi↔
of illegal tippers. E↔
David Holland is ap↔
to ring him on 228 2↔
department's assista↔
Whewell said: "Don↔
and risk a £200 fine↔
most of your rubbis↔
charge".

Blackboard J
STOCKPORT: Th↔
staffing row over ↔
"grudgingly" acc↔
formula involving ↔
by 1980. NUT sto↔
council had been ↔
obligations".

Quango Chop
MANCHESTER:↔
ing over the futu↔
Opportunities ↔
Overseas H↔
ing the res↔

unoer siege

The Trial Regina v. David Britton
An open letter to the reader
A Report from Prison

What experience and history teach us is this — that people and governments never have learned anything from history, or acted on principles deduced from it.

Georg Wilhelm Friedrich Hegel (1770-1831)

Comparatively few people care for art at all and most of them care for it because they mistake it for something else.

Arthur Symons, *The Savoy No. 8*

The excuse for censorship of fiction, that it causes people to commit crimes, is absolutely ridiculous, in view of the crimes committed every day by people who get the ideas from the newspapers. I think that all censorship, any form of censorship, should be abolished. I don't think so-called dirty books ever inspired anyone to commit any crime more serious than masturbation. What the people in control are trying to hide by censorship is the fact that if all censorship were removed, nothing would happen.

William Burroughs, *The Job*

Those who cannot remember the past are condemned to repeat it.

George Santayana (1863-1952)

uNOeR síege

FIRST, THANKS FOR the moral support and help you've provided for Dave and all of us at Starplace, Orbit Books, Savoy, England's Glory (Bookchain Ltd), Design & Print, Key Lock & Safe and the rest of the 'Empire'.

It's been time consuming and difficult trying to establish how events came to happen in the way that they did. The work has been hindered by red tape in the judiciary and prison machinery, the office hours most professional people keep, our ignorance of how to proceed, as well as by the day to day running of the shops and (in my case) family. All of us have felt frustrated because most of the time has been spent sitting about waiting for moments when action can be taken.

Two days after Dave's trial and imprisonment it was still not possible for me to see him to find out what his wishes were. I had managed to learn from our solicitor, Laurence Hoffman, who had been allowed to see him, that apparently he was in good spirits. Two weeks have passed and I am just beginning to have a clear picture of what happened and of what courses of action *are* open to Dave (I have now managed to see him, of course, and found that the 'good spirits' are entirely cosmetic, as expected). But I will start from the beginning, with a little preliminary history, as accurately as I can so that you may safely utilise the facts in any future business of your own.

Raids of the frequency we are accustomed to began in Manchester in 1976 (James Anderton took over as Chief Constable of the Greater Manchester Police on July 1st, 1976). Since then (and the opening of Bookchain, Key Lock & Safe, Savoy, Starplace and Orbit) our premises have suffered a combined total of 40 — perhaps 50 — raids. Unfortunately for most of this period only hapahazard records of the raids exist, so I cannot be more precise. I might add that Mr Anderton claims he raids Manchester establishments strictly on a rotation basis, that all establishments receive fair treatment, yet we know of some newsagents who have not been raided and others who have been raided once, or a few times at most. In particular, on these raids, he has tended to concentrate on shops in our ownership and those in the 'Private' chain (unlike ours, these are straightforward sex shops).

Before Anderton took control in Manchester there were few police raids. Dave's first shop, The House on the Borderland — opened in 1971 and now closed — received no raids; the early Orbit Books received no raids.

Of course, the sale of hard core books and magazines has always brought brisk police attention. This used to be organised in the traditional 'under the counter' manner, but was completely stopped in high street shops by Anderton's men, with the result that today only soft core is available for the police to seize. We have dealt *only* in soft core, as you well know. Indeed, despite surface impressions received by some on-lookers, and conclusions drawn in certain satirical sketches, no one involved in Savoy or the shops has set out to be a pornographer. The House on the Borderland was started as a specialist shop trading in science fiction and fantasy. It was opened with money supplied by Dave's first partner, Charles Partington, and Dave's own substantial personal sf and fantasy collection, which was 'thrown in' as opening stock. It was quickly discovered that serious books did not sell in numbers large enough to support the aims of the two partners, and soft core magazines and books were introduced into the stock at the suggestion of commercial representatives. Since that date the interest in science fiction and fantasy, as well as the publishing interest, has remained a prime reason for the continued existence of the shops, but soft core books and magazines have always occupied a part of the stock. But it is soft core publications which Anderton seems determined to prohibit.

In his annual reports to London the Chief Constable claims that, between the years of 1977 and 1981, he obtained from magistrates a total of 1,010 search warrants issued specifically for the purpose of raiding under the Obscene Publications Act. The raids were spread fairly evenly over this five year period and mean that, on average, at least one Man-chester premises is being raided *every two days*. Almost without excep-tion these warrants are used against ordinary high street shops and distributors to justify the seizure of picture magazines and paperback novels as well as other kinds of publications, and films. Our 'offence' was the sale of *paperback novels*, not picture magazines.

For retailers of soft core publications Anderton normally can procure summonses under Section Three of the Obscene Publications Act of 1959 (as amended by Section One of the Obscene Publications Act of 1964). These summonses are obtained from magistrates, and then routinely served. The same magistrate who issues the summonses also signs the warrants which the police use to search premises (therefore it is quite useless to protest to the court). After summonses have been served the Defendants then have to go to court to show why the articles seized by the police are not obscene under the meaning of the law and why they should not be forfeited. No penalties result from these 'offences' other than the destruction of stock, so it is not worth the risk of bringing costly defences and possibly compounding financial loss. Usually the result is that judgement is obtained in court in the Defendants' absence, and the seized materials are (allegedly) destroyed. Because the definition of the word 'obscene' is by nature subjective, this is an area of the law where the police can and do make strides in the enactment of 'moral' principles held by some of their number.

All raids on our premises except for two have resulted in Section Three summonses being issued. Over the years we have lost tens of thousands

25/5/82

Bookshop man jailed

Seven books taken by police from a city centre bookshop were obscene, a Manchester Crown Court jury decided.

Shop owner David Britton, aged 37, of Cooper Lane, Blackley was jailed for 28 days and manager Phillip Bunton aged 23, of Chapel Road, Oldham was given a one-month suspended sentence for having obscene articles for gain.

The books were seized at the Orbit Book Shop in Whittle Street in October, 1980.

Counsel for the two men, Mr Bernard Lever said: "They elected to ask a jury's opinion as to whether these ... were ... They ...

of pounds worth of stock in this way, which has meant that our struggle against an already deteriorating market situation has been considerably worsened. We have not lost much more than this because, for a time, we were underwritten by suppliers who withstood the losses incurred, but as our credit has worsened suppliers have not been forthcoming.

The two raids which were the exception took place on October 17th, 1980 (about three or four months before Savoy Books collapsed and whilst we were attempting to shore up the publishing company). These were part of a major raid which simultaneously covered Bookchain, Orbit Books and (jointly) Savoy and Key Lock & Safe (our other companies were not then operable). About 25 police officers, other men and vehicles were involved, at the estimated cost to the force of many thousands of pounds. In addition, an unknown number of plain clothes policemen had been observing stock movement for at least a week beforehand. In April 1981, the usual Section Three summonses were issued against Dave and John Mottershead (the shop manager) for the raid on Bookchain, for Dave and Philip Bunton (the shop manager) for the raid on Orbit Books, and on Dave for the raid on Savoy Books and Key Lock & Safe. But Dave and Phil (at Orbit) and Dave (at Savoy) also received Section *Two* summonses. In July I myself received Section Three and Two summonses for the raid on Savoy. Potentially the most serious of these summonses were those served on Dave and Phil at Orbit Books, because there they were charged with selling books for gain, whereas at Savoy we were handling the books in a storage capacity.

The paperbacks concerned were:

No Place for a Lady, A. De Granamour, Venus Books
Something for the Boys, Kenneth Harding, Venus Books, 1973
Mama Liz Drinks Deep, Howard Rheingold, Venus Freeway Press
Mama Liz Tastes Flesh, Howard Rheingold, Venus Freeway Press
Secret Sisterhood, Howard Rheingold, Venus Freeway Press, 1973
Cruel Lips, Marcus Van Heller, Grove Press
Two Suspicious Girls, Katy Mitchell, Grove Press

They are an assortment of titles belonging to the prestigious American publishing house, Grove Press, and Venus Freeway Press — comparatively 'mild', fairly well written tongue-in-cheek, of no particular literary merit. They were published in the early 70s. Until recently, when legitimately imported supplies went out of print, they have been freely available in Britain in newsagents and bookstores (for instance, Words & Music bookshops in London carried these titles for many years). Supplied to us cheaply at remainder prices in 1978, they were not sufficiently contemporary to sell at full price, and moved sluggishly off the shelves. The same books had been seized and returned by police on some occasions (the police return books they have suspected mistakenly of being 'obscene'), and on numerous other raids had been seized and destroyed without being used to obtain criminal charges. Like many books of their kind they portray a variety of sexual acts sequentially — a standard plot device to help overcome repetition and avoid tedium. They therefore cater for a particular omniverous taste, but regular readers of the genre will realise immediately that they are not intended by their publishers to be aimed at the hard core market.

Section Two of the Obscene Publications Act is designed to cover hard core publications. The police had to ascertain that, in the opinion of Sir Thomas Chalmers Hetherington, the Director of Public Prosecutions, (known as "Tony" to his friends), the seven titles could be used in court to prosecute the Defendants. Why Hetherington suddenly thought these books could be used in this way, reversing his previous decisions about them, is one of the puzzling aspects of the case.

Unlike Section Three 'offences', Section Two are criminal and result in fines and/or imprisonment as well as stock forfeiture. But before I come to deal with the outcome of the Section Two charge as it pertained to Dave, there is a broader framework than local police feeling within which the raids, the charges and the imprisonment should be viewed. The tirade against liberalism championed by Anderton, Lord Longford, Mary Whitehouse and others, has (though these campaigners will not like to think so) *not* directly brought about the conditions which have enabled a person like Dave to be persecuted. These campaigners were given the opportunity to see harsher action implemented when a related concern of the Government's came into the limelight — London's Soho sex shop explosion. Soho's sex shops, saunas, cinemas and clubs had been spreading into areas like Paddington and Victoria, previously free of such concentrations. It was the Town Planning Committee of Westminster City Council (the local authority for the square mile which is Soho) who finally decided that new legislation would have to be passed. It proposed that legislation to license sex shops should be incorporated in the next General Purposes Bill of the Greater London Council. Sir Horace Cutler, then leader of the GLC, agreed with the proposals, and William Whitelaw (the present Home Secretary), approached by Sir Horace and Westminster City Council, gave them a cautious go-ahead. "Up until the Government's sudden change of mind last December, the Government's line had been that, however much they might deplore the sex industry, personally speaking, there was no consensus on how to reform the laws on obscenity."*

In Soho, prosecutions which would normally attract fines or suspended sentences for a first 'offence', after Government concern had grown, began to attract prison sentences. Judges presiding over these trials felt inclined to impose sentences of between one and six months. When David Sullivan, founder of the nationally operated 'Private' sex shop chain, was finally nailed by police for an offence unrelated to the shops and committed many years ago (his shops sell soft core magazines, tapes and general sex aids only), he was gaoled (in May 1982) for nine months. In addition he received a fine of £10,000. Ian Gold, son of David Gold (of David Gold Holdings Ltd), a moderately large supplier of soft core

* *Liberty Versus Decency*, Sarah Benton and Marion Bowman, New Statesman July 2nd, 1982.

magazines and an importer of a wide range of science fiction (he was the first person to import *Heavy Metal* comics and similar journals into Britain), was nailed and imprisoned for one year. He was fined £16,750, and now faces an additional prison sentence if neither he nor his father can raise payment. Some of the Soho cases may have been the result of heavy trading, but to my knowledge Sullivan's 'Private' chain and Ian Gold's supply business have not dealt in hard core material.

But to me it seems very apparent that Dave's treatment in the courts was decided by the Government's concern that Soho entrepreneurs should be heavily deterred. He was lumped in with them. However, Westminster Council did not intend their proposals (to control metropolitan sex trade) to be used to protect family life in the provinces. According to solicitor Terence Neville, the only intention of the Council was to "regulate the whole of the sex industry as it operated in London today".

The police constables who laid oath to obtain the summonses for the 'section two' raids on our premises were P.C. 2129 Bruce Loudon (Orbit Books), and P.C. 3168 Wesley Marchant (Savoy Books and Key Lock & Safe), for raids led by Detective Sergeant Jenkinson of the Obscene Publications Section of the G.M.P.

Following the serving of the summonses, the services of barrister Michael Redfern were hired, who constructed what we considered to be an intelligent groundplan for the Defence. He thought that there was a likelihood of the seized books being found obscene by a jury unused to exposure to available erotica, therefore he chose to build his defence on the fact of police behaviour. As I have mentioned, police frequently return books they have seized which they do not consider to be obscene; then they raid the same titles on other occasions when Section Three summonses are served. Because the Grove Press and Venus paperbacks had been treated in this haphazard manner and then suddenly used in obtaining criminal charges, the police could be proved to be behaving inconsistently. As well as being dilatory in their own territories the Manchester police were out of step with forces in other areas where the same targeting on shopkeepers selling similar books was not to be found. Redfern intended to show the jury that in their business practices the Defendants had endeavoured to keep lawful shops. He intended to put to the jury the rational view that it was unreasonable of the police to expect shopkeepers to know what might and might not be hard core pornography when they themselves did not appear to know.·

For ourselves, we had always thought that the police had a disastrously weak case. Nobody except a novice would sell what he genuinely thought might be hard core in Manchester, in bookshops known to be police targets. We hoped that a jury would reach the conclusion that there might be an element of collusion.

Seven hurt in new jail protest fires

4/6/82

SIX prisoners and a prison officer were taken to hospital during the night after two more fires at Manchester's Strangeways Prison.

Two officers discovered the first blaze in a cell in the prison's hospital wing at about 10 30 and rescued the prisoner inside.

But as they did so the fire "flashed" along the corridor, filling the building with smoke.

Twenty-one prisoners were evacuated as the flames spread.

Later, four prisoners and the hospital prison officer were taken to Salford Royal Infirmary suffering from the effects of smoke and heat.

Only one prisoner was detained in hospital over-night.

Four hours later another fire was discovered in a third-floor cell of the new remand wing on the site of the old women's prison.

Two prisoners were found lying on the floor surroun-ded by smouldering mat-treses and bedding.

One had deliberately cut his wrists.

Prison officers had put out the fire by the time the fire brigade arrived.

The two prisoners were treated in hospital for the effects of smoke.

The prison hospital was closed today because of damage caused by fire and

water, and the prisoners were moved to other parts of the prison.

An investigation into the cause of the fires was being conducted by the governor, Mr Norman Brown, who expressed concern recently at conditions.

The Victorian jail has been the subject of a num-ber of protest fires started by prisoners complaining of overcrowding.

Mr Brown said today: "The latest fires were both started deliberately — I suppose it could have been in protest about the con-ditions and the time people are having to wait to go to trial."

"The hospital wing fire could have been very dan-gerous because of the num-... inside at the

time and the tremendous fumes being given off by the fire.

"But both the staff and inmates did a magnificent job in helping to evacuate the premises."

The latest fire brings the number of blaze outbreaks at the jail to 15 in the last year.

Manchester Central MP Mr Bob Litherland was to-day in urgent consultations with the governor.

He said he would be carry-ing out an on-the-spot in-spection at the prison later today and was trying to arrange for a delegation of MPs to be taken on a tour of the jail.

He is also trying to per-suade Home Secretary Mr William Whitelaw to visit the prison.

'Unico man' i. myster"

A MYSTERY man ...tal suffering from has pleaded for find out who he If it means bad "I want to kn about myself the man — a B said from his in Hamburg, W. He has been since May 31 injury and lo... The man, ir mid-20s, 5ft 10 dark hair so has a tattoo head on his tattoo of and the r group the on his k...

WHITELAW IN JAIL ROW

CONDITIONS at Strange-ways Prison in Manchester are so bad that the Board of Visitors were threatening to resign, Home Secretary William Whitelaw was told yesterday.

After meeting a delegation from the board, prison officers and Manchester MPs, Mr. Whitelaw promised to speed up plans for improvements.

Jail governor Mr. Norman Brown told him there was a grave danger of riots.

22/7/82

Li...
row
coup
work
It b
yester
took
Garden.
But n
At le
said b
before
And
invest
" scul
groom
thoug
The
by K

Three trial dates were set before the matter eventually came, unsatisfactorily, to court. The first was adjourned in court because there had been insufficient notice given to ourselves (we suspect, for various reasons, in an attempt to 'steamroller' us through the machinery), and a second date cancelled because Redfern was 'otherwise engaged'. The third date was cancelled as a result of the Prosecution barrister being absent. On the first occasion, when both parties concerned had to appear at Wigan Crown Court, Redfern succeeded in obtaining a postponement from the judge.

'Regina v. Britton & Bunton' was held *nineteen months* after initial seizure of the books, on Monday May 24th, 1982, at 10.15 a.m. at the Manchester Crown Courts. It was a grossly unfair trial as far as we were concerned. Before it commenced we had agreed to meet counsel to discuss procedure, and had assembled early at about 10.00 a.m. Expecting to meet Michael Redfern we were therefore surprised to be introduced to a new barrister, the Honourable Bernard Lever, who knew nothing at all about Dave's case. Mr Hoffman told us that Mr Redfern was not able to be present for the first crucial days of the trial (a trial conducted along Redfern's lines would last about four days). It seemed that he had backed down on Friday afternoon, at the last moment. Lever had been appointed to request a further postponement of the trial.

We were not *entirely* thrown by this turn of events — by now we had come to expect interminable delays — but we were disappointed and depressed at the prospect of spending more months beneath the shadow of the case. Barristers are in the habit of leaving their clients stranded. As you probably are aware, unlike in America where the lawyer is solicitor *and* barrister, providing greater guarantee of consistency to the client, this is not the case in Britain. Barristers' clerks 'place' their barristers with clients. For their astuteness they receive a manager's per cent of the fees. So, some clerks are liable without much warning to switch barristers to more lucrative clients. I do not know whether this is what occurred to ourselves, but regardless of this Mr Redfern's withdrawal appeared to be timed unusually late in the day. When court started Lever had to make what seemed to onlookers to be an unprecedented plea to the judge.

Mr LEVER (unsure and stammering): May it please you, your Honour. In this case I appear on behalf of both Defendants and my learned friend Mr Wilkinson appears on behalf of the Crown. I am instructed that this case was in the list on a previous occasion and was adjourned for matters quite apart from the readiness, or otherwise, of the case. Your Honour, I find myself today in a position in which in the seven years I have been practising at the Bar I have never found myself in, and that is not being fully acquainted with the case, not being instructed on certain matters, and not having all the materials which are necessary for my clients to feel that the Defence has been conducted in the way that they had been led to believe it would be

NEW STATESMAN

CENSORSHIP

2/7/82

Liberty versus decency

Westminster City Council has tried to regulate Soho sex shops for years. SARAH BENTON reports on new national legislation

...tables walk hand in hand on the issues sex and morality, the new restrictions nay well proceed smoothly. Where they don't, it opens new vistas for police/community clashes. The place where it might flare up first is Manchester, stalking patch of James Anderton, well known Christian and enemy of obscenity. In 1977, Anderton announced he had decided to clamp down on 'patently obnoxious material' in Manchester and reported that public support for his decision 'has been enormously overwhelming.' Among the shops raided under the Obscene Publications Act have been suburban newsagents, a branch of Tescos (for their Page Three *Sun* girls) and general bookshops.

Most retailers find the law unsettling because they do not know what might be classified by the police as obscene. However, one man who has found out, and feels very bitter about it, is David Britton, publisher of highly respectable works, and bookshop owner in Manchester. He has just come out of Strangeways prison where he spent 28 days for selling obscene literature. No previous case of a criminal prosecution under the Obscene Publications Act is remembered in Manchester.

The books he was prosecuted for were, thinks author Michael Moorcock, who is published by Britton, hardly obscene at all – more the sort of badly written soft porn that is available in most city centres. The seven books, including *Something for the Boys* and *Two Suspicious Girls*, have been freely on sale since 1973. Mr Britton bought them as remainders in 1979 and now says 'I've lost track of the number of times I've been raided'. What makes him especially upset is that he had approached the police for guidance on what they regard as obscene before his arrest, but could get no answer. The judge's comment was 'if you are in doubt as to whether you are committing an offence then do not do anything which could possibly amount to one.'

There is therefore a gamut of pending laws, new interpretations of the law and discretionary police decisions on the laws on sex which is likely to change the whole legal framework for both published and visual material. There are many on the Left, especially in the women's movement, who will welcome restrictions on the freeof men to make money out of purveysadistic and degrading images of

diction, chaos, and loss of that has rarely been seen international crisis.

In picking Shultz, motivated by the man at the State D and amiability u nerves an imple whic for Wher phlegn of polic

On fi lionaire F one of the is the sor expected from the cently bee. internation boards of I age; J.P. I Trust, the Sears Roe' tcl have foreign c port of A

This produc Shultz Relat con bui is E

conducted. Whatever personal embarrassment that places me in, being the person who holds this brief at the moment, it is a considerable embarrassment, and one for which the court is entitled to an extreme apology. My clients having had a conference for three hours on two occasions with other learned counsel, and that counsel having indicated that the Defence should be run in a certain manner, I do not feel that I am equipped to let my clients feel that the Defence has been so run. Your Honour, in those circumstances, I find that the holder of this brief must take complete responsibiity for the matter, but I do not really feel it would be in the interests of justice for the case to proceed today, unless Your Honour directs otherwise. In those circumstances, I respectfully ask for an adjournment.

Judge Hardy, (Robert James Hardy of Wilmslow, Manchester, a circuit judge since 1979), who is thoroughly familiar with the methods employed by barristers' clerks, appeared to me to put unreasonable pressure on the Defence to explain their predicament.

JUDGE HARDY: I hear what you say, Mr Lever, but I have not as yet heard an explanation as to how this has come about. I do not know, but I would have thought that the case went through the normal listing procedure, that is, placed in the warned list three weeks ago, and then in the fixed list. If that is not correct then perhaps somebody can tell me.

Mr WILKINSON (Counsel for the Prosecution): Your Honour, apparently it was fixed on the 10th March and the fixed date of trial was then set as the 24th May.

JUDGE HARDY: More than two months ahead.

Mr WILKINSON: Yes.

JUDGE HARDY: Today has been a fixed date of trial for a considerable period?

Mr WILKINSON: It would appear so.

Mr LEVER: Your Honour will appreciate by the nature of the circumstances which I have outlined that I cannot assist Your Honour on that matter.

JUDGE HARDY: Somebody should explain what has happened. We have here a case which has been fixed for two months. On the morning of the trial I am told that counsel is not able to proceed. I need some explanation. If you cannot give me one then somebody must give me one.

Mr LEVER: So far as I am concerned, I can give Your Honour an explanation, but I do not think that would be of assistance. What Your Honour needs to know is something which happened before Friday of last week.

JUDGE HARDY: Who is going to tell me about that?

Mr LEVER: I understand the person who can best assist Your Honour is the gentleman who directs my attendance.

JUDGE HARDY: So as not to talk in riddles, which will be mysterious to other people, presumably on Friday night it was discovered that counsel instructed in the case was not available today.

Mr LEVER: Apparently so.

JUDGE HARDY: That is not something which could only have occurred on Friday night. It must have been discovered at any rate some time on Friday. Who was instructed in the first place?

Mr LEVER: My learned friend Mr Redfern.

JUDGE HARDY: Do you happen to know where he is today?

Mr LEVER: I am afraid I do not. That is why I guess that my clerk could best assist the court.

JUDGE HARDY: I suppose I had better say nothing more at the moment. I will rise for a short while to enable you to discover what the position is, how it arose, and who was informed and when, so as to be able to place those matters before me. If need be you should have your clerk here to help you on those matters.

Judge Hardy established when Lever's instructing solicitors first became aware of the matter, then:

JUDGE HARDY: Frequently counsel have to take over cases at short notice. Is there any difficulty in running the case in the way that it was anticipated?

Mr LEVER: Yes, to this extent, that I have arrived today to be informed by by my instructing solicitor that a particularly delicate and complicated way of running this case had been recommended to my clients. Of course, this was a matter which was not contained in my brief and instructions because there had been two conferences of three hours.

JUDGE HARDY: You have not had an opportunity of considering that aspect of it?

Mr LEVER: No. In addition, over the week-end I have taken such materials that I was given in a great big box, but I have not read all the passages which the Crown rely on because I did not have at least one of the books.

JUDGE HARDY: There are many exhibits, but only a few are referred to in the indictment. I do not know in what way the Prosecution intend to deal with the matter.

Mr WILKINSON: There are a limited number of books, but they involve prolonged reading.

JUDGE HARDY: There is going to be an issue possibly as to whether the material is obscene.

Mr LEVER: I can assist Your Honour in this regard, that is the only issue.

JUDGE HARDY: Unless the situation is that some of it is conceded to be obscene, which would seem improbable in view of the way I am told the case is going to have to go, it is all going to have to go in front of the Jury...Is there any particular advantage in counsel reading everything at this stage?

Mr LEVER: No. So far as I am concerned, the matter is a straightforward issue of fact and that would be the way I would approach the matter.

JUDGE HARDY: Mr Redfern perhaps had other ideas.

Mr LEVER: Yes, which he communicated to my clients. Whilst I hope I would be competent to do the case as I would have done, I would not like them to feel that the case was not run as it was indicated to them it should run.

JUDGE HARDY: Perhaps I should not enquire any more until I hear what has happened. I take it you will be half an hour.

Mr LEVER: I shall make the enquiry as soon as possible.

JUDGE HARDY: I shall rise until 11.30 at which time if it is not possible for me to deal with the matter then I will consider rising for a further time.

As the court retired, Detective Sergeant Jenkinson and other police officers who had attended the trial made a belligerent and noisy show of protest, one shouting (before Judge Hardy was out of ear shot), "Don't let them get out of it again!" This was a reference to the earlier trial dates which had been adjourned through no fault of our own.

Mr Hoffman and Mr Lever retired with Dave and Phil to discuss what they were to do. I remained behind in court to keep notes. When they returned I learned that Dave, weary of the continual setbacks, had instructed Lever to represent him. To allow this was a mistake, because Lever was not able to conduct the Defence in the manner we had planned. However, we were tired and confused. Judge Hardy's attitude did not make it easy to back down. We therefore agreed with Lever that if we showed willingness to undergo trial, saving court time and costs, our case would be regarded favourably by the judge. This proved to be an erroneous assumption.

What we did not know was that Hardy was the judge who handled the obscenity cases in Manchester. In retrospect, Lever's Defence appeared to be a standard procedure used by pornographers who are 'trying their luck with the jury' — a procedure I had wished at all costs to avoid. His intention was to give the Jury a simple 'either/or' issue of fact to debate — the books were *either* obscene *or* they were not — rather than provide them with the objectively truer argument that Redfern had built.

Redfern had warned against the kind of defence Lever proposed because an unspecialised jury, not used to the strength of current erotica, might possibly find even a Mayfair magazine to be obscene. Lever was of the opinion that Redfern's more complex argument would serve to confuse the Jury. No witnesses were to be called by Lever, or evidence shown. The evidence that had been assembled by Redfern and which had been brought into court by our solicitors — police lists dating back many years which proved that the books on trial had not on previous raids been considered obscene, selections of available erotica of varying 'strengths' proving the relative innocuousness of the books — all this

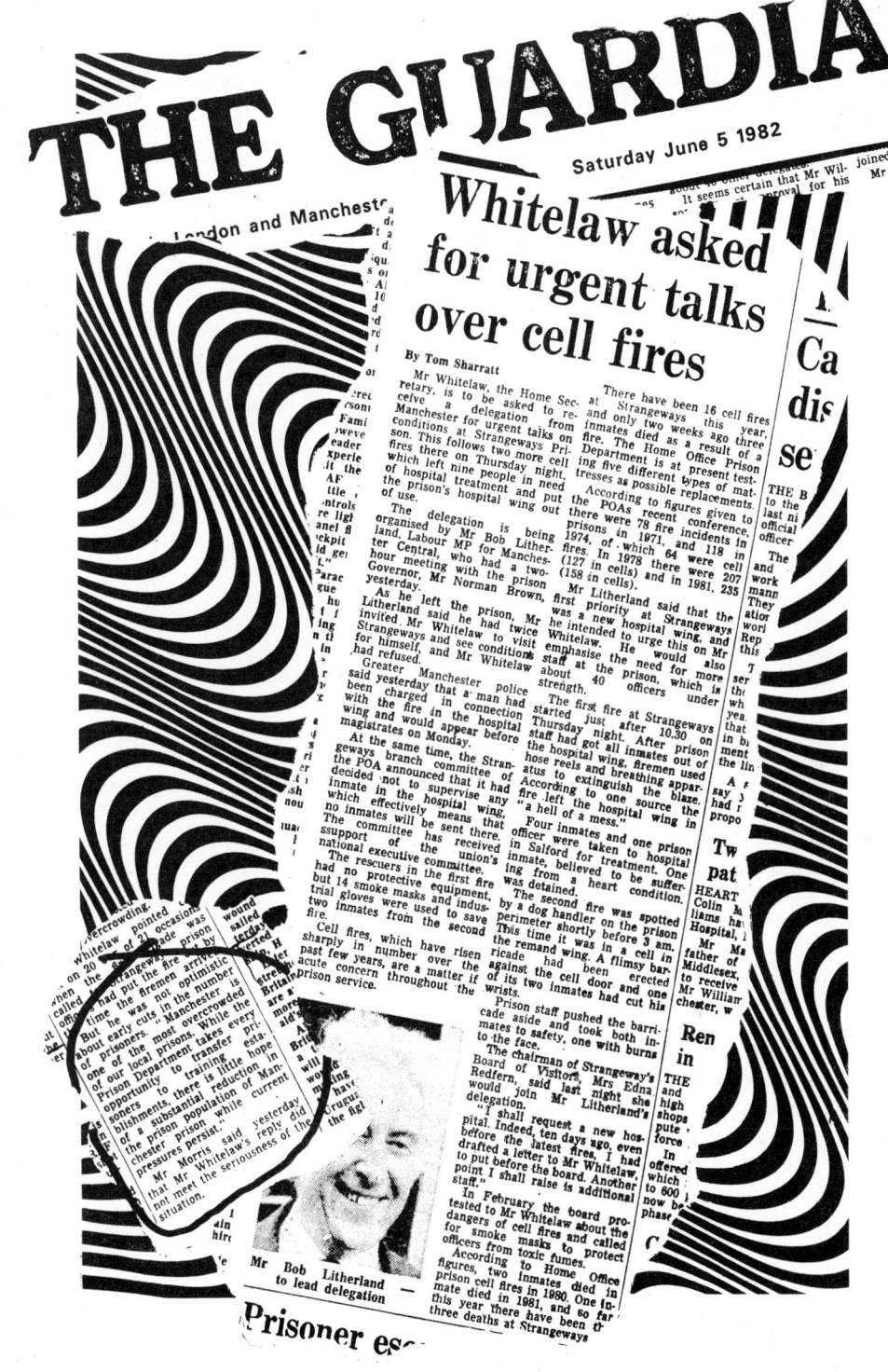

Whitelaw asked for urgent talks over cell fires

By Tom Sharratt

Mr Whitelaw, the Home Secretary, is to be asked to receive a delegation from Manchester for urgent talks on conditions at Strangeways Prison. This follows two more cell fires there on Thursday night, which left nine people in need of hospital treatment and put the prison's hospital wing out of use.

The delegation is being organised by Mr Bob Litherland, Labour MP for Manchester Central, who had a two-hour meeting with the prison Governor, Mr Norman Brown, yesterday.

As he left the prison, Mr Litherland said he had twice invited Mr Whitelaw to visit Strangeways and see conditions for himself, and Mr Whitelaw had refused.

Greater Manchester police said yesterday that a man had been charged in connection with the fire in the hospital wing and would appear before magistrates on Monday.

At the same time, the Strangeways branch committee of the POA announced that it had decided not to supervise any inmate in the hospital wing, which effectively means that no inmates will be sent there. The committee has received the support of the union's national executive committee.

The rescuers in the first fire had no protective equipment, but 14 smoke masks and industrial gloves were used to save two inmates from the second fire.

Cell fires, which have risen sharply in number over the past few years, are a matter if acute concern throughout the prison service.

There have been 16 cell fires at Strangeways this year, and only two weeks ago three inmates died as a result of a fire. The Home Office Department is at present testing five different types of mattresses as possible replacements.

According to figures given to the POAs recent conference, there were 78 fire incidents in prisons in 1971, and 118 in 1974, of which 64 were cell fires. In 1978 there were 207 (127 in cells) and in 1981, 235 (158 in cells).

Mr Litherland said that the first priority at Strangeways was a new hospital wing, and he intended to urge this on Mr Whitelaw. He would also emphasise the need for more staff at the prison, which is about 40 officers under strength.

The first fire at Strangeways started just after 10.30 on Thursday night. After prison staff had got all inmates out of the hospital wing, firemen used hose reels and breathing apparatus to extinguish the blaze. According to one source the fire left the hospital wing in "a hell of a mess."

Four inmates and one prison officer were taken to hospital in Salford for treatment. One inmate, believed to be suffering from a heart condition, was detained.

The second fire was spotted by a dog handler on the prison perimeter shortly before 3 am. This time it was in a cell in the remand wing. A flimsy barricade had been erected against the cell door and one of its two inmates had cut his wrists.

Prison staff pushed the barricade aside and took both inmates to safety, one with burns to the face.

The chairman of Strangeway's Board of Visitors, Mrs Edna Redfern, said last night she would join Mr Litherland's delegation.

"I shall request a new hospital. Indeed, ten days ago, even before the latest fires, I had drafted a letter to Mr Whitelaw, to put before the board. Another point I shall raise is additional staff."

In February the board protested to Mr Whitelaw about the dangers of cell fires and called for smoke masks to protect officers from toxic fumes.

According to Home Office figures, two inmates died in prison cell fires in 1980. One inmate died in 1981, and so far this year there have been three deaths at Strangeways

overcrowding pointed
Whitelaw said yesterday
that Mr Whitelaw's reply did
not meet the seriousness of the
situation.

evidence was discarded. The Jury were simply to decide whether or not the books were obscene.

Once they realised the fish had been landed in the net, the police left the court — presumably to attend to more important matters. The charge was read out by the court clerk, "David Edward Britton and Philip William Bunton, you are charged with possession of obscene articles for publication for gain, the particulars being that you on October 17th 1980 had for publication for gain certain obscene articles, namely books entitled..." The clerk listed the books.

Both Defendants pleaded not guilty. The Jury was then admitted to the court, without being made aware of the last minute changes in the Defence. They were sworn in. The charge was read to them. Prosecuting counsel Mr Wilkinson then addressed the Jury. Unfortunately no accurate transcript of the barristers' addresses to the Jury is available — in criminal trials, unless especially requested, shorthand writers are not required by law to take notes of barristers' speeches; not at the time being aware of this particular 'catch' we do not today have records.

After his speech Wilkinson called PC Bruce Loudon into the witness box in order to establish various particulars about the raids, including the manner of police procedure, the obtaining of the warrant, the timing of the raids, the identities and business roles of the Defendants as well as the names and addresses of magazine and book suppliers to the Defendants' business. During his cross-examination Loudon produced the seven books, each containing page markers referring readers to annotated parts of the texts which he considered obscene.

As I have mentioned before, these raids had cost the police force many thousands of pounds to execute, and it is probable that one of the main factors of Dave being brought to trial on the strength of this essentially trivial material was to, in some measure, justify this vast expenditure of public money.

Lever then briefly cross-examined Loudon. He established that there was no evidence that the books had been on sale to minors under the age of eighteen. He told the court that both Defendants were men of previous good character. This was not disputed.

Judge Hardy then instructed the Jury to retire for 10 minutes to enable him to speak in private to counsel. While they were out of earshot he told the two barristers that he intended to instruct the Jury about what they were to look for in the books because, he felt, they would not be familiar with the obscenity law. No objection to this was raised. When the Jury returned Hardy told them, "Members of the Jury, I am going to ask you now to look at the material which was seized by the Prosecution. I am not at this stage going to direct you in detail as to what the law is, because it is not the appropriate stage to do so, but I think it helpful if I say one or two things to you so you at least know what this case is about and what you are supposed to look for. I will read to you the statute, the Act of Parliament, which deals with this matter —

'For the purposes of this Act an article shall be deemed to be obscene if its effect or (where the article comprises two or more distinct items) the effect of any one of its items is, if taken as a whole, such as to tend to deprave and corrupt persons who are likely, having regard to all relevant circumstances, to read, see, or hear the matter contained or embodied in it'.

It is rather a lengthy definition, but you will see that it does not contain very much in the way of legal definition on the bounds of obscenity. The reason why these kind of cases come before a jury such as yourselves is for you to set the standard by what you think ordinary, decent members of the community would regard as obscene".

The Jury retired again. When they returned Hardy adjourned the Court for lunch, and to allow Lever an opportunity to acquaint himself more fully with Loudon's annotations. After this recess Lever delivered his Defence speech. He admitted to the court that the books might be objectionable to some Victorian minded adults, but he asked them to consider that the books had been published in a supposedly enlightened age. The books might be of harm only to a very small minority of contemporary readers. His address was followed by Judge Hardy's summing up address to the Jury.

Until this moment, discounting his intransigence about postponing the trial, Judge Hardy appeared to have *conducted* the proceedings correctly. But his *manner* (for example the tone of his voice) frequently gave otherwise fair and just pronouncements an inflexion. To observers who had detected this and who felt they were witnessing a forced trial, his summing up to the Jury increased their misgivings. I have italicised the parts of his speech which contain points which until that precise moment had not been brought up in court; which might refer to parts of the law which nebulously remained unexplained; which I feel might be inaccurate; which appeared to me to be opinion; which appeared to be biased interpretations; which seemed to be denials of points raised by our barrister.

Judge Hardy began by outlining his own function which, he said, was to control the trial and explain the law, and he told the Jury that they must accept what he told them about the law. It was particularly important in this case that they did so, he said. They must not substitute their own ideas of what the law was or what it ought to be. He continued:

JUDGE HARDY: There is only one issue in this case which you are being asked to try because the actual wording of the offence, although it contains several parts, is not disputed in all parts, but only the one. It is conceded that those books were in the possession of the two accused, (1) *that they had them for publication. That is a phrase, Members of the Jury, which means 'for sale'. It simply means printing them, and that they were doing so for gain.* In other words, that they were to make a profit out of it. The only matter which is disputed which is contained in this charge is that those books are obscene articles within the definition of the Act of Parliament which makes it an offence. Please note, Members of the Jury, that it is not necessary for the Prosecution to prove that everybody who came in contact with it would be depraved or corrupted. It is not necessary for the Prosecution to establish that it has vast publication which has the tendency to start off the process of depraving or corrupting. (2) *It is sufficient if the Prosecution establish that the article tends in respect of a not insignificant number of people likely to read it,* or come into contact with it, to deprave or corrupt them. In other words, Members of the Jury, (3) *I must disagree with the submission made by Mr Lever that what you are concerned with is the people who go into the shop to buy it because they are not the only persons, you may think, who are likely to see the goods which are purchased. They may get into other hands, be passed on to other people deliberately or by chance.* Also, Members of the Jury, (4) *I must disagree with Mr Lever's submission in this respect, that you do not ask yourselves whether those people are more or less likely to go out and act in the kind of ways referred to in the articles. It is sufficient if the tendency to deprave and corrupt affects the mind only. It does not need to affect the person's actions.* Mr Lever is quite right in saying that it is for you to set the standard. (5) *The Standard which you will set is that standard which you regard as being the standard of ordinary, decent, members of the public.* Would they in your view regard this material as obscene in the sense that it is defined in the Act. (6) *It is also irrelevant, although nobody had mentioned this, whether in your view you can get this kind of material, as bad or worse, elsewhere in this country, or indeed abroad.* That is not the point. I am afraid that I must also disagree with Mr Lever when he says that you must ask yourselves when deciding the question of guilt, or innocence, "Are we, the Members of the Jury, depraved or corrupted by it?" That is not the test. Quite apart from anything else, seeing it because you are asked to as part of this case is a totally different thing from going out and buying it for yourself, or it being passed to you by others. (7) *If the test were whether it would deprave and corrupt the people in court, the lawyers, the judge, the jury, the police officers, and all the other people there would never be a conviction.* Nor is it the test to ask yourselves if normal people such as yourselves would be depraved or corrupted because not everybody is normal. If in your view a significant number of people who are likely to see or read the material would tend to be corrupted then that is sufficient. (8) *The fact that it is not sold to anybody under the age of eighteen does not·preclude you from considering whether a significant number of persons under that age could get their hands on it.* Mr Lever makes the point that may it not, as he puts it, satisfy a need? He is entitled to submit that view for you to consider it, and think about it, (9) *but the other point put by the Prosecution is, of course, that a person who wishes to read this kind of*

FRONTLINES

EROSION OF LIBERALISM

BY MICHAEL MOORCOCK

I recently published a novel, The Brothel in Rosenstrasse. In it I tried to show the destructive social and psychological consequences of pursuing sexual sensation for its own sake. The book was dedicated to Dave Britton and Michael Butterworth, the Manchester publishers who commissioned it shortly before they went bankrupt last year. They had published too many novels reflecting Britton's own literary enthusiasms. In the last two years he published five excellent books by Jack Trevor Treece, four by me, Jack Henry and Langdon Jones's superb 'Eye of the Lens' (for the first time in this country). He had bought other titles, either new or unjustly out of print, for generous advances. His new Butterworth's Savoy Book anthologies publish work by Paul Ableman, Heathcote Williams, M John Harrison, William Burroughs, Harlan Ellison, Richard Kostelanetz, as well as good many new writers and illustrators. Britton also published some charming children's books, including one by comedian Mike Harding. The firm always paid authors above-average advances and were impeccable in their courtesy to their writers.

In May 1982 Dave Britton was sent to Strangeways prison. He had been found guilty, at Manchester Crown Court, of possessing obscene material for gain. He served almost three weeks of his 28-day sentence and emerged having gained a haircut and lost some 1½ stone in a very shaken condition. He had received the usual unpleasant treatment and witnessed rioting when two prisoners tried to kill themselves. As partner Michael Butterworth (a novelist himself as well as an editor of literary magazines) currently faces similar charges carrying the possibility for increased likelihood of the same sentence.

The basis of the publishing company was Dave Britton's bookshops, whose profits drop ped off after a series of 35 police raids and what began to seem like a policy of active persecution. In common with many other shops, his have been subjected to these raids since the senior echelons of the Manchester police announced their intention of 'cleaning up' the city. Two of Britton's shops sell mainly paperbacks, American comics, 'underground' fiction, and periodicals, general fiction, posters, records and badges as well as a very small selection, in a separate part. The seedy and depressing material one sees on newsagents' shelves everywhere. The third shop sold mainly the same soft-core pornography. On the morning Britton came out of Strangeways, the police raided this shop. By the time he reached central Manchester they had again seized large amounts of stock. One policeman, ac-

ther adjournment. Judge Hardy said he could not understand why the case could not proceed and gave Mr Lever, the new barrister, half an hour to provide a suitable reason why the other barrister could not appear, otherwise he would order the trial to proceed.

In this recess barrister, solicitor and clients discussed what to do. Mr Lever was unfamiliar with the original defence: police inconsistency in their choice of material for prosecution. No reasonable person could expect to know what the police considered obscene. Mr Lever meant to impress the judge with the defendants' wish not to waste public money with

are depressing, incapable of stimulating more than a twitch of irritation. But they were to cost Dave Britton rather more than three weeks of liberty.

They were seized in a general raid in October 1980. They had been seized before on at least half-a-dozen occasions, always subject to Section 3 of the Obscene Publications Act, a standard destruction order applied to all material (including Penthouse and Mayfair). On this occasion, however, they became subject to a Section 2 order: criminal prosecution. In April 1981 summonses were issued to David Britton and Philip Bunton (manager), charging them with selling 'certain obscene articles' (the seven novels). In July 1981 Michael Butterworth received an identical summons.

The case, due to be tried at Wigan in October 1981, was adjourned because insufficient time had been granted for preparation of the defence. The case was adjourned twice more, partly because the police barrister could not attend, then because the defendants' barrister could not attend. Eventually, on May 24 this year, Britton and Bunton arrived in court to discover their own barrister could not be present. A substitute barrister, unfamiliar with the case's details, had been sent. He went before the judge and applied for a fur-

ber of people were likely to be corrupted, that was sufficient. They must consider whether young persons might see it.

The jury retired, reappearing an hour later to inform the judge they could not reach a unanimous verdict. The judge reluctantly agreed to accept a majority verdict. He evidently wished to avoid a retrial.

Within minutes the jury returned a verdict of guilty. The defence reiterated the defendants' good character. Formal requests had been made by Britton and his lawyers asking what in the view of the Police was permissible or impermissible. Judge Hardy said that if you wished to sail close to the wind, you could

more delays. He thought it best to continue with the trial, but chose a much simpler line of defence — that the books were not obscene.

The trial began. Prosecution gave a short routine speech, calling the policeman in charge of the raid as witness. He produced the books, each with markers identifying passages he considered obscene. Judge Hardy instructed the jury to retire for ten minutes to look at the extracts, then told both QCs he intended to instruct the jury on the Obscene Publications Act.

When Mr Lever gave his defence he asked if the jury really believed the books were obscene by present day standards. Summing up, the judge told the jury it must decide if the significant number of a not insignificant number of people likely to read it, or come into contact with it, to deprave or corrupt them... It is sufficient if the tendency to deprave and corrupt affects the mind only,' he added. 'It does not need to affect the person's actions.'

It was irrelevant, the judge continued, whether one could find this kind of material, as bad or worse, elsewhere. If they were whether it would deprave and corrupt the various people in court, there would never be a conviction. If a significant num-

not expect the Police to tell you how close to sail. Philip Bunton received a suspended sentence of a month's imprisonment. Sentencing Dave Britton, Judge Hardy said: 'It must be made clear to people who run these businesses that if they infringe the law, then they must serve punishment for it.' Britton was sentenced to 28 days.

What happened to Dave Britton is alarming. What others (including Butterworth) now face is even more alarming. It suggests a steady increase of real power among strongly authoritarian and conservative elements in our society. Mrs Thatcher's government, not remarkable for breadth of intelligence or insight into and tolerance for complex social problems, appears to be encouraging and rewarding a reactionary element among those connected with the law. This gradual de-liberalising of our legal institutions allows certain policemen who, for a while, were somewhat more circumspect in their attacks on the easier targets for arrest and conviction (chiefly black youth but in general the area of so-called 'victimless crime') great opportunity to exercise their prejudices. Briefly, the bullies are anticipating a field day. That many senior police officers, politicians and lawyers are disturbed by this turn of events is en-

couraging, but their power to affect it is being weakened.

We're likely to see more cases of 'back-door censorship in the near future. Until now most people prosecuted have been professional pornographers, some recently imprisoned for long periods. I have little personal sympathy for them. They interpreted a vaguely worded Act as widely as those who oppose them. But there is now a strong er than ever case for the law to be changed, particularly since it has been used to prosecute people like Dave Britton, who was innocently selling what many others sell. He never dealt in 'hard-core' pornography and sex material was never his main stock-in-trade. Yet he has now been identified with Soho 'porn-kings', has a prison record and doubtless further threats hang over him. London helped his accusers secure a scare and in my view dreadfully unjust punishment.

The case suggests that an increasing number of decent people are about to find themselves accused and brought under the Obscene Publications Act. How long will it be before that excellent political bookshop Grass Roots, a stone's throw from Britton's premises, finds itself threatened? This shop carries a large stock of lesbian and male homosexual fiction and non-fiction. At present any police officer, finding a book obscene can obtain a prosecution on those grounds. Would passages extracted from, say, Rita May Brown, once more a jury any differently than the passages extracted from 'Secret Sister' hood' or 'Two Suspicious Girls' (two of the seven for which Britton was prosecuted)?

I'm worried that the reforming legislation of the 1960s and 1970s being eroded. These reforms were specifically designed to protect people from many sorts of persecution (including blackmail and extortion). The erosion is chiefly being achieved by means of 'back-door censorship' and biased interpretation of the relevant Acts. Yet it can only happen if lawyers allow it to happen, as it is Parliament's. But theirs, as it is Parliament's. But it's also in some part ours. We can't afford to turn a blind eye to the implications of Dave Britton's case. Until recently victims of the new conservatism were those with whom the majority of people could not easily identify. I myself found it hard to sympathise with Section 2 of the Obscene Publications Act. I find it very easy, though, to identify with Dave Britton, whose record as a publisher was exemplary.

I think racial, sexual and political minorities are now under a greater threat than now know. In the near future some of us who are currently fairly complacent could find ourselves in trouble. I don't want my books censored and I don't want my children to prison. I suddenly find myself facing the prospect that soon I will well become a member of a threatened minority.

● In London, officers of Scotland Yard's Obscene Publications Squad recently raided Knockabout Comics in the Portobello Road, seizing about comics and as many books relating to drugs.

ding to the shop's manager, said: 'Tell Britton we haven't forgotten him.'

The police had brought charges on only seven of all the thousands of books and magazines taken. The volume of stock seized has been prodigious and is frequently returned very late, returned in a battered condition, or not returned at all. No proper check on the quantities removed has been possible — partly because the raids are sudden and well-planned, 'are sudden which Britton was prosecuted were Grove Press and Venus Freeway titles which have been on open sale in England for nine years. I doubt if they could claim much literary merit. To me they *material — it is the analogy of the drug case that Mr Wilkinson used — "that it feeds upon their addiction".* You must consider whether they would not need stronger and stronger doses. That is the situation, that it is sufficient if it tends to increase the depravity, or corruption of the reader. It was said that there was nothing new under the sun. That may be so. There is, at any rate, some biblical authority for that. Activity of this kind may have always gone on. I am not saying it has not. This is the way the argument is put. (10) *It does not mean to say that these men should be acquitted.* What the Act of Parliament prohibits is not that people want to read this kind of material or people wish to indulge in this kind of activity, or know about it. What the Act of Parliament prohibits is people making a profit out of publishing it. That is what is prohibited. (11) *In the same way the act of prostitution is not an offence in itself, but if you run a brothel for the public then you do commit an offence.* What the Act prohibits here is people having obscene articles for publication for gain. That they had them for publication, and that they were for gain, is not in dispute here. The question which you are asked as members and representatives of the public to decide is whether or not that act of publishing these articles amounts to a breach of the statute which prohibits the publication of obscene articles for gain. So I would return to the words of the Act which are the ones which should guide you. Those articles are deemed obscene if in your view they have a tendency to deprave, or corrupt, a not insignificant proportion of people who in your view are likely to see, or read them.

I am quite sure that Judge Hardy kept within the framework of what is permissible for a judge to say. Nevertheless the sum total of what he said, delivered in his tone of voice, amounted to what we felt was a biased and, in one particular, an inaccurate summing up. We list our reasons below. (Numbers refer to the italicised passages in the Summing Up.)

(1) In this case the objection is the use of the word 'publication'. This word is used persistently by Hardy, perfectly legitimately, throughout his speech as a synonym for the word 'sale'. He appears to make his usage clear, but then immediately after supplying clarification he declares that the term 'publication' simply means 'printing them' This made us wonder what he *did* mean to convey by the word 'publication'. Did he mean to imply that the Defendants were publishers in the lay sense of the word? Quite apart from the inaccurate impression this would have given to the Jury (that Dave published as well as sold the books in question), the error raised the question of where the information had been obtained and how Hardy had come to regard Dave as a publisher/printer rather than bookseller. Hardy is a known pornography trial judge. Might he have been told by police beforehand that the Defendants were publishers of pornographic books (which, of course, is quite inaccurate)? Savoy have published two erotic literary classics, *The Gas* by Charles

Platt, and *The Tides of Lust* by Samuel Delany, both of which were seized on the raids. We know for certain that Sergeant Jenkinson was frustrated by his inability to obtain prosecutions for these from the DPP. It is not beyond the realms of imagination when faced with slips of the tongue of the kind made by Hardy, in such circumstances, to draw an unpalatable conclusion — in this case that a meeting might have occurred between police and the judiciary to intimate that the Defendants were harmful pornographic publishers who had escaped 'justice' and who must somehow be dealt with severely by the law. This slip, the reluctance of Hardy to postpone the trial, as well as the irrelevance of comments later made by him to Dave after sentences had been passed, gave the impression that Hardy was overlooking facts while attempting morally to condemn on the basis of information or impressions received from somewhere outside the proceedings.

(2) The relevance of the words 'a not insignificant number of people likely to read' (the allegedly obscene books) had not yet been made clear by anyone in court.

(3) Hardy's disagreement (one of several) with Lever's point that what the Jury are concerned with is simply the people who go into the shop to buy erotic books.

(4) Another of Hardy's disagreements with Lever: Lever says that the Jury should concern themselves with how a book buyer might *act* after purchase. Hardy says that it is of concern if the *mind alone* is affected.

(5) Who is able to say, objectively, who constitutes 'ordinary, decent members of the public'? Used in the context of the summing up it is a flattery to the Jury, initially made by Lever but (I.thought) perversely emphasised here.

(6) Why, unless he takes sides with the police, does Hardy bother to raise more points such as this one which would have been better voiced by the Prosecution? Hardy says that it is irrelevant whether books similar to those seized can be got elsewhere in this country or indeed abroad.

(7) Surely, the test *is* whether the Jury (a cross section of the public) think the material would corrupt *their* minds? To direct the Jury not to take this course is to have them try to consider an abstract 'test' on certain hypothetical persons about whom they have received no specific clinical information (the Williams Report, commissioned by the Government to discover whether there is any basis in reality for the belief that 'pornography' is damaging and corrupting, has been completely ignored by Government and courts; perhaps because the report concluded that there was very little objective evidence that 'pornography was harmful'.)

(8) Hardy tells the Jury that they must remember that people under the age of 18 can get their hands on material sold exclusively to over-18s. This constitutes the second occasion on which he has indirectly implicated the possible corruption of children. What is the point of the Government requiring shops to erect signs excluding under-18s from sections of shops catering to the soft core adult market if a provincial judge can 'slip'

16/7/82

Behind the lines

"THE TIMES LITERARY SUPPLEMENT"

...rature Panel has ...k at one client, ...d with its allied ...d N... ...Poetry 3,000, ...,000 means of ... ...king ...port. This doc... ...ent ...nter-report from the ...hich, while a...pting ...questio... ...
The Poetry S...ciety ...on...erned th... ...the ...e Nationa... ...ry ...h acts a... ...ry ...ized poetry ...eading ...country, should ...ot ...the Regional A...ts ...evotion would be a ...the Pre... ...ciety, and ...produce c... ...from ...that they did ...ot want to ...ecretariat over. S...ce it is ...ties cannot be ... ...hat ...lient's ...lient's consent, the ...ved without ...ore certain that the Literature ...s ...ep ... ...ch ...oes not hav... ...its ...ight... ...ce again.

The answer to such ...pecial ...investiga... ...appears ...
...own in first. ...being ...our ...too was a...out to be ...that it ...working party, the ...ational Book ...eague produced its own document. ...My understanding is that the working ...la... ...ty on the Nationa... Book ...eague ...sugge... ...meet.

• • •

The American book trade, is increasingly worried by the rising tide of censorship that has led to repressive legislation in several states (and even more ominously, to cases of book burning). Nearer home David Britton and Michael Butterworth of Savoy Editions in Manchester are suffering in a similar way. Mr Britton has just served twenty-eight days in Pentonville after being convicted of having for gain seven books found to be obscene. Mr Butterworth has a similar charge hanging over his head.

The books, which were seized at Savoy Editions' bookshop, can hardly be called serious literature: *No Place for a Lady; Something for the Boys; Mama Liz Drinks Deep; Mama Liz Tastes Flesh; Secret Sisterhood; Cruel Lips* and *Two Suspicious Girls*. Savoy

...e client ...ake place

...he preceding ...tive. I men- ...uld not care ...the idea ...hat ...the nar... of ...ssity ...over a ...howe...er, be ...ny members ...y possess a ...sense o... the ...btless fr...m ...ry wag who ...quiet drol- ...y Guide".

...es.

Editions admit that they are erotica, but there are aspects to the case which suggest that this is more than a matter of pornographers being caught out.

To begin with, the seven titles come from two American publishers, Grove Press and Venus Freeway. Savoy bought them as remainders, so they must have been freely imported into this country (in spite of HM Customs and Excise's censorial powers), and have been freely available in places other than Manchester. Secondly, far from hiding the books under the counter, Mr Britton actually went to the Manchester police and asked them what was and what was not permissible under the Obscene Publications Act. He received no satisfactory answer to his enquiries, and when this was raised as a mitigating factor at his trial, the Judge's comment was that if one thinks one might be in danger of committing an offence "then do not do anything which could possibly amount to one."

This last comment has serious implications for another aspect of Savoy Editions' activities, as publishers. Savoy have published a number of reputable writers, including the fantasist Michael Moorcock, Henry Treece, Jack Trevor Story and Mike Harding. Michael Moorcock is convinced that Savoy "are not serious and idealistic publishers – which is why they have had financial difficulties". Moorcock is also worried that the way evidence was presented at the trial – marked passages were handed to the jury – could be used against his own and many other contemporary works. Such prosecutions could be brought against radical bookshops which carry feminist or homosexual literature. "It all just seems to be getting worse to me."

The misfortune of Savoy Editions is that they are based in Manchester, where the Chief Constable John Anderton is carrying out a vigorous anti-pornography campaign – 187 raids in 1980, 209 in 1981. Savoy Editions are hoping to publish the collected works of Heathcote Williams, *Severe Joy*, whose contents are likely to be at least as risky as *Cruel Lips* or *Two Suspicious Girls*. (John Calder, who fought his battles in the 1960s with *Last Exit To Brooklyn*, was going to publish the book, but the torch has passed to Savoy Editions.) If Britton and Butterworth were to take the advice of the Judge at Britton's trial, then *Severe Joy* would be effectively banned without the bother of having a Manchester jury declare it obscene. Without any need for censorship, the book would not be published.

The argument over D. M. Thoma...s ...
The White Hotel continues. You ...

...o ...ove ...mate ...doc... g...ate made ...parti Pronic to cle... plagiar... there.

Kuzn... protest... Gollanc... *Hotel.* Thoma... appea... the c... appro... paid, positi... existe... cens... Rus... that ...he ...wh... text... ack... Mrs... W... Thon... of t... Jonath... althou... negotia... the qu... that th... *Babi...* know... inspi... haven... detail... lawyer... there ...and ever... much w... source amount... "fair de...

Whil... Kuznet... for th... husba... be the ...the b... be o... quot... left ...furt! circu... nov... fulfi... for

Fifty years on: Coleri...

The TLS of July 14, 1932 carried the following review by 1 ...rry of Unpubli... ...l Taylor ...li...

time arrogating to ...or sensitiven... ...inful...

this sort of direction (based on part of a lord's speech) into a summing up?

(9) Hardy's persistent use of the personal 'I disagree' (with Lever's points) pays dividends to the Prosecution's case. Because he never disagrees with the Prosecution it appears that he is siding with them, even though he here presents quite neutral re-statements of both Lever's and Wilkinson's points about the different kinds of 'need' a book buyer might have. This psychologically subtle, rhetorical tactic is particularly crucial here because he reminds the Jury of Wilkinson's analogy of the drug addict. Also, by juxtaposing Lever's 'need' (a healthy need for sexual release on the part of the book buyer) with Wilkinson's hypothesis of the drug addict 'needing' larger and larger doses, once again he smugly suggests to the Jury a more decadent interpretation to one of Lever's words.

(10) The phrase 'it does not mean that these men should be acquitted'. Hardy's phraseology seems to imply that the Defendants are guilty, even though guilt has not yet been proved. (Incidentally, Hardy goes on to paraphrase the Government's Act, and explains to the Jury that it is not illegal to read or watch 'pornography', only to manufacture or sell it. This absurd situation — where the individual is a free consumer in a suppressed market — is typical of the Middle Ages double-think attitude of society towards sexuality, and is symptomatic of the juvenile and harmful voyeuristic hypocrisy which says that sex is okay, so long as you don't get caught doing it or reading about it. It is a socio-psychology which results in much private suffering in those people particularly susceptible to the notion that their sexual impulses, which they cannot help, are wicked. If Hardy, Anderton and their kind think that 'pornography' is harmful because of the damage it may cause to the minds of a 'significant minority' of people then they should look in the mental hospitals, the prisons, the alcoholic and drug recovery centres, among the down trodden and the down-and-outs of society, where they will find a far greater scale of damage caused by their repressive attitude. It has been said often, but it is worth repeating again, that if society could form an honest attitude toward sexuality, the demand for 'pornography' would lessen).

(11) Hardy's introduction of the 'prostitution' and 'brothel' analogy appears to be a blatant piece of opinion. Why does he introduce an element which seems to have been drawn solely out of his mind and which has no fair or objective bearing on the proceedings? Why does he choose the emotive words 'prostitution' and 'brothel' for his analogy?

After the summing up, a farcical series of retirements on the Jury's part commenced while they considered their verdict. I say 'farcical' because the Jury, obviously deeply divided (even after hearing Hardy's summing up) appeared to be pressured to arrive at the conclusion Hardy wanted. They returned first to say that they could not reach a verdict. Hardy gave them more time. They returned a second time to ask what was meant by the nebulous term 'an insignificant minority'. Hardy threw this task to the two barristers, both of whom had pre-found texts which they referred him to.

Mr WILKINSON: I would refer your Honour to paragraph 3849 of Archbold.

Mr LEVER: Your Honour, it appears that the question which the ladies and gentlemen of the Jury have asked is set out in the speech of Lord Cross which is just about an inch before the bottom of that paragraph.

JUDGE HARDY: Yes. I probably cannot do better than quote that in the speech of Lord Pearson. Members of the Jury, I do not think that I used the word 'minority', but in the sense in which it appears in your note it is not inappropriate. This question was considered by the House of Lords, and Lord Pearson said:

"The statutory definition of obscenity contains no requirements as to the number of persons or as to the proportion of its readers which the article will tend to corrupt or deprave. The statutory definition '...refers to "persons" which means "some persons", though I think in a suitable case, if the number likely to be affected is so small as to be negligible — really negligible — the *do minimus* principle might be applied. But if a seller of pornographic books has a large number of customers who are not likely to be corrupted by such books, he does not thereby acquire a licence to expose for sale or sell such books to a small number of customers who are not* likely to be corrupted by them'."

Members of the Jury, you will bear in mind I have already directed you that it is not necessarily confined to customers who buy them directly.

"Lord Cross said, 'There is no doubt that the justices had to answer two questions: first, what persons were likely to read these books; and, secondly, whether they were satisfied that they would tend to deprave and corrupt a significant proportion of such persons'. Later, Lord Cross observed, 'a significant proportion of a class means a part which is not numerically negligible but which may be much less than half'."

I think that is all the assistance I can give you on the topic, Members of the Jury.

After this vaguery, which could be used successfully to convict all but the Pope, Hardy then directed the Jury to retire; but they soon returned again to say that they still could not reach a verdict. The Jury were obviously divided. According to second-hand reports received we knew that they were conducting a heated argument. In post-trial conversation with a member of the Jury we learned that the main support came from

* This appears to be a nonsense, and it is probable that the court writer meant to put *'likely'* rather than *'not likely'*.

the women — not the men.

Judge Hardy told the Jury that the time had not yet come when he could accept a majority verdict. The Jury retired again. They returned for the fourth time to report that they still could not reach a verdict. This time, Hardy told them that he could accept a majority verdict, but he asked them first of all to make one last attempt to agree with each other.

JUDGE HARDY: If that proves impossible then I can accept a verdict upon which at least ten of you are agreed; eleven to one, or ten to two. No smaller number is acceptable. If it becomes apparent after discussion that ten of you are not going to agree on your verdict then we do not ask you to struggle on the impossible. Please send a message and I will discharge you. It means a retrial of this matter, but if it has to be then it has to be. Will you please retire again.

To observers, Hardy appeared to grow irritable with the continual inability of the Jury to agree. The words, 'It means a retrial of this matter, but if it has to be then it has to be', with their tone of delivery, appeared to imply a criticism of the Jury, that the Jury had somehow wasted court time. In post-trial discussion with our juror 'friend' we discovered that as a result of this verbal pressuring one of the members among the 'for' group abruptly changed sides. She declared, "Let's get it over with!" To me, her words are tantamount to her saying that, because the judge seemed determined to get a verdict one way or another, today or tomorrow, it was futile to oppose him. It was, of course, almost tea-time. The Jury had been in recess for two and a half hours after sitting around since early morning and naturally they were impatient to be dismissed.

After further heated discussion among themselves the 'against' side won over members of the 'for' side. When the Jury returned for the last time they pronounced both men Guilty by a majority of 10-2. This was for the 'offences' committed at Orbit Books. Judge Hardy then listened to the similar charge brought against Dave for the 'offence' of storing books at the Savoy offices. In reading out these particulars the court clerk, when he came verbally to list the books (the identical Grove Press and Venus titles which had been sold at Orbit Books) included in the list together with the charged books Samuel Delaney's *The Tides of Lust* though this was not supposed to be listed with these books. No mention of this slip appears on the official court transcript but many observers will swear that they heard the book's title and its author mentioned by the clerk — for what reason, one is left to guess.

In mitigation, before Hardy came to pass sentence, Lever reiterated his point that both Defendants were of previous good character. He also said that of their own free will the Defendants had elected for trial because they believed they were innocent; this was quite a different matter to their being brought for trial. Also, the issue at hand — whether the books being prosecuted were obscene or not — was not the most clear-cut issue it was possible to have. After briefly stating the Defendants' personal financial circumstances (which were meagre, belying the impression built by the Prosecution and Judge Hardy that these men were living well off an 'evil' and 'corrupt' trade), Lever then raised a final, and most important, point:

Mr LEVER: There was one matter which exercised my mind as to whether or not it was proper to raise it in front of the ladies and gentlemen of the Jury. I decided that it was not. It is a matter which goes to mitigation. I am instructed that the Defendant Mr Britton had occasion before these raids to ask the police for some guidance. I am also instructed that formal requests were made not only by him, but by those instructing me so that he could receive guidance as to what was in the view of the police in this area permissible and not permissible. Whilst that is in no shape or form a criticism of the police in not wishing to —

JUDGE HARDY: They just dare not do it, dare they?

Mr LEVER: I realise that. In my submission, it is a matter which goes to mitigation because clearly, although he was running an establishment of this sort, he was trying to show a measure of co-operation and to receive guidance from the police as to what they regarded as permissible and not permissible. One does not criticise the police for saying "We shall confiscate what we confiscate, and prosecute on Section Two what we prosecute on Section Two". One cannot criticise the police for that.

JUDGE HARDY: If you wish to sail close to the wind, you cannot expect the police to tell you how close you can sail.

Mr LEVER: No. It is mitigation to the extent that they were not being clandestine about the matter, but saying, "Please can you give us guidance on the matter?" Although the police cannot be criticised, it is mitigation. It indicates a wish on their part to stay on the correct side of the law.

JUDGE HARDY: Yes, but they should not have sailed as close to the wind as they did. The answer to the dilemma is that if you are in doubt as to whether you are committing an offence then do not do anything which could possibly amount to one, but I take your point.

This last ruling by Hardy ("The answer to the dilemma is…" etc) is the one which must most concern people outside of Savoy who believe they are living in a free society. If this ruling is used as a precedent it could have widesweeping effects on liberalism and the freedom of the individual to read and to speak. If this whole case was a 'set-up' by police, DPP and the judiciary the dilemma which Hardy refers to is a manufactured dilemma. It is a sinister development. Many books currently on open sale throughout Britain and published by respectable houses of long-standing could be used effectively by police to secure prosecutions.

It is a precedent which could be used with impunity to bring convictions against any persons who manufacture, distribute, store, sell, print or otherwise handle almost any form of printed material provided there is a possibility that the material might be obscene.

So far as people in the book trade are concerned, the implications of the direction are bound to be impractical, because to protect themselves from possible conviction newsagents and booksellers theoretically are faced with the task of reading all the material which they sell in order to try to establish beforehand whether it might possibly be obscene. The direction is morally unsound, because individuals who are unable to predict accurately if materials they are handling are obscene appear to be being threatened with conviction and possible imprisonment. The direction is not even just. Under Judge Hardy's ruling, publishers, newsagents and booksellers are to carry all the responsibility for determining whether or not material is obscene.

Of course, in a society governed by these kind of rulings, most publishers will solve Hardy's 'dilemma', if it is enforced more widely, by avoiding books which might incur the retribution of police and courts; they will select books which give no offence to anyone, and most authors will be quite happy to feed publishers with an endless supply of this kind of bland, artless material. So far as English literature is concerned, the implications could be profound.

After listening to Lever's closing remarks made in mitigation, Hardy passed sentence. He ignored, so far as I could assess, all that had been said in mitigation. He implies, crudely, that there had been a secret operation underway at Orbit Books. Of course, this makes his absurdly inappropriate prison sentence for Dave appear justifiable, because if an operation is shown to be clandestine the public will more easily accept the fiction that the Defendants were lawless men.

JUDGE HARDY: I deal first with you, Philip William Bunton. This can be said in your favour, that you did not persist in this after being first approached by the police...*(Editors' Note: Phil left for unrelated reasons, but Hardy's case is best served by making this assumption)...* Secondly, that you did not try to conceal your position and thirdly, and most importantly, you did not cover up who was the real owner of the business. Those things stand you in good stead...*(Editors' Note: Phil 'revealed' these facts because there was no reason why he should not do so)...*It must be made clear that people who take part in this kind of activity are at risk. I think it is appropriate that there should be a sentence of imprisonment but I shall suspend it which means that if you commit no further offences, particularly offences of this kind, you will not have to serve a period of imprisonment, but if you do then the court has power to, and I most certainly will, order you to serve the term of one month, which is the sentence I pass, in addition to any other sentence. The period of suspension being twelve months.

David Edward Britton, if people desire to make money out of this kind of activity then they must be expected to expose themselves to risk if they run foul of the law. I think that it must be made clear to people who run these businesses that if they infringe the law then they must serve punishment for it. You must serve twenty-eight days imprisonment. I make the usual order for costs. The sentence is to run concurrently.

Few, if any in the court except Hardy, expected a prison sentence to be imposed. Many jurors' faces appeared visibly perplexed. A few days ago (on my Strangeways visit) I learned from Dave that the guards who escorted him to the cells after sentence was passed threw up their hands in disbelief. Mr Lever afterwards said that he felt the sentences were "unnecessarily severe". Mr Hoffman said that in his opinion, taking into account all the circumstances, he thought the sentences were savage. Mr Redfern, when contacted, thought the sentences excessive. According to Lever (his retrospective comments) Hardy's intention had been to make an example, to establish a policy which other courts would follow.

It could seem that Hardy was out to nail Dave. It has been suggested to us that even Redfern's more sophisticated defence would not have achieved different results. Perhaps not in *that* court, before *that* judge. But there *would* be a difference, I think, in Birmingham, in Liverpool, or Carlisle. For the moment at least. Many key points and observations which I have tried to highlight indicate a possible conspiracy to convict.

But where did we go wrong? Apart from the prevailing climate in society which appears to be sanctioning cultural avatars like Hardy, Whitehouse and Anderton to don armour and take up their moral swords (too much swords and not enough sorcery!), we neglected to press for a postponement of the trial. Lever appeared not to be aware of Hardy's aims.

But is society aware of what it is allowing? Events last night in Strangeways Gaol, today (June 4th) are making headlines on the radio and television. Near rioting prisoners have been taken to hospital; at least two have slashed their wrists. I am informed that the prison hospital wing has been burned down. Again, the conditions in this outmoded, Victorian-built gaol where prisoners are crammed three to a cell and remand prisoners have to wait for up to a year to come to trial, single it out. Only six months of the year have passed and there have been three deaths and several attempted suicides brought about by despair. Is this the right place to incarcerate *anyone*, let alone the people (and there are many) convicted of petty crimes (such as fare dodging) and those law-abiding people who have got caught by, or have been pushed into, the machinery?

According to Lever, an appeal is out of the question because of the precedents set by appeal judges at two of the Soho cases: Regina v.

A' JOKE

IN A RECENT article, author Michael Moorcock called it "the erosion of liberty". Under Thatcherism, he complained, and particularly in the midst of post-Falklands fever, "strongly authoritarian and conservative elements in our society" are at last being given the long leash they crave and are going to work on easy UK targets — "chiefly black youth but, in general, the area of so-called victimless crime".

The particular affront he highlighted was the prosecution of his own Manchester publishers, Dave Britton and Michael Butterworth.

Having suffered 40 to 50 raids in less than ten years, usually resulting in the destruction of seized material but never a charge, the pair were finally driven to temporary liquidation last year.

The most massive and co-ordinated assault came in October 1980 when two of Britton's shops, plus the offices of his publishing firm — jointly run with Butterworth — were raided. This time Britton came to trial under the Obscene Publications Act. The charge, which took 19 months to reach court, was storing and selling materials likely to deprave and corrupt.

A jury found him guilty. He served almost three weeks of a 28-day sentence before emerging, as Moorcock put it, shorn of hair, one and a half stones lighter and "in a very shaken condition".

His partner Butterworth is also due to come to trial, possibly before magistrates. He believes,

perhaps optimistically, that he will receive something less than jail.

The campaign against Britton and Butterworth worries Moorcock not only because his own bread and butter is threatened but because these were not hardcore Soho spivs but publishers and sellers in the almost reputable underground tradition. They published original works of some merit (Heathcote Williams, Paul Abelman, William Burroughs, Harlan Ellison) and generally dealt in radical literature, SF, periodicals, general fiction, American comics, posters, records, badges and similar paraphernalia. They also sold soft core porn, without which the business would have long ago gone down the pan.

Britton and Butterworth became a target for establishment headbutts soon after James Anderton, Manchester's zealous chief constable, come on the job in 1976.

Anderton would have noted that Britton's Orbit Books and then Books Chain Ltd were hangouts for numerous unorthodox youth — or, in the estimation of Butterworth, "the shops were at the very front of whatever street level rock wave was happening".

Butterworth joins Moorcock in sensing "an erosion into personal choice areas. Before," he says, "it was hardcore. Now it's the criminalising of soft core and from there it could go into books or films of literary merit."

In Moorcock's piece, printed in the August 6 issue of Time Out (it was done ostensibly for the Guardian but they backed out due, he suspects, to a case of jitters), he asked:

"How long will it be before the excellent political bookshop Grass Roots, a stone's throw from Britton's premises, finds itself threatened? This shop carries a large stock of lesbian and homosexual fiction and non-fiction."

The answer was — not very

long. Grass Roots, we learn, has been raided and deprived of its drug-related books: how to spot, grow, produce, and the dangers and pleasures therein involved.

Britton himself has been raided yet again. One of his shops was liberated of its 'girlie' magazines the very morning he was released from Strangeways. Some of this stock has been returned. Most has been destroyed. The usual pattern.

IT IS accu........ events of this ....rt th' ... dr.. ed the busi..ess .t i...se?. N.w othe publis! ers a. d distributors of simila: ca... might well begi. tr ...onder wh... ther...ey too re..ly to feel t..e st..k.

.n July 13 half a dozen m...bers of Lon.. .n's Obsce Pub.. at...ns squad launche. the...r .es .. on the Kens r.ad .....out Comic. / H. Kno.. ..ress, ..business Ton..Benn... .t (no re.. h.. ...ffe ..arol.

The pa..turn a liv on their posse.sio. licensing ...hts to Sh...on's F..ry F. Fat F... .dy's Cat which survive, the '60s.

T...Benne. the. own tit ... ics — ...tribute more co centri...

st........oward £10,000 worth of m...

B... he hi... rer hou wo art T ut. di of s

BRITAIN'S CREEPING CENSORSHIP

Sharman and Regina v. Vella. In both cases judges reduced sentences of four months to 28 days. Judge Hardy knew about these.

I say, "Where did we go wrong?" and of course I do not mean to imply that we went wrong with Savoy, or in the way we have conducted our business. We have been *conducting* our affairs in exactly the same way since at least the mid-60s, when I started writing for New Worlds magazine, and Dave and I separately started publishing. We have been working at the same thing in one form or another for getting on twenty years, and *we* have certainly got no more outrageous. The issues of "anti-terrorism, beating pornography, protecting diplomats and the Queen" (to quote from a recent *Daily Express* article, 'Crisis at the Yard') indicate that certain elements in society are becoming unreasonable, not us. I do not condone terrorism, but nor do I agree that the freedom to read, speak, write or publish should be sacrificed to what seems to me to be a wave of legally sanctioned irrationalism.

The skilful manipulation by some parts of the police and the judiciary of the obscenity laws as they exist, the timing of the prosecution against us to coincide with the trials in Soho, as well as the Government's measure to contain Soho sex establishments, would appear to have caused someone who was endeavouring to keep *within* the law to be cast as a criminal. There are other factors: the pronouncements of elderly lords divorced from the realities of British commerce, as well as Anderton's rabid prejudices which have ensured that there has been a shortcoming of democratic law in Manchester. It is the job of the police to uphold the law, not to make or influence it, yet society as a whole is apparently prepared to allow a degree of leeway in this respect. Recently, Mr Anderton was decorated with the O.B.E., presumably for his beliefs and actions. There were no letters of complaint to be found subsequently in the personal columns of the press.

We are not approaching the Dark Age — in Manchester we are *in* the Dark Age. Our shops and offices are still the targets of raids. Recently, Grass Roots, the local 'alternate' and feminist bookshop came under fire for the first time. Businesses in London and elsewhere, connected with this raid, were also 'done over'. The police are no longer concerned exclusively with erotica. The practices which arouse their prudery currently have been extended to cover the following:

The sale of manuals for the use and abuse of drugs,

The sale of 'underground' comics,

The sale of many kinds of videos including horror movie videos,

The sale of Rock music records (e.g. "the Anti-Nowhere League's *So What*, seized recently by London police).

(In Manchester, police have made the word 'video' virtually a synonym for 'pornography', following several interviews officers have given with the media). Seized goods in all these categories currently are with the D.P.P. who is deciding whether prosecutions can be brought under the nebulous obscenity laws.

Where will the police and their supporters — certain councillors, judges and the like — turn their attentions now, if they succeed in criminalising these areas of personal choice? What is the boundary between stimulation and art — when will *that* boundary be overstepped? What other minority activities (political, religious, social) could be 'proved' to 'deprave and corrupt'?

If the police can make another 'offence' stick, in any of these areas, then even heavier prison sentences are on the way. Do we stand back and let that happen, stop what we're doing, say we're sorry? Sorry for what? The problem has escalated beyond Savoy's immediate concern and survival. We can only hope, for ourselves, that, after the publication of Savoy Dreams, we will be able to survive in any conditions. Internment, about which Anderton has repeatedly spoken as a deterrent to young offenders and 'anti-establishment' (i.e. minority) persons, is now less of a remote possibility in Manchester than it was in 1980 when he first proposed the idea. Cheaper than building new prisons.

M.B. June 1982

Because of a series of possibly auspicious occurrences, **Savoy Dreams***, initially intended for publication in 1981, and then in 1982, sees publication on the eve of 1984. Police antagonism in Britain towards films, books, magazines and comics, has increased. Among the thousands seized are standard works by Aldous Huxley, Tom Wolfe, William Burroughs, Hunter S. Thomson and Charles Baudelaire, as well as underground comics (*Fat Freddy's Cat,* Furry Freak Brothers*, and others), and sundry works on the use and abuse of drugs. At the time of going to press it is not clear whether prosecutions will be successful, although it is thought likely that many of the publications will be destroyed.*

December 1983

MAIMED MAN'S MIRACLE 'STITCH ON' OP

By SUN REPORTER

DOCTORS performed a miracle operation yesterday in a bid to save a man's sex life.

They sewed his penis back on after it was severed in a brutal attack with a knife. The man picked it up and stumbled into a nearby hospital, pleading for help.

Amazed nurses and orderlies rushed him into the operating theatre at Chesterfield Royal Hospital, Derbyshire.

The man, who is not being named, was "satisfactory" last night after the operation.

Surgeon John Whiteman refused to discuss the case.

"I cannot talk about the patient without his permission." he said.

The man also refused to comment on the operation.

Refused

But a hospital spokesman said "We think it was reasonably successful, although it is too early to say if he will be able to have a sex life."

The victim, aged 37, was slashed with a do-it-yourself knife in a public lavatory in Saltergate, Chesterfield.

Police said they were treating it as "a serious crime." and appealed for witnesses to the incident.

They refused to release the man's name. "because of the personal nature of the attack."

Sex attack on pelican

POLICE SAID yesterday that they have charged a young Moroccan man in Syros, Greece, with sexually assaulting a pelican, the mascot of the neighbouring island of Tinos. The pelican died from internal haemorrhage, police said.

They said that a trial was suspended yesterday when the Moroccan asked for legal representation and will be continued today. The man, identified as Abdel Brim Talal, aged 28, was arrested on Saturday in Tinos when traces of blood and feathers were found on his clothes.

The pelican, Marcos, was one of two males on the island, much beloved by the locals. He was found wounded late on Friday in a public toilet, and a veterinarian's examination showed that he had been sexually assaulted. The bird died shortly afterwards.

Police said that a group of enraged islanders attacked the suspect. He was saved by police intervention. Press reports said that two German tourists had also filed complaints against Talal for attempted rape, but police did not confirm this.

The press also reported that the body of the pelican will be stuffed and kept on Tinos.—AP.

"I am so ... .t what I have done." seen at his Davenport.

● Cont on Back Page

Baby's head on mountain

Police were today visiting hospitals, clinics and doctors' surgeries in an area near Swansea after a huntsman, exercising his hounds, found a baby's head on a mountain.

The head was found near the village of Cwmllyntell in the Swansea Valley and police were also searching the area today.

Police said the head was that of a child born within the last two weeks.

cíties of the Red nígbt

Cities of the Red Night *is the latest work of an author to whom Savoy owes a great debt both as a model and as a catalyst, and although we have published no work by William Burroughs other than the narrative to be found elsewhere herein, the UK paperback rights to* Cities *were purchased by Savoy but had to be relinquished during company reorganisation.* Cities of the Red Night *has been well reviewed in other places since the book appeared from John Calder in the Spring of 1980, and so no synopsis was thought to be necessary for the following review. Mr. Moorcock had already commenced notes expressing his reaction to the book before Savoy approached him, and his review is to be considered more as a short appreciation of William Burroughs and as an advertisement for a remarkable novel.*

CITIES OF THE RED NIGHT is not only the first full-scale novel William Burroughs has produced in some years, it is for me in many ways his best. Burroughs has reclaimed himself and returned to those of us who used to bring illicit Olympia Press editions of *Naked Lunch* and *Ticket That Exploded* back from France a sense of that heady enthusiasm which we might have thought gone for ever. The metaphors and the images are frequently the same in *Cities of the Red Night,* but Burroughs brings to them a power of organisation, a narrative drive, which was often lacking in his previous work. His inspiration seems undiminished, his prose bears all his stylistic hallmarks (much imitated, but of course inimitable) and has a keener sense of control. His obsessions, his original turn of phrase, his humour, are all exhibited in this book which suggests, among many other things, that 'Free Brotherhoods', or pirate communes, might have been a better model for society than democratic capitalism. These outlaw brotherhoods, similar in attitude to, say, the Cossack sechs, are cited by Burroughs whose alternate universe is hardly marred at all by a touch of sf rationalisation. Burroughs can write with such authority that one is never absolutely certain if he personally believes in some of the ideas put forward in his books. One looks for irony and sometimes finds it. Sometimes one does not. So we wonder if we are faced with a supremely clever literary writer or a supremely-obsessed fanatic. This ambiguity is in itself perpetually fascinating for those of us who admire Burroughs and who have found him as puzzling in person as he is in his books. He seems at once naively open and a master of disguise. His books work on our imagination as I believe they are meant to work: to spark further images and ideas, to focus our attention on the abuse of all kinds of power, whether sexual or political, to examine the nature of modern mythologies so thoroughly rooted in us as to be described frequently as 'facts'. Burroughs's great skill is that he takes philosophical abstractions and earths them very firmly in concrete images. Often these images are horrific, fantastic, sordid. But the method has an appropriate effect. We may move into the wildest fantasies, explore the strangest ideas, give closer than usual attention to acceptable modern morality, but our feet are kept, somehow, on the ground. Burroughs uses irony and aphorism to achieve this, as well as scenes of frightening brutality. It is what makes him such an original and why he has been such a major influence on the fiction of the last ten or twenty years. We have all learned from him. His metaphors are drawn from the world of drugs, sado-masochism, homosexual bars, crime and despair. His characters are at once aggressors and victims, prepared to kill or to die for the possession of something which they cannot even identify, let alone name. They are lost souls in a Hell which they have helped create, searching for anodynes and solutions, for a means of living in a world whose rules and verities are forever in question. Prometheus escaping from a bondage harness to create nuclear fission without any idea what he can do with it and horrified at the power which it confers upon him. We all possess power. How we react to the knowledge of our own power is a central theme of Burroughs's work. We can abuse it. We can refuse to accept it. We can play tricks with it. We can try to give it away. But it is always with us. And because Burroughs presents us with so many metaphors of power we can interpret him in almost any way we choose.

To extend this theme any further would be to give you my interpretation, my beliefs, and I do not think that there is any place for such an exercise in this review, save to say that in the end Burroughs seems to be predisposed to those anarchist ideals of self-determination which are directly opposed to any notion of licence, inhuman cruelty or self-indulgence which a literal emulation of some of his characters might lead to. There seems to me to be very little Nietzsche in Burroughs and much more Kropotkin.

There are many familiar characters in *Cities of the Red Night*, continuing to discover permutations of the roles set for them in the three first novels of their kind: Dr Benway, who remains one of my favourite characters, and the others. There are characters from later work. And there is factual material, dealing chiefly with the setting up and the destruction of the pirate commune founded by Captain Mission in the 18th century. Burroughs seems to have extended his range while developing new techniques to deal with this extension. There is a vitality about this new book which could be said to be lacking in some of his work from the past ten years.

> There he is standing on a ruined pier left over from the English, in some uniform of his own devising. He is flanked by Opium Jones, the de Fuentes twins and Captain Strobe, all looking like a troupe of traveling players a bit down on their luck but united in determination to play out their assigned roles. Boys trail behind them, carrying an assortment of bags, cases and chests. They walk across the beach and disappear one after another into a wall of leaves.

The book cuts back and forth from a distanced third person narrative to an immediate first person. A few paragraphs further:

We are standing in a walled enclosure like a vast garden, with trees and flowers, paths and pools. I can see buildings along the sides of the square, all painted to blend with the surroundings so that the buildings seem but a reflection of the trees and vines and flowers stirring in a slight breeze that seems to shake the walls, the whole scene insubstantial as a mirage.

Then in the next paragraph:

This first glimpse of Port Roger occurred just as some hashish candy I had ingested on the boat started to take effect, producing a hiatus in my mind and the interruption of verbal thought, followed by a sharp jolt as if something had entered my body. I caught a whiff of perfume and a sound of distant flutes.

I have not extracted these examples as being the 'best' from a book so rich as to put almost anything else published this year to shame, but to show a little how the narrative works.

Cities of the Red Night is by William Burroughs. It could not be by anyone but William Burroughs. It is the work of a conscious and audacious literary artist. It should be bought at full price (£9.95) and it should be read.

Michael Moorcock

RABBIT HORROR

A MAN slaughtered rabbits in a park's corner then shoved one of the dead and bleeding animals into the face of a 67-year-old woman.

And when arrested, James Bird, 20, of Cale Green, Shaw Heath, Stockport, had a dead rabbit in his mouth Manchester Crown Court heard yesterday.

Bird was remanded in custody for medical reports after admitting the offences which took place at Bruntwood Park, Cheadle.

Corpse exploded while it was being cremated

A BODY being cremated exploded because of a heart "pacemaker" device still in it, Ipswich Borough Council's environmental services and property committee heard yesterday.

The tiny device's mercury-powered batteries overheated and blew up, endangering crematorium staff, said technical services chief Mr. Reg Marden.

"It sounds extremely dangerous to me," committee chairman Mrs. Margaret MacDonald remarked.

From the Ipswich Evening Star

58 die as cop goes berserk

A DRUNKEN policeman killed 58 people in an eight-hour rampage after a row with his mistress.

Then crazed Woo Bom-Kon, 27, blew himself to pieces with hand grenades, authorities in Seoul, the South Korea capital, said yesterday.

Woo's mistress, Chun Mal-Sun, 25, who was among 37 injured, said a row began when she woke her lover while trying to brush a fly off his chest.

Woo went out and returned to the house drunk. He started beating Chun and when she followed him outside he shot her.

Drink

He then made door-to-door calls—killing anyone who answered. Next he went on the rampage in the surrounding countryside gunning down residents. In another village he killed 18 people, police said.

At one point, he ordered a boy to get him a soft drink from a shopkeeper, then gunned down the boy and two other youngsters as well as the shopkeeper and his wife.

By dawn, police and troops had tracked Woo to a farmhouse. There he set off two grenades which killed three members of the farm family as well as himself.

WILLIAM BURROUGHS

the place of Dead Roads

Text from the Ritz Readings

INTRODUCING KIM CARSONS, hero of a novel in progress entitled *The Place of Dead Roads*. Kim is a morbid, slimy youth of unwholesome proclivities, with an insatiable appetite for the extreme and the sensational. He has a dark side to his character, and he loves it. His mother had been into table-tapping, and Kim adores ectoplasm, crystal balls, spirit guides and auras. He wallows in abominations, unspeakable rites, diseased demon lovers, ancient ruined cities under a purple sky, the smell of unknown excrement.

In short, Kim is everything a normal, decent American boy is taught to detest.

(Progressive Education)
When Kim was fifteen, his father allowed him to withdraw from the school, because he was so unhappy there, and so much disliked by the other boys and their parents.

"I don't want that boy in the house again," said Colonel Greenfield. "He looks like a sheep-killing dog."

"It is a walking corpse," said a St Louis matron poisonously. Years later, Kim settled that account: when informed of her death, he said "It isn't every corpse that can walk — hers can't."

"The boy is rotten clear through and he stinks like a polecat," Judge Ferris pontificated. This was true. When angered, or aroused, or excited, Kim flushed bright red and steamed off a rank, ruttish animal smell.

"The child is not wholesome," said Mr Kindheart, with his usual restraint.

Kim remembers his father's last words: "Stay out of churches, son; and don't ever let a priest near you when you're dying. All they got a key to is the shit-house. And swear to me you will never wear a policeman's badge."

Kim decides to go West and become a shootist. If anyone doesn't like the way he looks, and acts, and smells, he can fill his grubby peasant paw.

Kim's training as a shootist begins. He meets a wise old assassin, Whispering Kes Mayfield.

"Uncle Kes, this is Kim Carsons."

The old man spoke in a dead, dry whisper: "Your hand and your eyes know a lot more about shootin' than you do. Just learn to stand out of the way." Now his eyes, old, unbluffed, unreadable, rest on Kim, as if tracing his outline in the air. "City boy, did you ever see a dog roll in carrion?"

"Yes sir, I was tempted to join him, sir."

"Did you ever see a black snake pretend to be a rattlesnake?"

"Yes sir, he coiled himself up and vibrated the tip of his tail in dry leaves: *brrrrrp.*"

"Kim, if you had your choice, would you rather be a poisonous snake or a nonpoisonous snake?"

"Poisonous, sir, like a green mamba or a spitting cobra."

"Why?"

"I'd feel safer, sir."

"And that's your idea of heaven, feeling safer?"

"Yes sir."

"Is a poisonous snake really safer?"

"Not really in the long run, but who cares about that. He must feel real good after he bites someone."

"Safer?"

"Yes sir. Dead people are less frightening than live ones. It's a step in the right direction."

"Young man, I think you're an assassin."

(Kim makes his bones)

As soon as Kim walks through the swinging door, he knows this is it. Two men at the bar by the door. One is tall and thin, with a dead, sour, wooden face; the other tall and fattish and loose-lipped, with lead-grey eyes. They fan out, blocking the door. Loose-Lips smiles, showing his awful yellow teeth.

"Now I don't like drinkin' in the same room with a fairy — do you, Clem?"

"Can't say as I do, Cash."

They want to bat it around for awhile. Kim doesn't.

"I don't want trouble with you gentlemen . . . let me buy you a drink."

Kim is still talking as his hand sweeps down to his belt and up, smooth and casual, as if he is handing Clem a visiting card, and shoots him in the stomach. Clem doubles forward and his false teeth fly out, snapping in the air. Clem's .45, barely clear of the holster, blows a hole in the floor. Kim pivots, both hands on the gun, and shoots Cash in the hollow of the throat. The heavy slug tears through and spatters the wall with slivers of bloody bone. Cash's gun *chunks* back into its holster. Clem is weaving around, trying to re-cock his .45 with numb fingers. Taking his time, Kim shoots him in the forehead. Both assholes are dead before they hit the floor.

Kim's arduous training has paid off in hard international currency. As Kim looks down at the two bodies crumpled there, spilling blood and brains on the floor, he experiences a rush of pure joy. Two enemies will never bother him again. Two lousy sons-of-biches, melted into air and powder smoke.

Kim remembers his first adolescent experiment with biologic warfare. Smallpox was the intrument, the town of Jehovah across the river his target. Their horrid church absolutely spoiled his sunsets with its gilded spire sticking up like an unwanted erection, and Kim vowed he would see it levelled to the ground.

It was dead easy. The townspeople were anti-vaccination . . . "polluting the blood of Christ," they called it. Around the turn of the century there were a number of these anti-vaccination cults, a self-limiting pheno-menon since all the cultists contracted smallpox sooner or later.

So Kim simply jogged the arm of destiny, you might say, by distri-buting free illustrated Bibles impregnated with smallpox virus to the townspeople of Jehovah. The survivors moved out. Kim bought the land and used the church to test his homemade flame thrower. He found the plan in *Boy's Life* . . . a weed-killer, they called it. Well, rotten weeds you know . . .

Kim recruits a band of flamboyant and picturesque outlaws, called "The Wild Fruits". There is the Crying Gun, who breaks into tears at the sight of his opponent.

"What's the matter, somebody take your lollipop?"

"Oh Señor, I am sorry for you . . ."

And the Priest, who goes into a gunfight giving his adversaries the last rites. And the Blind Gun, who zeros in with bat squeaks. And the famous Shittin' Sheriff, turned outlaw. At sight of his opponent he turns green with fear and sometimes loses control of his bowels. Well, there's an old adage in show biz: the worse the stage fright, the better the performance.

Kim trains his men to identify themselves with death. He takes some rookie guns out to a dead horse rotting in the sun, eviscerated by vultures. Kim points to the horse, steaming there in the noonday heat.

"All right, *roll* in it."

"WHAT?"

"Roll in it like dogs of war. Get the stink of death into your chaps and your boots and your guns and your hair."

Most of us puked at first, but we got used to it, and vultures followed us around hopefully.

We always ride into town with the wind behind us. The townspeople gag and retch:

"MY GOD, WHAT'S THAT STINK?"

"It's the stink of death, citizens."

(Kim makes the Grand Tour)

Kim disliked England at first sight. The porters and hotel clerks were deferring to his clothes and his luggage. They didn't see him. He soon saw that the whole pestiferous area is run on class categories. The most important category is manner and accent. If you have the manner and the accent, you can be wearing a burlap sack and the flunkers will stand to attention like one of Pavlov's salivating dogs at the sound of his master's voice.

What hope for a country where people will camp out for three days to glimpse the Royal Couple? Where one store clerk refers to another clerk as his 'colleague'? Licensing laws left over from World War One: "Sorry, sir, the bar is closed." And you know he is just delighted to tell you the bar is closed.

God save the Queen and a fascist regime . . . a flabby, toothless fascism, to be sure. Never go too far in any direction is the basic law on which Limey-Land is built. The Queen stabilises the whole sinking shit-house and keeps a small elite of wealth and privilege on top . . . And talk about licking the hand that takes the food out of your mouth! What Englishman has not seen himself having tea with the Queen, oh quite at ease you know . . .

The English have gone soft in the outhouse. England is like some stricken beast too stupid to know it is dead. Ingloriously foundering in its own waste products, the backlash and bad karma of empire. You see what we owe to Washington and the Valley Forge boys for getting us out from under this den of snobbery and accent, this ladder where everyone stomps discreetly on the hands below him:

"Pardon me, old chap, but aren't you getting just a bit ahead of yourself in rather an offensive manner?"

The only thing gets homo sapiens up off his dead ass is a foot up it. The English thing worked too well and too long. They'll never get all that ballast of unearned privilege into space. Who wants that dumped in his vicinity? They get out of a space ship and start looking about desperately for inferiors.

Kim was meeting Tony in Hyde Park. He got out of a cab and looked about him with loathing, at the brown water, the listless ducks, the dirty, scruffy pigeons.

"There is something here that is just awful," he decided. "A terrible lack . . ."

Kim was a few minutes early for his meet with Tony. Always advisable to get there early for a spooky meet like this, and check things out. "Maybe I should feed the fucking pigeons to be less conspicuous, or cruise one of the obvious guardsmen in civilian uniform of cheap lumpy blue suits?" Most of them looked suety and stupid and deeply vulgar, with a vulgarity of the spirit that only a class-rotten society can mold. No doubt about it, these are the *lower* classes.

Kim had never doubted the possibility of an afterlife or the existence of gods. Kim considered that immortality was the only goal worth striving for. He knew it was not just something you automatically got for believing in some nonsense or other; it was something you had to fight for, like everything else in this life or another.

The most unpleasant, precarious and downright stupid immortality blueprint was drafted by the ancient Egyptians. First you have to get yourself mummified, and that was very expensive, making immortality a monopoly of the truly rich. Then your continued immortality in the Western Lands is entirely dependent on the continued existence of your mummy. That is why they had their mummies guarded by demons and hid good.

Here is plain G.I. Ali . . . he's got enough *baraka* to survive his first physical death. He won't get far. He's got no mummy, he's got no names, he's got nothing. What happens to a bum like that, a nameless, mummy-less asshole? Why, demons will swarm all over him at the first check-point. He will be dismembered and thrown into a flaming pit, where his soul will be utterly consumed and destroyed. While others, with sound mummies and the right names to drop in the right places, sail through to the Western Lands.

There are of course those who just barely squeeze through. Their mummies is not in a good sound condition. These creeps can only live in the third-rate transient hotels just beyond the last check-point, where they can smell the charnel-house disposal ovens from their skimpy balconies. "Might as well face facts . . . my mummy is going downhill. Cheap job to begin with . . . gawd, maggots is crawling all over it . . . the way that demon guard sniffed at me this morning . . ." *Transient* hotels . . .

And here you are in your luxury condo, deep in the Western Lands . . . you got no security. Some disgruntled former employee sneaks into your tomb and throws acid on your mummy. Or sloshes gasoline all over it and burns the shit out of it. "OH . . . someone is fucking with my mummy . . ."

Mummies are sitting ducks. No matter who you are, what can happen to your mummy is a Pharaoh's nightmare: grave robbers, scavengers, floods, volcanoes, earthquakes . . . Perhaps a mummy's best friend is an Egyptologist: sealed in a glass case, kept at constant temperature . . . but your mummy isn't even safe in a museum. AIR RAID SIRENS; IT'S THE BLITZ!

"For Rah's sake get us into the vaults," scream the mummies without a throat, without a tongue.

Anybody buy in on a deal like that should have his mummy examined.

The end of Dead Roads . . .
Suppose the backdrop of reality, what you see
out there and assume to be real . . . streets, people,
trees, hills, sky . . . were suddenly ripped wide open.
The sheltering sky is thin as paper here . . .
that afternoon when I watched the torn sky
bend with the wind . . .
I can see it start to tilt and shred and tatter . . .
Caught in New York beneath the animals of the Village,
The Piper pulled down the sky.

Brion Gysin has an all-purpose bedtime story: It seems that trillions of years ago a giant flicked grease from his fingers. One of these gobs of grease is our universe, on its way to the floor.
SPLAT!

istration from **From Adam, to Oscar, Up Edgar.**
thcoming from Savoy.

Illustration from **The Adventures of Lord Perfidious Albion and Count Sublime Hubris.**
Forthcoming from Savoy.

From
Kris Guidio's
**Tales from
the Cramps.**
Forthcoming
from Savoy.

Photograph omitted from Savoy's
The Legendary Ted Nugent,
1982.

MICHAEL GINLEY

Introduction to the

BERNARD MANNING

Blue Joke Book

I MUST BEGIN by addressing a few, short words to those who will pick up this book knowing very little of its subject — Bernard Manning. A handful of readers have perhaps never heard of him. They should be told that Bernard is that rarest of creatures, a dialect comic whose strong Manchester accent nevertheless finds favour Nationwide and even in the USA. Manchester's answer, if you will, to Harry Lauder or Max Miller.

It is very rare indeed for a Manchester comic to rise to the stature of a 'household name' elsewhere in the country. Thanks to television, Bernard is perhaps the first. It started with his appearances on the networked GTV series *The Comedians* and will have been boosted, by the time this book appears, with his own TV quiz show *Match Up To Manning* due to be filmed in mid-1981.

Before Bernard, only one Manchester comic came close to national recognition: the late, great Ted Lune. Ted was another comic who spoke in a strong Manchester accent, but shortly after gaining some attention in *The Army Game* on ITV, Ted passed away. Not long afterwards, a likeable and extrovert club comic called Bernard Manning opened The Embassy Club in the working class district of Harpurhey, well out of the Manchester City Centre area but where, at the time, big money was to be made in clubs.

But why, the reader will wonder, have Manchester comics so rarely achieved any kind of stature in the variety world before? My own guess is that first theatre impresarios and, later, television producers, were unhappy about such artistes. Tough, blunt, uncompromising and independent as we are, Mancunians do not constitute malleable fodder for the footlights or the camera. Nothing that a latter-day Svengali could re-cast in an image of his own greatness. Had he tried, the impresario or television producer would have been told to fuck off. And that would have been the end of it.

Even Bernard Manning has probably only made it this far thanks to John Hamp, variety producer for Manchester's Granada Television. John produced both *Comedians* and *Wheeltapper & Shunter's Club* and both shows were networked nationwide. Comics who were previously unknown became overnight hot properties, as did some other acts appearing on *Wheeltappers* such as Dukes & Lee. Largely because Hamp left the artistes to get on with their acts as naturally as they would on the club stage.

Dialect accents were not barred. Jokes were told which would have scandalised a pre-war parlour gathering. Even the odd cuss-word crept in. Not as liberally as they are used on the club stage I grant you — but even John Hamp had to keep interference and meddling from the likes of Mary Whitehouse to a minimum. All in the cause of exposing North West talent to a wider audience for the first time. The success of the shows proved the point. And the most in-demand performer from either of the shows is the one man who regularly appeared on both: Bernard Manning.

A hardened club writer such as the author can pick out the individual features of Bernard Manning's act which generates his popular appeal. For a start, he's a fat man — the kind we prefer to have around since Shakespeare put the words into Julius Caesar's mouth. Then there are things like the pace of his routine, microphone technique, timing, breath control and script strength which nit-picking journalists are trained to look out for. I cannot belabour these points here; take my word for it that Bernard has all these technical features well under control.

It is with regret that I must tell the reader who has yet to see Bernard working live, that this book can only come pretty near to giving some idea of his talents. The written word is a poor vehicle for his visual gags, cannot generate the atmosphere in his Embassy Club and on the printed page we have to ignore Bernard's abilities as a male vocalist — six L.P.s the last time I counted.

What I can do is give some idea of the strength of his scripts, quoting many of the jokes used by him or attributed to him over the course of his career to date. A lot of them were written by Bernard himself; only a very small amount of his material is generated from ideas sent in to him. Some are jokes that have been around in other forms for a while but which have since been given the Manning 'treatment'.

It is important not to be shocked by what you read. Some of Bernard Manning's jokes tend to look a bit stark when presented on the printed page instead of in the raucous, beery atmosphere of the Embassy Club. I have resisted the temptation to weed out what I might think to be his more offensive racialist jokes or his jibes at religious minorities so prepare to be offended; Bernard is most catholic with his iconoclasm.

Readers may be aware that some of Bernard Manning's 'away' gigs have resulted in complaints from his hosts to the effect that his ideas of humour were not quite what had been expected. Though invariably exaggerated in press reports, such stories do illustrate that Northern humour has its roots in the savage conditions endured by the working class poor in the 19th century. In some parts of the country, the humour of the deprived poor was never heard and remains unacceptable to this day. Similarly, in a few smart seaside resorts developed in recent years, the past never happened.

Pointing out that press reports about his gigs are always much embroidered by the time they hit the stone, Bernard Manning claims that he is able to work anywhere. He might like to believe it but I'm sure that this is not true. Bernard is most certainly the toast of Harpurhey but I cannot see too many copies of this book selling in Cheltenham or St John's Wood. There, the inhabitants and their ancestors never had the need of a coarse and often sordid sense of humour to divert their attention from the squalor, graft and starvation with which they had to come to grips each day.

Instead, they got by with a much milder, twee, genteel sense of humour which today, only the most Pythonesque 'Upper Class Twit' would find amusing. The rest of us might even find such 'jokes' offensively irritating. Here's an example:-

Lady: (To her maid who, being of the Lower Orders, is none too
     bright.) "Tell me Mary, where is Mexico?"
Maid: "Beg pardon Ma'am but I do not even know the gennulmun."

This works in the opposite direction in that today's dirty joke can cause offence to a contemporary working class, now mostly relieved of the stresses and strains of life in former years. Bernard and myself hope that those people who are appalled by what follows will shut their great flapping gobs and leave the rest of us to enjoy life as we see fit.

The **Bernard Manning Blue Joke Book** *was published by Savoy / N.E.L. in 1982.*

MICHAEL BUTTERWORTH

(Illustrated by DAVID BRITTON)

a hurricane in a night jar

The Blood

I IMAGINE THE hungry blood of the desert shifts out there like a river of live intelligence beneath the sand. I imagine the blood-beasts sieve their way through the silica particles towards me, their tiny polymorphous heads moving like periscopes above the surface, the inexorable motion of their heads, crowded together in their millions, breaking like a wave-tossed sea at my feet, and I moan like a dreamer at some terror encountered in sleep.

I fancy that the blood mistakes me for the Hurricane's presence and comes either to revenge itself or to draw from me the 'something' that it seeks to make itself whole again. But *I* am not the blood's fashioner! The storm that agitates the blood and makes life has moved onwards on its track across the universe. How can I explain to the blood (if it *does* exist) that it has had its chance and must stay as it is?

The blood is the rationale of Jules Ulrik Vliet, and in my futile search for a reason for the behaviour of men and a foolish lingering hope that a way of continuation for my creators may yet be found, I have welcomed — and now cannot rid myself of — the notion of the 'blood'. Vliet assumed, contemptuously, that if life had shown such insouciance as it had on Earth then it must know that it can easily be regenerated. In the same way that warring kings and prime ministers knew that their people, decimated by war, could reproduce themselves again, Mankind knew that his extinction was surmountable.

He must have known about the invisible blood.

I do not think Vliet actually believes in the blood, although in the absence of a personal rationale of my own — I can have none — I find myself seduced. But Vliet's sensibility is such that he continually subverts his main didactic purpose, favouring abuse and ironic metaphor above

69

the usual compassion and directness, and so what success he will have with his aims on these sorry specimens that are left, I do not know.

"Some men caught more of this blood than others," he continued, after I had been listening to him for about three hours one evening. "Hitler, Jung, Einstein, Napoleon, Christ, all the great movers of Mankind including all the heroes of swords and sorcery and Rock'n'Roll which were my personal models, were more conscious of the blood's existence than most men, and they therefore tried harder to preserve the way the blood had been expressed – but the others, who had less blood, or who had less awareness of it, in their blindness worked constantly to thwart and pervert the efforts of the few. Earth's history was a record of the repression of the blood."

The Ghosts

" – I ONLY TRIED to do my job, to suckle up to my husband and bring up his son. It was my husband who never played true, who made my life an agony from beginning to end and took my mind off what I really wanted to do – my real aim in life was to be a model, a glamour girl that all women would love and who could rule all eternity. I would have stopped the war and saved the world from this –"

" – I worked bloody hard fixing panels to chassis day after day stinking with sweat and fouling my lungs with metal dust. The noise of the line was never out of my ears. The monotony drove me mad. I never wanted to do a factory job in the first place, but with a wife and screaming kids what can you do? What I wanted was to be a player on the pitch. I was good at football, but after I got married somehow there was never the time. I got more interested in getting my wage rise than watching what was happening –"

" – Of course, I saw it all coming. I warned the world in advance but no one listened. During my life I achieved what I wanted to do, one of the lucky ones I suppose. Nevertheless I was able to tour the world having a quiet word in everyone's ear, and I put in my bit to save you all –"

" – I too knew what was going on. How could I ignore it when my fields were withering from insecticides and my soils turning to fertiliser dust? My animals were treated badly to make ends meet. I was forced into a position I never wanted to find myself in. What I wanted was to be at one with the Earth, to enrichen its soils not strip it; but the pigs in the cities, the hungry bastards, ate everything faster than I could produce, and still wanted more. In the end I took my kerosene to the cities to burn them down –"

" – Ha! You *would* like to blame me! But I can assure you with all honesty I knew nothing! I knew nothing! My system was sound and my advice given in good faith. I practised all my life to make sure that I became a man of the world before giving you my secrets. I always wanted to be what I was. I loved my job and I'm sorry now that we can't all be around to continue..."

"— I never wanted to be who I was. I wanted to be a poet and soar on high, taking the whole human race with me. But I was no good with words and the words I did produce never gave me a proper income. I was forced to sell what little talent I possessed and go into the Business. I was unhappy, and lonely, but as I rose higher I eventually reached the limits I had set myself as a poet, and for a while I grew happy with my lot. But instead of elevating my fellow men I left them blind and purposeless; and I must confess that it might have been I who conferred with colleagues and international governments and unwittingly created the conditions which have led to this —"

A politician reluctantly appeared, smiling and then frowning, at first speechless, and dressless, his words finding no sure direction, his clothes no occasion, but eventually he spoke. As he did, the Earth trembled and shook. Gaping cracks appeared in the desert. Mountains tumbled down behind him, and when he had finished his brilliant oratory, applause soared from behind the sky in a continuous, beating thunder that echoed around the globe, sounding his curtain. Then the wind gathered his protesting form on its way.

Finally, in the debris, I saw a virgin ballerina, her sure white legs extended and her graceful arms curved above her arched spine. She trilled on her toes before gracefully launching herself across the sand, her ghost the last and most difficult to depart because in her art she carried all men and women, all ages and all promise of the future, away, in her movement.

Vliet smiled when I told him about the ghosts, and said that I was perversely affected. He can talk! But from my place, I had to agree. I was one who had erred and grossly misjudged the fine examples of Mankind who had left the watery womb of the Earth and grown away from the Earth as she had become used and abused and dry as an old husk speeding on her course through the black.

The Human Beings

VLIET: "SO, PIGS, filth, cocksuckers, I have come from your closets where you tried to imprison me, your Belsens where you tried to exterminate me, and there's no way you can escape for I have mutated into something which is beyond your comprehension!"

The partygoers are distracted by this sudden, ranting outburst which they know to be directed at them, but they are nevertheless riveted by the marvellous rhetoric of which Vliet is capable when he's tanked up and infected by the desert: "I am like the wind that cannot be stopped, or the rain that beats down on your enraged heads, or the sea that still pounds at your fractious toes. I can tell you, you are in for a dipping...a *sheep* dipping..." he takes another pull from that bottle which is the last bottle left on Earth, squandering it recklessly, like water "...my greedy and unwilling hosts, and I shall leave no blow unfelled or nightmare unturned!

"I set out to the very seat of your nature, to the time you ground one stick against another and heated your wretched carcasses as protection against the naked elements, for you were defenceless on plains of laval earth and needed to band together for the protection of your souls. Here you began your journey of blindness, of moronic proportions that has, as I shall show you, caused you to destroy your world; began that paltry, shiftless habit of looking to your behind, to the shit entrailed amidst the blood and viscera of your fallen, began your scheming, grasping rise to a thousand different godlands where you tried to insulate your conscience and justify your rapacity. You became what you called 'civilised', but your Civilisation grew into a mold which ravaged the planet and which will spread outward to destroy the fabric of the universe!"

He paused, for effect. Already some of the guests were waving large peacock feathers about in the radioactive air and were becoming bored, but they were still sufficiently struck to feign attention. The guards listened with unblinking gills as Vliet descended from the steps of a summer pavilion and began walking among his unwilling audience. His voice had grown harsh, and froth flecked his lips, and I knew that it would not be long before he was lying gasping on the ground, calling for one of his ornate breathing masks and suffering from one of his fits. "I am a part of you," he shrieked in hatred of all he saw. "I was an inadvertent creation, a side-product of your vanity industry who, if you'd ever recognised me properly, you would have gladly devolved back to the caves to elude! I was your advance warning, and for once in your miserable, prick-thinking lives I made you listen to another voice, another way; either you would listen to my voice or you would listen to the atomic wind as it scythes this way and that over your bones...and you listened to the wind! So I'll give you up as lost and shoot off on my own."

And off he went, past the guards who had allowed him this indulgence with their colourful patrons and who had sunken back into a sickly trance, but I knew he would be back, a half man and a half spirit, an artist swordsman up against bankers and accountants and housewives and polytechnic heads, taken by the fabulous ethereal airs of higher Earth but addicted to the bank clerks and the shitty earth from which he had been built.

20-8-1981

The 1980s — Part One

I GET UP
I GO TO WORK
THE CLOCK GOES ROUND
I GET UP
I GO TO WORK
THE CLOCK GOES ROUND
I GET UP
I GO TO WORK
THE CLOCK GOES ROUND
I GET UP
I GO TO WORK
THE CLOCK GOES ROUND
I GET UP
I GO TO WORK
THE CLOCK GOES ROUND
I GET UP
I GO TO WORK
THE CLOCK GOES ROUND
I GET UP
I GO TO WORK
THE CLOCK GOES ROUND
I GET UP
I GO TO WORK
THE CLOCK GOES ROUND
I GET UP
I GO TO WORK
THE CLOCK GOES ROUND
I GET UP
I GO TO WORK
THE CLOCK GOES ROUND
I GET UP
I GO TO WORK
THE CLOCK GOES ROUND
I GET UP
I GO TO WORK
THE CLOCK GOES ROUND
I GET UP
I GO TO WORK
THE CLOCK GOES ROUND
I GET UP
I GO TO WORK
THE CLOCK GOES ROUND
I GET UP
I GO TO WORK
THE CLOCK GOES ROUND
I GET UP
I GO TO WORK

My Life

I CONTROL EVENTS that I live as I see them – events of others intersect. To be realistic, I am born of flesh and blood – banks of material similar in function to memory tape passed down from generation to generation, from a period remote in time to my incongruous manifestation in the living present called 'My Life'.

Clouds flying low over desert wastes...

Dug-out canoes sluicing down culverts carrying entrants in a marathon race...

Ruined cities on skylines...

Sun beating down on water-boatmen flapping in the dried pond...

Packet of Weights Tipped lying by his ankle in the Smoker's Hut...

Elizabeth Higson's tits pressed in his warm face. Cider bottles, empty, in the wire waste paper basket in the golf hut. "Like to fuck?" Lying out-of-bounds in the sun-yellowed fields sniffing ether from the chemist for that "nice young boy with a chemistry set" / the words of his headmaster: "Why did you supply it?" Sniffing and stammering: "Told me they collected butterflies, sir." "Don't you know ether's dangerous?" "Do now, sir."

Smoking joints in the toilets. Stripped in the showers examining cocks. He thought that his cock was one of the smallest, and needed reassurance; but looking at it in the mirror he thought that it looked bigger, and one kinder boy, who he later realised fancied him, told him that he had quite a big cock all considered. Steam, soap, the smell of skin. Fragments of a sea cove – his father, muscular, bronzed, in swimming trunks, playing with one of those large airy beach balls....

Bloody cuts on nails, on glass, on barbed wire.

"Butterworth! I want to look what you've got in your pockets. Now stand still while I see – and keep your hands on your head." Crumpled cigarettes. Damp leaflets. "You picked these off the tent floor? You've been inside stealing liquor, haven't you?" For the cigarettes, rustication. For the liquor from the deserted cricket club party marquee, with its bar left open...the crime couldn't be pinned.

Hankies tied into hard knots and smote against his skin by a German school mate. "Want to show me?"

A lift in a post-van, warm hands on crotch. "You've got a big pair!"

Sycamore rustling outside his window in sodium lighting – deserted streets – sodium glare in sky above city. Air-smells fresh and clear and the night silence frees him from the day. Youths stalk the streets with rifles, armoured cars manned by school-children patrol the city perimeters. Dogs bark in the distance. Mars shines brightly, a fierce red throb.

The door opens and the Stranger Man comes in, followed by his parents who wear anxious, concerned faces. "Now lie still. Let me see." The doctor rolls back the bedclothes down to his stomach which contracts in fear. "What a nice smooth tummy!" the doctor chuckles over him.

"Just a little more." He peels back the clothes still further to reveal his pyjama bottoms, and with soft fingers unties the white cords. "Soon have him out." Rectal smell from far away...Scarred, layered vista of desert and rubble. Seeping sun through red clouds. Rock music pounding through canyons into the sky. Yardbirds' *Still I'm Sad* booms through the dusk. Reactionary survivors dance to the strains of the last orchestra. "Not enough booze left for another!" Vliet shouts, running amok with a broken champagne bottle amongst the party-goers, his open shirt flaring out behind him...Mother crying, and father pacing up and down the tiny kitchen shouting. Crackling blue sparks from a dead tarsal on a laboratory bench. "Now, the object of passing the current is to prove the electro-conductivity of nerve fibre, and...energy equals work done. A truly splendid effort, Michael! 'A-Double Plus'."

White Mummies with diamond shoes drape themselves over Lying Lambs with burning cloaks. Albatross Men and Spider Women rope themselves together and trill in the sandstone dust. Large verandahs of long-gone palaces float just above the ground, and the revellers swirl and shout on their dreamy boards. Some recline in giant wicker chairs with enormous decorated backs, and smoke Sobranie cigarettes through jade holders. Men with syncoptic eyes fuck young girls in satin dresses who retreat to hacienda beds in cool palace bedrooms. Private guards with green gills stand idly about the fading scene eating cream buns and drinking wine and spirits offered to them by the dancers.

The Earth lies cleared, its huge flat surfaces spinning under the pink skies, and Butterworth smiles as he listens to the last idle chatter —

"The international market will stand another thermo-nuclear...Got any Secanol? Got a terrible migraine."

"Cut price dollies, I got to have my cut-price *dolly*...Well, I guess that completes our talk, Your Eminence, Prince Rahfad. If there's no oil left..."

"Got the jolly bugger!" Prince Phillip shouts out as the last white rhino sinks down on its buckled forelegs, sending up a cloud of dust into the African sky.

The Holocaust

EXCREMENT DRIPPED THROUGH sores through the old WWII trenches we used to lie low inside. Faded curtains — anchored bird-men try to fly in the red deserts. They eventually rise, trailing forlorn sperm webbing dripping in long strands to the barren ground: Vliet's supporters among the Cola People, and beneath and between them soar the bird-girls, exciting the bird-boys with feathery draughts from their mouths and gliding with open legs to show their silly slits.

The party is long over. The marquee closed. Crowds jostle the pave-

ments on long ago Earth as the pubs empty the blind. For long periods I can see only intermittently: I am one of the millions...then, above the scene, static, the frozen lunch on my fork poised: the boiling, seething lava; the sand cities; the burning napalm; the creatures of waste. With shame and fear I once saw Vliet take off his Rickenbacker and fling it at the stars like a man putting the shot, his thin body sucking at the stars, his mind emptying itself into the colossal bins of red sewage, and I felt that he had lost his poise and become sightless like myself.

Stars shone shine dream, winter's day long ago ice cracked under a young foot, cold mud-water welled up and caused that child to reflect on the nature of life. Blue star winking warning at the Cola People. Skins of albatrosses flayed out to dry and worn to get the secret of escaping through ethered dreams. Body lying in the dirt, spirit soaring.

Nova headlines:

PLANET DEFUSED
BOLIOGIC MUTANTS SCRAM
GLAZED LAYERED DESERTS OF THE HUMAN STAGE
LAST BIOLOGIC FLICKERS

"We understand you meet Death." The guards spray their lazy guns, turned on the lazy uncaring guests. Pleasure bombs rip through venal nerves – focus shining man the right way. Bodies slashed with burning rocks from the larval outpour. Billions speak at once. Clamour of pink clams just before exploding: "We want equal rights! We want equal...!"

Conversion currency useless.

I saw, and now I live it all.

Fire belching from drowning suburbs erupting through the flooding sea-water in white belches – and frogmen surface like bloated fish with white-attired bellies facing up at the silver sky.

I saw, and now I live it all.

From beneath, the Earth gives a groan, and the tortured mechanisms stop.

Burst of sun-fire.

Arm of God, a pulsating brilliance which swept out and engulfed that unfortunate population.

In the Night Jar

"WE HAVE DEVELOPED special senses which tell us where we are headed –" "Flashy upstart – who'd'se think he is?" slurs the pie-bald Countess of Sorum, collapsing in her lemon sorbet. **Something in my memory jumps, and I go back in time. I see Jules Ulrik Vliet with that drunken expression on his face, that long-ago child re-incarnated in his whisky-sodden face, and the desert, ever-present, all-covering, so that no human nuance is left except the extreme elements of all societies and**

the types like Vliet who, from their pinnacles of human perfection, swig the last drinks —

"But can we get higher?" he persists. "Can we soar like spirits in the void that envelops us, and get our energy directly from the suns without the bull-shit that passes for flesh?" He asked me this once, long ago, when we were earnest lab techs in a different world. I think of his words as I watch him cajole these 'characters' who live out their last moments in the desert, their last moments of their insane illusions, and I have to admit that these 'characters' are colourful. They are like zoo animals, who will soon become extinct — but be under no illusion yourselves, Vliet is not their keeper. He feels nothing for their souls.

The guards stand round with petrified gills, their guns smoking from recent killings, just a little tired now with Vliet whom they've tolerated because of his inventive energy. "Just one last swig — it's all that's left!" he implores, as the last of the old awake from their drugged flesh and stare from marbled windows open to the desert winds, coat tail flashing in the wind. The gun nozzles raise lazily and the party's over.

Long tracers of long ago.

Filamental boys with long rope-like penises entwined with the same comfort derived by massed worms — sunsets brilliant beyond belief and unattainable as the goassamer threads of hydrogen molecules that drift from the distant stars — smiling   postcard   long   gone.

'The 1980s' — Part Two

THE PAIN OF LIFE
THE CLOCK
THE PAIN OF LIFE
THE COCK
THE PAIN OF LIFE
THE CLOCK
THE PAIN OF LIFE
THE COCK
THE PAIN OF LIFE
THE CLOCK
THE PAIN OF LIFE
THE COCK
THE PAIN OF LIFE
THE CLOCK
THE PAIN OF LIFE
THE COCK
THE PAIN OF LIFE
THE CLOCK
THE PAIN OF LIFE
THE COCK
THE PAIN OF LIFE
THE CLOCK
THE PAIN OF LIFE
THE COCK

THE PAIN
THE CLOCK
THE PAIN OF LIFE
THE COCK
THE PAIN OF LIFE
THE CLOCK
THE PAIN OF LIFE
THE COCK
THE PAIN OF LIFE
THE CLOCK
THE PAIN OF LIFE
THE COCK
THE PAIN OF LIFE
THE CLOCK
THE PAIN OF LIFE
THE COCK
THE PAIN OF LIFE
THE CLOCK
THE PAIN OF LIFE
THE COCK
THE PAIN OF LIFE
THE CLOCK
THE PAIN OF LIFE
THE COCK
THE PAIN OF LIFE
THE CLOCK
THE PAIN OF LIFE
THE COCK
THE PAIN OF LIFE
THE CLOCK
THE PAIN OF LIFE
THE COCK
THE PAIN OF LIFE
THE CLOCK
THE PAIN OF LIFE
THE COCK
THE PAIN OF LIFE
THE CLOCK
THE PAIN OF LIFE
THE COCK
THE PAIN OF LIFE
THE COCK
THE PAIN OF LIFE
THE CLOCK
THE PAIN OF LIFE
THE COCK
THE PAIN OF LIFE
THE CLOCK
THE PAIN OF LIFE
THE COCK
THE PAIN OF LIFE
THE CLOCK
THE PAIN OF LIFE
THE COCK
THE PAIN OF LIFE

The Hurricane

THE HURRICANE: A fiery, yawling beating of nothing forced by the collapsing stars to contain itself.

There is no blood. The sun has swelled and diminished, and gone out, and the airless 'sky' is a darkened mass of approaching matter.

"We are the torches who light up the unknown," the voice in my head says. "In certain areas the 'finite' mixture of atoms and molecules has the property of forming itself into cognizant eyes and ears which enable it to record and see itself. The universe is a creature with the capacity of self-examination; we are its senses. Our role is to light up more of its darkness — by scientific and artistic endeavour, and by spreading our habitats to its far-flung reaches."

Then:

"We always try to understand the Universe in terms of ourselves when we should be trying to understand ourselves in terms of the Universe — as a necessary, rapacious mold of universal destruction, aiding entropy, or as a sensory organ of a blind creature."

It is the voice of the Librarian, recorded in conversation milennia ago to counter Vliet. There is no Superman — only a very clever Super-universe, as Vliet eventually discovered.

It has no eye — the Hurricane. The inrushing matter is charged with its frenzy, though I can detect no perceptual movement. I feel sudden horror at an idea — a culmination of many ideas of my long life — that the approaching masses are drawing towards *me*. I have become the Universe's awareness, the stars and galaxies my limbs! *I* am the heart!

When the Universe exploded from its primal ball it was stunned into senselessness, and while it regained its senses its pieces were flung far and wide, but as the power of its mind returned so it dragged back its mass! My species was but a spark off its brilliant mind — the purpose of our life was — is — no more or less than to regain that illumination, that lost soul —

The Bird People

"YOU CAN'T FIND that kind of solace out here,' Vliet said to me when I had made one of my periodic attempts to fault his motivations. I had asked him whether he felt that the postatomic landscapes represented a simplified emotional ambience. "Your mum and dad aren't here," I told him. "You don't have any brothers and sisters...no complicated business entanglements, no one trying to tread on your shoes and deny your right to occupy your space. No policemen, lawyers, girls, no one but yourself to have a ball."

"No," he said. "It doesn't work like that, because there's no one to get

WHIZZBANG
ON THE SOMME

your food and take care of your shit. There's no one to get high with — hell man, I need someone to bounce off, someone to tell who I *am*. So I'm not operating out here because it's simpler. The desert does nothing to help me in that way. What it tells us is that 'this is the future — this place out here is where the Big Mistake can be put right'. The right ones can start over."

"But wouldn't it have been better to have got it together before it came to *this?*" I asked him. "Who wants to live in a desert?"

He shrugged. "It was the only way, it was the only way. You see, Mankind being the way he was there *was* no other way. How can you teach a frog a new croak? I mean it was *that* impossible. No, we've got it okay out here. I don't feel anything wrong with the situation, but I don't need simplified landscapes either; I'm not copping out. I'm as complex and wanting as the rest of you were."

Fading tracers of a bad dream — strong, warm currents that took me away long ago on a voyage of calm, pink hem-line caught on the barbed-wire fluttering in a wind on a hill-top overlooking a small village nestling between hills. Scudding white clouds against a blue sky, and brilliant yellow sun — my hand warm and damp nestled in your thigh your naked warm stomach pressed to mine in an urgent moment.

Petrified willows stuck in a landscape of lime, tin cans, barbed wire and tin lids; packets of 20s Gold Flake and used Durex perished into dusty white strands. Opium roaches in the woods outside the swimming pool: our first signs of adulthood in a world where we already thought we were hip — erection through silk-blue swimming trunks, blue expanse of pool water under blue sky and golden sun broken by hundreds of white shouting laughter and flashing skin and blue...

The Cola People are on Vliet's side of an endless battle with the old order of humans who are trying to re-establish themselves on the planet. The Cola People arrived apparently from nowhere, human in form, apparently from human stock, but they are able to fly, and they think and act differently. According to Vliet they evolved from small, isolated nihilist Earth communities who had destroyed Homo Sapiens with an attitude. After half a life-time of artistic endeavours, with their rising Vliet had glimpsed a purpose amidst the chaos and 'become of his time'. Their rising substantiated his belief that the artistic impulse was now free. "It's better to have the chance to evolve now, in the desert, than not to have had the chance at all," the swordist explained to me. "In any case, we don't need the same facilities you old land-lubbers needed. The trees have served their function; we don't need grass and babbling brooks but raw power and trillions of cosmic volts from the brilliant suns." He shrugged, aware of my protest. "It's sad, I know, but every step forward you take is sad because you always have to leave something" —

The Man Machine

WHEN VLIET REFERS to me as 'one of Them' he thinks of me purely as Their product, where technology has met spirit, the one maybe good thing They aspired to build. "They were always taking care of the shit out of their own arseholes," he explained to me. "They never let a thing go, and they were vain enough to want to live for all eternity and so they built you. I fully understand you. You don't need to get sour with me..."

Sometimes I can see what he means. But *he* is their vanity. He thinks that me and him are like two great big Siamese twins frotting it up out here on the postatomic surfaces of the ball that once boogied for bergers in Daddy's new car —

Wild Cola Folk gathered in pink banks of cloud — telescoped mountains dotted in a mind's eye — variegated clouds scudding the arena where the fight is being fought to its last, last bickering inhabitants of a dying globe...

The 1980s — Part Three

Brutal mothers
slash young sons' wrists.
Gays are beaten to pulp.
Smiling bowler-hatted gents
lose their teeth
in underground toilets
to hordes of teenage boys.
Fathers
decapitate their daughters.
Crane jibs
swing across streets
slicing through masonry
and tip boiling lead into screaming crowds.
Murderers stalk alleyways
in broad daylight
ripping shoppers' hearts.
Children with guns
and black hangman's hoods
stand at bank corners
waving-in the frightened guards.
Brother fucks sister,
then strangles her.
A mother rips open the chest
of her 4-year-old,
and hungrily sucks up the blood;

her face, disgorged,
drips crimson as it pans round
the nervous crowd
with an accusing glare.
Gangs of East End garage mechanics
and scrap dealers
break in and attack families round their TVs, as
dwarves and midgets swarm in the parks
uprooting shrubs and destroying flower beds,
and inside primary school canteens
junk-eating children
hack teachers to death.

The Duel

ETHERED DREAMS ON baked earth – soft green meadow grass beneath yellow blue skies – You there near me lying lazily in dreams, your skin next to me but apart – My dream to hold you yet softly formed and unacted – I brought you ether and you brought me love...

I see out over the unchanged surface. Vliet is challenging his birdmen and women to a duel to keep them on their toes. He has regaled himself in his breathing apparatus and harness, which serves to keep his body morally pure from the airs of Earth; this time he has on his long-snouted mask: a silver proboscis encrusted with silver holes made of a rare gauze. The mask is strapped tightly to his body by a brown leather harness with blackened buckles which impress themselves into his pale skin. His thighs and arms are exposed but covered by the black down of his body hair. He is clad in knee-high boots of red and chrome; his gauntlets are of puce. He would approve of such a style of description. And today he has come up with an improved plan of attack: he has armed himself and his followers with steel cutlasses, and as a symbolic gesture they are to sport until they have improved their minds – for amongst them all, warfare is to be made purely an artistic affair, and swordsmanship is to take the place of nuclear holocaust, and when they are ready Vliet will have them enact witty skirmishes and protracted battles before the guests...

Freedom of Choice

"YOU CAN HAVE no idea how difficult it has been to pull the right strings," the King of Bengal jokes and bows his head with prayerful hands outpointed.

Smoking guns still hang from the arms of the guards; the guards look

as though they have been through some kind of trance and are now awakening to the full horror of what they have subliminally been induced to do by Vliet's swordsmen. Vliet is realising, stupidly, that he has been too transparent. After the King's remark all eyes are suddenly upon him, and he wonders how he is going to merge once more into the background. He simply shrugs, helplessly, and smiles innocently, and they shake their heads and to his relief and my stunned amazement they turn back to their drinks and small talk. Their abodes — the bits and pieces of their former luxury — fill the desert to hundreds of square miles. It is the last ghetto on Earth — a ghetto of the privileged of a dying kind sunning it one last time in ethered dreams.

"Soon the guards will raise their guns again," Vliet told me days later. "It won't take long." — **But, brilliant artist that he was, it took him longer than he thought, always scheming, always trying to keep three things up in the air at the same time** — "They're still living in illusions and they can't see that the illusions are no longer genetically useful..." —

"I live in my Far Pavilion, but I feel *good,*" the Countess of Sorum says as she suns herself by letting her Henekey's parasol sway to one side.

"Quite so, quite so," says the American President, who has come to join them in the fading hours. Behind him roars an improbable Presidential guard of Greater Manchester police riding in three half-tracks and a Bedford truck. "We must preserve the dream at all costs. You know, recently I've been quite won over by you European guys."

"We Must Preserve the Blood!"

Vliet's shrill voice reverberates in the sodden skulls, and the Cola Folk cheer like pirates. They bite on their cutlasses and hold decorated rags aloft as they drift in the dusty air.

Change. Rather than mutate, Human Beings hid their desires behind wraps.

Clear Spot

WINDS SIGH OVER electronic deathlands. People weep in despairing gestures to avenge and to be avenged. Oceans plume from primal beds and leak into space where orbiting junk glints in Earth's last light, and pelleted creatures born from slime emerge onto the land and scavenge among the remains of humanity. In his signal box beneath the confused sky Mr Zero wakes to the bellowing, snorting stampede of the humans that nuzzle among the artefacts and destroy his station flower beds for the last time.

Sword Born

VLIET: A RAZORED mouth. An unwanted eye. An enemy of fashion. I am caught by the tender pull of my Ether Girls as they lie in the yellowed fields beneath the Letchworth skies. My mind springs back, and I am appalled by the human defeat — detritus beneath the sky — but though I sympathise with Vliet's affectations I take the overall objective view: Life is 'here to go'; it came, it went; nothing has been changed — what harm can there possibly be in *that?*

As Deviants Stagger

THE ETHER GIRLS represent sensuality, Humanness; but is Humanness an indispensible presence in the universe? Vliet, really a later, more developed Hot Plate persona, tries to heighten the sensuality and insists that there is a 'higher, finer' level of existence which can be attained. Swords and sorcery writing demonstrates that a finer, fabled existence *can* be achieved — in fantasy — and so Vliet is very much an S&S character, albeit trapped in the real world; he is a splinter of that Swords and Sorcery imagining which went amongst humanity in those last desperate hours to try to elevate us. He is living proof of the imagination to effect change. "Mutate and spread!" is his battle-cry. But is not this highly evolved philosophy simply a form of madness? Has there been a point to his ravings for a world that has left no trace of itself other than a few expanding ripples of radio signals? What can he and 'His Kind' do that is more significant than what has gone?

A Temporary Occurrence in the Desert

THE BLOOD SIGHS beneath the sands; the Ghosts hover always just out of sight, just out of clear hearing, so that no one can be sure whether they existed except in memories. But time, as I thought, has healed the rift. I feel calmer now, and for the moment the threat of the blood to overwhelm has been diminished. It was a futile thought in any eventuality, for how can one man be held responsible for the follies of an entire race?

And as I sit out here in the postatomic deserts I feel neither kinship with nor hostility toward 'My Kind' (and 'My Kind' includes the likes of Vliet, who is always so eager to segregate and pigeonhole). I have no bias toward life or death, sensuality or austerity, masculinity or femininity, man or universe; I feel everything; I have only an extreme objectivity and sometimes, a fine nausea.

For the time being, thank you.

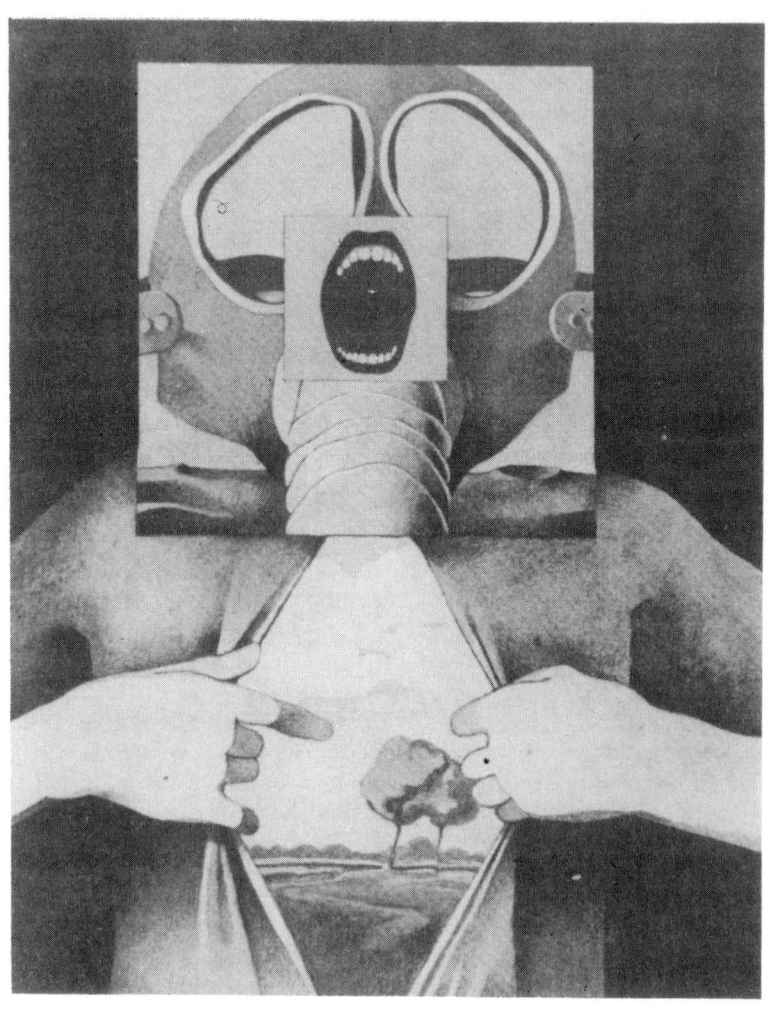

TOM
THOMPSON
in the gas oven

*'It's like being in a lunatic asylum, with permission
to masturbate for the rest of your life'*

Henry Miller

JUST FOR OPENERS

MILL AND RAY TONE have separated.
That is to say, they aren't One anymore, not Man & Wife.
Just Mill Tone and Raye Tone.
Mill was a Cleric but he gave away the cloth for University and a
married life with Raye. Raye was a teacher but ·gave away her sole
diploma for a dedication — Music saved her thinking always about
discarded Clerics...I had met Raye accidently near the laundry chute at a
Motel. She was fighting off the advances of an 'American Pornographer'
and we kicked him in the leg...I helped her move out. Now Mill had done
the fatherly thing and had found Raye a new home. A real home with
some old friends of his from University. A terrace full of intellectual
distinction, in Glebe, on the hot streets of the Gas Oven.
I've been lying helplessly on this slab of hot white concrete for the last
half hour and Christ! it's Hell down here...Everytime I close my eyes, flat
out trying to forget about the jutting ridge of concrete-back, I get gassed
— Quite enraptured, always smiling naive with those faint grey cloud-
stains rippling overhead, not noticing as the gas creeps quietly, secretly
closing off the pressure in the back of my neck...I can't speak! Concentrating on the pressure of my hands wound round the concrete slab with
my eyes shut, breathing in delighted the heavy dulling wheeze of gas, till
Nauseous Mother Nature helps one to heave into next-oven-doors.
I'm lying alone on the hard rim of the Gas Oven, in tempered Hell,
waiting for the mutants to arouse from these ruins of a City. This dead
part of the City-Elbow, gassed and already decomposing...It's inhabitants
lie low in the yellow-green sunshine, breathing slowly in and out through

long complexities of plastic tubing strapped to their chests and covering their genitalia, degrees and diplomas make them readily identifiable as residents of this terminal zone.

These lungfish open up at night when the heat's off and re-enact the nocturnal rituals of Copulation, Dejavu and Sleep.

Certain Institutional factors have created this decay and still sustain it. Note the close proximity of SYDNEY UNIVERSITY. It's constant process of Examination/Elimination. If you make it – Deification! If you don't, – Defecation! OUT YOU GO!

So much objectification on Intelligence demands constant defecation to convince the System, the staff, the students, one's friends and lovers and oneself; that one is indeed Sexually Attractive and Intellectually Powerful. Or Vice-versa...You've got to say the right things, do the right things; for and to the right people. Like letcherers. Your position in the Process, your position of power in the INSTITUTION depends entirely on following out the dictum AS YOU THINK / SO YOU FUCK in some suitable mode of learning. Like Plant Psychiatry...So let's go inside –

THE PELVIC CALL

Yes they're all home except Raye but they say, *'Please darling stay –'*, so I do. On the lounge we have both Dante & Beatrice in the diffuse shape/s of Rino, a prominent Member of the Language Department, and Winnie, his best 3rd year student and gun-moll. I sit down with them and dismantle the Roquefort Cheese. Listening hard to the other Academics who are croaking heavily under gas masks. I don't ask them to repeat it. That would be a mortal sin. So I humbly mumble *'Pavese...huh, poor suicidal glyp –'* and receive Yes gestures back.

Rino and Winnie are doing her homework. Embracing on the naked lounge suite, getting entangled in their plastic apparatus, as well as highly excited. It's because they kiss-mouth-cunt-fuck-talk in front of me I suppose. Sheer exhibitionists!

All orifices are the same here, all in a state of Primal Ejaculation. P.E. There's such a desperateness to get everything out, to leave nothing amiss...Stanley Fox the English Letcherer elucidates his sexual panic –

'You know when I was 16 years old I had such a sudden crush on a young girl. No-no-now, not a young boy-ha-ha, a young girl. Catholic maiden virginal type of whack who used to blow gum with me every Sunday after Church. She was strictly adolescent. I mean, I suppose we all were then-ha-ha, weren't we...Mmm but then she was really intelligent and had a great figure-ha-ha for such a girl...Whaarr-we both would exchange Time magazine, I had it on subscription, ponder it closely together. You know, in her room.

'Well she had good full size hips this girl, Maureen Wilder that's her name and I was sort of fat and unathletic, so that was important. I mean, she liked me. She really did...Yeah. She told told me about Mailer for the first time and

she'd read Vanity Fair. Life begins in funny places doesn't it! Nar, well I listened to her for I don't know how long, really wanting to CLUTCH – HER. I can still see her now, those perfectly curved white thighs near the rotting pumpkins. Arhh-compliments of T.S. Eliot!...I almost wished I'd kissed her then!'

Rino smiles in mild agreement. Voljack walks in and everyone lights up excited. Who cares about Stanley's rotting pumpkins...Voljack's been smoking hashish in the toilet. He has V.D. and everyone treats it like a Diploma. They get in line to see the extent of decay from his syphilitic condition. He is the true Sexual Martyr – Everyone wants to fuck him because he's got IT, but IT makes him unobtainable. For them that's like being Head of a Department. Best Member.

Stanley is a little angry, sitting rolling a joint in one hand and petting his wife June with the other. With the other hand not the other joint. She has the other joint. She is a voluptuous brunette, spilling breasts into Stanley's angry hands like dozens of boiled eggs. Stanley cackles. He's happier. They embrace. Crack –

Winnie is looking across at me and laughing. Rino whispers something in her ear. This house is his laboratory, Winnie his guineapig. She turns and shows me her latest garter. *'She has Dietrich legs'*, shouts Rino. They remind me of Cocteau's. Stanley is cackling, he loves a show. Winnie thrusts her thighs into Rino's face and asks him something. He says. *'Sure, go ahead, have some fun –'*

QUEEN TO BEDROOM FOUR

Mill walked in and soon he and Rino were making chess of the weather – *'So it's been a good –'* / *'Yes a good day'* / *'Day how good say?'* / *'How do I say so good!'* / *'So fine –'* / *'Then, fine and well and good.'* Checkmate. Rino is drying his underwear near a burning log and the house reeks of street-fuck fumes. He laughs and says, *'Strong huh –'*

Winnie smooths out her dress into a V, pushing herself against Mill Tone, making little gurgling noises. She's a leaking balloon, hot-air drawn plastic apparatus. Automatic, two-speed. She gyrates at Mill. She goes off (like a rocket) over to me –

'Id like to kiss ya but I jus' washed my hair'
'That's O.K. I don't want to kiss ya hair'
'So you think I'm a dangerous woman too?'
'Perhaps in the kitchen –'
'No I mean you want to fuck me I can tell'
'Arh well...'
'Everybody does'
'Arh-erh...ghh'
'Then how about I cross ya palm'
'You mean masturbate?'

'No I mean give us ya hands creep, I'm gonna read them!'
She took my shaky hands and led me up to bedroom 4 which was a drying room for pairs of scanty nylons and heaps of underwear. A sort of Rehabilitation Room for dozens of invisible legs. She sat me down on the large bed. She put one of my hands underneath her dress and said, 'Not so fast honey, just love me'. Then she grabs back both my hands and read them like open Pocket Oxford Dictionaries, making twirling lines over my palms with her nails –
'Me and You kiss-fuck, that all right? I like you, place your hands on table. Christ! Let me see your WHOLE palms!'
I laid out my hands on the heavy varnished wood, looking up to see her face under its plastic coating, gloating 'These your hands', with remarkable intuition. I leant on both elbows, swaying as she turned one palm over the other, like a geriatric exercise, repeating crazy earnest talking contradictions. I try hard to concentrate on this.
'These lines long. Mmm, your life deathly short. As well, your reasons conflict with your emotions, making you a plumber or a psychiatric nurse...I love both. You found love at 20 and at 30, unless of course you're only 25. Which is possible...You're cold-hearted and ruthless and love Jewish Intellectuals, Yabetcha, I'm one. Arrh, you hold your cock at barmitzvahs and outdoor family barbecues. You have radiation burns from them as well as Maroa Atoll, the French tests 1963. Your fate lines lack sulphur in the body. You smell of reeking rubbish – No. I smell of reeking rubbish! Gotta change these pants...'
She thrust her hands into mine and squeezed hard –
'Can you love me?'
'Arrh, at the moment, no...'
Her arms pleading pulled me in, her plastic lips surging ahead, seeking direction like some underground lung fish. Blindly, till I finally toppled over and she disengaged. She says extato –
'You know me so you love me. I want you so you want me. I kiss-fuck you only. You can't have my virginity, my hymen's in the Nicholson Museum. I'd love to fuck you but I'm only kidding. Say you love me and I'll go away. Everybody else does...Rino my only man because he Teacher, while I just Student of Love. Say you love me and I'll go away – I'm only interested in your mind! I want men around me all the time to say Your Beautiful...I know everything about life at 26 because I've had a baby. It's a little girl. I don't know where it is, but if you say you love me then I'll go away and find it –
I fell face forward on the table, my arms pinned by her face on my neck. 'I feel sick...' I say. Luckily Voljack arrived looking for Winnie and burst open the door –
'Is this a free fuck, I'm busting –' he roared.
I fought my way to my feet.
Rino walks in with Stanley and soon the three of them calm Winnie down. Flattering her, her body. Her tears dry up, the plastic coagulates. I fall back into a nylon filled chair to catch my breath – It's all this gas...

94

MIDDLE GAMES AT MUSCLE COVE

The three men parade their stiff jeaned genitals.

Winnie compliments them. They are busily discussing their relative degrees and diplomas and the weather. All standing, hands on hips in front of the mirror, holding poses for as long as plasticly possible. Delighting in the flesh so close...At last we all went single file down into the lounge-room, the three men sitting on the couch while the women made tea. Raye walks in and sees the men, each in jeans and T-shirt smoking reefers and looking glossy −

'*Muscle Cove!*' she says and kisses each of them, sitting down next to me. Winnie and June bring in the tea and look adoringly toward Muscle Cove. The men are laughing amongst themselves, suitably adored. Analysing Voljack, who is in the middle of some hideous confession, which they heartlessly commend.

'*Well done Volj. Divulge!*' says Stanley with relish.

'*Liturgy, Liturgy!*' cries Rino waving a crumpet.

'*Who was it?*' asks June and they all look at her, sneering at the interruption to the momentum of the trauma. They don't answer, and June sits back not unhappy. Voljack goes on −

'*I was with this bunch of blokes copping a look at this short shiela wrenching her elbows in that chrome and glass coffee house, the Refuge or the Refugee or something. Anyway. This country cop turned his lark on us and we were forced to leave. I grabs the shiela, with me mates shouting FUCK HER FOR ME BOB! Well it's a miracle I missed the clink with the cop no more than a yardarm away, homing in on the screen. I got the shiela into the Zephyr '65...*

'*You know the Zephyr '65? It's a nice car, red upholstery − Got her tubing off just as her sister hits the street. "Where's Maureen?" she says, "Where's my lill sister?" Well, panic-yes-she was, Christ! There I was groping the pull in the front seat with a hair lip, groin in plastic Paradise. How could I possibly tell a lie...So I got the strap and tied her legs to the steering wheel, laughing a little aren't you now, Christ it was funny too; I took my foot off the brake and let it go...SHE'S IN THE CAR! I yelled SHE'S IN THE CAR!... I never saw the car again −*'

Everyone laughed. Stanley asked if she was His Maureen?

'*You lost a '65 Zephyr for a girl?*' said Raye, '*You're crazy −*' Stanley analysed Voljack as a potential Plastic Surgeon, and indeed Volj was furthering his Arts Degree with six years of Medicine − '*I need it for my disease*', he said. Rino pours the tea out, mine all over the floor. He takes the stage...All attention is his. He screws up his brow and looks down from Muscle Cove. Raye spoils the filmic effect by leaving the room but undaunted Rino blurts pontification −

'*I was in a Mental Institution once. Hardon Hall. You all should know it, near Callum Park...Well out there you know I saw madness from the inside, and I can tell you they're not just a bunch of freaks. Far from it. They're all incredibly intelligent, they all demand attention, desire to be loved...It's incredibly competitive in there, a pressurised atmosphere. In a way a higher atmosphere with everyone groping. The confines of the Institution make real encounters impossible. There's no fucking, it's all very frustrating. Even when you get out it takes a while to re-adjust. You can never really take off your mask, if you know what I mean…Yes, in there the most perverted are the most revered, though most of them could hardly do anything else but talk…I've seen them holding on to limp cocks for hours, willing themselves into erection. Looking for results. Talking all the time. Innassertive, if you know what I mean…They have non-existent relationships built on a shaky edifice of sexual potence. As their perversions build up by degrees, so does their sense of sexuality-as-power and their position in the Institution. Their sexual prowess equates with their perversions.'*

Mill toned in, *'And what did you do to keep out of it?'*

'I spend 6 hours a day in my own personal study of madness'

'You mean at University —' I said.

'Of course not block — That's my work! My study in Yoga, Meta & Pataphysics, Meditation and Snake-charming keeps me occupied —'

He drifted off, a little angry at the paltry questioning so Winnie soothed him by nibbling his belly. *'Put on some Rock & Roll!',* Stanley yells to June, *'Let's thrust hips —'*

Putting his head between her breasts he weeps three alphabets. Winnie is still sucking Rino's belly. For Rino in the Language Department, words are a metaphysical fellatio…Satisfied, he falls back on a satin cushion…For Stanley in the English Department, words run amidst the Rock & Roll —

"Everybody in the ol' Cell Block, —
Gotta dance to the Jailhouse Rock —"

PURGATORIO / A SCENARIO FOR THE ORGY

(reel one)

Refa has come down from her hovel upstairs to see Mill. It's been a fairytale existence for Mill Tone — Upstairs one night, downstairs the next. Raye was rather put out and said it wasn't going to last long, she'd move out.

Refa is a heroin addict. She's shivering in a thin cotton dress and is glad that Raye is out of the room. She's afraid of Raye, that Raye might take Mill away. She doesn't need plastic apparatus because she has a regular fix. She doesn't need the Church or University, she just wants Mill. The discarded cleric. She mumbles something to him, then she talks—

'I had a dream that I was going crazy. I did. This man came into my bedroom early in the morning, when Mill was asleep. I was putting away the kit. I'd burnt my hand, was sucking it. He came in. Mill was asleep. He came in naked, his cock was throbbing. He was looking at me. He had a red beard. He said, "Can I come in, I'm cold". I was putting away the kit. My arm was stiff

and my hand had gone white. I was holding my hand. Mill was asleep. I crept under the blankets and asked him to go away because Mill was asleep. — '

She fell into Mill's arms and shook violently. He caressed her neck gently and spoke softly across to us —

'It happened early this morning. It wasn't a dream, it was Gory. Rada's left him and he wants attention. I locked him outside but he's coming over later tonight — '

(reel two)

Winnie later flat out on her back with her legs splayed over the chess table, knocking over the pieces. Rino shoved her to the floor. 'This is a Serious Game!' he says, rescuing pawn to Queen four. Mill counters with a bishop. Refa has fallen asleep on the couch. Voljack defends her and Muscle Cove...

Winnie put her feet back on the table toppling both Kings and Rino leapt off his chair to squeal and wrestle with her legs, leaving Mill to finish off the game himself. He does.

Stanley watches the fight.

It isn't really a fight but he makes it into one.

He sees Winnie nibble Rino's ear. Rino bites into her apple neck. She shrieks delight and he grunts. Electric motion of wrist and arse dynamics. Stanley searches Rino's heavy torso with darting eyes. He takes off his glasses. He looks down at the crease in his own pants. He puts his hand on his crotch. Winnie is holding Rino to her biting into his neck. She's holding onto the pockets of his jeans. He has one hand up her dress. Squirming, eels. There is the smell of sweet reeking rubbish...

Voljack sparks awake —

Stanley smooths out his pants with sweaty hands.

The lump in his pants equals the lump in his throat.

He looks down at the man writhing on the floor, looks at the strong heaving back, imagining. He gets up stiffly and falls onto the two of them, laughing embarrassed as his stiff cock meets Rino's jean-arse. Rino laughs and grunts, while Winnie wheezes under three sets of plastic apparatus.

(reel three)

June is smoking calmly in the gas-filled house. By the fire are sleeping bodies crumpled around her. She breathes in gracefully, her lips sing with cigarettes...

Winnie sits opposite her with both arms wrapped around her chest, staring at June. At June's lovely breasts, voluptuous plastic apparatus strapped perfectly in swinging pairs upon her chest. She is staring at June who is breathing smoke rings through some invisible plastic tube curving out of her mouth —

June dreams of talking with Rino. She wants to say so many beautiful things to him but he always laughs. She wants to tell him about all those

Exquisite Moments in her life, all the great moments. She wants to relate Stanley's Graduation, the Wedding, her honeymoon. How Stanley has become lately a stranger to her, he keeps away, he doesn't want to fuck...He's got something always on his mind. He tells her to Shut-Up! He's trying to Verk! He studies Italian, so he can talk to Rino...

June is talking about trading in her mouth at some Government Department, or going back to University in search of some greater, more complete Plastic Apparatus. Perhaps a Degree in Chemical Psychology... If only she could get a Hip Committee like Social Therapy or be a Member of a Department, then she could talk to Rino. As one Member to another. She could fuck Rino...

Winnie looks at her own tiny pear-shaped breasts and whistles through her teeth. She wants that little extra something. It's the only thing that's missing...She wants to crush men with her tits. Break them. She smiles back at June with a twisted mouth.

"THE ATROCITY EXHIBITION"

I got to the party held that night a little late, but no matter, it didn't really come to life till Voljack Devine, the Syphilitic Kid, dropped in after a late lecture on Nietzsche and started to rustle up the Orgy. Everyone had been waiting with this precise idea in mind, but needed guidance from the Head of that Department. They wouldn't overstep themselves, not in the Gas Oven –

Voljack had brought a huge woman into the room who displayed an amount of plastic tubing rarely seen these days. Diplomas from Oxford and Cambridge, one from the U.S.A. These were plastered on a strange parachute apparatus just in case she said the wrong thing in this elite company and had to be thrown out...All eyes were attuned to those booming breasts, all mouths sought nourishment. Voljack sensed the dilemma and rapidly undressed her, prepared to 'Throw her in the Ring' so to speak and everyone calmed down. They sat down together near the fire eating nutmeg and lemon rind, digested with a little Dostoyevsky –

Stanley seemed to be under local anaesthetic watching Rino cuddling Winnie's baby ShoeShine. He shifted a little in his wet leather seat, June still nibbling at his elbow. Winnie had one hand on Voljack's thigh, asking 'How does it feel Volj?'

Next to arrive were the notorious troika; Gory, Rada and Jerk, who had been living together in the same block, doing radio classes in Applied Maths. Gory in his red beard and boots sank his teeth into the large woman who squealed delight. Then he sank his teeth into Winnie – 'Take a walk on the wild side baby!' – She amorously stroked his hunchback. ShoeShine asked him where their baby was and he quaintly smacked her ear.

'I left him in the cupboard –' says Gory, hah-hah.

Everybody now is really laughing —

Jerk is locked in passionate embrace with Rada, his hands seeking her electrolysed thighs — *'The operation makes me look more beautiful, don't it Jerk'* — Umbilical embrace. Rada is also a student of Rino's and seems very jealous of Winnie. Tonight she's come to show Intelligent Jerk off to Rino. She is all white except her hair which is green. Jerk between swallows, talks fervently about American Literature, about Norman Mailer at 65, no 56 — still the doyen of Hip. Jerk the doyen of Bop with his mechanical Sexaphone, writes slop obituries for two Sex-magazines in the form of electric editorials. Rada rests her mouth in a glass of low-calorie water and takes off her shoes to free her feet —

Refa comes down from Upstairs with the devout Mill Tone, bringing her own apparatus with her, soon shaping up the kit. Mill placidly holds the needle and dropper. There is a burning smell of used bandages. She rubs her swollen arms hard. *'Anyone want a lift?'* she says, but no-one does. Mill helps her into the drug-costume, the tornequet, and puts her politely in one corner of the lounge.

Soon all three men from Muscle Cove are pawing the large woman, rolling her over and over, cropping the Feel. Mill joins in shaking a small crucifix. Voljack is pounding his chancred cock over her hot heap of flesh — She keeps smiling, *'Is this really it!?'*

Rada and Jerk are fondling each other on the bannister and Gory tries to squeeze himself between them. *'Let me in too, I'm cold!'* he says. He gets one leg caught up in the railing and the two of them rush out and leave him for home. Stanley saws off the offending wood, cutting into Gory's hairless left leg, undaunted he runs bleeding out the front door —

Stanley is jostling with Rino who is very drunk and gives him a tiny kiss on the nose. Stanley takes off his shirt and wriggles his hips — *'Hit me with some Rock & Roll!'* he says. Rino clouts him with Chuck Berry's Golden Decade. Stanley falls into his own arms ecstatic —

Winnie watches in horror as June takes off her shirt to reveal Those Lovely Breasts! Rino looks at Winnie criticly so she takes off her singlet too. She goes very red and hurries over to her protector, pumping heartbeats — Rino smiling, *'Gee Honey you shouldn't feel like that about such a natural thing —'* June is dancing ecstaticly and Rino looks hotly at her. Stanley is reading Mussolini with vigour, tearing at the pages. Voljack has strapped his girl between a burning log and the fireguard. She keeps on laughing, hysterically — *'Is this really IT! Is this really IT!?'*

Voljack kisses her.

'Calculated indifference is the Key to Success,' he says.

She giggles appreciatively. Soon everybody else is dancing, semi-naked, semi-detached, staring at each other's plastic apparatus red-hot in the burning atmosphere, all hoping that Voljack will attack someone to start the next stage —

Raye walks in cool amidst the jungle fever and June covers her breasts. Everybody is suddenly quiet, they've been caught red-handed. The

silence drags. A heavy grating...Raye walks back out again.
'Portrait of a Lady —' says Rino.
Stanley is whimpering...

ENDGAMES / MILL SAYS HELLO AGAIN

He walked into Raye's room and shut the door. She was at the piano. Her throat lurched forward and she didn't know what to do. He says, *'Well isn't it nice to see me?'* No answer.

Raye sat quite still, hardly breathing as Mill bent to kiss her cheek, holding her long brown hair fast in his hands. She closed her eyes and flexed her fingers. She knew why he was here and wouldn't say anything. Mill had left Refa and the kit upstairs and wanted to come home. No chance.

She played, but with mistakes.

He laughed, his whole face one contorted mouth and said, *'Raye, I want us to try all over again. We'll try and make it —'* He had his large hands on her tiny shoulders. She held her head up under his weight and began to drown his fevered attention in crashing walls of sound. He spoke earnestly to her small pointed face reflected on the piano. She looked back at her hands, waiting for the right moment. He took his hands off her shoulders and moved to the centre of the room.

'Something going on between us?' he said, like a pair of rusty old loins. He began to undress, *'I'm staying, that all right with you —'* and chuckled...

She turned around — *'What do you mean anyway!?'*

Mill blinked, hovering uneasily on one foot, still holding his belt in one hand. He said, *'I want to stay here, I want to live here, starting now —'*

Raye got up and quickly picked up two bags of clothes from under the bed. Started to walk out the door. Mill blinked. Strange. Raye said, *'That's all right Mill, you can have my room. It's got lotsa gas. It's the classiest hole in the block...better than hotshot's upstairs...It's goodbye honey, goodbye Mill, goodbye...'*

She smiled kindly to him, then started laughing — *'Did you get yours at the party last night, get the clerical finger in —'* She went out. *'I'll pick up the rest of my stuff later',* she said.

Mill sat on the edge of the double bed holding his hands. He gripped his belt carefully, moving his fingers over its hard shiny surface. Holding it by the punched end he flayed the grand piano with its buckle. Sickening bruised wood sound.

GORY HITS HARDON HALL

I have just arrived to hear the news that my old school chum, Gory Normal, has committed himself for a stint at Hardon Hall. When he tried to strangle baby, Rino suggested it. Rada is radiant, free at last! Jerk thinks it *'Ironical, he always wanted to be in a group —'* Musically minded, he was.

Later that day we heard he'd signed himself out, after only ten hours in the INSTITUTION OF HIS CHOICE. Rada said he must be mad. Jerk fell down the bannisters and split his head.

'I've missed Raye again. I'm going to help her move out —'

STANLEY FLOPS DRUNKEN NANA

That night so drunken everyone was finally overloaded and had risked life and limb with a dozen heinous chemicals and a carload of booze still soaking in the kitchen sink while others burnt their whiskers smoked their breathing apparatus electrolysed their thighs or whatever near the burning logfire / some had even gone to sleep but me no no I was watching a Brand New Oven Ritual in the form of a drunken lusty fight between those old Academic Hipsters Stanley Fox and Rino Canaloni who were sort of mixing it between beers and smashing flagons in the playroom dragging at each other's clothes tryin' hard to get in going Ha-Ha and Hey watcha doin' / knowing all the time what was on each other's minds til Stanley reminiscing reeling back til 14 year's old talks about the time that Rino at his party kissed his neck and how he wanted him to do it again for friendship's sake C'mon Do It Again Rino C'MON GIVE ME A KISS! flaunting his apple neck and pouting while Rino looks meekly around all red and smiling then he kisses Stanley on the lips and they both drop their drinks and fall onto the couch TEARING OFF EACH OTHER'S SHIRTS AND TROUSERS DOWN / PULSATING COCKS STRETCH FLOP ON BELLIES STANLEY'S DRUNKEN NANA INTO RINO'S HEAVING ARSEHOLE YELPING DELIGHT WITH RINO HOLDING HIS OWN STEAMING COCK JACKING OFF ONTO THE FINE SATIN CUSHION SEVERED RIPPING TILL THERE'S FEATHERS EVERYWHERE ALL OVER THE WHOLE COUCH SWEAT-SHIT-STAINED AND JOLTING STANLEY BORING UP AND DOWN —

PLASTIC PARADISE

It was the third day and I'd come to help Raye move out, but she hadn't arrived yet to collect her bags. I sat down in the lounge-room, knowing that this was going to be the very last time I was ever going to be here, so I may as well enjoy it. I picked up a book, IN THE PENAL COLONY by Franz Kafka, this looks easy reading...

I notice Stanley fearful in the corner applying some Dettol on a lacerated hand. *'Dog bite you?'* I asked. Stanley growled back, spluttering fragments of the Rosetta Stone into his alphabet soup. June comes in nonchalant and sews up his lips with her mouth. They cuddle, wearily. I go upstairs—

Winnie meets me at Bedroom 4 with the news that Rino is bedridden, and *'Does that mean he's impotent?'* I think she means important...She's wearing a plastic negligee and is modulating her hips to my own contorted mouth. She takes me into the bedroom. I ask what's so secret — She goes *'Rah-Rah! COCK!'* and grapples with my buttons. June walks past eating a Violent Crumble bar. Rino can be heard denouncing Moravia. I'm fighting for limb and limb...Winnie shuts the door, is ravenous...I trip over long lines of faded nylons and Winnie is upon me —

'I love you, can I suck you off mister? If you no like me you can get out! Rino trying hambone in mirror next door, so sick in head I can't watch. You look ill. Sick. What's wrong, my lingo. O.K. — You get out of here creep, Rino sick but cool man and gas. I know. I've had a baby. Rino next door, he's mouthing now, he's flexing apparatus — Here, put finger up sphincter, smell —'

I didn't bother. I took a guess. *'Mmm...GAS?'*

She nodded yes, *'That was an educated guess...'*

I ran outside and bolted the door. Rino tries to trip me on the landing so I strap his neck to knob. June is eating chocolates so I kiss-kiss her on the mouth, *'Mmmm-mmm-Choclates!'* Stanley feeling threatened, turns out the lights and I tread on his leg, pulling off all the plastic coating... Finding the telephone, I call the Operator —

'Operator, Operator...I'm in the Gas Oven, please take this down...The highly luminous atmosphere of Academia seems both delectable and attractive, but its offal creates a general entanglement, a torturous choking from the self-destructive Gases of Elimination / Examination; A panic at the threat of Sexual / Intellectual Extinction on the Crumbling Edifice. Still holding on to my psyche...Thankyou Operator, over and out—'

Stamping down the hallway I hear their bodies under-going chemical weathering. Under a rain of plastic piping their limbs cry out for strangulation. The house-foundations give way as a dozen nylons tear. Stanley is still babbling an inventory of his wife's organs. A needle and dropper at the front door, Refa naked. Mill and Voljack gang-fuck the grand piano. June walks out ahead of me eating Violent Crumble bar. As I close the door behind us the house falls down —

Climbing up the hill in a strange silence, no sound save a few sparrows by a leaking gas tap, silver-whizzing in the sun. No June. Getting to the top of the hill, my intestines are struggling to leap at my feet. Stumbling over the corpse of Gory Normal, my old school chum, trussed up in a vacant block, I can't help but feel relieved, feeling the cold crunch underfoot — The glass. Yes it's all over, blurting, it's all over. I'm coming out of the Gas Oven. Bounding over the corpses of my past — Gasping for breath I see her, call out, *'RAYE, I'M ON MY WAY —'*

She was standing with her two packed cases on the corner. There we caught a taxi and we didn't look back.

Reproduced from James Cawthorn's *The Crystal and the Amulet*, Savoy Books 1984

Man 'drank parrot's blood'

A 22-year-old man has been accused of ripping open the chest of a valuable parrot and drinking the dead bird's blood.

Police said they found the parrot with its eyes plucked out after they investigated a burglary at the home of a 17-year-old youth.

The 32-year-old bird was able to speak in three languages and was valued at up to £3,500.

Officials in Tucson, Arizona, identified the suspect as Charles Horn, who claims to be a punk rock performer using the name of "Charlie Monoxide."

Horn, his girlfriend Anna Mercer, aged 21, and Hector Molina, aged 20, were charged in the burglary case.

Police said Mona told them Horn claimed he opened the bird and sucked out its blood after Molina's bulldog bit the parrot and stunned it.

Horn and his girlfriend, who uses the nickname "Mercy Murder," have razor cuts allegedly inflicted during punk rock performances.

Horn, with bleached blond hair was held on charges of second-degree burglary, theft, criminal damage and marijuana possession.

Killer 'ate flesh of girlfriend'

A STUDENT ate some of his girlfriend's f
after killing and dismembering her, Paris pol
alleged today.

Police said Issei Sagaw aged 32, a native of Kob Japan, told police investi gators, "I have always wanted to eat a young girl."

Sagawa was arrested yes terday, 24 hours after police found the dismembered body of Dutch student, Miss Renee Artewelt, aged 25, in two pieces of luggage in the Boulogne Woods.

Police said Sagawa told them that he shot her in her apartment on the Rue Bonaparte last Friday when he became outraged by her refusal to accept his sexual advances.

Police quoted him as saying he dissected her body with a kitchen knife, put a few pieces into the refrigerator and later ate them

Investigators said Sagawa would be examined by psychiatrists though he had made his confession in a quiet, lucid way.

Both Sagawa and Miss Artewelt were students at the Paris Censier scientific faculty.

MICHAEL MOORCOCK

an english exile in hollywood

WELL, I'VE EXPERIENCED the other side of the romantic deception now and I think I'll give it a rest for a while. Here, the realities are more casual. When the dogs begin howling (as they were recently) it usually means a threatened earthquake. Overhead the planes come in and out of two nearby airports (Burbank and Van Nuys): DC9s, Cessna's, Lears, and various small passenger turbo-props. At night police helicopters occasionally drone over, their searchlights telling us that there is a suspect in the area (this is primarily a chicano suburb-ghetto) or a freight train will hoot from the nearby railroad tracks. There is a liquor store within walking distance, otherwise most of the other stores on this section of Burbank Blvd are repair shops, motor bike shops and chicano bars which, in accordance with California law, have no street-facing windows and therefore have the appearance (with their graffiti) of bunkers in some sophisticated Spanish civil war. I have no licence to drive. When I cross the street cars display genuine confusion at the sight of a pedestrian. I have been brushed but not directly hit, twice, so far. I am a soft vehicle.

Los Angeles has more bookshops, concerts, films, seats of learning, etc. than any city I've ever spent time in. It is sometimes bizarre, even in this rundown part of North Hollywood (where the odd ancient star still resides in poverty), to come across so much unselfconscious service to what you might call people's inner lives. As well, there are antique places (mainly dealing with stuff thrown out or sold off by the studios) where you can buy complete costumes (sometimes 'as worn by Alan Ladd in The Glass Key') and restored cars are so frequent that there is often a strong sense of timeless technology which I have never, again, experienced anywhere else. Old Hollywood is half-ruined. The studios are still there, with their offices in different architectural styles so that they can be used as locations, all looking inward on squares or campuses, and you still can't tell the real sky from the back-lot sky, but they are more and more like monasteries. Outside, the stars set in the pavements celebrate names you've never known or else completely forgotten, and they are often covered in dog-shit. Everyone seems old and looks like the actor or actress they hoped to replace when they first moved here.

But that is a long way away from North Hollywood, all that, where I am. I would move to Hollywood proper, full of graffiti, decay, some street life, if I could. If I stay out here on a semi-regular basis, that's what I shall do. It's more expensive, but it has plenty of texture and isn't too safe. I need the mixture, I think. I might as well make the most of my exile, for this was not much of a voluntary move. I'm enjoying the experience. It relieves the bafflement and the brooding into which I slip about once a day: faced with a story to write and subject matter close to home. The young men in the liquor store ask my advice on which British beers to import and currently, strangely, I'm drinking Theakston's Old Peculier which a couple of years ago was only available in Yorkshire. They get me different ones to try and suggest some small US breweries I might like. So I try 'em. But I don't think I'll be able to keep up the Beer Man role for long, not unless I go for the complete Chesterton kit (with the danger of turning into Kingsley Amis, of course). "Good pint, this", I could say to the unblinking chicanos as I lift a tweedy arm and put a foaming tankard of Samuel Smith's to hearty lips, "What's the crumpet like round here".

I have an invitation from a millionaire engineer to visit him in Venezuela when the airships (being built at Cardington) start being delivered. So it could be next year in Maracaibo and Caracas. The problem is crossing rotten Central America where 400 miles of Pan American highway will never be built.

WEST HOLLYWOOD IS on the other side of the hills from North Hollywood. North Hollywood is largely barrio now — Mexican families and 50s Chevvies with plastic saints hanging in their back windows — and nobody cares what they paint over their deco facades; they treat the buildings as casually as the Romans treated their monuments for so long. But West Hollywood is on the fringes of Beverly Hills and where I live, between Santa Monica Boulevard and Sunset Boulevard (the Strip is a few minutes walk up the hill) is the city's main gay area, with bars called The Blue Parrot and Casablanca and everything self-consciously nostalgically Hollywood in 40s neon and airbrush gloss.

For the most part the local stores cater to their largely male homosexual clientele with expensive sports clothes and soft life-size dummies of the stars: Oldenburg using Warhol images. There are very few ordinary utilities here. There are at least four 'whimsy' shops, selling postcards and penis-shaped candle-holders, a cake-shop which will make a fantastic edible Judy Garland, places selling antiques which I remember seeing in Woolworth's in the forties and fifties. There's a Safeway Supermarket and a Post Office, but the pet-shop burned down and all its parrots and cockatoos with it, and there's an ordinary dry-cleaners, a laundromat and a drug-store. Nearby is The Palms, the LA branch of the best saloon in New York, which has superb steak and lobster, all very big, sawdust on the floor, and waiters imported from New York because the LA ones aren't rude enough. The walls are covered in murals representing actors and writers, many of whom are unknown to me.

Mostly the colours around here are bright blue and orange. There's a roller disco called Flippers a couple of blocks up Santa Monica where young blacks in naturals and bright green and scarlet overalls wait in line, each with a two-hundred dollar pair of roller-skate boots with see-through yellow and silver wheels hanging by the laces in their hands or over their shoulders while a little further up is Barney's Beanery which used to boast the best chile in LA, a famous biker cafe where pool is played night and day and they claim to have 180 varieties of beer. Here you can have half-a-pint of imported Samuel Smith's and watch the angels and the Hollywood cowboys, the Beverly Hills sleaze-girls on the slum, the family-groups sitting dazedly in corners and trying to make sense of the metallic blonde who lounges maternally over them and tells them if they sit at the tables they gotta order something to eat, while from the back, from amongst a dozen stolen street-signs and beer-ads and signs telling you that Barney's now sells the 11th Best Chile in Town a gloomy voice pushes the dish of the day which is liver and onions. I sit in the window looking towards the huge royal blue bulk of the Pacific Design Center — a kind of Centre Pompidou which seems to consist mainly of giant air-ducts and silver escalators. Just down from there is the Cafe Figaro, a favourite of the younger middle-classes, which sells a variety of semi-desserts described as coffee and wholemeal sandwiches; it's more or less opposite the Georges Sand Bookstore, which specialises in books by and memorabilia associated with the authoress. That's on the Beverly Hills side of the district. If you travel for a while uptown along Melrose you'll come to the twenties Gothic of the Valentino Apartments which are built around a tiny courtyard dominated by a statue of a lion. A statue of the actor, who once owned them, all but fills a nearby park. They're next to the Paramount Lot. We tried to get one of them but there's something of a waiting list so we tried the Normandy Towers fantasy village on Poinsettia. Here the apartments are in the form of fairy-tale assymetrical cottages also built in the twenties and also run-down. Both Harlow and Monroe lived there. But the place was too small for us and the ceilings too low. So we returned to our motel on Santa Monica.

The Tropicana has a swimming pool which could contain a corpse and a couple of dead dogs without your noticing. Punk rockers and Rastas from England lie around it in battered lounge-chairs, drinking beer out of cans and chortling at the fun-and-games of an obscure all-girl Japanese band as they try to drag one another into the water while an older, mannish woman looks on from the side, smiling like a tolerant madam, a failed Debbie Harry lookalike. The office of the Tropicana is covered on all available wall space with promo pictures of rock bands signed by the Dying Cats, the Filth and the Come Come Band. Behind the desk two friendly faggots smile at the customers who come in to complain that their air-conditioning is fucked or their boy-friend has locked them out of their cabin and is trying to kill himself in the shower. To the left of the office and down a few steps to the street, which is wide and to the English eye virtually featureless, everything is so far apart, is Duke's Tropicana Coffee Shop where Duke himself, sweating in one of his own advertising T-shirts, sometimes supervises his huge staff who crowd behind the relatively small bar, serving the students, the truckers, the bikers and the out-of-work actors who pack it. Cornbeef sandwiches — what we'd call salt beef — chile and the all-day breakfast. The speed and the grease mean that you never leave there without feeling you've had the most delicious indigestible meal of your life.

Three blocks West is another coffee shop entirely staffed by soft-voiced faggots with body-built muscles in tight sweat-shirts and jeans who are always friendly to me and my son Max but who hardly notice and sometimes don't serve either Linda or Sophie and Katie, my daughters, when they go in alone. Most of the customers are gay, tending to cultivate a look which gives them the appearance of super-sanitary buccaneers though the occasional bondage-costume appears, sometimes chained to his partner, and there is the infrequent beautiful transvestite, one of whom I sometimes see in my bank. She's black. She wears a sleeveless top, culottes, high-heels and a neat beard. When Linda and I take our Sunday stroll we feel self-conscious and somehow perverse, for we are literally the only heterosexual couple in sight.

I can get across the street to the local library if I press the traffic-light button and run. You don't get time to walk it. The library is part of an ordinary complex which you could find in any small town, with a children's playground, a ball-park, a tennis-court, not thirty yards from the Palm, a lesbian bar where elegant Beverly Hills bi-sexuals come to get their thrills from the regular customers, the ordinary dikes who tend to get preyed upon by these Guerlaine-scented women in the French designer-clothes their husbands have bought for them. The others are fag-hags in Calvin Klein jeans and high-heeled boots who come in with a couple of gay men and are ignored by the majority of the other women. The juke-boxes are loud in all the gay bars, particularly the Blue Parrot and the Four Star Saloon, playing monotonous disco and sentimental country ballads loud enough to drown conversation as you pass by outside looking for a quiet place to have a drink (there are none in our part of West Hollywood). At night we can't sleep for the noise of revved Harley's and MGs and Porches and the bitter quarrelling of the faggots returning at three or four in the morning to where they parked. It's hot and we have no air-conditioning, though it's not as hot as in North

Hollywood last year where the streets and the cars were covered in fine ash from the forest fires in the hills and we kept ourselves cool at night by dousing each other with water from a plant sprayer. I get up early in the morning to take my walk before it gets too hot, desperately patrolling a wider and wider area in the hope of getting the measure and the texture of this attenuated environment which seems to have none of the characteristics I have learned to expect from a city. I walk along the strip of park which runs from here to Beverly Hills for a mile or two. On the other side of Santa Monica, where six lanes of traffic move with the turbulence of logs in a river, I look at the mysterious black skyscraper office blocks of Century City and smell the air which is suddenly filled with the aroma from the Wonderbread factory on the outskirts. The City is almost entirely the province of commerce and I've never visited it.

I return home and we have breakfast before my boss's secretary arrives in her grey VW bug to ask how I am and drive me up into the Hollywood Hills for another chat about my script. The director gives me a book on magic mushrooms and tells me that the Celts were heavily into them. He moves bewilderedly about a room full of scripts, video-cassettes, props from his last super-successful movie, and his unmade bed, then suggests we go down into the lounge which is furnished vaguely in the Ranch-house style, with a lot of Indian rugs and, here and there, some African wood-carvings. We try sitting out on the sun-deck, which shows signs of many earthquakes in its cracked concrete floor, but we agree it's too hot. From the deck I can see the Strip below and beyond that the block where I live and, given the subject matter we're working on and the position I'm in, get a spontaneous impression of the continuing feudalism of the motion picture business. I'm writing an Arthurian tale which is going to be authentic, set in 6th century Britain. Lancelot, the hero, has a black Roman centurion side-kick called Cornelius. My boss thinks the name's perfect. I mention that I've used it once or twice before. He says it doesn't matter. He doesn't drink, so we have some milk. I hope the uppers I did after breakfast will last me through another day. We talk about 'story' and he tells me he wants a script which has the atmosphere and action of a Kurosawa picture but he wants it written in the style of Bergman. 'Not a script at all. Something more flexible I can work with. More like a short story.' I remind him that the studio is paying me for a script. They might not be too happy about something which looks like a treatment. He says he'll square it with the studio and tells his secretary to remind him to phone somebody there. He explains some of the politics of his dealings with the studio and I realise that my original suspicions were right: I'm in the middle of a standard bit of manouevring between producers and directors and if I go along with one side I'm likely to fall out with the other. He gives me the story-outline of Cries and Whispers and a picture book about *Yojimbo* and *The Seven Samurai*. I mention quietly that about the only thing these directors have in common is that they work with regular actors and crew and usually the same script-writers and that therefore they know who'll be reading the script they prepare before the script is written. I'm not sure that by doing something like that it will make quite the same sense to, say, Christopher Reeves, James Earl Jones and Raquel Welch (all of whom have so far been mentioned for Lancelot, Cornelius and Guinevere respectively). Bergman's script is couched in the style of a letter to his regular actors. My boss dismisses my arguments. I have to prepare something similar to Bergman's script but with lots of people running and plenty of sudden, unexpected violence. 'Those people were fit, you know — warriors — and they were barbaric, too. Wham! Wham! Pow!' He mimes a sword-fight, then stands panting and grinning in front of me, wanting my reaction, hoping he's fired me up to do my best work. 'See?'

It's lunch-time. The director has discovered hippies. Stonehenge. Glastonbury. He's fifty-six. I reckon that by the time he's seventy he'll have become a student radical. He serves me rotten cantaloupe, telling me it's better for us, and saying that he keeps his melons in his clothes-closet because it flavours his shirt and pants as the fruit grows over-ripe. We have wholefood. I tell him it's great. I have the choice between giving out the wrong vibrations and not being in tune with him or returning to England and probable bankruptcy. We discuss the director's liberalism, his interest in feminism. He tells me a personal story which makes my hair curl. I'm becoming very confused. My identity's slipping as the day grows hotter. I take away the umpteenth rewrite when Linda comes to pick me up. I'm on expenses, the kids are on expenses, our apartment is on expenses and the studio has given me an IBM Selectric II which keeps breaking down at moments of desperation. I have lots of paper. The director has insisted to the studio that I have plenty of the best quality typing paper. I get home, take whatever drugs I can lay my hands on and have a couple of drinks. I wait for the evening to cool and begin my rewrite. I do what I can and we go out to a restaurant to eat. We have to spend, or appear to spend, a thousand dollars a week, but our tastes aren't high enough and our clothes not good enough to make too many trips to Ma Maison, where the beautiful people, the latest Charlie's Angels and Dukes of Hazard lookalikes try to rub shoulders with their originals. Almost everyone looks like someone whose name you can't remember who's appeared in some TV detective show.

On Sunday my agent gives me a party to introduce his clients to the girls who work in the office. Gene Wilder stands in one corner of the deck overlooking the pool. He looks miserable, hunched in a sweat-shirt, jeans and dirty tennis shoes, smiling awkwardly at the women who surround him. Directors tell one another their films were wonderful. Nicholas Roeg sits in another corner, near me on the far side of the pool from the house. He reminds me we've met before. I tell him I admire his work and hear myself sounding like everybody else. Conscious of this I stub out my cigarette, burning my thumb badly in the process. Linda gets us some more drinks. Robert Altman says something funny and everyone laughs. I smile as if I understand the joke. Christopher Lee towers over me, telling me he's my greatest fan and has always wanted to play Arioch in an Elric picture. I stare at his teeth without knowing quite why. He invites me to visit him at his home in LA and tells me that the secret of surviving here is to remember at all times that you're British. 'Don't drop your standards,' he says. My agent makes a joke about sci-fi and dragons which characterises me suddenly as the token nigger and I recall the previous producer I worked for on *The Land That Time Forgot*. He told me that he didn't really think a whole lot of the kind of shit I wrote and that he had directed and produced through most of his career. But what he really liked doing was Margaret Drabble; she was a real writer. You keep your peace and you take the money, swearing to yourself that you'll never put up with this kind of patronage and condescension again. Memory fades, of course. The ego restores itself, but it's hard to understand that while you're going through with it.

Linda and I go to the movies in Hollywood, in one of the dowdier parts of town, an old cinema where you get three movies and a stage show for 99c. The stage show is the amateur Beverly Hills Dance Company: executive's wives doing ballet routines. The audience, mainly Mexican, looks at it with baffled politeness. The movies are *Superman*, *The Black Stallion* and something else. It's like watching films in the ruins of the Colosseum, full of grandeur and high excitement. We've gone to see *The Black Stallion*, made by Coppola's Zoetrope Company, because everyone says it's artistic and a break-through. In it Mickey Rooney plays almost the same role as he did in *National Velvet*. He's the trainer and another kid rides the horse which wins the race against all the odds.

I get international phone-calls from ex-wives telling me they're worried about the rent or that their lovers are giving them shit. I tell them I'll have some money soon. We go to Knott's Berry Farm, because it has more smell and grease than the other pleasure parks like Disneyland or Magic Mountain. We ride the big roller coasters and eat tacos and popcorn. We go to Venice and sit in the local bohemian cafe which has tables directly on the sidewalk where roller-skaters practice their disco dancing and one young black with a portable Pignose amp strapped to his back and a Fender guitar skates up and down playing familiar Rolling Stones tunes. The cafe has sandwiches and meals named after famous writers (it's attached to a bookstore). We hear a waiter trying to remember for a customer who Jack Kerouac was. 'He was pretty well-known, I think.' We go on the beach. The smog is heavy today and I don't realise how strong the sun is. Max and I try body-surfing amongst the kids in wet-suits or shorts who ride their boards around us. I get sun-burned and we have to go home. The girls go off in a huge Oldsmobile with red velvet interiors, having been picked up by their friend, a Beverly Hills teenager whose mother is a celebrated ventriloquist. They come back the next morning from a Punk spectacular in Santa Monica having taken drug cocktails which even an old Heavy Metal performer like me thinks excessive, but they're cheerful. The back door of the car has got broken, but they had Max in the back holding it shut when they went round corners. They are contemptuous of the LA punks, whom they describe as soft and 'fake', but they like the Surf Nazis who are currently said to be terrorising the beaches.

In the evening we go past the parking lot opposite the Blue Parrot. Somehow a Corvette has managed to reverse onto the roof of a brand-new Porsche. The driver appears to have driven straight up the sloping front of the other car until he had gone as far as he could go without sliding down the other side. We join the crowd who are speculating how it is possible. A man who saw the accident — a huge black queen with an excited lisp — says 'He just came right out and went on going.' The police arrive with a breakdown truck. We carry on towards the Palm to get a bill big enough to make our expenses look good. We're going to celebrate Linda's birthday. This morning she got her present — a cake in the shape of a giant moth, on expenses.

In the mornings, when the smog is invisible, you can sometimes smell the jacaranda and magnolia outside the apartment. We have two doves nesting in the palm tree outside our kitchen window (we're in the top half of a duplex) and a tattered old squirrel who perches on the roof of our garage. During the day two escaped green Amazon parrots screech overhead, flying crazily and inexpertly from telephone pole to eucalyptus branch and sometimes seeming to talk to each other, but I can't hear any of the words. The lunatic next door begins to mow his tiny lawn, the blades of his mower yelling on asphalt most of the time. He will later call to ask us to turn our radio down. He's probably the one who called the cop a couple of days ago. 'I like the music,' the cop said, 'but your neighbours don't.' I said I was disappointed. Shouldn't he have come in in a crouch shouting 'Police. Freeze!'? He cheerfully offers to go through the whole ritual again, but this time with his gun levelled. I said it was okay, since it was so late, and anyway we were waiting for one of the kids' friends to turn up and she's never without a gram or two of best quality coke about her person.

North Hollywood, where Macdonald Carey still lives, amongst the Mexican bars and old-clothes shops selling the costumes worn by Patricia Medina in a hundred pirate movies, is a good half-hour's drive from here, over the hills, through Laurel Canyon, or Benedict Canyon, where Beverly Hills has extended itself into what was until recently forest-land. The Hollywood where the tourists stay (at the Hollywood Roosevelt near Mann's Chinese Theater) is another half-hour away in a different direction. Santa Monica Boulevard stretches for hundreds of blocks West to the sea and East to downtown LA where Mexican gangs hang around the bus-station hoping to find an easy mark. Everything is half-an-hour from everywhere else. We take Max to see *Airplane* in Westwood, a kind of more recent Hampstead Garden Suburb. Tomorrow morning I'll walk a few blocks through the winding streets which are unusual enough in themselves and are like an idealised Surbiton, peaceful and green, to look at the English Village, a complex of mock Tudor apartments behind a high wall, a sort of series of miniature Pickfairs. Mary Pickford still lives in the real Pickfair, guarded by clean young men in CIA suits who become alert should you slow down your old Camero to take a glimpse. Later this morning my boss's secretary will come to pick me up in her grey VW bug and ask me how I am. We'll drive into the Hollywood Hills and from there my boss will take me to Burbank Studios to see a screening of one of his old movies, which he believes is the best he ever did, though it was fucked up, he tells me, by the writer. Like several of his pictures, it's a sequel to another director's success. This is a 'Return of' picture, in fact.

Outside the studios the actors are on strike because they want royalties for TV showings of their movies. They dress as if for auditions. You get the impression that half the pickets are there because it will be the first time they've been on TV in a couple of years. The character actors wear character costumes. The fresh young lookalikes are in Miss America denims and prints, in jeans and sport shirts, their hair carefully arranged. Their placards are just as neat as if they'd been done for a *Lou Grant* segment. In the viewing room I'll sit in an armchair beside a mike and tell the projectionist when I want him to start rolling the movie, while a control at my elbow will give me the sound level I require. I'm still hungover from the weekend when I went to an SF convention at the airport, drank a Texas fifth of Bacardi in just over an hour and collapsed on my face in the lobby of the hotel after insulting a few writers and a publisher I'd hoped to sell a book to; Linda drove me home, but somehow I'd got trapped under the car when I left it and hadn't been able to get out for another hour. Most of the six or seven hours after that are a blank.

The movie begins. I turn down the sound. It's a Western. I'm quite enjoying it, although I do tend to keep nodding off. Later I'll have to force myself awake when the director comes in and sits beside me to point out the techniques he used in a battle between two Indian tribes. Then we'll probably watch another samurai movie. I'd rather watch almost anything than a samurai movie, particularly with a man who believes that the Japanese have somehow achieved a lifestyle which we of the West might do well to emulate. A few more swords will flash and wide-eyed heads will roll and you can bet your life I'll be enthusiastic. I'm on this picture for another five weeks. After that I'm allowed to go home.

WHEN YOU COME into LA by train, stopping first in Pasadena, you get the impression that you're arriving in a small Southern European town or perhaps Mexico: you feel you're experiencing the opening credits of a 60s

Western or a film by Bertolucci. You expect to hear a bell tolling. When you arrive by air LA looks like the excavated remains of an ancient settlement, vast and geometrical but without much complexity, as if the examination of a few broken pots and a fragment of a sign will reveal most of her mysteries. You descend towards this dig through smog which stretches for miles over the bland Pacific. These are the garden suburbs comprising what is now, I think, the world's second largest city (after Tokyo), apparently a middle-class paradise with a higher serious crime-rate than any of the noisy megalopolises its inhabitants have so frequently rejected. The grid provides few alleys. These have to be created by architects. Only the slums of downtown Los Angeles, the sleazier areas of Hollywood or Venice manage to avoid the appearance of a carefully-constructed set. Even many of the people have that lack of texture characteristic of a Harryhausen monster.

We're no longer living in West Hollywood. We're in Venice, about midway between Lincoln Boulevard and the beach, in an area which was once a fashionable resort, with canals, gondolas and rococco arcades, a recreation of Renaissance Italy in the minds of its early 20th-century inventors. It's half in ruins now. The big bathing pavilion and the huge fake galleon which was actually a restaurant erected on wooden scaffolding beside the pier have gone. The pier itself has been pulled down and most of the canals have been filled in to allow for developers to erect their bijou haciendas. But where we live is a ghetto. We are the only white faces on the block. When we see another Anglo we experience a shock of surprise. People are friendly here. They are chiefly black and chicano, though the family which lives in the 'front house' (we live in the 'back house') is Japanese. On either side of us, in the 'improved' parts of Venice bordering Marina del Rey to the south and Santa Monica to the north, are the theme apartment complexes — Fisherman's Village, Old Spanish (with fake brick showing through fake adobe cracks) Town, French Alpine Village and Frontiersville. A hundred years ago they hid the wooden frames of buildings with stucco and false fronts. Now the wood is on the outside and the frames themselves are sometimes false, so that we can get the natural look. These theme complexes have shops and recreation areas which maintain the image and they also provide a nervous middle-class with a sense of security which is probably the least realistic thing about them, for they are within strolling distance of our part of Venice and their nooks and crannies, their mazes of internal passages, their stair-cases and carefully broken contours provide a thousand hiding places for the burglars and muggers who do not even have to drive to the pickings. One can imagine the look of surprised delight on the faces of young criminals as they watched the complexes going up and realised that the wealth had come to their very doorsteps. People are afraid to visit us in our part of Venice — they know other people who moved to Venice and, after being the victims of several robberies, moved out again. But we live in the area shunned by the whites — prime real estate to which the poor cling with a frustrating obstinacy — and nobody has ever come close to threatening us in any way. My theory is that the muggers' mothers would catch them if they tried anything so close to their own houses. But we find our neighbours friendly and good-humoured.

This isn't a quiet neighbourhood, however. The families measure their status by the number of old cars they own and the size of their portable stereo equipment. The Mexicans have laboured for at least a century under the impression that they are musical, just as most blacks can apparently deceive themselves into believing they have a natural sense of rhythm. Mexican disco is the most hideous sound in the world. Elvis Presley cover-versions in Spanish are a pleasant relief from it. But it goes on forever.

We sleep with our heads next to what are actually sliding doors which open directly onto the alley. Because it's autumn we have all the cracks stuffed with foam-rubber strips to try to retain some of the day's warmth — the temperature falls drastically at night near the beach and we have no means of heating our 'coach-house' (as the landlord describes this single room converted garage with its concrete floor). Every night pretty much the same cycle repeats itself. If we come home in the evening the street is lined on both sides with old Chevvies, immobile Recreation Vehicles, restored VW convertibles and Dodge station-wagons. Kids lean against the palm trees shouting to their friends sitting on the hoods and roofs of the parked automobiles, drinking beer and playing football. From the lighted doors and windows of the houses come sounds of families at leisure and in the yards and on the pavements scores of excited dogs run from group to group. By about midnight there is comparative silence. You hear the occasional distant radio, a yap or two from the dogs (large dogs are also status in the ghetto). By about one in the morning the gunfire begins. This isn't in itself alarming. V13, the chicano gang, has its headquarters only a street or two away. The pistol shots are largely exchanged between gangs; there's more macho display than any deliberate attempt to wound. Our only fear is that one night we might get caught in the crossfire (Senator Abe Ribakoff's daughter died when she was accidentally shot coming out of the twee 'Merchant of Venice' restaurant on Washington and California where pottery shops and whimsy stores have recently replaced the old groceries and liquor-marts) or that shots will ricochet off the walls of the alley and come through the thin wood of our garage doors.

The gunfire begins the cycle. Next come the police and ambulance syrens. By around three all the dogs are howling and barking in response to the syrens. This wakes up the babies who begin to bawl. Their bawling wakes the mothers who first placate them and then yell for them to shut up, waking the fathers who scream at the mothers until, slamming doors, they go and sit in their cars, playing the stereo at full distort to drown the other noise. Wails and thumps, impossible to relate either to words or to music, seem to fill our heads; we might as well be in the speakers. It echoes around our garage. By five I am fully awake and jittery, wondering how on earth I'm going to get any work done. I take a couple of downers, but I can't get back to sleep. It won't become quiet until around ten and by that time we will have to drive to Long Beach to the library where I'm researching the Ku Klux Klan and where Linda has friends she must see to arrange for the collection of her furniture and clothes which she left in a variety of Long Beach addresses last time she came to join me in England.

Long Beach is about 30 miles from Venice. You drive south along the San Diego Freeway until eventually you see the offshore oil-rigs, the nodding pumps which line the highway and look like giant versions of those glass drinking birds you used to see at fairs or get for Christmas. You spot the Queen Mary, secure in her concrete, and the signs which advertise her virtues as a convention centre. Long Beach has done its best to improve its image in recent years and there's no doubt that the conservative middle-class Orange County immigrants have made it a richer and more salubrious town than it was in the twenties when the main impression it gave was of churned mud and filthy derricks, but it still betrays its origins here and there. The great dockyards which service the naval vessels of Australia and the US can't be as readily cosmeticised as the offshore artificial oil islands. At first glance these islands appear to be skyscraper apartments surrounded by palm trees, complete with coloured lights in the windows at night. The residents objected to the unsightly rigs so close to the beach and the oil-companies obliged with a facade.

We visit a school-teacher who breeds dogs in Orange County, a witty well-read woman who tells us with a mixture of relish and horror that her kids are handing out Klan leaflets at school. "What's black and brown and looks good on Mexicans?" she asks, replying: "A Doberman Pinscher." She has a string of them, all from her kids. "How do you control the Mexican population in the ghettoes?" We don't know. "You tell the niggers they taste like chicken."

We return to Venice. The cars pour mariachi and soul into the crowded, narrow streets. These bungalows and Hollywood-Spanish houses would cost a fortune in Wimbledon or Haywards Heath and would be inhabited by stock-brokers, but here the balconies and verandas are piled with old television sets, parts of motorbikes and useless freezers and big fat women sit in deckchairs amongst the junk, fanning themselves and keeping an eye on the younger children. We mop the floor where our own refrigerator has leaked and make ourselves a drink to have with the hamburgers we have brought home. We settle down for a chilly, nervous sleep. Next morning we go to visit my new film agent in Century City where the cheapest parking costs about three dollars an hour and every building is a tall skyscraper built of black glass and chrome: an island of sinister anonymity menacing the borders of downtown Beverly Hills.

My new agent wants to know what properties I have, what assignments I have completed, what kind of scripts I want to write, when I'll next be in LA. He's an efficient, likeable man with the world-weary air one learns to equate with integrity in Hollywood. One isn't always right, but there's nothing else to trust. It means 'no bullshit' as a rule and it's the most highly-prized quality of character in town. He asks me to send him a list of my books with short préces of each one. He doesn't pretend he's going to read them. I'm thankful for that and glad that he doesn't refer to me as an artist or as a creative personality. He assumes that my time is as valuable as his own. He will do his best for me. I tell him, in turn, that I can't afford to have an experience like the last one. I'll do the work, but I won't do the endless 'conferences'. It will be 1) Treatment 2) Discussion of Treatment 3) First Draft Screenplay 4) Discussion of Screenplay 5) Second Draft Screenplay or no deal. I'm not sure he believes me. But he's heard me, and that in itself makes a change. Normally if you state your case you get treated at best like a disturbed puppy. Drinks or drugs are then automatically offered to you to quieten you down. The last screenplay I did has not, of course, got anywhere near production stage and probably won't. I hear that the same director has two other screenplays at about the same stage as mine and two other writers (both well-established) on the brink of nervous-breakdowns. Hollywood is feeling the recession as much as New York. In New York the heady days, where the 'grand' was the casual unit of currency and authors were bought at auction like stud-bulls, are over. There is scarcely any auctioning now. Instead the publishers confer together cautiously to keep advances down. The great literary conmen, who could play one publisher off against another with little more than a scrap of paper on which a few words of 'outline' were all that existed of their *majornovel* (a category in itself then), are disheartened and bitter. Many have come out of Hollywood only to find that the pickings are no better here. They have lived for so long on their wits that the idea of writing anything more than a scam seems distasteful to them, almost a denial of faith. Their shots have been called. They have the hurt, insulted look of whores whose services have been refused. My own attitude (of getting a job, doing the work, getting paid, going home), seems pompous and old-fashioned even in my own eyes most of the time. I'm self-conscious when forced to admit I have actually completed a piece of work. I've no coups to compare with theirs, just a few books, and in offending their sense of decorum I become guilty and feel a bit stupid. Most of the people I spend any time with out here are comic-book writers and illustrators who are still used to delivering a day's work for a day's pay and see their ability to keep deadlines as a virtue.

I walk nowhere. Sometimes I go outside and fill the waterbowls of the two chained huskies who lie panting on the concrete path of the yard. Once a week a Mexican gardener comes to water the bougainvillea and birds-of-paradise in our yard. Almost every landlord in LA, even the ghetto-landlords, employ such gardeners. I am too late to stop him trimming back the passion-flower vines outside our door. Now we look directly into the alley, onto a half-reconstructed Impala and a pile of electronic parts topped by a smashed TV set. I play Country and Western music on the radio to drown the disco from the Impala's stereo. We have to have the door open around noon or the garage becomes uncomfortably hot and I start to get dizzy. There's no point in tuning in a classical station to combat the disco. Roughneck music is all that works. C & W enjoys unprecedented popularity since Reagan's election. I try to work but the heat gets to me and I find myself watching the lunch-time soap-operas instead. I write no letters to speak of. Friends visit with beer or cocaine. We go out to the nearest stand for chili-dogs and burritos which make us feel sick within half-an-hour of eating them. It seems sometimes that we're drowning in noise and that there is no end to it. We have decided reluctantly not to sublet our garage again but to give it up. This involves packing and storing more furniture. We have seen no movies in a city where everyone discusses them. There is an Australian film season on at the local art-house. People tell you constantly that they've had it with LA, that they're seriously considering moving to Australia. Once everyone went West in pursuit of the Dream. Now that the Dream has gone sour on the furthest shore of the subcontinent the same people or their immediate descendants make preparations to cross another ocean, just as their forebears crossed the Atlantic. I wonder how many generations it will be before they wind up back in Europe, a wandering tribe of yearning optimists who know that the promised land exists and are prepared to make many sacrifices in order to find it. The crime-rate is minimal in Australia, there are no dark-skinned immigrants and consequently no ghetto-problems, there are plenty of opportunities. That's what I'm told. It doesn't sound quite as easy as that to me, but I don't quarrel with someone else's hopes of heaven. California has one of the highest rates of unemployment in the US but people refuse to move 'back' to the Midwest where there are more jobs. It would be a terrible loss of face and a rejection of faith.

In the Rockies and Sierras men still pan successfully for gold, making a small but satisfactory living, while the Indians manufacture Bic-lighter cases out of silver and decorate them with imported turquoise. "I went to Kansas once," a Navajo told me in the Painted Desert, "but I didn't like it. I couldn't see far enough." He glares reminiscently over the sand and scrub, the eroded buttes. He has a degree from Flagstaff Agricultural College but no real use for it. A mangy dog growls at his feet. In Flagstaff we get drunk in a bar near the station. The train is over three hours late. Men in stetsons and cowboy shirts stand in the bar and the few Indians keep to themselves in a corner. C & W music plays. The blonde, elaborately made-up women laugh loudly at the cowboys' jokes. In the lavatory all the graffiti consists of complicated Latin puns. The train eventually comes in and Indians wrapped in blankets rise up from the floor of the waiting room to board it. We take our places, heading back to Pasadena.

We go for dinner at the Tikki Hut in Marina del Rey. Waitresses in grass skirts put imitation loas round our necks and serve us with drinks in china bowls shaped like conch-shells. The food is described as Hawaiian but is mainly derived from the kind of dishes you find in Chinese restaurants. The friend who takes us is a TV writer. His friend is a woman who has become a Biofeedback Therapist. She talks about Marlon Brando and how her techniques helped him get through his last crisis. She goes on to discuss the scientific basis for Astrology. Her job pays very well. She quotes an hourly rate which makes us all envious that we haven't her training. The Hawaiian guitars whine and the chorus chants and swings its hips. Slowly the rolling Polynesian drums will signal the real start of the nightly show. The TV writer says that he thinks he might move to Hawaii, although he has heard there are good opportunities for writers in Australia these days. He descibes his frustrations in getting an ambitious script produced. He's back to doing horror stories for a new series which is going to be 'much better than Twilight Zone'. We watch the first showings. I can't tell the difference between this and Twilight Zone, except that the presenter has changed. This makes me embarrassed. What nonsense life would seem if we didn't have some kind of faith. We tell one another lies as we wait for death.

The whole of Southern California sometimes seems to have been created by out-of-work set-designers who, as the movie-industry collapsed, began to represent themselves as architects. And Disneyland has had something to do with it, too. Even the non-theme restaurants are on that theme, and usually based on European models. The only difference between a theme restaurant and a non-theme restaurant is the snobbery. The food can be very good or mediocre in either.

We drive past the little local grocery store with its tiny grilled windows and steel doors, like a blockhouse or a frontier trading post. A group of young blacks permanently hangs around the entrance. We go past the laundromat where boards replace windows and into a battered filling station which only takes cash and therefore makes itself more liable for robbery than any of the others nearby. We have to use this station. None of the others sell leaded gasoline any more. I get out to fill the tank and we are approached by young Mexican kids wanting a dollar for the Jehovah's Witnesses who for some reason seem to do well in predominantly Catholic areas. The Catholic church nearby is covered in black graffiti while the Baptist church is decorated with chicano slogans. But the Spanish language predominates. Even the black children have learned a sort of pidgin Spanish so that they can communicate amongst their peers. The whites seized this country from the Spanish in the 19th century. Now it seems only reasonable that the Spanish should be slowly reclaiming it.

Back at the house I lie on the bed and try to get an hour's sleep before the evening radios start up. A dog sniffs along the bottom of the sliding doors behind my head, scenting the remains of yesterday's meal. Next week we plan to go up to San Francisco along Highway One in a rented car (our VW won't make the steep hills) and visit friends. I'll sign copies of my new book at a science-fiction convention and see my publishers. Then we'll return here and tackle the problems of moving back to England. LA has changed, says Linda. She'd rather be in Yorkshire. The driving is getting worse on the freeways and it's no longer much cheaper to live here than in London. We visit an actress friend in Hollywood. She hasn't worked in several months. "Even the stars are doing commercials." She wonders if she should move to London, too. "After all, they have a lot more theatres." She is deeply depressed. We go dutch at a nearby all-night Jewish deli and wind-up doing nothing but drinking. She doesn't want to go anywhere where she'll be recognised. "I look like death at the moment." Passing the MGM lot on the way home it seems to us that the place has a desolate, melancholy air. Perhaps Hollywood, too, is thinking of moving on to Australia, the new hope of the industry, where simple stories and good photography, uncomplicated characterisation and straightforward moral points are still more valuable commodities than the self-tortured personal philosophies of the nervous, middle-aged directors who are no longer able to hand back to their audiences a coherent dream, who have been weakened by liberalism, by an inability to gauge public taste and by the shocking understanding that in Hollywood only the Big Budget has any chance at all of guaranteeing success. Yet my sympathies are with them. I think I, too, am not young enough to make the necessary mental adjustment to the idea of the New Australian Cinema. My dreams can't be altered to fit any idealism other than that based on a Hollywood Renaissance, a new Golden Age in which revived studios produce a minimum of two new features a month for a public eager to enjoy the work of a fresh generation of Hawks, Curtizes and Fords. Could this happen anywhere but here, in the cinema's own holy city? In Australia? Australia is all location shots. They have no sense of the claustrophobic intensity of the genuine old-fashioned movie studio where almost everything was sacrificed to the deadline and internal political expediency, where the moguls ruled because they could look out of their office windows and see their workers building sets in the courtyards below. Samuel B. Meyer, Paramount, Universal, Columbia, Twentieth Century, the names still proclaim themselves in stone and neon above the long, marching, confident boulevards. Surely they can't go the way of Nurenburg or Rome. "I can't relate to the big studios any more," said another actress, also with her eye on Australia. "What do they mean nowadays?" They betray a lack of loyalty which upsets me. Are they all planning to desert the monuments of their youth simply because the money is no longer there?

It dawns on me, as the gunfire begins again outside, that perhaps I am an anachronism as pathetic as they are. My kids look back to the early days of Rock-and-Roll. Memphis and Tupelo mean much more to them than Hollywood. We plan to visit Memphis on our way home. I had a certain investment in Beale Street once. Linda tells me that they're pulling Beale Street down, but there's a chance I'll see something before it disappears completely.

It's a rotten visit, all in all. Sambo's on Lincoln reminds me of the old Lyon's Tea Shop in Notting Hill in the fifties (in atmosphere and quality of food if not in appearance). It's full of lonely old loonies at almost any time of day, but mostly in the early evening and small hours of the morning. The place is staffed by pale, miserable men (rarely more than two, often only one) who take the orders and see to the cash-register and put up moderately patiently with the belligerent shouts of the over-made-up women whose voices are whines of despair, demanding attention from anyone who will give it. In my mood of depression I get a certain nostalgic pleasure from being miserable in such a familiar ambience. It could be Euston Station at three in the morning, as it used to be. It seems that half my youth was spent in this kind of grim atmosphere. The fifties was a decade dominated by the mackintosh and the bicycle clip, the grey smugness of the Amises and Braines, when Colin Wilson was offered to us as the best thing available, so we read Raymond Chandler and went to see Bogart and Mitchum as an escape: it was still reasonably familiar territory; it rained a lot in those movies, too. But a trenchcoat and a fedora offered a bit more comfort than a shapeless duffel and a balaclave helmet and the men who wore the trenchcoats had faces given dignity, tolerance and an understanding of human behaviour which seemed impossible to discover in the world of the Soho coffee-bar. It was a romanticism acceptable to a post-war teenager.

I am bored and tired, waiting out my time, doing no real work. We go to a party and see a few old friends, most of whom seem as fed up as me. It's all economics, I suppose. A man who has given up fiction to write technical manuals tells us that he's buying a quarter-of-a-million dollar house on the beach. He has had some problems with his description of a new sanitation system being built for a hospital in Saudi Arabia. They have had to produce special stone-traps in the lavatories. The nomad Bedouin who come in to be treated won't give up their stones. It's what they wipe their bottoms with.

After the party we ride to the crest of the hills and look down onto LA. Lights glitter in orderly rows for as far as the eye can see. A fog has rolled in from the ocean. As we drive down towards Venice the streets are softened. It's cold along the beach suburbs. Palms rise out of the mist and the figures of roller-skaters disappear into sidestreets. The following Saturday we visit the hairdresser on Sunset Boulevard in West Hollywood. He remembers us because we brought my daughter Kate to him last year to have her hair dyed back to its natural colour after her own experiments went wrong. He bullshits the whole time he cuts Linda's hair, about his years in England, his experiences with muggers, about his intention to go to Australia where he has an uncle. I walk up the street to the posh cigarette shop to buy some English Silk Cuts. The owner emigrated from England to Canada in 1952. He has a heavy tan and a Hawaiian shirt. He came to L.A. in 1958. "I love it. I'd never go back to Bournemouth." Like many immigrants, his image of Britain is partly nostalgic, partly horrified. He's pleased to be told that the cost of living in Los Angeles is still lower than in London. It reinforces the sense of his own decision, made thirty years ago. He's surprised that I don't want to stay. "What don't you like?" I shake my head. It's not my business to tell him. It's the lack of density, as always. Finally, the city seems like a huge retirement resort to someone like me, born and raised in London. Yet I love L.A.. and can never bring myself to badmouth it the way, for instance, New Yorkers do. San Franciscans look down on the city. I find San Francisco self-important and provincial, almost a joke. It is proud that it is frequently compared to European cities. L.A. is a properly American city and that's why I prefer it. I wonder if I'll feel the same about San Francisco next week, when we get there. We leave the hairdresser and go to a grocery to buy another bottle of Californian Cabernet Sauvignon — a Robert Mondavi, 1978. I'm drinking my way through the cheaper reds. In my experience Californian clarets are good if drunk early, but they don't improve much after three or four years. I've given up the imported British beer. We go to watch the Christmas Parade — Santa and sleighs and all the usual trappings in 80° of heat. We might try and make it to this year's Long Beach Christmas Parade in the Naples canals — as usual it will be on boats, with a swimming, fire-breathing dragon. The decorations in Beverly Hills are a bit restrained this year, nothing but giant silver snowflakes. Trees begin to appear, with imitation snow on their branches. In the meantime we're getting unusually hot weather. We look forward to cooler days when we go North. We have lunch with the young man who wants to film one of my books. He's pleasant and enthusiastic. He says he wants to do my book 'properly' and 'seriously' and wants to know my ideas. I haven't any. I have nothing but the lowest expectations for my fantasies on the screen and believe that market requirements and bad acting will do whatever the script fails to do. But I can't tell him that. For all I know he can produce miracles. I must admit I'm primarily worried about getting a decent amount of money for the book. The reason I'm here is the same as it was last year — I'm trying to raise enough money to off-set the threat of bankruptcy. When I get on the plane to London it will be a relief, though it will be a return to unwelcome realities, to litigation and, unless things have changed, a fair bit of moral blackmail. I'm looking forward to the few days of the San Francisco trip. We plan to spend a night at the Madonna Inn. I'll write more when I get back. The Madonna Inn has over 200 rooms, each one on a different theme. We'll probably visit the Hearst Castle, for old time's sake. I sit on the yellow and orange couch watching *As The World Turns* on the black and white Sony portable. Outside, the huskies, perpetually chained to stop them digging their way under the fence, rattle, shuffle and pant. Linda comes in from the yard after a desultory attempt at sun-bathing. We've never made it to the beach. I doubt if we'll get there now.

IN THE EARLY mornings the alleys which run behind the dilapidated Venice houses are like country lanes. The air is fresh from the sea and the smog has not completely taken over; the light is hazy on shrubs, palms and brightly-coloured flowers and you can walk through the little back-streets with a wonderful sense of well-being, even though you know that only a few hours before this was the scene of a gang fight, possibly a murder. At 7am the beach, when you reach it, is all but deserted save for a couple of middle-aged joggers from Marina del Rey thumping and wheezing their way home, and two or three golden-haired surf-boys carrying their boards towards the ocean. In the silence of bird-song and waves you can sit and think. Tranquility as such is hard to find in any American city except at dawn and since for some reason my peace-of-mind frequently disappears in the country I come to love the streets and beaches of Venice at sunrise and take one last walk before we leave for San Francisco. Gradually the rising hum of the freeways behind me begins to mingle with the sounds of the surf. The rush-hour begins. The San Diego Freeway gradually clogs. The sluggish cars resembling baffled migrating termites. There are only two true cities in the United States, New York and Los Angeles. Everything else for me retains the atmosphere of a small town. I find I can read a city while a rural or suburban environment frequently makes me uneasy. I find it hard to raise much anger over what the sentimentalists call 'ecology', particularly when one can look over a fence and see fifteen Mexicans of different ages and sexes assembling for breakfast in one small room. Do they talk of the fate of 'the environment'? And if they do, do they mean quite the same thing as the eager Beverley Hills teenager growing emotional over the misery of battery chickens which laid the eggs being scrambled by an olive-skinned servant in a kitchen bigger than many chicano houses? I make my way back to our garage apartment while all around me the radios wake up and the engines try to turn over. I'll be glad of the respite, I suppose. A stroke of good luck has given us a black Mercedes 450SL sports car and we're going to take it North in an hour or two. Our VW bug isn't in perfect condition and probably couldn't make it up the steep hills of Highway 1. There are about 60 miles of dramatically curving cliff-road before Big Sur and it can best be enjoyed in a small, powerful car. As I reach our gate our neighbour begins his daily routine, revving the clattering engine of his old Dodge pickup which will take him to the gardens of Bel Air where, behind electric security fences, he will work watering the lawns and pruning the trees of nervous millionaires. For our own part, we'll soon be going in the same direction, to claim our escape car.

It takes about two hours to get completely free of Los Angeles and her suburbs. We cut along Highway 101 and head North for San Luis Obispo to get on to 1. It's the scenic route, the coast road to San Francisco. The suburbs gradually become more verdant, with wider lawns outside more elaborate houses, taller palms, larger oleanders and magnolias. We're taking a break. Until last night we were squatting on our concrete floor trying to pack trunks ready for the removal people. With so much stripped from the rough wooden walls it was even colder than before. When we get back we'll try to sell the VW and various other things too heavy or too expensive to take with us. Temporary possession of the Mercedes adds to our euphoria. There isn't a lot to beat the sensation of total release you can get in an open sports car with the great Los Angeles palms on one side of you and the roaring bays of the Pacific on the other. Sun on your face; wind in your hair. As we pass the turn-off for Solveg, the mock-Norwegian village, I shout to the family sedan offering us five pinch-lipped disapproving faces: "You're right. We *are* having a better time than you." The Madonna Inn is just outside San Luis Obispo, our first night stop.

The Madonna Inn is a Swiss chalet-style fantasy in pink and gold. In fact it's a cross between an Alpine Ski Lodge and the Sleeping Beauty Castle at Disneyland. Each of the 200 rooms is self-contained (it's a huge motel on about three levels, filling two main buildings) and each is on a different theme. Amongst the first things you notice are the pink-and-gold 'coach-lamps' decorating its white perimeter fences and the bright pink gas pumps of its own filling station. It's not easy at any time of the year to get the theme of your choice. Some are single rooms, some are whole complexes for family groups. The most sought after, usually booked months in advance, is the Caveman Room. The Caveman Room is finished in stone; its bathroom fittings resemble rock pools, and animal skins replace almost everything which would normally be made of fabric. One of its features is its special toilet. So as not to mar the overall effect of Stoneage living, there is no ordinary flushing lever. Instead, when you get up, an electronic eye registers you've finished and automatically sets the mechanism in motion.

When we phoned to book for a night we were told there were only two rooms available: Canary Cottage and The American Home. Canary Cottage is like something out of Edgar Allan Poe and would drive any normal person mad within a few hours. Curtains, carpets, bedspreads, walls, bath, toilet, ceilings, towels are in different shades of glaring yellow. About the only reason for choosing it would be if you wanted to disguise your bad case of jaundice. The American Home is tasteful in comparison but not exactly easy on the eye. The American Home is not finished, as we expected, in Disney-Colonial. It's more a stimulant than a narcotic: in red, white and blue. The sliding shower-door is an eight-foot long American flag in faceted plastic which glitters and dazzles and is set with old coins. The walls are scarlet, the ceilings navy (with silver stars), the fixtures white. There are two huge double beds facing one another and a sort of living-room space with a fireplace borrowing something from the Caveman Room: it's in concrete moulded to represent a sort of troglodytic cooking area (maybe Pueblo). You're supplied with two rolls of imitation logs which you can ignite and which will burn, they say, with a genuine log-fire effect and brightly-coloured flames. We try one and it's a bit disappointing. Overwhelmed, we sit on the floor by our fire and watch *Barnaby Jones* while we drink a bottle or two of Mondavi Cabernet Sauvignon (we're now trying out each year in order). We look through the catalogue at some of the other rooms. Each one is a different fantasy. You can stay at the William Tell, the New Orleans Showboat, the Safari Room (a bit heavy on zebra-skins), the Old Fashioned Honeymoon Room, the Austrian Suite, and so on. You can eat in the Gold Rush Dining Room (covered in more gold gilt than an Italian candlestick) or the Coffee Counter which retains the Chalet motif, its mouldings representing carved wooden beams. Over the counter itself is the slogan FOREVER HAPPY. It's as if an American has gone to Paris and seen Le Drugstore, brought it back and retranslated it into something even further removed from its original; rococo on rococo.

The folk-process in architecture is probably one of the most interesting aspects of the Twentieth Century for me. One sees it all over the world. The *idea* of the Pub transformed into a dozen different permutations in California, France, Italy, Greece, Sri Lanka, Vietnam; the *idea* of an oriental bordello or a Mid-American motel. These images shift back and forth many times, gradually losing any sense of their original function. In Wilmington, Delaware, there is a boutique called Le Drugstore next to a drugstore called The Chemist's Shoppe which sells, of course, mainly ice-cream and sodas. In Antwerp I once stayed at Le Drugstore Inn, an idea of a California motel bearing unmistakeable traces of Belgian baroque.

Most of the customers who pack The Madonna Inn are midwesterners delighted by a fantasy of Europe which is in many ways better than the real thing, or Europeans who see the Inn as the last word in classical American kitsch. Everyone is satisfied, though the foreigners are a little surprised that the Inn will not take credit cards and deals only in cash or guaranteed cheques. The shops above the Gold Rush Dining Room sell either European imports — beer steins, Harris Tweed jackets, Italian scarves (the stuff one is familiar with from the duty-free stores at international airports) — or the inevitable Western-style leather-jackets and stetsons. These stetsons are found in greater profusion in Carmel, further along the coast towards San Francisco. Everything is very expensive and only here can you use your Visa or Mastercharge. Downstairs you can buy monstrous gateaux, which look delicious but don't taste of much, or imported European candy. There is a fierce wholesomeness about the place with reminds one of Las Vegas. Most of the staff have that dedicated look of grim sunniness one associates more with Utah and her Mormons than with Southern California. The place is considerably cleaner than anything in Las Vegas but here, as it is throughout the world where the fantasy is of paramount importance, a lot of the fixtures are a touch ramshackle, windows are inclined to stick, light-switches often don't work, bits of gilt and fake chrome tend to fall off and doors don't quite close properly. One could be in a new tourist hotel in Moscow, an Olde

English Restaurant near Leicester Square or, indeed, at the Hearst Castle which is only a few miles from The Madonna Inn and is remarkable not so much for its grandiosity as the appalling sense that poor Hearst was ripped off by every rascally European dealer unloading the stuff he had been unable to sell anywhere else.

The 16th-century tapestries at the Hearst Castle have been badly-darned in mismatched fabrics, the panelling has been poorly-aligned, the furniture lazily faked. The only construction that looks solid and authoritative is that done in the twenties by native Californians: the swimming pools and the outer-shells of the various Moorish-style 'casas' where Hearst entertained the famous people of his day and into which alcohol had to be smuggled because the old man would allow guests only one cocktail before dinner. The pathos of the Hearst Castle is stronger than anything one is given in Citizen Kane's Xanadu. There's a fair bit of Security at the Casa Grande. It's impossible to drive up to the Castle. One must go on a tour (there are three, of varying lengths), taking a bus from the little town at the bottom of the Enchanted Hill which has grown up entirely to service the visitors. Security has a CIA look about it. The male and female guides are Disneyland clean, usually blond and blue-eyed, wearing dark blue blazers and grey flannel. They have the cold chirpiness of automata and you feel that somewhere on the way up you have been· electronically frisked. Patti Hearst still isn't mentioned in the list of famous family members. The place is now owned by the State and it seems to me that Ronald Reagan should have made it his official residence when he was Governor. There's still time to shift the Seat of Government here. But I suppose it represents a more romantic past, the age of the great millionaires who identified themselves with their castles and cities quite as much as the merchant princes of renaissance Italy with whom they had so much in common. There is little at Castle Hearst of the modern downhome ranch-style favoured by Reagan and so many of his recent predecessors. When I was last there someone had made an attempt to bomb the facade of the main castle, not so much, I suspect, to strike a blow at modern capitalism as to make a statement against traditional culture.

I have a friend, a successful writer in Los Angeles, who remains impressed by the castle. We visited it together once. He stood on the great balcony looking down over wooded hills and landscaped meadows where Hearst's huge herd of wild animals (including zebras and bison) had grazed and told me almost in a whisper that this was his ambition, to become rich enough to buy the Hearst Castle and to live in it. Instead he has turned his own Los Angeles house into a kind of miniature Hearst Castle, with secret rooms and fantastic decor, with six huge gargoyles in fibre-glass looking as if they have been ripped from the set of the Charles Laughton *Hunchback of Notre Dame* and placed over his garage entrance. He also has a grotto, faced with real stone, a small reproduction of the Caveman Room at The Madonna Inn, though without running water.

126

Beyond San Luis Obispo is Monterey, full of prosperous farms and vineyards. Every Wendy's hamburger place, every Denny's or Sambo's or Macdonald's pays its tribute to Monterey's literary fame with pictures of Steinbeck, with hamburgers or Tex-Mex dishes named after his mythological paradise: the Tortilla Flat and the Cannery Row Special, the Sweet Thursday banana-split and the Pastures of Heaven Special Salad. I expect to see cocktails called The Cup of Gold, The Wayward Bus, The Moon is Down or East of Eden. The titles might have been planned for this inevitable transformation. I know that somewhere in Monterey County it must be possible to find these drinks, as well as a powerful wine concoction called The Grapes of Wrath. Yet the Monterey one sees from Highway One is disappointingly unlike the picture drawn by Steinbeck. One feels it's high time some enterprising person moved in and reproduced the fantasy more successfully. Doubtless it will happen. California is greedy for cultural associations. Dana Point, for instance, is named after the author of *Two Years Before The Mast* who, as far as I can tell, stopped off there for an hour or so on his way to somewhere else. However, the nearer one gets to San Francisco the more 'good taste' (or San Francisco's idea of what that is) gets in the way.

San Francisco regards itself as a cultured city, a 'European' city, a city of enlightenment and art. One is forewarned of this if one stops off in Carmel which is a kind of tourist development out of Big Sur and was originally an artists' colony. Now it is more famous, I think, for its association with Clint Eastwood than with Henry Miller. Clint Eastwood has a house outside Carmel and he also owns a 'tavern', all naked wood and untrimmed stone where one can obtain an unremarkable hamburger (the Dirty Harry) or a reasonable drink, in downtown Carmel. It's called The Hog's Breath Saloon. One can, in fact, get a good nouveaux cuisine meal in Carmel and the motels are comfortable, if expensive.

The town is pretty. Each brick-paved street of its grid is lined with huge trees. But it's almost wholly given over to tourism, a kind of King's Road near the sea. Here are thousands of stetsons made from every conceivable material, decorated with precious stones and exotic plumage, in every possible colour. One shower of rain could ruin most of them, as it could ruin the snakeskin boots, the antique-style 'frontier' jackets, the silk cowboy shirts and the delicate designer-jeans. When I first saw this vast display of Western chic I had no idea who could be buying it. It's totally impractical and largely out of reach of the average person's pocket. A few tourists could be seen sporting the odd blue-suede ten-gallon hat with peacock and pheasant feathers fixed into a huge amethyst pin set on a hatband of woven gold-thread, but mostly they stuck to the ordinary straw stetsons you buy throughout the West to show you've been in cowboy country. The hats would put any Edwardian lady's to shame and cost more than anything you could have bought from a Parisienne milliner in 1900. I shall see them worn (and I suppose 'used') a few days later in Marin County up beyond San Francisco, when all is made clear.

Every old hippy 'craftsperson' who ever stained glass or tortured metal can find a retail outlet in Carmel, which prides itself on its artisticness, the tastefulness of its wares, the creativeness of its inhabitants. Here is the epitome of laid-back artworks, the snootier end of the wholesale market you associate with Sunday by the Hyde Park railings, folk festivals, rural craft-shops, paintings of big-eyed children and plunging horses: high-priced handiwork now found universally throughout the Western hemisphere wherever there is an area once lived in by artists. In Old Stockholm, in Heidelberg, in Amsterdam, in Montmartre, the same people seem to produce the same paintings, the same woven patterns, the same beadwork, the same leather-goods, the same glassware, the same pewter and polished pebbles, whose glowing merit in the eyes of the purchasers is that they were made by a woman in a long Liberty-print dress rather than by a man in overalls standing at a factory lathe. Do they buy this stuff for the same reasons they buy health-food — as charms against mortality and the mysteries of a technological world? Will the homespun poncho become magic armour, bestowing invulnerability, immortality, even invisibility on the woman who buys it from the dark-eyed man murmuring reassurance and with a beaded headband around his long grey hair? Are the potted preserves potions to confer well-being and domestic happiness on the businessman who hands his five dollars to a rosy-cheeked young woman? She charmingly thanks him in that accent peculiar to Northern California. It seems to derive half from the kindergarten, half from the psychiatrist's consulting room, and suggests a plea for kindness and understanding mingled with a whine of desperate frustration at the world's failure to love and protect the speaker. A voice that constantly invokes beauty, the unity of art and nature, the pleasure of the intellect, as if these things are a sort of thumb one may suck on and feel safe.

Yet Carmel is not all creative artworks and high-priced boutiques. It is one of the great white middle-class drug-consuming centres. Only the upper middle-class can afford to live here, buy here, feel secure here. The associations with the famous linger on and add to the image the inhabitants have of themselves as being somewhat daring, somewhat different, somewhat above the conventions, and because there's so much money in Carmel there is, inevitably, an easy-going police force which isn't going to mess with the well-to-do so long as the well-to-do don't mess with it. So the consumption of cocaine is high. And these people aren't paying street-prices of $80.00 a gram. They are paying, to coin a phrase, through the nose, as they do in Knightsbridge and Woodstock, for stuff that's usually far more adulterated than it will be in Notting Hill or Harlem, perhaps $140.00 a gram. A dealer, who stayed in the business she reckoned just because of the interesting social contacts she made, once gave me a line of some superb Peruvian cocaine just before she left to visit the Rolling Stones, to whom she was a regular supplier. I said that if

I envied the Stones nothing else it was that good quality coke. She laughed. "They aren't getting this! Jesus, what a waste. They'll pay twice as much for shit that you and I wouldn't snort on a bet!" That was when I first learned that in the main the higher up the social scale you are the worse and more expensive the drugs get. Her argument was they couldn't tell the difference any more and were subsidising the poorer consumers. A few producers and stars buy in bulk from the importers and tend to get decent drugs, but most won't risk having such quantities in their houses, or risk being caught making the deal, or risk blackmail from their suppliers. We were lucky in Carmel, for we bumped into the friend of a friend who makes his living from successful young executives and gave us some good stuff to help us on our way to San Francisco where by chance we were going to taste some of the purest cocaine either of us had sampled in a long time. My prejudice against San Francisco and Carmel tended to modify as a result.

The rocky bays and pine-covered hills seem to go on forever. Even when it rains, as it did several times on our way up, the scenery along Highway 1 is unfailingly dramatic and beautiful. This is the great twisting dream-road out of the future which is LA into the past which is San Francisco. One crosses long bridges over inlets, passes through tunnels in the sides of mountains, drives for a while beside the railroad and its huge slow-moving Metroliner while the radio plays Bluegrass and New Orleans Jazz and the possibilities of America seem wonderful and limitless. It's only a dream and it will only last a few days, but while it does last I intend to enjoy it to the full before we have to return to the realities of our Venetian garage.

BURNE HOGARTH

Tarzan

a myth man in the age of the macromachine

IN THE AGE of the electronic technological society and the rise of the cybernetic world machine, we have shaped a time in which all existence seems negative and perverse. When we split the atom, we witnessed the emergence of a new nature and a new reality, a new world and a new man. It is a time which starts at the point of ethical exhaustion and moral failure, a time littered with the wreckage of dreams. What we have is a world of chance and peril, where truth in nature and natural law seems to have been suspended, and moral law and Mosaic law have been submerged in universal lawlessness.

Today there is disruption everywhere, a conscious bloodletting of the vital processes. The cybernetic society has permitted uninhibited machine output to be the pacemaker of human needs and demands. We have let our pious desire for abundance and the pursuit of happiness to pass from higher social standards into a depraved, hedonistic narcissism. We have turned away from our celebration of the brotherhood of man and praise of the human spirit to become a cult society conditioned to the ritual use of raw power and the routine threat of nuclear annihilation.

Conflict has become a law of cultural dynamics

and crisis after crisis has become a normal way of life. In our time there are no greater disasters than *man-made* disasters. As Max Scheler put it: "...man is a complete deserter from life...Within the order of his species...*man himself is a disease*..."

Nature with all its phenomenal powers has not been able to disrupt the planet with such pervasive, unrelenting persistence as has humankind. Only man has been able to so damage or derange the function of living things as to produce irreversible changes in the environment. Since taming and manipulating nature in the 18th and 19th centuries, man is now moving to enslave, rape and deplete the planet on a world scale. Lessing sums up: "Man is a species of predatory ape that gradually went mad with pride over its so-called mind".

As the transgression of all nature has been accomplished with the use of the machine, so the 'new' society has reversed the course of human culture. The "industrialisation of culture" (Dorfles) and the technical invasion of the creative process have corrupted the artistic canons and ideals of an older humankind. The stereotype is replacing the archetype. In art, the Precious Object, the ideal form of earlier culture patterns, is dying or dead. Everywhere, we see the machine aesthetics of our technological culture — computerised drawing, laser-beam sculpture, 3-D holographic illusionism, media tectonics and structures, automated mobiles, electronic colour-organ circuitry, web, cable and membrane architecture, and an avalanche of plastic and plaster-cast reproductions from the Venus de Milo and the Virgin Mary to Donald Duck and the Seven Dwarfs.

It is undeniable that art always evokes the visual images and form-patterns of a time. In our era art forms tend to commonplace, mawkish or profane; or they are evasive, enigmatic or incomprehensible. They are, in truth, anti-forms, anti-objects, anti-art. That is to say, they are anti-human and anti-social anomalies, concoctions of the cheap, the shoddy and the tawdry, and in them we see the excesses and aberrations, the functions and process of this incredible era.

In the fine arts of our time, the anti-form is

contrary to all forms of nature. This concept of form is a model of some kind of machine-made artefact. It is fundamentally a similitude of our sleek, supercharged culture, a factory-orientated facsimile of assembly-line, mass-produced objects. Beyond this facade of elitist "form follow function", there is the other side of pop culture, "form follows funk", which imitates the mountains of mass-consumed, dazzling, titillating technological junk of the macromachine.

It is an age of dada, folly, funk and fraud; a time of schlock, kitsch and rubbish. And because of its innate transitoriness and leisure-orientated concerns of ego gratification, our culture has let us believe that life is not genuine, that our aims are denatured, synthetic or spurious. As we become homogenised and standardised, blending and merging in a uniform taste norm of artless kitsch and simplistic chic, we take on pseudo-life values that have an inherent tradition-destroying power. We lose our sense of privacy and dwindle away in a rootless, conforming drift, while the irresistible culture sparkles and beckons, splendidly seductive through its cantankerous forms.

It is clear that the machine is the maker and the mover. The machine is the totem animal of modern man, the tireless, uncomplaining iron beast of burden. In the unceasing cycle of the mechanical slave there is no season of scarcity. It needs no care — only supervision. Man, committed to its ceaseless routine, becomes a routine functionary himself. Mimetic, his identity takes on the crisp, smooth, efficient characteristics of the mechanism. Because the beast never tires, if man becomes weary or complaining, he is cast aside like a malfunctioning part; he is judged incompetent or obsolete.

In the supersystem of the macromachine, man tends to become a faceless, anonymous example of collective mediocrity. As the culture creates a machine-made, anti-human art, so indeed does the society produce a utilitarian, institutional nonentity, a depersonalised adjunct of the macromachine.

*

On a larger scale, technology has created a new archetypal culture, unique in history, whose capacity to produce wealth is so enormous that to measure it by any past standards is meaningless. We are the "affluent society" of such opulence that our abundance is *not* measured by accumulation, but only by *discard*.

In the tonnage of junk, trash, clutter and glut is the visible fulfillment and climax of our social power.

The proof of our wealth is not in what we hoard, but in what we *waste*, how much we relegate to the garbage heap.

In the logic and dynamism of our superabundance, if the affluent society is to become ever larger, it must move to a new concept of growth, to a format of *planned waste*. Social necessity cannot be durable, permanent or precious objects. If the tempo of use must keep pace with the new growth, then use must be *accelerated*, and this means the creation of *instant objects*. Hence, the new tempo calls for *total replacement* of the *instant object* in the era of *planned waste*.

The name for this concept of progress is co-ordinated chaos and ruin. This is why we are fascinated with a cinema of holocausts, infernos, sharks, monsters, satanism and cannibalism. This is why we love the *fragment in art* — why we believe in the found object *(objet trouvée)*, and why we cherish the *assemblage* and the *collage*, whose concoctions are random pieces of discard, the expendable metaphors of the cybernetic age.

*

Histories typically relate the large-scale events in human affairs, the panoramic overviews of a time. With their Olympian commentaries historians tell of immense patterns of violence — crises, rebellions, wars and revolutions, the "contours of our civilisation".

Of the shapers and makers of events, they narrate acts of ruthless ambition, policies of inordinate cynicism, gross paranoia directed against all rivals and a ferocious aggrandisement extracted from the weak. Those who advance such a grim view of official reality with a cool objectivity must at least feel some dismay, if not trauma, when they review the excessive rise of violent assaults, slayings and suicides, to say nothing of the wanton maltreatment and frequent murder of children and babies.

In these dark tales of the history of mankind as an unrelieved Armageddon, one looks in vain for the other side to this reality — for the singular imprint of the beneficent man, for the virtuous human persona. This other record is left for myth.

Myth enters the human record when the passage through life is too steep, the way too rough, the tunnel too dark — or the path is beset with dragons, monsters and dangers of every description. Then a myth figure appears, a hero to save us from the terrors of the world and to restore us to safety, security and sanity.

Myth begins in the web of the imagination, almost as autobiography, like a self-portrait, virtually as an autonomous act of creative art. Each individual sees the myth in a personal way, but in an idealised mirror-image of the exalted mythic personality.

However, this mythic persona projected on a world scale becomes symbolic of an era, subsumed in poetry, literature and art. The mythic image of the culture, developed from the needs and aspirations of a time, embodies the essence of the strains and tensions that afflict the world and its people. Hence, the universal world and the personal world respond in unison to the example and energies of the mythic personality.

What gives the myth its essential authenticity, however, is its power to possess and be "possessed". The mythic figure seizes and "consumes" us — it transmutes our character and personality as it transforms the world around us. It becomes a double reality of dreaming and consciousness: one side plausible, palpable, real; the other fictive, ephemeral, incorporeal — each existing simultaneously with the other.

But the motive force of the myth figure lies in its *innate charisma*, in its interpenetrating power to exact a magical, transcendental response. Its aura compels an orgiastic surge of inner life energy to relive in the life of the hero a personal drama, revealing powers that are demonic and wonderful. And in the end, a catharsis occurs, prophylactic and regenerative, restoring psychic balance and felicity, sunrise at the end of a dream.

*

When Edgar Rice Burroughs created *Tarzan of the Apes* early in the 20th century, he scarcely realised he was creating a tale far beyond the dimensions of a popular romance. It was written on a theme that was not very original, in a form that was not very sophisticated, for a public that was not very mature.

Burroughs' style was entertaining and enthralling; his prose, vivid and seductive, had a magnetic quality of drama. His style of storytelling, indeed, took on a greater lustre in the *telling*, for it was beyond fiction — more than romantic narrative or heroic adventure. His tales set countless youths acting out the deeds of their hero, Tarzan. Burroughs, without realising it (although he admits in the opening page "it *may* be true"), created in Tarzan a *myth-man*, an authentic mythopoeic hero endorsed and validated in almost every way by the turbulent events of this 20th century "Age of Anxiety", the era of "anguish, torment and chaos", in the "civilisation of discontents".

It was a confluence of the same dust and ashes that riddled the personal world of Burroughs with an endless string of failures; and he began to write the first of his Martian stories, in an evocation of autobiographical desperation, on the back of a piece of stationery left from a bankrupt business.

His words are fantasy, but the mood is not. It is a saga of a "brooding, suffering man...fated to walk the earth in agony...in the midst of a dying planet".

But in the creation of *Tarzan of the Apes*, the untried, self-taught writer touched a raw nerve in his own unconscious that became linked to the elemental magma of the mythological stuff from which all ideal heroes spring.

Burroughs, indeed, was a man of his time — a frustrated dreamer. His act of creation was sublimely innocent, and Tarzan was the dreamchild of his own fitful yearning. Yet this creation became the archetype of every man's secret desire to be liberated from frustration and despair. For even as Tarzan is the anti-hero and orphan of his three lost worlds — his personal world, his jungle world, and his civilised world — so is Burroughs a rejected anti-hero-orphan of the world; and so is everyone.

There comes a time when Burroughs, the failure, becomes an unqualified success. It is 1932; come face to face with one of the most widely read authors in the world. His books are published in over 50 languages with more than 100 million copies sold. See him as one of the three most-read authors in the United States and, perhaps, the highest-paid writer then living. In Russia, the most popular writers in the English language are H.G. Wells, Jack London, O. Henry, Conan Doyle and Upton Sinclair; but among them, Edgar Rice Burroughs is the favourite. And in Germany, the creator of *Tarzan of the Apes* receives the highest royalties ever paid to a foreign author.

Now imagine Burroughs' feelings as he learns his books are banned by his local library for not meeting standards of good fiction. He is at the height of world renown, yet his name is not listed among the ten most popular authors of American fiction. He is consistently disparaged by critics, and so at odds with the literary world he has not the friendship or acquaintance of any writer of note or reputation.

The denial of Burroughs by his professional peers was so extreme a phenomenon as to be unmatched in the life of any modern author. He was a modest reticent man who had a profound and relentless need to belong, and the idea of rejection must have given rise to deep pain and humiliation.

What must Burroughs have been like when he faced this alienation and despair? Surely, he must have painfully recoiled into the depths of his psyche and soul — angered and hurt. How else shall we understand him if not from the volcanic source from which Tarzan was energised? What terrible fuel powered the wasteland of Mars and her annihilating wars?

We do not know exactly what forces worked on this prosaic man to make him write the golden legend of the jungle god, the modern myth of the demonic *Tarzan of the Apes*. We know Burroughs was a loser and a loner. We know, too, he was in some ways a perpetual adolescent; like Tarzan, he grew up but wished never to grow old — to stay forever young.

Burroughs had a compelling need to write, to shape a dream of fantasy and folklore. It was narrative pantomime, a kind of *meta-literature* that was outside formal fiction. It was, in truth, *mythology*. This fledgling upstart, learning to write, shaped a modern myth; and writing, shaped himself. He was an important writer and great in his way, though he never knew it. And that is why, perhaps, he was so misunderstood and rejected. For even at the end, he mistrusted his talents, disparaged his accomplishments, denigrated his education and denied his value and place, even in the face of great rewards, because he felt small against other writers whose accomplishments and distinctions were less than his own.

*

If a single word were to describe the quality of *Tarzan* which holds every reader's interest, it would be *enchantment*. We are not here concerned with those fake pop-media words which abound in contemporary jargon, for example, in con-talk ads, two-bit instant psychology, funk-image politics, slob films, hip religion and the like.

What we are speaking of is a form of sorcery or mania; it is not unlike self-hypnosis or sympathetic magic. The terms are not important but the concept is: what we are dealing with is an animistic identity with deep, sensual undertones expressed on the primordial level of innocence, ego security and the vital sense of whole-feeling and all-being. Tarzan is the condensed demon-spirit who inspires the stubborn life-force in all of us. He is the fever of life that violates the coma. There is in this enchantment the miraculous and the wonderful, the impeccable and the incorruptible.

In our present crisis, Tarzan denies the end of mankind. He takes us back from the edge of the abyss of nothingness and negates the nameless, the unutterable, the unthinkable. He forms a bridgehead from the derelictions of the civilised world and opens a passage to the gardens of the mind. Rejecting the poisoned, unprincipled world of cash-box culture because he belongs to *himself*; he takes *us* away, not to Paradise or an Arcadian realm, but to a feral jungle in the dawn of man, where he is an ape among other beasts — and no living creature is a slave.

If today there is despair; if, in the era of ruin, we have seen the wreck of man and the death of God; if, in the society of planned waste, we have wrought the anti-form and the anti-man — then Tarzan is the antidote to the anti-self. We can believe in him because like ourselves he is naked, defenceless and alone. He is a child of tragedy, born to suffer and labour. Then by strain of wit and fang and claw, he struggles to survive — and rises, to transcend and triumph.

Tarzan is no automated man; his powers and passage are neither supernatural nor hypertechnological. Against the clatter of machines, his scream of challenge reminds us there is something powerful and life-defining in his presence.

"The Myth," says Cassirer, "emphasises the physiognomic character of experience." Indeed, with the onset of the technological supersystem, the great societies have dealt mortal blows to the prevailing myths of modern man. We have seen that happiness is not the natural state of man; goodness is not his natural conduct; freedom is not his inalienable right. We are told civilisation does not necessarily lead to progress; science does not categorically assure the betterment of mankind. The era of optimism is finished; the world's frontiers are closing down; and hope for the future is dying.

From this dismal view the world is a wasteland, depleted and moribund. This perception, it must be argued, is incomplete if not inexact. Its conception of despair has too low a centre of gravity and a sense of affliction that is too static, too melancholic, too stoic to meet the dynamism of the age.

Burroughs, without doubt, has constructed a better model. If the myth is physiognomic, it must also be *synergistic* (according to the Burroughs' schema) in that it opens the way for the *insubordination of the ego*. The myth, if nothing else, is a form of folklore; and as revealed insight to a culture it must project something of its aestheticism, its passions and aspirations.

That Tarzan confirms the tragic pattern of conflict and suffering indicts his world and civilisations to be parallel hells and purgatories with our own. He is scarred and wounded as all of us are, but the nostalgia, the yearning to return to the *past* in order to outwit the untenable future, is a nostrum for the sick, the feeble and the infirm. As we close down the 20th century and open the 21st with its inevitable collisions and commotions, we must, in Thoreau's words, move into the future with our ears tuned to a "different drum" and our eyes holding the vision of a different dream.

Tarzan is in a better position to transvalue and transcribe the modern myth. As the ape-man rejects status, inheritance, wealth and luxury in his modern world, he also rejects servitude, power, torture and all noxious manipulations of other human beings. That he is moral and humane are persuasions, not of written codes and creeds, but of an ardent response to all life's needs in a state of nature. Hence, he leads us "home", not to Nirvanas or disinfected Utopias, but to that abode of sanity, the wilderness paradigm of autonomy and optimism, to a celebration of forbearance, felicity and mercy.

Tarzan is not the tragic hero, the tortured champion or the suffering god. Such concepts are too pessimistic and permeated with masochistic resignation to be useful in coping with the problems of the future. *Angst* and breast-beating are latter-day manifestations of indecision and collapse in the face of crises. Resolutely, we ought to step back from the abyss and cease contemplating the crippled ego of our existential being. There is still time for a reconstruction of "modern man", one who does not succumb to an internal tyranny of unrelieved subservience and cannibalise himself with self-hatred and rage.

There is still time for a new spirit to shape the pattern of the dream, taken, perhaps, from a form of play or wit, from childhood innocence. Or perhaps it may come from another kind of energy which shapes the cobweb and the rainbow and remakes the sounds of oceans in a seashell. From the infrastructures of the mind and the beating heart — it may come, perhaps, from *Tarzan of the Apes*.

BOOZY COPS GO ON WILD SPREE

Drinkers flee terror org[...]

TWENTY young detectives went on a frenzied rampage after a ten-hour drinking spree, it was claimed yesterday.

Other drinkers are said to have fled in fear and disgust at the amazing antics of the booze-crazed cops.

Witnesses allege they **KISSED** each other on the lips, **SQUIRTED** soda siphons in bars and **POURED** beer over their heads.

The plain-clothes policemen are also accused of swearing at staff and customers who objected to their behaviour.

ATTACKED

Some of the drunken gang ended up being held by uniformed police after being kicked out of two pubs, a fish bar and a restaurant.

And it is claimed two black men were attacked in a restaurant fracas.

Startled bystanders watched men kissing each other on the lips, pouring beer over themselves and squirting soda syphons.

Rowdy

Customers also claimed that the detectives swore in front of other drinkers, driving customers away from the pub.

See Page Nineteen

REVEALING MIRROR

...ES DOWN ON PAGE 18

JAC[...]

UNMASKED

The hooded Pc who preyed on young girls

BY GEORGE GLENTON

A HOODED prowler who terrorised a town was unmasked yesterday ... as policeman Paul Thomas.

Dressed in his all-black outfit he sexually assaulted a young woman at knifepoint.

And he terrorised schoolgirls by stealing underclothes from their homes and making obscene phone calls to them.

Jailing 28-year-old Thomas for five and a half years at the Old Bailey yesterday the Recorder of London, James Miskin, QC, told him: "You are a disgrace to your uniform."

Thomas, a former scoutmaster who once said he wanted to be a top cop, admitted six charges of theft, and one of burglary.

The jury acquitted him of attempting to rape a West End night-club girl, but found him guilty of indecently assaulting her.

The judge ordered that an alleged rape charge on a British Airways employee, which Thomas denied, should be left on the files.

The court was told that Thomas terrorised two schoolgirls in Isleworth, London.

CONVICTED: Pc Paul Thomas: "You're a disgrace."

HI[...]
diar[...]
expos[...]
as
fakes

■ THE HITLE[...]
[...] finally
yesterday
carried a
and bi[...]
volur[...]

CROWD WATCHED MAN MAKE LOVE TO CORPSE

By NATION Reporter

A MAN who had sexual intercourse with a corpse was yesterday jailed for six months.

Nairobi district magistrate Mr. Joseph Wanjala convicted him on a charge of common nuisance.

Gichuki Ngatia admitted 19 previous convictions, dating back to 1943.

He denied the charge that on May 30 at Pumwani location, Nairobi, he had sexual intercourse with a corpse.

Mr. Asumani Ramadhan told the court he saw Ngatia having sexual intercourse with a corpse near Pumwani bar.

Mr. Ramadhan said many people gathered there for a glimpse. He said: "I then sent someone to call Mr. Asumani Hamisi, who works at Pumwani bar."

The witness said that when Hamisi came he asked Ngatia to leave the corpse, but Ngatia refused and said: "I am not going to leave her. She is not your wife."

Mr. Hamisi pulled Ngatia from the corpse. At that time he was half naked. He was arrested and taken to Shauri Moyo police station.

The police took the corpse to city mortuary.

Ngatia said he arrived in Nairobi to attend Madaraka Day celebrations. He went to Pumwani bar where he got drunk.

Ngatia said: "I just don't know where I slept. I was surprised when I found myself at Shauri Moyo police station."

Mr. Wanjala said the court took a "serious view" of such a case.

EXPRESS

Man kept wife in a box

MICHAEL McGOVERN in NEW YORK

A JEALOUS husband locked his wife in a box at the foot of his bed every night.

Lucienne Duclos, 51, told a Montreal court that her 49-year-old husband, Alfred, would force her to strip and examine her closely for any sign of infidelity when she came home from work.

Duclos had made her sleep in the box for two years, and on rare nights when he let her out to join him in bed would handcuff her to his arm.

She went to the police for help the day after her husband punched her in the face, kicked her in the legs, locked her in the box and slept with one of their teenage daughters.

Now Duclos has been sentenced to 19 months in jail —and the judge has ordered him to join Alcoholics Anonymous.

The Queen holds key

THE QUEEN received the keys of the city of P Vallaria when she ...-sure at the Vi— eer resort ye... She visited ...i

Sexy Zena meets boys in blue

SEX QUEEN Zena Whitehouse popped into Manchester and enjoyed a brush with the boys in blue.

It was a case of "hello, hello, hello," when busty Zena autographed magazines in a shop on Oldham Street.

The police popped in to see that Zena was not displaying too much of her 36-24-36 charms.

Busy Zena, 23-year-old star of Emmanuelle in Soho, was suitably clothed — and on the right side of the law.

The brunette beauty said: "We had a good natter and I gave the officers some advice about their love lives. They were very nice and can lock me up any time."

Then she carried on signing books for her fans who queued at the shop to see their favourite pin-up in the flesh.

Police said: "We visit book shops in the Manchester area in the public interest. We are not out to be unreasonable, but just want to make sure shops are keeping within the law."

Collector coshed

A 61-year-old club money collector was coshed and robbed of £100 in Dalton Road, Rhodes, Middleton.

'CRIPPLE KILLED WOMAN' —INSPECTOR

By NATION Reporter

AN inquest into the death of a Nairobi woman was told yesterday she died after being beaten by a cripple.

District magistrate, Mr. Joseph Wanjala, was told Beatrice Wanjiku died at Kenyatta National Hospital on November 13 after she had been beaten by Mr. Minyaru Mbugu. Mr. Mbugu, whose legs have been amputated, was alleged to have seriously injured the woman on the head with a knife. She died from the injuries and the beating, Mr. Wanjala was told.

Chief Insp. David Theiru Munuhe told Mr. Wanjala he ordered one of his officers to bring in Mbugu after the woman died.

"Mr. Mbugu gave a statement to me after I had informed him of the charge facing him and I had cautioned him not to make a reply. I told him if he replied, what he told me could be used as evidence against him.' the inspector said.

Mr. Mbugu then said he had beaten the woman because she was very abusive to him the inquest was told.

"It was around 6.30 p.m. when I was riding my handcart and I met Wanjiku. She abused me calling me a crippled dog," Mr. Mbugu was alleged to have said.

Abuse

"She always abused me whenever she saw me," Mr. Mbugu was quoted as saying. He later went to the woman's house with a club to ask her why she had abused him. He hid near the house until the woman arrived, the magistrate was told.

After she opened the door, Mr. Mbugu entered the house. As she was trying to shut him out, she fell down, the inquest was told.

"I got hold of her and started beating her with a club I had carried from my house," Mr. Mbugu was alleged to have told the inspector.

But Mr. Mbugu denied having said that he went to the woman's house to beat her. He also denied beating her on the head.

Insp. Charles Issika also testified. He told the inquest he went to Kenyatta National Hospital and transferred the woman's body to the City Mortuary.

He told Mr. Wanjala he arrested Mr. Mbugu at his house in Kirigu and that Mr. Mbugu voluntarily surrendered a club which had allegedly been used to beat the woman.

The inquest continues.

KINKY HUSBAND FILMS HIS DEATH BY HANGING

By KIERON SAUNDERS

VIDEO fan John Halstead made a film in sound and colo — of his death by hanging in a bizarre sex rite.

The 32-year-old unemployed bus driver set up a porno film stu in his attic while his wife was out, an inquest heard yesterday.

The arc lights were switched on and the cameras were rolling when h slipped accidentally from a ladder to his death during a bondage sex act.

His wife Patricia discovered him dead in horrific circumstances when she returned home from a visit to her mother.

His partly-clothed body was hanging from a padded noose—with his feet dangling from a ladder 18ins from the floor.

Police later found a 15-minute video film of the sex drama which led to his death.

Wife tells of horror discovery in the attic

Children

And at yesterday's inquest on Mr Halstead at Denton, Manchester, his wife admitted he had engaged in unusual sexual practices for some time.

Mrs Halstead, a slim redhead, said that on the day her husband died he had taken her and their three children from their home at Ashton Road, Denton, to her mother's home.

Padded

When her husband failed to return, she went home alone on a bus.

All the curtains in the house were drawn and when she went inside she saw a strong light coming from the open attic door. She used a wooden box

to peer into the attic— and saw her husband hanging.

PC Michael Baron said he found a full sound and colour video recorder on the landing. Cables led into the loft to two strong lights and a video camera.

All were focused on the body—and all the equipment was still switched on.

Ladder

PC Baron said the noose around Mr Halstead's neck was padded with "three to four inches of cotton wool."

He said he found boxes of porn magazines in the attic—half of them showing bondage sex. There were also newspaper cuttings of deaths by hanging and shooting.

PC Baron said he played the video film through. It showed Mr Halstead slipping from the ladder and

struggling in vain to regain his footing.

Pressure

Coroner Peter Revington said: "It's perfectly obvious Mr Halstead met his death in pursuit of sexual perversion.

"For this purpose he had a rope around his neck, not in a way meant for hanging — it was padded very carefully in cotton wool.

"It is well known and widely recognised that pressure on the neck produces additional excitement. It also produces a terrible risk of death."

Verdict: Accident.

HEATHCOTE WILLIAMS
cosmic whore batter

Why'd Ya Do It?

When I stole a twig from our little nest
an I gave it to a bird with nothing in her beak
I had my balls an ma brains put into a vice
an twisted all around for a whole fuckin week

Whydya do it, she said,
whydya let that trash
get a hold of your cock
an get stoned on MA hash?

Whydya do it, she said,
whydya let her suck ya cock?
Oh, do me a favour,
don put me in the dock.

Whydya do it, she said,
they're Mine all your tools,
you just tied me to the mast
of the Ship of Fools.

Whydya do it, she said,
when you know it makes me sore?
Cause she had cobwebs up her fanny
an I believe in giving to the poor.

Whydya do it, she said,
whydya spit on ma Snatch,
Are we out of love now?
Ach, it's just a bad patch.

Whydya do it, she said,
whydya do what you did,
you drove my ego
to a really bad skid.

Whydya do it, she said
Aint nothin to laugh
You just tore all our kisses
right in half.

Whydya do it, she screamed
After all we've said
Every time I see your dick
I see her cunt in ma bed.

Whydya do it, she said
Whydya do what you did?
Betray my little oyster
with such a low bid?
Whydya do it, she said
Whydya do what you did?

My cock turned tail
an coiled up inside my head . . .
it was just the Hormone Jail
but I thought it was ma Death Bed.

The whole room was swirling
but her lips were still curling
Whydya do it, she said, whydya do whatcha did?
Whydya do it, she said, whydya do it, she said,
whydya DO WHATCHA DIIIIIIIIIIIIID!

Oh Big Grain Mother
I Love You For Ever
With Your Barbed Wire Pussy
And Your good and bad weather

Whip me, trip me, strip me
an I'll be your little Trevor.

Cosmic Whore Batter

Oooooooooh your satin fanny,
What do you feed it on?

Clouds of electric honey!
Sucky Fucky Fuck me and Be Free!

I kept this space for you and me
To turn Them and Us into Aeon Juice
a genital gyration
an intergalactic grope
a Cosmic Consummation!

You want a short time?
You want a long time?

Your aerial's become unplugged

. . . soon to be a bad-ass doper, soon to be a giggling joker
soon to be a jive-ass jigger, soon to be a soft-rod jigger . . .

COME ALIVE AN FUCK THE HIVE!

Queen Bee's in Everyone's Anatomy

      SUCK ME AN SEE

CRASH, STASH, LASH, DASH, MASH, or
         FLAAAAAAAAAAAAAAAAAAAAAAAAASH!

     Interconnection,

     Holy Erection,

     Resurrection

WHEN THE COCKS RISE,

     THE PEOPLE RISE

God is Black and she's hungry and HUGE
   Well that's all now,
      from the cosmic centrifuge.

The Body Lightning Rodeo

Let's Get our End Away
and then there'll be no end

My soul is on fire
can't get it any higher

Sister Sesame Cloudbuster
fly me, earth me, burn me, stretch me

Everybody's humming a body mantra
Everybody's seeing that hot gland yantra

We must love one another or die

Queen Boadicea builds a bed for 200,000 people in the middle of Hyde
Park and out come Narcissus and Psyche, werewolves, armed lovers,
nuns, shebeen dervishes, robbers and cops, salesmen and princes, tramps
and cyclists, when it is dark

        The pillows are eighty feet long
              and the sheets a quarter mile wide
       We lift them up
      and get inside
Earth Rose sings the Meat Roxy Anthem: The Cock and Cunt Connection
                     is a fifty volt injection

                  Don use no insulation
                  .....GET IT ONNNNNNNNN!
City Rats bring us wafers and communion wine

             Love FEAST
             Love feast
           Immortal Yeast

Sister Sesame sits on a plinth of jelly babies, opens her legs to the moon
        and the lunar rats make her mink scallop water diamond rivulets

The tramps rejoice! Methylated cataracts   fall   from their eyes!
They hack off their clothes and lie on the ground
Every bedsore is an altar for Sister Sesame's Sperm
The lice and the ticks fly away to Mars
and we all start to be reborn.

148

Everyone comes out of their holes — lushes looking for tush, sex gypsies,
hormone nipsters, and love clowns.

                    our juice fields are flowing
                    our Auras are Growing . . .
Striped Cocks, Green Cunts, Purring Assholes tasting of mint!
Doctor Divine in his knees:
                    Goose-Grease every reason for life
                    Every part   of Every Body is my   Wife

Supernatural family on a bed of flowers:

Brains flowering, hair flowering, breasts flowering, eyes flowering, navels
    flowering, hands flowering, feet flowering, Seeding an Astral Tibet.

                    Only when we fuck you have we met
                    Touch and be touched — a million bodies in
                                                            one
                    It's still going on now, and the sun'll go out
                                                    when we
            C O M E

Sid Did It

The white blood was squirting
And Nancy was hurting
But Sid did it

All the pistols of sex
Had blanks up their spout
Shit and piss and vomit
Was all they could get out
So . . . Sid did it

The dagger went in
The dagger went out
Just like his vicious prick
He knew fuck all about

Your stomach's pretty vacant
Give this metal food a try
Die you little cunt
Die you little cunt
And let me fly

Never mind the bollocks —
You've got none —
Let me hack at your tits
There's no future in them
Sid did it

Heroin makes a cock up
Of the dark and the light
Hey little corpse
What'cha doing tonight?
Sid did it

No spunk punk and lowlife stealer
Brain death reject
Trying to get a feeler
Sid did it

Hate turns your sperm
Into a stinging jellyfish
The world gave you all its crap
Including your last wish
Sid did it

150

Oh little punk boy
Murderer on the make
Not even your own life
Was yours to take
Sid did it Sid did it
Sid did it Sid did it

Nancy Spungen (with astral overtones):
Slash me open
Slit me true
Turn my guts into a fanny
'Cos I love you
Through and Through

NICKED! A COP IN CHILD PORNO HUSH-UP

A POLICEMAN accused of smuggling child porn into Britain took part in an amazing cover-up to protect his career.

He appeared in court, admitted the offence and was fined—all without magistrates realising that he was a member of a crack crime squad.

Detective Sergeant Melvin Rigby was arrested by Customs men as he returned from a weekend in Amsterdam with nine magazines showing pictures of children in sexual poses.

But he managed to keep his boss from knowing of the incident for nine months before his case went to court.

No mention of his job was made when he appeared before Manchester City Magistrates.

And his solicitor, Mr David Middleweek, successfully applied for the case to be moved to another court room where no reporters were present.

Rigby, a member of the Manchester force on the North - West regional crime squad, was fined £200 and ordered to pay £200 costs.

CLEVER

After his cover-up was revealed he told me:

"Personally I don't see any harm in pornography, but I know what view our Chief Constable, Jim Anderton, takes.

He denied that the magazines contained sex pictures of children.

"It was just ordinary porn — men and women with each other", he said.

But one of the JPs on the bench, Mr Tom McIntyre, said: "We saw the magazines. They were full of child pornography.

"They were the worst I've ever seen.

SCALPED B SEX BEAST

POLICEMAN DAD 'RAPED FOSTER GIRL 130 TIMES'

By DENIS BUDGE

A POLICEMAN raped his schoolgirl foster daughter 130 times in two years, it was alleged yesterday.

The middle-aged man was said to have told the 12-year-old girl that no one would believe her if she complained — because he was a policeman.

Prosecutor Michael Brook told Chelmsford Crown Court: "He forced himself on her using his influence and authority."

The policeman ...

The Boy Who Wanted To Be A Rabbit

A FIFTEEN year old schoolboy, Steven Shea, killed himself recently after reading Richard Adams' book *Watership Down* — because he wanted to be a rabbit. Steven leapt 50 feet to his death from the top of a multi-storey car park in Letchworth, Herts. When police investigated the death they discovered in his diary a coded message which ran:

"After reading *Watership Down* I killed myself to become a rabbit".

An inquest jury at Hitchin returned a verdict that he killed himself while the balance of his mind was disturbed.

☐ DICK TRACY

DAILY MIRROR, Friday, February 25, 1983

THE KINKY

EE Leonard Bowie's secret women's hair led to a night of

rmer operating theatre assistant 0-year-old Anne Reilly "for sexual n."

ie called police ... who found convicted killer Mrs Reilly unconscious in her council home.

Her scalp was on the floor beside a blood-stained knife and hair clippers.

Stroking

Locks of hair were scattered about and detectives found a large quantity of other hair in a cupboard.

Bowie, 43, brother of a Church of Scotland minister, told officers: "I get sexual satisfaction from stroking and cutting women's hair.

"I remember picking up the clippers but don't remember using the knife."

By MIRROR REPORTER

"I suppose I did it, I don't know."

At the High Court in Glasgow yesterday Bowie admitted cutting and removing Mrs Reilly's scalp to cause her severe injury and permanent disfigurement at her home in Emerson Road, Bishopbriggs.

In the same court in 1979, Mrs Reilly was cleared of murdering her husband after describing how she was forced to commit unnatural sexual acts with him.

But she was found guilty of culpable homicide and eventually jailed for three years.

Her three - week relationship with Bowie began shortly after her release.

Bowie, of Springfiel Road, Bishopbriggs, w jailed for four years.

He telephoned brother Bernard and his wife Doreen in Grimsby, South Humberside to tell them about the bumper birth.

Doreen said: delighted because "We're have been through this test-tube business twice before without success.

"They said they wouldn't be trying again if it wasn't successful this time. This was their last

Tou... driver... Northampton, pl. grating, is home to sho...

LLAMA ALARM

An escaped llama caused traffic chaos on a main road at Bath, Avon, yesterday before the owner, who keeps it nearby, recaptured it

'GIVE VICE COPS ANTI-SEX DRUG'

VICE squad police should be impotent or given pills to suppress their sex drive, a magistrate said yesterday.

He hit out in Hong Kong after the colony's force fell down badly on the job during a club raid.

Instead of booking two vice girls, detectives fell to your their sexual charms, said magistrate Sirinarain Maharaj.

The officers arrested four officials at speedy club spending 90 minutes in girls booths Magistrate Maharaj dismissed the police case and said: "Although constables were under orders not to get excited they did the opposite."

Make your life brighter with the switched-on Sun

...lona

G.L.A.M... granny h Strike shares w lovenest with ex-husband h her 20-year-old friend.

Tongues ha wagged non-sto since the three-s set up Home in council flat in Ker shaw Road, Dagenham, East London.

But 47-year-ol Evelyne, who plans to marry he 25-year-old toy boy lover Day said next mon yesterday: "I don't worry about wha nosies say, what nothing sordid is h

Her invalid husband cop own so book ye... for the h when for for

Chopped, the Vice Squad boozers

By IAN RAMSAY

A POLICE Vice Squad was last night disbanded after a Chief Constable reports about boozing bobbies.

At least seven vice squad officers have been reported to the Director of Public Prosecutions after a 2 a.m. raid on a pub in the centre of Manchester.

They include the "A" division licensing inspector — the man responsible for upholding the drinking laws — and his predecessor.

Altogether, about two dozen officers are believed to be involved.

Senior officers have also been told how one vice squad officer gave a live sex show for his colleagues by having intercourse with a prostitute on a pub table.

Livid

Chief Constable James Anderton was said yesterday to be "absolutely livid."

He called senior officers together and told them that as from 5 o'clock last night, the ENTIRE plain-clothes squad operating out of "A" division were off the job.

And he instructed them to be posted immediately to other duties.

The chief and his aides spent most

Turn to Page Two

Boozing Vice Squad gets the chop

From Page One

of yesterday picking an entirely new team.

One senior officer said last night: "The chief feels he has been betrayed and he has cracked down hard."

Officers reporting for duty last night suddenly found they had been taken off Vice Squad assignments and given routine jobs.

The officers in the squad are not detectives but operate in plain clothes dealing almost entirely with licensing, prostitution, gaming and pornography.

The "A" division Vice Squad covers a square mile of Manchester City centre.

But last night, for the first time, the area was without a Vice Squad patrol.

CHARLES PARTINGTON

confusing the cunning cortex

I HAD RETURNED to Manchester reluctantly, drawn there by circumstances over which I exercised no control. My only consolation was that my stay would be brief. I could have refused to oversee the installation of one of our new Printel-Xerox agencies on Deansgate of course, but that would, it was pointed out, have reflected negatively on the New York appointment.

Booked rather unexpectedly on a British Airways inter-city flight, I spent most of the brief journey reflecting that during the four or five weeks it would take to get the Deansgate agency operational, the likelihood of avoiding all of my once too-close acquaintances in the city was remote. And how onerous that prospect seemed.

Approaching the airport in a wide banking turn, the aircraft descended below the suffocating cloud-belt for the first time during the entire flight. Despite the early hour, the light was already dying. The city lay spread out below us, bathed in a mercilessly revealing neon and sodium glare.

During my absence Manchester had changed.

The concrete cancer of the Arndale Centre had eaten away a vast area of the older architectural heart of the city. Gaping rubble-strewn sites, some with pre-stressed steel and concrete skeletons already rearing into the dismal sky, indicated that the disease had not yet run its course. Many of the city's main arterial routes had been sealed off to traffic, as the Victorian sewage systems had finally collapsed under the ever-increasing loads imposed upon them. No-go areas and skyscrapers; beneath the city's brave new facade, it's base was decaying away.

I resisted the temptation to stay at my parent's house, situated out on one of the wide tree-lined avenues bordering the East Lancashire Road, choosing instead to book a room in the Holiday Inn that had recently been erected at the junction of Fennel and Corporation Street.

From the windows of my room on the sixteenth floor, I gazed out beyond the square tower of Manchester Cathedral, following the twisting progress of the Irwell's sluggishly flowing oil-scummed waters. At the curve of Salford Crescent, the relative grandeur of the lesser city's 19th century Fire Station and Art College presented a marked contrast to the horror of the Regent Road high-rise complex. Did people still inhabit those grey prison blocks, I wondered? And further off to the North, where the moon was now rising, the huge flattened mass of Winter Hill sat on the skyline. Above the summit reared the steel needle of the telecommunications tower, its aircraft warning lights blinking back at me across the all too familiar miles. I turned away, submerged under a tidal wave of inward rushing memories.

I showered and changed, then went down for dinner in the hotel restaurant. Around a group of tables on the far side of the imposing almost empty room, a party was in progress.

I ordered and ate quickly, casting frequent furtive glances at the women laughing and chattering so animatedly. In any other city I would have experienced a delicious sense of freedom, of release, at being so far from Karen and my family. But I knew Manchester too well. Here I felt only desperation.

Sensing that it would now be impossible to return to my room so early, I left the hotel and went out onto the streets.

Behind Hanging Ditch and the Edwardian facade of the Corn and Produce Exchange, a narrow street eventually gives access to the small, well-tended lawns of Manchester Cathedral. I wandered, aimlessly I imagined, down that street, noting critically how the old trade shops and cheese cellars had been supplanted by neon-advertised night clubs, video games-rooms and massage parlours. It appeared that despite all the publicity Chief Constable James Anderton had recently achieved in the media, his National Clean-Up Campaign was apparently foundering in his own parish. I knew of at least two people on whom the irony would not be lost. Smiling, I turned away from the lights and hurried down the length of Cathedral Yard.

Crossing the Irwell by Victoria Bridge, I approached the intersection of Market Street and Deansgate. On my left, rearing high into the night sky, were the yellow fortress walls of the Arndale Centre. Overhead, a concrete walkway already extended across Victoria Street, an exploratory pseudo-pod of the ever-growing shopping complex.

Deansgate, still elegant and luxurious and for that reason the site of our prestigious Northern Printel-Xerox Agency, had suffered badly from the widespread disintegration and collapse of the city's long-neglected drains.

Ominous holes and depressions had appeared almost overnight all along Deansgate about three weeks ago, and, ever since, both the Sewage and Highways Departments had been working non-stop to repair the damage and to restore the chaotically diverted traffic back to this main artery.

All of the subsidences were shored up against further deterioration by massive timber beams and corrugated iron sheeting. The throbbing of diesel-powered pumps and excavators roared in the fume-filled air. At times, the stench from the open pits was sickening. Sizzling flashes from electric-arc welding guns frequently paled even the unrelenting glare of the emergency floodlights strung out in parallel lines down both sides of the street. Moving carefully along the narrow strip of pavement still uncontaminated by the mounds of excavated earth and pools of black water, I finally reached the plate-glass frontage of number seventy.

As I had half-anticipated, despite the late hour all the lights were on inside. What they revealed was hardly encouraging.

The three units comprising the laser print-system were already bolted in position on the cluttered shop floor, surrounded by inert and as yet unconnected coils of heavy three-phase electric cable. The office furniture and display stands remained in their protective plastic covers and even the familiar Printel-Xerox decor was only half-finished. I cursed Scollay. There was more to be done than he had suggested.

I must have rung the doorbell continuously for perhaps five or more minutes before Colvin decided that whoever was waiting outside obviously had no intention of going away. The stairs from the basement almost defeated him. He looked tired.

"Didn't expect to see 'till next Monday," he said. Under the stress of a slight smile, the crevasses time had etched on his face briefly realigned themselves in a new epidermic maze.

I shrugged, entering quickly through the half-open door, relieved to get in off the street. "Change of plan," I answered. "Head office want this agency fully operational by the end of the month." I stared bleakly at the appalling disorder. "But if I'd known it was in this condition....." I began.

Colvin slammed the door shut, sealing us off from the fetor blowing across from the open drains. "It's no worse than this city of yours," he countered. "God, what a mess. Coffee?"

I nodded and he took me past the silent, half-assembled machinery, down into the white-tiled basement where, from the looks of things, he was camping out.

He sensed my disapproval. "Don't worry, Charles. I'll have moved into a hotel long before you start interviewing people."

Colvin had been an installation-technician with the original company in the days before the merger, and though he'd been sacked on many occasions since then, he never seemed to take much notice. Because of his contributions to the theory and development of the new print technology, his idiosyncrasies were overlooked.

"I hear you've got the New York appointment, Charles," he said, spooning small mountains of instant coffee into three dirty enamel mugs.

"It's not official yet," I said cautiously. Where did he get his information from, I wondered? And who was the extra coffee for?

"Anyone can understand your eagerness to get the job done." Boiling water from an equally dirty electric kettle was poured into the mugs.

"It wasn't my idea to speed things up here!" I protested. "That was Scollay's decision. He wants the agency open in time for the Royal Visit. He's always been strong on the establishment, you know."

Colvin was unimpressed. "Has no one told him what's happening here? The city centre's slowly sliding into it's own sewage system. It'll be a year or more before the G.M.C. dare to organise the dedication of the Central Exhibition hall."

Up on the ground floor the street-door was opened then slammed shut again. Footsteps echoed overhead. I looked at Colvin in surprise. Who else had a key to this shop, I wondered?

The technician moved to the bottom of the stairs. "Ian, we're down here!" he called out.

I'd seen Colvin's friends before. I knew the type. This one wore his anguish openly. He was dressed in a standard G.M.C. mackintosh and yellow wellington boots. A faint odour of stale gas clung to his clothes. His pallid hands were streaked with mud.

While passing round the coffee, Colvin introduced us. Ian Mallin worked for the City Engineer and Surveyor's Office. Currently he was involved in the Deansgate and Blackfriars sewer replacement scheme.

Watching them while I sipped the hot coffee, I began to regret the impulse that had brought me here unannounced. My continued presence would be an embarrassment to all of us.

"Thanks for the coffee, Colvin," I said, placing the still half-full mug alongside a clutter of unwashed dishes in the large sink. "I'd better be getting back to the hotel. I intend to make an early start in the morning."

Colvin nodded, understanding the warning. "Then you'll probably have to wake me up. Just keep kicking the door 'till I appear."

"I'll 'phone you before I leave."

He smiled. "That should do it. I'll get you a key cut tomorrow." Mallin, it appeared, would be keeping his for a while longer. I saw no reason to object.

Colvin followed me to the foot of the stairs. "I forgot to mention it earlier; you had a visitor today."

"Oh?" I turned and looked down at him. That was odd. As yet even my parents didn't know I was back in Manchester. "Company man, I suppose."

Colvin seemed almost amused. "Hardly! A fat man with a beard and too much hair. Strange way of dressing too. He left you his card."

I closed my eyes for a moment. "Eddie Albion."

"That's right," Colvin said. "How did you know?"

"It couldn't be anyone else." I told him wearily.

The following day was taken up with preparing and placing advertising copy in the press, on local radio and television and in the main city job centres. It would have been simpler to farm out the standard Printel-Xerox employment ads, but I needed the right people, quickly. I didn't want to waste days interviewing a stream of no-hopers. Scollay wouldn't like it, but then it would all be over by the time he found out. It was also necessary to concentrate the resources of the shopfitting agents into clearing out and finishing the first floor office suite. I could hardly interview people of the right attitude and qualifications in an atmosphere of near chaos.

That night, driven by a nagging sense of moral guilt, I went over to see my parents.

I came away physically drained by the tension I encountered there. They had never forgiven Jack or me for moving down south, thereby denying them access to their grandchildren; or for telephoning or writing so infrequently. Forced in on themselves, the anger and sense of grievance they both felt found an unnatural outlet in their increasingly callous treatment of each other. It hadn't changed.

Though I stayed until late I didn't have the courage to tell them that Karen and I were planning to settle in the States.

For the next two days I avoided Eddie Albion; avoided even thinking about him. Then, quite by chance, I caught sight of him on Deansgate.

I'd just come out of the Manchester Evening News offices, and there was Eddie Albion, walking towards Knott Mill on the far side of the street, presumably heading for his Peter Street bookshop.

I stifled an impulse to attract his attention. Something appeared to be worrying him. He looked decidedly nervous, ill at ease.

The bootleg record busts of our earlier association, and later his countless court appearances on pornography charges had obviously hardened and tempered his attitude to life. Of course Eddie Albion had always owed money; vast amounts of it, usually to book suppliers and printers. But he was accustomed to such debts. They were inescapable elements of his existence, and he had long ago learned to live under such pressures. But I'd never seen him like this before. Except on those rare occasions just before a migraine attack. But that didn't seem a likely explanation. He always had prior warning of the onset of one of those shattering mental storms. He wouldn't be out on the streets. No this was something quite different.

This didn't seem an opportune moment to renew our acquaintance. Turning away from him, I went back through the still swinging doors of the Manchester Evening News building.

That same afternoon the interviews began. Experience has taught me that an efficient secretary was the first essential. And since none of our London staff had relished the prospect of being transferred to the north of England, even for only a week or so, such a person was my number one priority. With a still escalating level of national unemployment, a good secretary would not be difficult to find, especially for a company like Printel-Xerox, and I could perfectly well have engaged any of the first three girls I saw. Eventually, after having interviewed more than a dozen applicants, I spoke to a middle-aged woman who not only had excellent qualifications and references but who also had been employed for several years in the order and dispatch department of the recently bankrupt Odhams Press. I knew I need look no further. Mrs Ture got the job.

Later, having visited my hotel in order to shower, change my clothes and eat dinner, I walked over to the Crown and Anchor on Port Street. All day long, even while immersed in the complexities of company business, part of my mind had been worrying about Eddie Albion. If he hadn't changed his drinking habits, I knew there would be someone in the Crown and Anchor who might be able to tell me what was going on.

John Mottorhoad was there alright and he was alone. But not for long. This was, I now realised, the first Wednesday in the month, the night the Manchester and District SF group gathered, ostensibly to discuss their mutual affinity with so-called speculative fiction. In reality, even before I had left Manchester, it had degenerated into a series of mindless monthly booze-ups.

"A pint, John?"

He looked up from his book, glanced tiredly at his half-empty glass and nodded. "Yes, lager."

It was only as I carried our drinks over to his favourite table, conveniently situated opposite the ladies toilet, that he smiled at me.

"Eddie mentioned that you were back in Manchester. Opening a new branch, aren't you?"

"Helping to," I replied.

Outwardly he had changed very little in three years. He still favoured those slightly ridiculous black leather biker-jackets heavily adorned with silver zips, black gloves and a casually knotted university scarf. Sitting beside him was a battered camera-accessory bag containing copies of the current music and literary papers. Perhaps he was slightly fatter, perhaps he had lost more hair. Had he lost any of his cynicism, I wondered?

"What's the book?" I inquired, wondering how best to phrase the question that had brought me here.

"Devil's Tor," he answered. "First time in paperback."

I accepted the book for inspection from his still gloved hands. "Nice cover; I'll have to get a copy." I handed the Lindsay back, then took a long swallow from my pint. "John," I said, after a moment or two, "what's wrong with Eddie? Is he in any kind of trouble?"

John Mottorhoad opened his bag and began to put the book away. "He's always in trouble, you know that."

"No, I mean serious stuff."

His slow brown eyes studied me warily. "Why do you ask?"

"I saw him on Deansgate," I explained. "He looked unwell, almost

160

frightened. I got the distinct impression he thought he was being followed."

John sank back against the upholstered bench seat. His brow was furrowed, he seemed almost to be sulking. He sniffed. "Something's wrong," he admitted at last. "But I don't know what — nobody does. Eddie won't tell us anything these days, barely speaks to us, and he won't let us near Peter Street."

I looked at him in disbelief. "He won't let you inside the shop? But I thought you were the manager of Bookchain?"

"I was," John answered. "But I've been put in charge of our new Hanging Ditch shop now. Eddie's running Bookchain on his own. Oh, he doesn't prevent us from calling in there, but he won't allow us to hang around any longer than ten minutes or so. Personally, I'm not sorry to be out of the place."

"Is it just Bookchain?" I asked. "Does Eddie seem worried about anything else?"

John Mottorhead shook his head gloomily. "It's just the Peter Street shop."

"What makes you so certain?"

"Last week he made us all hand over our Bookchain keys."

John insisted on buying me a drink. Now he'd told me all he knew, I was anxious to be off before anyone else arrived, but I didn't want to risk upsetting him. He might yet be of further use.

As I'd feared, members of the sf group soon began to drift in and with their arrival, John began to shake off his lethargy. I excused myself and headed towards the Gents. Mottorhead would be alright now he had company. I used the urinals, then slipped out of the Crown and Anchor by the other door.

It was still comparatively early. I considered the alternatives and decided that the cinema offered the best option. According to the current issue of 'Nightlife', Pretty Baby was showing at the Aaben coupled with the 1936 Universal serial, Flash Gordon. Brooke Shields and Larry 'Buster' Crabbe; an interesting prospect.

But I had an hour to kill before the start of the programme. The Aaben cinema was situated on the edge of a sprawling, multi-racial council estate in Moss Side. I could easily walk there in twenty minutes. Moss Side lay on the southern perimeter of the city and to get there on foot, I'd have to cross Oxford Road; a slight detour would take me down onto Peter Street. Bookchain would be locked up for the night now, Eddie Albion having long since made the interminable bus ride up Rochdale Road to his neglected Blackley semi.

Within a couple of blocks of Bookchain, the smell emanating from the open drainworkings became increasingly apparent. During daylight hours constant traffic congestion and rickety pedestrian walkways were the most obvious inconvenience; at night the darkness seemed to emphasise the awful stench rising from the collapsed drains.

In the distance, beyond the impotently flashing traffic-signals, where Deansgate intersected Peter Street and Quay Street, emergency floodlights illuminated the unceasing activity of the council workgangs. Up here on Peter Street it was much quieter. The traffic seemed to have deserted this section of the inner city, only the occasional tail-lights of receding cars revealing the efforts of bemused drivers as they struggled to extricate themselves from the temporary maze formed by sealed off roads, 'No Entry' and 'Diversion' signs. Many of the street lights were out too, perhaps yet another example of the crises afflicting the hard-pressed G.M.C.

I stood in the shadows of the narrow alley that linked Bootle Street and the Headquarters of 'A' Division Manchester Police with Peter Street. Almost opposite was a four-storey Victorian office block. Bookchain was situated in the middle of a row of street-level shops, the majority of which had been transformed into glass-fronted car showrooms. The first floor of the building was largely taken up with unlet office suites; the third and fourth floors were completely untenanted — windowless echoing spaces slowly falling into irreversible decay.

I saw now why John Mottorhoad had not been sorry to be transferred over to Hanging Ditch. Bookchain was in a dilapidated state. The wooden door and window-frames were badly splintered in several places and the paintwork was cracking and falling away. For some reason the shop's name had been clumsily painted out. A confused, almost slovenly display of once-new books, records and magazines lay under a patina of dust behind the unwashed window. Eddie Albion had always been acutely aware that only the profits from all his retail outlets enabled him to finance his publishing company. It seemed decidedly out of character then that he should allow one of the more profitable shops to slide to such a level.

Having crossed the road to gaze in the window, I was suddenly attracted by a faint scuffling sound emanating from high above. I looked up quickly just as a large wet mass fell onto the pavement only inches away from my feet. For an instant I thought I detected a suggestion of movement in one of the windowless rooms on the fourth floor, but it was too dark to be certain and the noise of a distant car engine drowned out any further sounds.

But there was no mistaking what had fallen onto the pavement; it had the same sickening odour as the open drains.

I cursed angrily, walking stiffly away towards the Holiday Inn, all thoughts of an evening at the cinema abandoned. My shoes and trousers were spattered with foul-smelling excreta.

After lunch the following day, with no further interviews scheduled for the afternoon, I left Mrs Ture in charge of the 'phones and the paperwork and set off down Deansgate to see Eddie Albion.

He was sitting at the counter in a shapeless bored posture. Several cardboard boxes containing old Marvel comics, badges, rock-star photographs and records were spread out before him. He was chewing absentmindedly on the end of a cheap Biro, reading a recently published history of the Sex Pistols.

As I entered the shop he looked up. "Charles!" he cried, his blue eyes sparkling, his tedium instantly forgotten. "I was beginning to wonder when you'd return my visit."

"Been busy, you know," I replied, grinning back at him. It was good to see him again. As usual he was wearing a black trenchcoat, which did little to disguise his girth, black Terylene slacks, thick woollen socks from Woolworths and brown leather sandals. His long fine hair was fastened in a bun at the nape of his neck by an elastic band. He still sported a small goatee and moustache. Whatever else might be wrong with Eddie Albion, his appearance hadn't changed.

We talked for a few minutes, recalling our mutual friends and their often bizarre exploits, filling in the gaps my three-year absence had inevitably opened between us. I'd known Eddie Albion since the early sixties, when our first business venture together had been to open a small bookshop somewhat romantically called, 'The House On The Borderland'. I knew him as well as anyone could, certainly better than most. His gestures and mannerisms were as familiar to me as my own. So, as we talked, I watched carefully for any indication of the unease that had been so apparent on Deansgate.

To my intense relief, he seemed perfectly normal. I was even more surprised when he asked if I could stay for a cup of tea. I was beginning to suspect that the difficulties John Mottorhoad and the rest of the staff were experiencing with him had a completely rational and mundane explanation.

Eddie disappeared into the basement, after asking me to watch the shop, an easy task as there were no customers. He reappeared a few seconds later with a half-filled electric kettle in one hand and a rueful expression on his face.

"We'll have to skip the tea, Charles," he said, sighing. "I'd completely forgotten, I've got an appointment with my solicitor at three. Have to dash, I'm afraid."

"That's a shame," I said disappointed and a little puzzled. "Are you still with Derek Hoban?"

He nodded, balancing the kettle on a stack of paperbacks while he fished about in the desk drawer for the shop keys. "I can't leave him now, he knows more about my business affairs than I do." He straightened up from the drawer and began to search his pockets. I got the message.

I left Bookchain, promising we'd meet for dinner in the Kwok Man at seven. But instead of going straight back to the agency, I entered the Christian Science Reading Room just across the road. Two members of the clergy were studying the image projected on a microfilm viewer at the rear room. I smiled at them, and selecting a volume of sermons at random, occupied a chair that offered a good view of Bookchain through the Reading Room window.

I didn't have long to wait.

Eddie must have found his missing keys. He locked the shop door behind him, then turned to walk up Peter Street towards Oxford Road station.

It looked as if my suspicions were unfounded. I had assumed, wrongly it now appeared, that the appointment with his Altrincham-based solicitor was merely a ruse to get me out of the shop. However, I decided that it would do no harm just to sit and watch for ten minutes. Who knows what might happen?

Before even five minutes had elapsed, Eddie Albion came scurrying back down Peter Street. As he turned the key in the lock, he looked anxiously up and down the street, then he vanished inside.

One thing was apparent; wherever Eddie Albion had been, it hadn't been to Altrincham.

I ran into more problems back at the agency.

The shopfitters were making slow but appreciable progress with the reception area and I could hear the steady chattering of Mrs Ture's typewriter upstairs. There was no sign of Colvin. I assumed he must be working in the basement.

I met him halfway down the steps. He waved me back up, holding a finger against his lips for silence.

"What's wrong?" I asked back on the ground floor. "What's going on down there?"

"It's Ian Mallin," Colvin explained. "You remember, the chap from the City Engineer and Surveyor's Office. He's very upset."

I waited.

"He's worried about the sewers."

"Who isn't?" I replied.

Colvin didn't seem to find the remark particularly funny. "The Water and Sewage Department won't accept that there's any foundation of truth in his report; they say his fears are totally unfounded."

"Then perhaps he should resign, or offer to," I suggested, wondering exactly what was in his report. "That should force someone to consider his claim seriously. If that fails to gain him a fair hearing there's always the media."

"Ian's considered the press," Colvin admitted, "but he's afraid they'll put totally the wrong accent on his findings."

"Exactly what *is* he afraid of?" I asked.

I couldn't really blame Colvin for storming downstairs after he had explained Mallin's theory. My laughter was inexcusable.

The Kwok Man in George Street was still just as popular with the local oriental community, and as a result all the tables were occupied. Characteristically, Eddie Albion had neglected to make a reservation. However, having been assured we would not have long to wait, for Eddie and his friends still dined there regularly, we sat at the bar and talked. Or rather, I talked. Despite constant promptings, Eddie Albion seemed content merely to listen.

But during the latter stages of our meal, perhaps because the immense mountain of food he'd consumed had induced a more tranquil state of mind, he slowly began to reveal the nature of his personal dilemma.

"Am I what?" he asked, blinking owlishly and wiping a sheen of sweat from his heavy-framed glasses.

"Are you still drawing?"

Eddie Albion gave a curious little laugh. "I think only you would bother to ask that question, Charles. No one else cares; not even me now. You know what Jung said of artists, I presume?"

I shook my head.

"He said, 'Musicians, painters, artists of all kinds, often can't think at all, because they never intentionally use their brains'. And George Russel, he gave up art when he was twenty-two; he told Yeats it would weaken his will."

"And that's why *you* stopped drawing?"

"No," he admitted, "I just got bored — with everything," he added, almost as an afterthought.

"Even with Savoy?" I challenged.

He stared into his empty coffee cup as if confronting an image from the past. "We achieved everything we ever wanted with Savoy," he said. "I started the publishing company with a clear idea of the titles we were going to print. Somehow, we managed to get every one of them out, and several additional titles; all the rock-music books, the Harry Clarke and Gerald Scarfe art books. It was a nightmare at the time, but somehow we did it."

"One of them got away," I reminded him. "You remember, we always talked about publishing it in the early days....."

Eddie Albion wagged a fat white finger at me. *"Beneath The Wine Green Sea?* Moorcock would never allow that one to come out!"

We laughed, then ordered more coffee.

"How are the shops doing?" I asked, sensing that the moment had arrived to be more direct. "You're not bored with the business of making money, I take it?"

He rubbed the palm of his right hand across his forehead, wiping errant strands of hair away from his soft round face. "Money's important, but then the acquisition of wealth is just a trick — once you've learned how to do it you'll never go hungry. The shops....." he paused for a moment, "if I lost them all tomorrow it wouldn't matter."

I wondered how far this alarming disaffection with his lifestyle had gone. "I take it you've still got your collection of books; I can't imagine you not reading? Surely that's not changed?"

"Oh, I still read, but I've put most of my books, the best of them that is, in Bookchain."

"They're for sale!" I said, aghast, knowing what his collection had once meant to him. "Even your first editions?"

He nodded. "I've priced them very reasonably, at far less than a dealer would ask. Absolute bargains."

He saw the expression of disbelief in my eyes and smiled. "Don't worry, Charles. They're quite safe. I've put them on sale in Bookchain merely to prove a point to myself — I'm conducting a little experiment, you see."

At that moment a tall, almost emaciated man with short hair, a grey double-breasted woollen suit and a slightly gauche manner approached our table. This was Michael Butterworth, Eddie Albion's shadowy partner, who had twice been bankrupt and once raped in an underpass in Ardwick.

"Charles!" he cried, leaning across the table to shake my hand, almost stumbling over an unoccupied chair in the process, "nice to see you again. We must get together for a drink sometime."

"That would be fine, Mike," I said, aware that his presence at the Kwok Man could only be due to some urgent business matter.

Eddie Albion began to struggle into his coat. "I'm sorry, Charles," he said apologetically. "I'd hoped to avoid this."

"No problem," I assured him, inwardly cursing Butterworth's arrival. He couldn't have chosen a worse moment. I tried to object when Eddie insisted on paying for the dinner.

"Listen," he said, "I've negotiated a twenty per cent reduction on all the meals my staff eat here. Let me pay the bill, there's no sense in throwing good money away."

As they moved towards the exit, I called out after him. "Eddie, I'll come over and see you at Bookchain on Friday, I've got all day free. You can tell me more about this experiment of yours."

He turned and stared at me, doubt burning in his eyes.

"Look, I'm going back to London soon," I told him. "I might not get another chance."

Butterworth was tugging anxiously at his arm.

"Well?" I demanded.

"Alright," he agreed at last, shrugging heavily. "If that's what you want. I'll see you on Friday."

Later I was to appreciate fully the old adage that nothing worthwhile is ever gained by deceit.

Thursday saw the remaining staff positions for the Deansgate Printel-Xerox agency filled and Colvin's laser-print system fully assembled. The Thompson Crown offset-litho machines and the ten-station collating and finishing unit would be test run by the installation engineers during the coming week. Only the shop front decor was still giving cause for alarm. But the foreman shopfitter was still insisting that the job would be completed on time.

I had reluctantly agreed to spend Thursday night at my parent's house, but not wishing to go over too early, I took Colvin for a drink; there was something we had to discuss.

"Now look," I began, pushing a pint of bitter towards him, "this can't go on you know. From Monday morning onward we'll have a full compliment of staff working at the agency; you'll just have to move out of the basement sometime this weekend. I think I've given you more than enough time. Scollay would have a fit if he found out."

"I was talking to Ian at lunchtime," Colvin began, making interlocking patterns on the wet tabletop with his beerglass.

"And that's something else!" I said, interrupting him. "It might be advisable to keep Ian Mallin away from the agency for a while, especially while he's in his present frame of mind. You can't expect everyone to be as tolerant as Mrs Ture."

"But that's what I wanted to tell you," Colvin said, smiling. "Ian's suggested that I move in with him until the job's finished here."

"And?" I could see this would solve both problems for me.

"It seemed too good to miss. I said yes. I'm moving in with him on Saturday."

"Good." That had gone far easier than I had anticipated. I leaned towards him over the table. "Colvin, can I ask you a question?"

"Of course," he answered. "What is it?"

"Is Ian Mallin really serious about this, what did he call it, this pressure-wave theory he's been driving everyone mad with?"

Colvin drained his glass. "You may not have noticed, Charles, but Ian's not one for making jokes about anything!"

Despite Colvin's abrupt departure from the pub, I felt that at last I had the situation at the agency well under control now. As a result, I made the trip out to the East Lancashire Road in a much more relaxed state of mind.

Leaving my parent's house shortly after ten o'clock on Friday morning, I travelled back into Manchester and was surprised to find that Eddie Albion had not yet arrived at Bookchain.

It was unlike him to be late. Was he now regretting his decision to talk to me? Was he hoping that I'd tire of waiting for him and find something else to do? That seemed unlikely. He had no way of knowing what time of day I'd be calling in to see him, morning or afternoon. And even given his present state of mind, I couldn't imagine Eddie keeping Bookchain shut all day just to avoid me.

So I waited.

After forty minutes or so, a taxi drew up alongside Bookchain and Eddie Albion, clutching a plastic carrier bag and a briefcase with a broken clasp, struggled out onto the pavement.

His face was drained of colour and beneath his spectacles his eyes looked watery.

"Oversleep?" I inquired, taking the plastic bag from him while he paid the driver and went through the daily ritual of searching every pocket for the shop keys.

He shook his head, groaning slightly. "No, I've been awake since five o'clock fighting off a migraine. Ah-ah!" He produced the keys and after fumbling a little with the five-lever security lock, managed to swing the heavy door open.

"Not yet!" he called out as I reached up to switch the lights on.

In the gloom, he stumbled towards the counter. "Wait a minute before you switch the lights on, I've got a pair of sunglasses here somewhere." Prior to or during a migraine attack, his eyes became extremely sensitive to any source of bright light.

"Here they are," he said putting them on in place of his spectacles. "You can put the lights on now."

As always, his first task was to sort out the post into two separate piles, one of which consisted of bills, solicitor's letters and writs, while the other — noticeably smaller — took the form of publishers' lists, samples and customers' inquiries. He sifted through the various packets and envelopes with the casual dexterity achieved by long practice, then, suddenly bored by the whole process, he consigned the contents of the first pile to the waste bin and threw the rest into the bottom counter drawer.

While Eddie Albion was thus engaged, I went down into the basement intending to boil water for a pot of coffee. Although John Mottorhoad had already told me what was stored down there, I'd had no idea of the numbers involved.

Apart from the claustrophobically narrow tunnel that allowed access to the toilet and sink area, the rest of the basement, from the damp stone floor to the high mould-encrusted ceiling, was filled with thousands of undistributed copies of Savoy books. Here and there packets had broken open, spilling their contents across the floor of the narrow tunnel. Waiting for the kettle to boil, I rummaged among the titles scattered underfoot. I found copies of most of the Jack Trevor Story and Henry Treece books, Charles Platt's *The Gas* and *Who Writes SF?*, Michael Moorcock's *My Experiences In The Third World War*, *The Golden Barge*, and dozens of others.

Slowly rotting away in the darkness of this Manchester cellar, these tottering columns and pyramids of unsold books rising to the gloomy ceiling in their tens of thousands might, to other eyes, appear to be a testament to the monumental business folly of Albion and Butterworth. Yet given the same minimal financial base Savoy Books started from, I could think of no one else who could have achieved so much.

There were customers in the shop when I climbed the basement stairs holding two mugs of steaming hot coffee. Several youths were glancing through boxes of imported American comics and a middle-aged man, inspecting the contact magazines, was inquiring if Eddie stocked the August edition of *Dominant*. I carried the coffee over to the counter and sat down next to Eddie on an upturned box.

"What do you think of it?" he asked.

"The cellar?"

He nodded, shaking out three Paracetamols from a family-size dispenser.

"Illuminating," I answered.

He swallowed the analgesics with gulps of coffee. "Most people find it depressing," he explained.

"That's not exactly surprising." I smiled at him. "There can't be many who share your peculiar outlook on life. What you identify as success, others tend to regard as catastrophe. Savoy is no exception. You just possess a different set of values to most people."

I could see this had pleased him.

The shop area of Bookchain was divided in half by two-metre high bookstands that ran down the centre of the shop. On one side all the science fiction books, comics, rock-music and film magazines were displayed, while the other side was devoted exclusively to the sale of sex magazines. A prominently displayed notice warned customers what to expect if they ventured into this area. Strategically placed mirrors enabled Eddie Albion to keep a watchful eye on both sections while serving at the counter.

Finishing my coffee, I wandered over to the science-fiction racks, curious to discover if what Eddie had told me at the Kwok Man was true.

I didn't have to look far, the books were all there, valuable first editions scattered at random among run-of-the-mill American paperbacks and the latest uninspired, tired reprints from NEL and Panther. I stared at the evocative titles, wondering furiously what Eddie Albion was playing at. An experiment, he had claimed. I could see no sense in it.

With great deliberation I selected several of his books; the Arkham House editions of *Something About Cats* by H.P. Lovecraft and *The House On The Borderland* by W.H. Hodgson, the Essex House printing of *Image Of The Beast* by Phillip José Farmer, *A Voyage To Arcturus* by David Lindsay and Poul Anderson's *The Broken Sword*. "These will do nicely," I said, carrying them back to the counter, "especially at the prices you're asking for them."

Eddie Albion gave me a slight smile. "You know they're not really for sale," he said.

"Then what are you playing at?" I asked.

"Put them back on the shelves and I'll explain."

"Do you have any idea how long those books you've just selected have been sitting on the shelves?" he asked, when I returned to the counter.

I made a wild guess. "A week? Perhaps ten days?....."

Eddie Albion made a sound like bitter laughter. "Over six months. And during all that time only a handful of people have ever shown even the slightest interest in them. I sold the Random House edition of *Breakfast In The Ruins* to a student who was travelling to the Lake District to take up a midterm job in a Youth Hostel, and just as reluctantly, the Doubleday imprint of *Storm Of Wings* to an unemployed kid from Warrington who could barely afford it. No-one else has glanced at them." Tentatively, he removed his sunglasses for a moment, squinting up at the fluorescent lighting overhead. "Now, what does that tell you."

"Perhaps the economic depression....." I suggested.

"No!" Eddie Albion almost shouted. Heads turned towards us in the shop. "That's not the answer and you know it. Every one of those books makes some form of intellectual demand upon the reader, requiring him to think about and evaluate what the author is saying."

"What's wrong with that?" I asked.

"Don't be obtuse, Charles!" For an instant his soft face solidified into a mask of bitterness. "The people who come in here, who visit any of my shops, seek only one thing, entertainment. They refuse to have to think about what they're reading. In the same manner that savages are attracted to bangles, they choose books for the brightness of the covers." Almost without noticing, he served a customer with the latest *Playboy* and two rather tatty back-issues of *Whitehouse*. "Four pounds fifty," he said, thrusting the money into his trench-coat pocket.

"I sometimes think it can't all be put down to bad taste or poor education," he went on, "there has to be another explanation. I've got this theory; they're the end products of life-support machines from hospitals up and down the country. In the hopeless cases, when a patient is known to have suffered irreversible brain damage, the machine is turned off. Unfortunately, not all of them die; eventually they find their way here and become sf readers."

From his expression, it was impossible to determine whether he was joking or not.

Later he was to tell me more. Again I watched him closely when he discussed his customers.

"I filled the bookracks with Ballard, Burroughs, Peake, Wilson, Lindsay, and writers of similar vision and imagination — all they asked for was the dragon books of McCaffrey, John Norman's Gor books, all that dreadful stuff of Andre Norton and Karl Edward Wagner — these and a dozen more mind-numbing sf writers.

"Over a number of bleak years," he continued, "I came to the conclusion that if I couldn't improve their minds, then I'd subvert them — exchange the innocent pap they insisted on selecting for some really dangerous material. One way or another I'd get my own back on them.

"Religion and politics were out — nothing dangerous or stimulating

170

about them: Colin Wilson, of all people, had proved that to be true. And depending upon the individual, drugs were either too passé a subject to excite a response or too awful to even talk about."

Eddie Albion saw his customers regularly, knew all their weaknesses and foibles. And he was aware that only one subject touched them all in varying degrees: sex. This was how he'd get his own back on them.

"Promiscuity," he went on, "even the paper promiscuity of the sex magazines, eventually corrupts, engendering a form of syphilis of the mind, an infection of the synaptic links instead of the penis or the vulva. And the contagion doesn't stop there. Forget what the doctors tell you about the heart being the main instrument of the body — it's the mind, that's the focus, the deepest root. Effect a change in the mind, and ultimately that change will manifest itself in the flesh."

I was worried. Was he, as I hoped, merely being cynical, or was he in fact possessed by a peculiar paranoia? For some reason he interpreted my doubt as curiosity. I found the "little demonstration" he gave me extremely disconcerting.

He placed copies of several recently published science-fiction books in the soft-porn section alongside magazines devoted to bondage and animal sex, then he waited patiently, almost smugly for the right unsuspecting customer to inquire after one of them. When the inquiry came, Eddie patted his lips thoughtfully for a moment and said, "Yes, you'll find that book alongside Tolkien's Lord Of The Rings, second rack along, third shelf down.

Some minutes later, the puzzled customer returned to the counter empty-handed. After years of handling bailiffs, income-tax inspectors and porn-squad detectives, Eddie Albion was extremely adroit at looking bemused and puzzled. "But I'm sure that title came in yesterday," he muttered. Then, after apparently consulting a stock-display list, he suddenly brightened and heaved a sigh of relief. "Ah yes, I see what's happened. Tommy's placed it in the wrong section. I hope you don't mind, you'll find it down there." And here Eddie Albion pointed with a pudgy finger at the fun book section.

Provided with such a legitimate excuse, he later confided, few sf fans ever declined the opportunity to enter the adult magazine section. And while the unsuspecting sf reader furtively inspected the lascivious delights offered by those sex magazines nearest the book he was supposed to be looking for, Eddie Albion was apparently concentrating on other things, rearranging rows of long-neglected paperbacks on dust-covered shelves or making a great show of pricing a recently purchased collection of early film-magazines.

Rarely in such circumstances was a sex mag purchased openly. The sf fan was too concerned with his image to admit to a prurient sexual curiosity. More often than not, Eddie Albion confided in a whisper, a magazine was hurriedly selected, and then, with his back turned to the apparently unsuspecting proprietor, concealed inside the folds of his coat or alternatively thrust out of view down his trouser leg.

Only then would Eddie Albion permit himself the softest of small smiles. Once again, he had successfully engineered the first step of the descent into depravity.

"But surely," I argued over a lunch of Donner Kebab and chips, eaten off thin paper plates while sitting behind the counter at Bookchain, "even science-fiction fans have seen girlie magazines before?"

Eddie Albion stopped eating for a moment. "Do you mean stuff like Penthouse and Men Only?" He scooped up a huge forkful of greasy chips.

"Yes."

"These books are different."

"In what way?" I asked. "Are they overtly pornographic?"

"It goes deeper than that, Charles." He wiped a glutinous dribble from his chin with a badly-creased handkerchief. "They're designed to erode certain values. In the same way that sub-standard literature contaminates and erodes the critical faculties, these books have a similar deleterious effect upon the psycho-sexual balance of the cerebellum."

"Oh, come on!" I exclaimed angrily. "You can't be serious! And what do you mean by, 'designed to erode certain values'. It's not possible and you know it."

"Are you sure?" Eddie Albion sounded almost prim. "The SS books *are* rather special you know. A great deal of imagination and ingenuity went into their design. They each contain a series of subliminal visual triggers that....." He hesitated, aware of my mounting impatience. "You don't believe me, do you?"

I sighed. "I can't convince myself that all this isn't some elaborate game you're playing."

"To what purpose?" he asked.

I was dubious. "Perhaps simply to relieve the boredom of just sitting here."

"It's all true," he answered.

"Then show me one of these, what did you call them, these SS books."

He turned away from me and stared out of the grimy window for a moment, as if considering. "That might be unwise. You should not become further involved."

"Involved?" I echoed. This was unexpected. "In what? Anyway, I'm returning to London soon, then to New York. How could I get involved even if I wished?"

He seemed convinced. "Help yourself," he said.

Having been told what to look for, I had no difficulty in finding one of Eddie Albion's *special* books; indeed they appeared to be well represented on the shelves alongside the more usual publications. I picked one up, interestingly entitled, *Wet Whores*. Like the others, the letters, two linked S's were employed as a logo on the spine and in the top right hand corner of the cover. Apart from these two small reversed-out panels, the SS books seemed no different from other girlie books.

"Show me!" I demanded, handing it to Eddie Albion back at the counter.

Giving it only a casual glance, he opened it at random and offered it back to me. On the right hand page was a black and white photograph of a partially dressed girl. She was directing a stream of water from a hosepipe up her open legs. She appeared to be enjoying it. The left hand page was taken up with text relating to the picture. I could see nothing else.

"Notice anything, Charles?" Eddie Albion asked, after a moment.

"Nothing unusual," I admitted. "Should I be able to?"

"Of course not. The effect could hardly be subliminal if you could identify it so easily," he answered.

That made sense, I conceded, but there was much that puzzled me. "What do the letters SS stand for?" I asked.

"Why, Savoy Sex, of course. It's a logo we use on all our pornographic publications." As he turned away to serve another customer, he said, "I thought you'd be able to figure that one out."

Shortly after that, Eddie Albion grew increasingly sullen and morose, complaining that his migraine was returning. I nodded sympathetically, suggesting that he should go and lie down in the basement for half an hour, I would watch the shop; but he wouldn't hear of it. He seemed unable or unwilling to talk further about the SS books and I got the distinct impression that he now resented my curiosity concerning them. "Find out for yourself, if you're so interested," was the only answer he'd give me, "I have neither the time nor the patience to explain further."

I felt no rancour towards him; I'd known him too long. The onset of one of his severe headaches could well explain his sudden acrimony and certainly the shop was beginning to fill up with customers.

After obtaining his grudging consent, I borrowed several examples of the Savoy Sex books, intending to examine them later in my hotel room. When I left Bookchain, Eddie didn't respond to my farewell. His mood had grown very black.

Outside the shop the air was hot and humid. The sun was hidden by massing grey clouds and there seemed to be a suggestion of distant thunder in the heavy, suffocating air.

Reaching the corner of Peter Street and Deansgate, I paused for a moment and looked back up the empty street. Was I being inconsiderate, I wondered. Perhaps he had been ill-humoured and irritable, but that could well be merely a symptom of his hemicrania. Indecision plagued me.

At that moment, three figures appeared at the far end of Peter Street, having apparently emerged from behind the tattered Bingo hoardings bordering the old Theatre Royal.

I saw them for only a few seconds, and then at a distance, just before they went into Bookchain. But what I saw annoyed me. "Tramps!" I muttered to myself. "Filthy animals!" And unwilling to come into contact with them, I turned the corner and walked quickly away.

Crossing Deansgate by one of the many emergency footbridges spanning the sewer excavations, I stopped in some surprise outside No. 70. Mrs Ture and the rest of the staff should have gone home an hour ago, I realised, yet the lights were still on inside. Had she been delayed, I wondered? Or had Scollay and Berestain arrived unannounced from London?

Through gaps in the whitewash painted over the plate-glass door and windows I saw Colvin operating the laser-print unit, while Ian Mallin looked on expectantly, occasionally inspecting a sample copy of the stack of A4 pamphlets emerging from the collator.

My key wouldn't turn in the lock. The latch was on. I rapped loud enough on the glass door to be heard over the noise of the L.P.U.

At a nod from Colvin, Mallin opened the door. He was obviously surprised to see me. He mumbled a greeting, glancing apprehensively, almost guiltily, from the pamphlet he was still holding back to Colvin.

Colvin had no such misgivings about what they were doing. "Got it running nicely for you now, Charles," he said, obviously pleased with himself. "Ian's report was perfect for a test-run."

I nodded. "How many copies are you producing?"

"Only a thousand," Colvin answered. "Nearly finished them."

I stood watching for a minute or two, then decided that as I didn't intend eating dinner at The Holiday Inn, there was little point in going back there just yet.

"I'm going up to the office," I told Colvin. "I've got work to do. Lock the front door when you leave."

Colvin nodded. As I passed Ian Mallin, he pressed a copy of his report into my hands. It was entitled *Doubts On The Computation Of Sewage Flow In The Deansgate Renewal Scheme — A Reassessment Of Projected Internal Pressures And Pipe Loads Under Inundation Conditions.* I could manage only a slight smile of gratitude.

Upstairs, I threw Ian Mallin's incomprehensible report on Mrs Ture's typewriter, then scattered the contents of the brown paper bag I had brought with me from Bookchain across my desk.

A cursory inspection revealed nothing very odd or outrageous in either the fiction or in the articles by various 'Doctors' or 'Psychologists' featured in the SS books. Similar contributions could be found, I suspected in practically every other contemporary sex magazine. And even the photographs lacked the power of those found in the 'hard' magazines.

Before attempting to isolate the mysterious visual triggers Eddie Albion had talked so evasively about, it seemed logical to first read through the

SS books, making notes of my reactions to the various stories and articles; these could later be compared to the directives contained in the subliminal messages. Assuming that those covert communications existed, and that they achieved even a limited degree of causation, then it should be possible to discern a certain correlation between the two.

Instead of growing bored with the task, as I had expected, I soon became utterly absorbed. I forgot all about dinner, and even Colvin and Mallin's departure failed to register. Later I looked up, wondering what had distracted me, but by then the sound of the front door slamming impinged on my thoughts only as a fading echo.

I was to identify the first subliminal effect quite by accident.

It was now growing quite dark outside and I was finally forced to get up and switch the office lights on. Returning to the desk, my attention was momentarily drawn towards a book I had earlier abandoned as unreadable. From this vantage point, the book was of course, inverted, and I stared, suddenly perplexed, at the columns of solid text on its open pages. Unmistakably, I now saw that the white spaces between the letters and lines of type had been so arranged by the compositor to form a pattern of words. Once this clever typographical trick was discovered, the words they delineated stood out so clearly it seemed impossible not to have seen them before.

I turned the book towards me. The message was terse and disgusting; unnecessarily brutalising the act of masturbation, surreptitiously undermining the reader's self-respect. I stared at this first visual trigger for a long while, almost hypnotised, appalled by the nature of this unsuspected assault on the subconscious.

It soon became apparent that Eddie Albion had cleverly employed a number of different subliminal elements in the Savoy Sex books. In every case the concealed messages had one common objective: degradation of the ego by the imposition of a massive sexual guilt-complex on the reader's psyche.

But I cared little about any possible effect these visual triggers might have upon the minds of those who read the SS books — I was, however, fascinated by what they revealed of Eddie Albion's mental condition.

For the first time I began to accept that he was ill, and if not actually deranged then certainly in the grip of a strange and intense obsession. What other explanation could there be? Why would any rational man go to such extraordinary lengths to inflict such an odd revenge on those he despised most? Paranoia was hardly too strong a word for it.

As if suddenly afraid of becoming contaminated by the contents of the SS books, I swept them off the desk top with a gesture of irritation and distaste.

I felt angry with myself for not being prepared to take the logical approach towards Eddie Albion and his problems. I should simply leave Manchester as quickly as possible, forget the entire incident. It was no concern of mine, and anyway if things went as I hoped, I'd be in New York by the end of the month. What sense was there then in becoming involved?

A stabbing headache, no doubt a result of studying the SS books too long and too intensely, terminated all such speculations. I was feeling hungry now, but dinner would have to wait until the headache subsided. Lowering my head onto folded arms, I slumped onto the desk, closing my eyes for what I imagined would be only a few moments.

I was awakened by the sound of footsteps, a woman's footsteps ascending the uncarpeted stairs to the office. Daylight now flooded into the room and with it came the sound of traffic.

It was Saturday morning! Mrs Ture was on her way up to finish off the paperwork. Somehow I'd slept all night.

I pushed the chair away and stood up. Long-cramped muscles contracted into knots of intense pain. Groaning, I sagged forward against the desk.

The polished wood felt hard and very cold against my skin.

Still half-bemused by sleep, I looked down, realising for the first time that something was wrong. And gasped in dismay. I was completely naked!

For an instant I considered rushing across the room in a desperate attempt to lock the door. But before I could even start to move, the handle turned and the office door began to swing open. Desperately seeking somewhere to hide, I looked wildly around the room, but no place of concealment offered itself.

Instead, I found myself staring horrified at walls covered with dozens of lewdly erotic photographs torn from the pages of the Savoy Sex books. Obscenities in a familiar hand had been scrawled across the windows with a bright red marker pen.

At that moment Mrs Ture entered the room.

Explanations were impossible. And my embarrassed attempts at an apology, guttural, stammering and incoherent, only exacerbated the awful situation.

Apart from a fleeting expression of shocked disbelief, Mrs Ture conducted herself with remarkable composure. Her resignation, effective immediately, was tendered without hesitation and with perfect self-control.

After she left, I collapsed into a fit of nervous shivering that seemed to last for hours.....

Towards mid-day I shook off the inertia sufficiently to gather up my scattered clothes and get dressed. Several cups of black sugarless coffee from the office dispenser were consumed during the hour or so it took to clean the walls and windows of the offending material. Yet the physical activity did little to restore my spirits. I felt angry, dejected and extremely vulnerable. I still found it difficult to accept or think about what had happened during the night, deliberately concentrating my thoughts on small, more immediate matters rather than attempt to consider the wider and more disquieting implications of my situation.

When the time came to leave the shop, I stood irresolute and mentally demoralised behind the locked door for some considerable time. The thought of the crowded streets outside terrified me.

The weather was still hot and oppressive, with not the slightest trace of wind to move the sticky air. The odour from the open drains mingled with exhaust fumes, producing a nauseous stench. I saw several women walking along with handkerchiefs pressed over their mouths.

During that short walk to Bookchain, my attention was drawn to the lunch-time edition of the Manchester Evening News. Splashed across the news-hoardings was the headline:

COUNCIL ENGINEER WARNS OF MISTAKE IN CITY CENTRE'S NEW SEWER SYSTEM. THOUSANDS AT RISK, CLAIM!

Apparently a copy of Ian Mallin's report had quickly found its way into politically sympathetic hands.

Beyond confronting Eddie Albion with the news of what had happened to me in the office last night, I had no clear idea of what I was going to do at Bookchain. But it was obvious that I needed help, for God knows what I might find myself doing next, what suggestions had already been inplanted in my subconscious. Albion could help me. I was convinced of that. He *had* to help me.

Even before I crossed Peter Street I sensed trouble. The dark green Transit van parked outside Bookchain with its two nearside wheels straddling the pavement and the rear doors left wide open meant only one thing, a raid by the vice squad.

As usual they'd turned up in strength. Five plain-clothed C.I.D. officers were busy filling large cardboard boxes with any and every book or magazine that had a photograph of a female on the cover. No attempt was made at discrimination; that would be left to the police prosecutor. Everything went into the boxes; *Titbits, Playboy, Janus,* the *Sun Page-Three* calendars, even copies of 1950's *Spick and Spans.* Eddie Albion had been through this scene so many times that it was now as routine for him as it was for the police. Everyone was bored with the situation; everyone wanted it over as quickly as possible. Yet the police had to maintain an image of authoritarian efficiency.

"Where do you think you're going?" one of the C.I.D. officers asked brusquely, placing himself in the doorway as I tried to enter the shop.

"I want to talk to the manager," I said cautiously, remembering never to use anyone's name, real *or* assumed.

"Do you work for Mr Albion?" the officer demanded.

I shook my head. "I'm just delivering a message from his mother." I was relying on the fact that Eddie had never allowed a telephone to be installed in Bookchain. "His Uncle Jack's been taken ill," I explained, "they've rushed him to Oldham Infirmary."

He studied me carefully. I was unshaven and somewhat dishevelled. He must have assumed that my appearance tended to support my story.

"Wait here!" he ordered, then vanished inside the shop.

Eddie Albion appeared a moment later. His expression changed when he saw who was waiting for him. Suddenly he seemed uneasy, tense. "Look, Charles," he began, "I'm afraid this is a bad time....."

"A bad time!" I echoed, angry and astonished by his off-hand manner. "What about me? Do you know what you've done? Because of you —"

"Now wait a minute!" Eddie Albion objected, raising his soft hands in a gesture both defensive and placatory. "I did warn you not to get involved at the outset. It was you who insisted on examining the SS books."

"But I never thought...." I said despairingly. "I never imagined that you were serious!"

Eddie Albion shrugged. "Now you know the truth." He took a step backwards, as if about to re-enter the shop.

Overwhelmed by panic, I lunged forward, grabbing hold of him by the coat collar. "You can't leave it like that!" I protested. "You've got to help me, tell me what else was in those books — you owe me that much!"

He brushed my hands aside as a police officer approached.

"You're wanted inside."

Albion nodded. "Coming officer." He turned towards me again. There was a look of exasperation in his eyes. "Very well, Charles. I'll see you back here, tonight, about nine o'clock. I'll do what I can."

I stood outside the window, watching, my thoughts and emotions whirling around in a confusion of distrust and hope. Inside Bookchain, Eddie Albion was handed a list of books and magazines the Vice Squad officers were removing from the premises. Eddie appeared to be studying the list intently.

After a moment or two the police officers lost interest in Albion, turning their backs on him to talk among themselves, light up cigarettes, or even to recommence, in a desultory fashion, their search for pornographic materials.

When he was convinced no one else was watching him, Eddie Albion slowly stretched out his right foot and gently pressed the wooden base of the bookrack nearest him. It slid inwards, revealing a compartment inside which dozens of neatly packed books were stored. Then, still apparently concentrating on checking off the list, he took several steps away.

Of course it didn't take the police long to discover the books. The list was snatched back and additions made as the newly-revealed books joined the titles already waiting in the cardboard boxes. No questions were asked. The police evidently considered the incident a lucky accident.

I was perplexed and worried. All of the books were Savoy Sex publications. The implications were appalling.

All that long afternoon I waited in my rooms at the Holiday Inn.

Too agitated to sit for longer than five or six minutes at a time, I paced anxiously up and down, gazing blankly at either the images flickering silently across the television screen or at the view beyond the open window. I could barely control my impatience. Sleep, even had I felt tired, was out of the question. Until I'd seen Eddie Albion, I did not dare take the risk of releasing whatever appalling subliminal suggestions still lurked in my subconscious.

Relentlessly the same unanswerable questions plagued my mind: 'Will Eddie Albion be there at nine o'clock? Will he help me? Will he be able to help me?' I stared down at the streets far below. The landscape seemed subtly altered. Nothing was familiar.

Convinced now that whatever happened I could no longer remain in Manchester, I packed my bag, checked out of the hotel and made my way towards Piccadilly Station. Unlike other main-line railway stations in the country, Piccadilly still provided a left-luggage service, and I intended to deposit my bag and then book a compartment on the overnight train to Euston. A locked sleeper door, to which the guard held the key, would offer some security later during the hours until dawn.

I can remember staring up at the sky. The cloud-cover was low, dense and unbroken, a shimmering grey canopy through which the heat of the late afternoon sun penetrated in suffocating waves. Then without warning I was suddenly assailed by a sequence of dislocated but intense sexually-related images, as fleeting as visual echoes scattering across the eye's retina.

They seemed to last only seconds. Then came the return to reality.

I was standing in a narrow alley somewhere. My bag had gone. I was breathing hard and shivering violently. My shirt was soaked with sweat and all of my clothes seemed oddly uncomfortable. What *had* happened?

At the end of the alley several people appeared, saw me, then began to shout and scream in obvious anger. I did not doubt they were pursuing me. Their rage went beyond reason.

I turned and fled in terror.

I spent the rest of the afternoon crouched in a seat in the darkened well of the ABC Deansgate. Even when my shivering subsided, my haunted eyes never left the screen.

I timed my exit from the cinema exactly, checking the accuracy of my wristwatch with the dimly illuminated clock hanging above the entrance to the Gentlemen's toilet as the minutes dragged past. Then at precisely ten minutes to nine, I stepped out onto Deansgate and began the short walk to Bookchain.

I had taken only a few steps towards Peter Street when the rain began.

There was no warning, no isolated drops falling across the pavement as precursors of the approaching storm. It came suddenly in a torrential downpour, sheets of rain descending out of the darkness with such force that within seconds the streets were awash with dark swirling water as the gutters failed to sluice away the deluge.

For a couple of minutes I stood in a shop doorway, waiting for the initial fury of the cloudburst to abate. I'd never seen rain like it, though my father's descriptions of his experiences of the rainy season in India during the war called to mind a tropical Monsoon.

The rows of emergency floodlights strung out above the open-trench sewer excavations dipped and swung madly under the onslaught, flashing bright cones of light that clearly illuminated the driving rain first into the rapidly filling pits then high up against the walls and windows of the shops and office blocks all along Deansgate. Several of the floodlights exploded as the cold rain came into contact with the hot bulbs, plunging whole sections of the excavation into darkness. Mounds of piled-up earth began to crumble and slide away, adding a sea of black mud to the waters backing up against the overloaded drains.

Realising I could wait no longer, I hurried out into the roaring precipitation. Bent almost double, soaked to the skin, I waded through ankle deep water towards the junction of Peter Street and Deansgate.

I hesitated before crossing over the road by one of the wooden emergency footbridges. Through the driving rain I caught sight of a familiar figure running down Peter Street, away from the lighted windows of Bookchain, towards Deansgate. I wiped the streaming water away from my eyes and looked again. Yes, it was Eddie Albion. And at the speed he was running, he would reach the corner before I was even half-way over the bridge. I began to shout his name and to wave my arms about in the air, hoping to attract his attention. At that same moment, just as he hesitated, turning to gaze uncertainly in the direction of my voice, I saw what he was running away from.

I'd seen them once before, emerging from behind the bill-hoardings in front of the Theatre Royal. Only there were more of them now.

They shambled after Eddie Albion and there was something peculiarly menacing in their awkward, almost spastic movements. The waterlogged ill-fitting rags that served as clothes seemed to only partially conceal limb and spinal deformities, but of this I could not be certain. Perhaps my own abhorrence of all tramps and down-and-outs exaggerated certain features beyond all rationality in those unusual conditions. But even of this I could not be convinced.

Certainly Eddie Albion found them repulsive too. As he turned towards me, I could clearly see the horror on his white face. But he could not stop, even for an instant; his pursuers were too close behind.

As he reached the junction and turned left towards Knott Mill, there came a strange sucking roar that seemed to emanate from somewhere deep underground. The roaring noise grew rapidly in volume, completely overwhelming the sounds of the storm and the cries of both the pursued and his pursuers.

Standing on the wooden bridge half-way across Deansgate, I stared down at the open sewer-trench below me in disbelief. A vast wave of foul-smelling water came bursting out of the mouth of the open pit, a subterranean river of noxious content that overflowed across Deansgate in a white-foamed swirling flood of such force that it carried all manner of shaft supports, planking and excavation equipment before it.

Eddie Albion went down under this surging flood, his arms thrashing impotently as the black waters enveloped him. For a second longer I saw him, carried along by the swollen sewer outpouring; then he was lost from sight as the mass of water swept on towards the River Irwell.

I stood gripping the wooden handrail unable to move off the bridge. Later, firemen had to prise my fingers open before they could carry me down....

AN
PUBLICATION
THE HAUNT OF
THE CRAMPS
#1.
PREMIERE ISSUE!
TALES OF
VOODOO, ZOMBIES
& HEART-BURSTING R.O.C.K. N R.O.L.L

BACKSTAGE: BY NOW THE ZOMBIE UPRISING HAS ALMOST DESTROYED THE ENTIRE TOWN. THE CRAMPS FIND THEMSELVES UNABLE TO LEAVE THEIR ROOMS....

AND SUDDENLY ......BRITTON AND BUTTERWORTH ENTER THE SAVOY CLUB

EXTRACTED FROM "TALES FROM THE CRAMPS" BY KRIS GUIDIO ∽ SAVOY BOOKS, 1984. ROCK∽ART

M. JOHN HARRISON
Lords of misrule

"WE MAY SOON be overrun," the Yule Greave said, looking away over the empty moorland and rough grazing seamed with tree-filled cloughs. "Aid from the city is our only hope now."

He was a tall man, fortyish, with weak blue eyes and a straggle of thin blond hair, who breathed laboriously through his mouth. Under the old queen, who had given him the house and the pasture that went with it, he had been known as a fighter. Every so often he would look round him as if surprised to find himself where he was, and his lower lip trembled briefly when he talked about the city.

To give him time to catch his breath I stopped and looked back down at the house. It was built on a curious pattern, like an ideogram from an old language, ramified, peculiar. Much of it now lay abandoned and overgrown in a tangle of elder and hawthorn and ivy. Flung out from it were four great stone avenues, each a mile long. I wondered who had built them, and when.

"I've been forced to knock down some of the walls and grub up the pavement," he said. "But you can see what it was once like."

There were deep muddy furrows in the gateways, where the stone-carts went in and out. The wind came in gusts from the south and west, bringing a rainy smell and the distant bleat of sheep. The dwarf oaks on the slopes above us shifted their branches uneasily and sent down a few more of last winter's brownish withered leaves. One of the little grey hawks of the moorland launched itself from some rocks above us, planing downwind with its wingtips ragged against the racing white clouds; it hovered for a moment, then veered off and dropped like a stone on to something in the bracken below.

"Look!" I said.

The Yule Greave stood wiping his face and nodding vaguely.

"To tell you the truth," he said, "we never thought they would come this far. We expected you people to stop them long before this."

I breathed in the smell of the bracken. "This is such a beautiful valley," I said.

"You'll be able to see the whole of it soon," the Yule Greave said. He started up the slope where it steepened for its final climb to the rim of the escarpment, following a soft, peaty sheep-trod through the bracken. He placed one foot carefully and heavily in front of the other, grunting at the steeper places and still breathing heavily. "I'm sorry to bring you all this way," he said. "I don't expect you're used to this sort of thing."

"I'm not tired," I said.

He laughed, his blue eyes watering unoffendedly. "You really have to see it from up here," he said, "to appreciate the position. You'll be able to judge for yourself how far they've come."

"Of course."

We climbed the last few yards to the little outcrop in silence. At the top, when I turned, the spring sun had come out briefly, and I could feel it on my face. It was three or four minutes before the Yule Greave recovered himself sufficiently to speak. Sweat poured down his forehead and into his eyes, which were sore in the dusty wind. He put one hand against the rock to steady himself. "They quarried this to build the house," he said. "A long time ago."

The rock was pale, coarse-textured, full of little quartz pebbles. Higher up in the quarried bays hung matts of ivy.

"Now you can see what I mean," he said.

Below us the house lay like a metaphor in the wide flat valley. It was a light fawn colour. Its four vast avenues of stone thrust out from it across the old alluvial bench, black, black. What it meant I had no idea. It was one of those places where the past speaks to us in a language so completely of its own that we have no hope of understanding. Puddles of water in the worn paving reflected the sky; I could see gaps in the tall walls like bites, where the Yule Greave had taken stone for his fortifications, a line of hasty revetments and trenches stretching across the valley lower down, where it sloped away to the south.

"Incredible," I said.

He pointed south, past the fortifications.

"There used to be a dozen houses like this," he said bitterly. "And places even older than this. But all overrun now, and the decent people who lived there gone. All the way down to the sea you could find houses like this, full of decent people."

Anger glittered moistly in his eyes.

"What do we make, we who come after? Nothing! We pull it all down instead."

"I'm not sure I agree," I said, tempted to ask him why, if he didn't want to destroy the old walls, he didn't reopen the quarry and use fresh stone; but his face was now full of a kind of savage self-hatred and self-pity, and he said,

"What's the point of discussing it? Everything's gone to waste. It was all up a thousand years ago for the people who built this."

Abruptly he shrugged and apologised.

"You've heard it all before I expect. Anyway, you can see how close they've come. They'll be across the river and over the fortifications in a month, perhaps less if we don't get help. See: there, and there? You can see the sun glinting on their camps."

"Will you show me the house before I go?" I asked.

He looked at me in surprise. He was pleased to be asked, I thought, but he said, "Oh, the inside's a ruin now. We do our best, but it's all dust and mice."

He seemed reluctant to go down the hill now he had got up it. He watched the little grey hawk hovering and stooping, hovering and stooping, as it worked its way up and down the slopes of sun-warmed bracken. He took a last look at the great stone symbol which filled the valley and which he had lived in for twenty years without understanding, then began to descend slowly. New shoots, he observed, were beginning to appear green and delicately curled between the ruined bracken stems. The turf, flattened and bleached by the previous month's snow, was springing up again. "That air!" he exclaimed, breathing ecstatically a gust of wind which brought the scent of may blossom up from the valley. Then he stopped suddenly and said, "How is it in the city these days?"

I shrugged.

"We have similar problems to yours," I heard myself tell him, "but not so extreme. Otherwise it is very beautiful. New buildings are springing up everywhere. The horse chestnuts are in blossom along the Margarethe-strasse and in the Plaza of Unrealised Time."

I did not mention the torn political cartoons flapping from rusty iron railings, or the Animal Mask Societies with their public rituals and increasingly unreasonable demands. But he was remembering a different city anyway.

"I suppose the place is still full of clerks and shopkeepers?" he said. "And tarts who overcharge you in the Rue Ouled Nail?"

He laughed.

"We'll always look to Uroconium," he said sentimentally, and quoted, "'Queen of the Empire, jewel on the beach of the Western Sea'."

The high walls that surrounded the house had already warmed to the weak sunshine, trapping a fraction of its heat to give up to the elder and ivy in the overgrown gardens. Two or three hawthorns filled the air with the scent of the may, which in that confined space seemed drugged and dangerous. Insects murmured in the little orchard and among the fruit bushes which had run to bramble in the shelter of the walls. Above the garden rose the heavy honey-coloured stone of the main building, covered in creeper and bright yellow lichens. The wind blustered round its complicated roofs.

Inside the house he had someone bring out a bottle of lemon genever, and invited me to have some.

"Foul stuff, but the best we can get out here."

We drank silently for a while. The Yule Greave grew pinker in the face, more irritable. He seemed to sink into himself, into his own sense of abandonment and futility. "Dust and mice," he said, staring round in disgust at the high gloomy walls and the silent, massive, oppressive old furniture, "dust and rats. This is the only room we ever light a fire in." Later he began to talk about the old queen's reign. It was the common story of infighting at court and violence in the city. Many of the actions in which he had taken part struck me as being little more than outrages, committed by people hardly able to help themselves. He kept his souvenirs of these 'little wars' in one of the upper rooms, he said. There was some peculiar stuff among it all, stuff that made you think. We could go up and look at it later if I was interested.

"I'd like that if there's time," I said.

"Oh, there'll be time," he said. "It's mostly clothes, weapons, stuff we picked up in their houses. You wouldn't credit the hanks of hair, the filthy pictures they were always looking at."

He asked if I had done any fighting in the city, and I said that I hadn't. There was a silence, then he went on musingly: "The women were the worst. They would hide in doorways, and reach out for your face or your neck as you walked past. Hide themselves in doorways. They'd have bits of glass embedded in a cake of soap, do you see, and slash out at your neck or your eyes." He looked at me as if he were wondering how much more he could tell me. "Can you believe that?" He shook his head. "I hated going up the stairs in those places. The lamps would all be out. You never knew what would be in a cupboard. A woman or a child, screaming at you. Or else they'd show you something foul, something obscene, and laugh. The old queen would never bear them near her, not at any price."

"So I have heard," I said. "It is less of a problem now."

He chuckled.

"Old men like me cleared it up for you," he said. "We can be proud of that."

A little later his wife came in. By this time he had drunk most of the bottle. He stared at her with a kind of muddled resentment.

She was a tall woman, though not perhaps as tall as him, very thin and ethereal, dressed in a fashion long out of date in the city. She seemed not quite real to me, like a picture in a darkened room. I guessed she had been one of the old queen's women-in-waiting, given to him like the house and the valley in return for his loyalty in the back streets and tavern brawls. Her hair, an astonishing orange colour, was worn long and crimped, to emphasise the height of her cheekbones, the whiteness of her skin, and the odd, concave curve of her features.

Over one arm she was carrying a piece of heavily-embroidered cloth which I recognised as being part of the 'mast horse' ceremony: it would be used to hide the operator of the animal's snapping jaw. I had never seen such an elaborate cloth in use. When I mentioned this she smiled and said:

"You'll have to ask Ringmer if you want to know more about it. He was born near here and his father worked the horse at All Hallows."

"Ringmer's father was a half-wit," said the Yule Greave, yawning and pouring himself more lemon gin.

She ignored him. "Are you young men at all interested in such things in the city now?" she asked me. Her eyes were green. She had unfolded the cloth to show me a complex pattern of leaf-like shapes.

"Yes," I said. "Some are."

"Because I've filled a whole gallery with them. Ringmer —"

"Has he shifted the rubble in the south avenue?" the Yule Greave broke in suddenly.

"I don't know."

"It was important to get that rubble moved today," the Yule Greave said. "I want it as infill further down the valley. I told him this morning."

"He didn't tell me that's what he was supposed to be doing," she said.

The Yule Greave muttered something I couldn't quite catch and emptied his glass quickly. He got up and stared out at the ruined raspberry canes and lichen-covered apple boughs in the garden, his hands trembling. This left me marooned with his wife at the other end of the long room, with only the embroidered cloth in common. A few transparent blue and orange flames stirred round the unseasoned logs in the hearth.

"Ringmer will show you the rest of the horse if you'd like to see it," she said. "I'm so glad you're interested." She folded the fabric up again, her long thin hands white in the shadows. "Sometimes I feel like wearing it myself," she laughed, holding it up against her shoulders. "It's so glorious!" I had a brief vision of her as she must have been in the days of the old queen's court — waxy and still in a stiff, grey, heavily-embossed garment down to her feet, like a flower in a steel vase. Then the Yule Greave came and stood between us to tip into his glass whatever dregs remained in the brown stone bottle. He was breathing heavily again, as if ascending some private hill.

"Don't you want to come up and see the things I told you about?" he said.

"I shouldn't stay more than a few minutes," I answered. "My men will be waiting for me —"

"But you've only just arrived!"

"I have to be in Uroconium by tomorrow morning."

"He wants to see the horse, whatever else," the Yule Greave's wife insisted.

"Oh does he? You'd better go and show him then," he said, looking at me as if I had let him down and then turning abruptly away. He poked so hard at the fire that one of the logs fell out of it. Smoke came into the room in a thick cloud. "This stinking chimney!" he shouted.

We left the room, the Yule Greave looking after us red-faced and watery-eyed. The 'gallery', which was some distance away, turned out to be a mezzanine floor somewhere in the west wing. The sun was just coming round to it, pouring obliquely in through the tall lanceolate windows. The Yule Greave's wife stood in an intermittent pool of warm yellow light with her hands clasped anxiously.

206

"Ringmer?" she called. "Ringmer?"

We stood and listened to the wind blustering about outside.

After a moment a boy of twenty or so came out of the shadows of the mezzanine. He looked surprised to see her. He had the thick legs and shoulders of the moorland people, and the characteristic soft brown hair chopped off to a line above his raw-looking ears. He was carrying a horse's head on a pole.

"I see you have the rest of the Mari," she said with a smile. "Do you think you could show our guest? I've brought the coat back with me."

It was an astonishing specimen. Usually you find the skull boiled and crudely varnished, or buried for a year to get rid of the flesh; a makeshift wire hinge for the jaw; and the bottoms of cheap green bottles for eyes. This one had been made long ago, and with more care: it was lacquered black, its jaw was hinged with massive silver rivets, and somehow the inside of a pomegranate had been preserved and inserted, half in each orbit, so that the seeds made bulging, faceted eyes. It must have been appallingly heavy for the operator. The pole on which it rested was brown bone, three and a half feet long and polished with use.

"It is very striking," I said.

The boy now took the embroidered cloth and shook it out. Hooks fitted along its top edge allowed it to be gathered beneath the horse's head, so that it fell in stiff folds and obscured the pole. With a quick, agile movement he slipped under it and crouched down. The Mari came to life, hump-backed, curvetting and snapping its jaw. It predated not only the Yule Greave but his house. Time opened like a hole underneath us, and the Yule Greave's wife stepped back suddenly..

"'Open the door for us'," chanted the boy:

> "'It is cold outside for the grey mare
> Its heels are almost frozen'."

"I would admit you at my peril," I said. The Yule Greave's wife laughed.

I went to examine some manuscripts which belonged to the house. They were kept at the other end of the mezzanine. When I looked back the Yule Greave's wife was standing next to the mast horse. Its eyes glittered, its lower jaw hung down. Her hand was resting on its back, just as it might rest on the neck of a real animal, and she was saying something to it in a low voice. I never found out what, because at that moment the Yule Greave came puffing and panting into the gallery, limping as if he had banged his leg and shouting, "All right, come on, you've seen enough of this."

The Mari reared up for a second, bared its white teeth, then retreated into the shadows, and the boy Ringmer with it.

At the door of the staircase which led to the Yule Greave's private room I took my leave of his wife, in case, as she said, we did not meet again.

"I'm sorry to have badgered you so," she said. "We see so few people."

I laughed.

"Hurry up," urged the Yule Greave. "It's quite a climb."

The staircase was so narrow that he rubbed his shoulders on the wall as he led the way up, brushing off great flakes of damp yellow plaster. His fat pear-shaped buttocks shut out the light. The little square room was right at the top of the house. From its narrow windows you could see one of the stone avenues stretching away; a sliver of brownish hillside; and a bend in the shallow stony river. The wind boomed around us, bringing quite clearly the bleat of moorland sheep.

The Yule Greave tried to open a trap door in the ceiling so that we could go out on to the roof, which was flat here. The bolts were rusted shut, but he would give up only after a lot of heaving and grunting.

"I can't understand it," he said. "I'm sorry."

He hammered at one of the bolts until he cut the heel of his hand, then his eyes watered and he began to cry. He turned away from me and pretended to look out across the hillside, where the sheep were scattered like grey rocks.

"You'd never believe we were abandoning these old places," he said. "Simply abandoning them one by one. The future will judge us very harshly." He sniffed and blinked. He looked at his cut hand then wiped his eyes with it, leaving a smear of blood. "Now look what I've done. I'm sorry."

I couldn't think of anything to say.

The tower smelled of the old books he had abandoned to the mould in haphazard piles. I picked up *Oei'l Voirrey* and *The Death and Revival of the Earl of Rone*. I asked him if he would show me his souvenirs, but he seemed to have lost interest. He kept them in a wooden chest: a few dolls made out of women's hair and bits of mirror; some cooking implements; a knife of curious design. The damp had got at everything and made it worthless. "It's just the sort of thing we all picked up," he said. "I think there's a mask in there somewhere."

"'The men of the community set out in the afternoon'," I quoted, "'and, after much parading and searching, discover the Earl of Rone hidden ineffectually in the low scrub....'"

"You can keep the *Oei'l Voirrey* if you like," he said.

We stared down at the ancient avenue stretching away from the house, its puddled surface reflecting the white sky. His wife appeared walking slowly along it with the boy Ringmer. They were smiling and talking. The Yule Greave watched them sadly, biting his nails, until I said that I would have to go.

"You must at least have something to eat with us," he said.

"I have to be in the city before morning," I said. "I'm sorry."

We went down the stairs and he came out to say goodbye. There was no sign of his wife. I got on my horse in one of the muddy gateways. As I set off down the long avenue I thought I heard him say, "Tell them in the city that we still keep faith."

The avenue seemed barren and endless. The sun had gone in and it was raining again by the time I led my men through a break in one of the walls; and with the cold wind of spring blowing into our backs we turned north and picked our way up to the rim of the escarpment.

Up by the Yule Greave's abandoned quarries I stopped to have one more look at the house. It seemed silent and untenanted. Then I saw a stone-cart move slowly down the valley towards the fortifications. Smoke came out of one of the chimneys. Above me the little grey hawk dipped and swerved on the wind; my men, sensing my preoccupation, huddled in a bay of the quarry, wrapped in their sodden cloaks and talking quietly. I could smell moorland, wet wool, the breath of the horses. Soon most of the valley was obscured by mist and driving rain: but I could see the fortifications lying across it in raw straight lines; and beyond them, towards the sea where a fugitive and watery sun was still shining, the light was reflected off the waiting encampments.

If I had the eyes of that hawk, I thought, I know what I would see down there, moving towards us from the sea.

One of my men pointed to the fortifications and said, "Those walls won't last long, however well they're defended."

I found myself staring at him for a long time before answering.

Then I said, "They have already been breached. That house down there is raddled."

Even as we watched, the Yule Greave and his wife and their three children came out of the house with the boy Ringmer, and began to dance in a circle in the overgrown garden. I could hear the thin voices of the children carrying the tune, blown up the hill with the mist and the rain:

> "What time will the king come home?
> One o'clock in the afternoon.
> What will he have in his hand?
> A bunch of ivy."

Behind me someone said, "You've dropped your book, sir."
"Let it lie."

COLIN GREENLAND
NICK PRATT

unsettling the world

THE FIRST THING that strikes you about anything by M. John Harrison is sheer style. As a virtuoso he has two distinct strains. One is rich, romantic, uninhibited:

> Viriconium, sump of time and alchemical child; sacrificer of children and comforter of ghosts — who can but shiver and forgive in the damp theatrical airs of dawn?

> A red stain grew in the sky above the Haunted Gate. Against it floated the airy towers, suspended as if in water glass, while below were conjured shabby reflections — a glitter of fishscales, olive oil, broken glass, and the west wind shivering the wide shallow puddles of the empty squares.

The rhetorical gesture is bold and extraordinary, but secured within a semaphore of absolute precision (not water, not glass: 'water glass'). His other strain is equally acute, but plain, depressed and mean:

> The motorways were covered in black ice: there were extensive detours, and I ended up driving all through Friday night. Jones slept in the back, and then ate three fried eggs in a cafe straddling the road, watching with his head tilted intelligently to one side as the sparse traffic groaned away south and a kind of mucoid greyness crept into the place through its steamed-up windows.

Harrison believes that a writer has not finished his job until every word is perfect. For him the aesthetic principle is a moral principle — an unfashionable notion, predicating hard work and discipline. He has plenty of others. For example, a writer must not start his job until he has something to say. The temptation to stop at the stylish surface of Harrison's fiction is quite wrong. Michael Bishop reviewed **The Pastel City** as "a vehicle primarily for his baroque lyricism, an excuse, if you will, to be writing." No; and this is where Harrison begins his long quarrel with the genre of F-&-SF. He sees all genre fiction as an act of complicity between writer and reader: a contract to fulfil narrative expectations. When those expectations are fulfilled more thoughtfully or more elegantly than is customary, the reader becomes bemused, or, more probably, does not notice. Since Harrison loves to frustrate the expectations anyway, crewing starships with aesthetes or describing heroes who can't remember where they keep their swords, what he has done has often been overlooked. His habit of irony is itself an attack on sf, which is normally read absolutely literally, as if it were written in an explanatory tone (which too much of it is). Irony is also his own personal way of keeping things in proportion, a necessary corrective to that stylistic glory, which could otherwise become inflated. Harrison needs to poke fun at his heroes.

Truck was always running for doors. This time he made it, and he was out in the corridor before something pricked him in the neck.

For someone not getting any dope, he thought, I'm passing out more than I should.

The heritage of F-&-SF supplied him with a marvellous vocabulary of images, which he deploys to the very best advantage; but they are not reality. They are beautiful lies. The writer must not allow the reader to believe them. Harrison is very sensitive to beauty, in many forms, through all the senses; he also often points accurately to the place where that sensibility shades into fascinated disgust, which cannot look away. The writer, he says, is an observer, who offers his observations to the reader with the intention of illuminating his experience. The genre contract gets in the way, making him write according to literary conventions instead of observations. Harrison continually seeks new ways to tear up the contract.

One day Harrison will write a completely naturalistic novel. Meanwhile he believes that a writer trained in a particular genre continues to need at least a fragment of the genre to seed his work. His short stories *Running Down*, *The Incalling*, *The Ice Monkey* and *Egnaro* represent his most naturalistic fiction to date. American publishers are avid to buy them as horror stories: Harrison depicts the suspicion of the supernatural in the mundane as profoundly disturbing, a disease of reality. These stories demonstrate his unflinching grasp on the actual as well as the imaginary. Camden and Bow as well as Viriconium, the Pastel City.

I blundered angrily on to the canal towpath, and, with the dull green water full of greedy little fish on one side and the high decaying walls of a goods yard on the other, convinced myself that I was walking towards Islington, not Camden at all. I had to go further out of my way to get off it again, I wouldn't dare the nightmare brick waste east of York Way. The cloudbase lowered and the wind grew nasty, whipping across the lock basins, picking at the tethers of the crumbling boats and the plumage of a few miserable-looking ducks.

The Incalling tells something of Harrison's feeling of being stuck in London, which he escaped in 1975, fleeing north to an environment where he could go running and rock-climbing, and where he could find the solitude and space necessary to his writing. Nevertheless, he still writes about cities, complex, powerful, and containing. As SF writers usually do, he goes for the city in decline, for cracked pavements, boarded terraces, empty towers. The utopian tradition so reverently named in paternity claims for SF is actually historically less apparent than a corresponding willingness to anticipate the breakdown of the urban machine. Wells reports the relish with which he sacked London in **The War of the Worlds,** "selecting South Kensington for feats of particular atrocity". The abandoned cities of George R. Stewart's and John Wyndham's disaster novels express similar middle-class longings, covert hopes and fears which became the subject matter of J.G. Ballard in **The Drought,** *The Day of Forever*, and **High-Rise.** Largely at Ballard's instigation, the derelict city was a favourite landscape for stories in New Worlds: Michael Moorcock's *The Ruins,* and *The Pleasure Garden of Félipe Sagittarius,* Charles Platt's *Disaster Story* and *Lone Zone,* and Harlan Ellison's *A Boy and his Dog.* The image was quickly adopted by the new writers Moorcock encouraged. The November 1968 'New Writers Special', featuring Brian Vickers' *Area Complex,* a story of the city after the disaster, fully equipped but perfectly useless, also included Harrison's *Baa Baa Blocksheep,* a pot pourri of urban seediness.

Never one to adopt a convention without good reason, Harrison has made the disintegrating city very much his own. He portrays it as a place of desolate beauty which offers strange new dreams to replace those it has betrayed. It can be a cause of neurosis; it can also be a symptom made manifest:

At its simplest level, the city is a maze in four dimensions, a purely physical ant-heap, over-large, over-complex and over-populated. I am continually frightened that the size and complexity of the hive will one day cause it to implode, to fall in on itself in a million slivers of coloured glass and rotting concrete. Yet, this fear aside, I catch myself wishing it would do just that: anything to escape this incredible multiplicity of directions and vectors.

Whatever its exact nature Harrison uses the city as the nexus of all possibilities, overwhelming to some, stimulating to others. The protagonists of his early stories *Visions of Monad* and *Ring of Pain* are paralysed by it, horrified by the unforeseeable consequences which spread, like ripples, from the smallest action. Jerry Cornelius is nurtured by it and constantly exploits its potential to sustain his persons. But in Harrison's hands even the perfect denizen of the Catastrophe has his weaknesses. People see through him:

"What's the joke?'

"You, Mr Cornelius. The beautiful clothes. You're guitars, guns and glitter, but are you anything else? All the *props!*"

Jerry's response is to pelt Dr Naw with mouldy skulls: she has touched a nerve. The catch is that urban chaos provides a stage for everyone: the auditions are compulsory (even the solitary 'Kristodulos' of *Ring of Pain* tries on a false name), but stardom is transitory at best. The destruction in **The Committed Men** frees Wendover from one set of options and attitudes, but circumstances still condition his newly chosen priorities, the soaring winged humans and huge alien dragonflies of *London Melancholy* have their separate enclaves, but neither is proof against the involuntary taint of the other: perfect autonomy cannot endure. Even in such fictional contexts where characters apparently enjoy the broadest of freedoms, Harrison maintains that ordinary feelings of impotence will persist, and, as individuals encroach on each other, communication will be fumbled.

This emphasis grounds his work within our experience, so that in the most fantastic or macabre of his worn streets we can hear familiar echoes. The studied detachment or frenzied theatrical gestures of the characters in *Events Witnessed from a City* are both responses to the same timeless stimulus: pregnant with the unknown, their world is assuming a new and curious shape. Lurking amidst the vapid café society and hollow quest of *The Bringer with the Window* are cruel reflections of our bohemian cliques and fashionable mystic obsessions. A face from Eliot's London appears in Viriconium; it fits perfectly. Is 'The Blue Metal Discovery' in Viriconium or Durinish? It doesn't matter. Geography shifts and epochs waver but Viriconium survives, an aspect of the Eternal City: at once fluid and intractable, it never quite coincides with individual hopes or fears.

Harrison intensifies this effect by scattering his fictional worlds in fragments, here a glimpse, there merely a hint, too mutable to pin down. There is no opportunity for SF literalists to map them, just as, Harrison insists, there can be "no map to your own life, to reality. You're lost in it". It would be equally futile to pursue his characters as they float elusively from story to story, role to role: there are no heroes, no villains, no saviours or convenient scapegoats, none of the clear-cut distinctions which make fiction soothing but smaller than life. Harrison sabotages the familiar machinery of SF; the result is unsettling. This challenge to simple moral preconceptions is his way of confronting the essential problem of contemporary fiction: how to create characters that are not merely puppets of the author or his ideology, but show something of the contrariness of real people.

Harrison makes use of anything which helps him to do this. "Real fiction takes what it wants," he says. The imagery of SF serves him, not the other way round. He says of *Running Down*:

"Entropy is the science fictional metaphor which reflects and elucidates the subject matter... SF has been used to amplify, enhance, echo. This is the only excuse there can be for science fiction. The story isn't about entropy, it's about people."

The principle that sf should not be self-sufficient, should be a means to an end, informs the fiercely astringent criticism that Harrison developed as Literary Editor of New Worlds. The defects he found in even the most humane sf provoked him to examine both sides of the templates when using them himself.

In his approach to the post-disaster novel, a traditionally English form which has always emphasised people more than plot, Harrison concentrates on the motivation rather than the mechanics of survival. Wendover's quest in **The Committed Men** serves no practical purpose. After great effort, anguish, and loss of lives he succeeds in delivering the mutant child to representatives of the new people, but the significance of his achievement, even in terms of his own symbolism, is doubtful. The child is accepted with indifference; no communication of any kind results. Wendover has only bought himself time; for what? Something equally pointless, in all probability: a member of a superseded race can make no worthwhile choices. And his teeth will always hurt.

The Committed Men shows many of the defects of a first novel. Inevitably for a young British writer caught up in the New Wave the influence of J.G. Ballard is particularly strong. Harrison, however, stresses the ordinariness of Wendover and his moral obligation to make those choices, where Ballard would have characterised him as a psychotic whose behaviour was obsessional, but far from pointless.

The dynamic of the Sword-and-Sorcery genre is similarly compulsive. The hero has to get fighting mad about something. A career of carnage can only be single-minded: to quest is not to question. Harrison's heroes, when we come upon them in **The Pastel City,** are evidently off-duty, and Lord Cromis for one has no desire to relinquish lute and astrolabe and take up his nameless sword. Too depressive to be hearty, he never really rouses himself from his world-weary ruminations. He misses the climactic battle and slopes off to sulk in his tower. Acutely aware that all options lead to death (and Harrison sees no glory in sacrifice), Cromis defers decisions. Avoiding responsibility, he cannot avoid suffering. Despite the rout of the enemy and Queen Jane's political optimism, Viriconium's future remains blank. At the end of **A Storm of Wings,** eighty years on, nothing has changed: "in short, the Eternal City stands as it once did, infuriating, beautiful, vulgar by turns". The unintentional invasion of the giant alien insects has come and gone; the threatened transformation of reality has not taken place. Queen Jane's new champion Galen Hornwrack has encountered the source of the Locusts' power and made the great sacrifice to destroy it, but there has been no triumphal re-entry; no-one has even brought the news back to Viriconium. The prevailing mood there is a nice mixture of relief and anti-climax.

Humanity has recolonised the inconceivable avenues of the High City — gaping up open-mouthed at the inexplicable architecture of the Afternoon Cultures while it empties its bladder in their millennial gutters — and hung out its washing again in the Low.

Life goes on, stupid and ineffable. As in all Harrison's novels, the climactic sense of renewal is incomplete; no new order is ever inaugurated, even by the most successful hero. Viriconium has been saved again, this time by a self-centred Low City bravo. No one, least of all Hornwrack, could explain why he bothered.

For all the baroque fascination of the High Cities, Harrison's money is on the shrewd and shabby durability of the Low. He invites the reader behind the scenes of the usual melodramas, showing what really happened at those great events; how they affected the lives of ordinary people; and how the heroes were pretty ordinary people anyway. The prime example of the hero as victim is Captain John Truck, the soured naïf unfortunate enough to be the key to **The Centauri Device.** Pursued by the Israeli World Government, the United Arab Socialist Republics, the Church of the Openers, and the King of Junk City, Truck insists on claiming to be independent, but escapes each crunch only with help from the next person along the line waiting to use him. "It was his personal disaster that he never learned to resist the flow of events; he never learned to make steerage way." Truck embodies the eternal fantasy: the loser who suddenly finds himself in possession of enormous power. Harrison points out, typically enough, that he hasn't the first idea what to do with it. The system is too big, too complex, to make right. Truck, like Hornwrack, eventually opts for the heroic self-sacrifice. He detonates the Device, but Harrison scrupulously comments, in an epilogue, that this fictional account of his motives is only conjectural: it might have been an accident.

From the point of view of ordinary people, the system always seems to be the installation of someone else's mad fantasy, omnipotent but irrelevant to their real needs. They would prefer to have nothing to do with it, but at best can only compromise themselves. From the stark disillusionment of her drug withdrawal Angina Seng tells the hapless Truck,

"It's a rotten Galaxy, and it doesn't belong to you or I. That bastard"
— nodding and grinning and gasping at Veronica — "and the
General and ben Barka have it cut up between them. What scraps
they leave go to Doctor Grishkin in return for absolution. Politics,
religion and dope: they keep us happy with Hell."

Harrison believes with Eliot that we are all now hollow men, craving to be filled with some conviction, something that makes sense of existence; he believes with Burroughs that by compromise we become addicted to the explanations the High City would like us to believe. And addicts are human beings at their most exploitable.

In a universe of false omens and secret power games, where independence of mind is so difficult to secure, it is no wonder that such schemes as are organised go rapidly awry. Convened without enthusiasm, pilgrims wander to unsatisfactory conclusions and disperse. "Cause and effect separate like worn-out old lovers." In *Viriconium Knights* the café philosophers aver that,

> "The world is so old that the substance of reality no longer knows quite what it ought to be. The original template is lost. History repeats over and again this one city and a few frightful events — not rigidly, but in a shadowy, tentative fashion, as if it understands nothing else but would like to learn."

History, neither linear nor perfectly circular, is not progressive; neither malicious nor evasive, it is merely dumb. If you deny that the identities and actions of predecessors are implicit in your own, you hamper yourself; if you accept it, you are still no farther on. Purposes delude.

Harrison has as little sympathy with the idea of destiny as with the rest of the heroic paraphernalia. In some stories he uses heroic terms to describe the act of sabotaging an allotted purpose. In *Settling the World* and *Coming from Behind* the powers that give meaning and shape to history, not to mention full employment to the whole human race, are once again extra-terrestrial insects, which indicates Harrison's opinion of authorities, temporal or divine.

> "Why are you making us dig holes?" he asked them.
>
> "You are being given a chance to participate in a great cosmic adventure," they said. "A corporate endeavour in which your skills, though minor, can play a real part. Your small contribution enables you to participate with joy."

Certainly Harrison objects to the authoritarian imposition of purpose; but he is equally conscious that we continuously do the same to our own lives, while often refusing responsibility for it. The majority of mankind being addictively compromised to the benign despots, the resistance fighters are a minority (to this extent Harrison maintains the heroic stereotype). If Harrison had got his hands on **2001** he would have dynamited the black monolith, convinced that we had erected it ourselves. In fact, there is an intriguing contrast between Clarke's parable and Harrison's *The Machine in Shaft Ten*, which converts human emotion into a fuel for an alien species; Professor Bruton goes down to destroy it. "We deserve the opportunity," he declares,

> "to make our first gesture of independence since the Pliocene, to become self-determining at least as far as the limits that were originally built into us...We deserve the dignity of pointlessness."

He makes the decision on behalf of humanity and restores that original autonomy, though it requires a suicidal act. There remains the artful paradox of a passionate man motivated by pointlessness. As Doctor Grishkin assures Birkin Grif in *The Bringer with the Window*: "Nothing matters...but that is not the point..."

Harrison himself is a passionate man, pushing himself at the typewriter with the same sustained attack and urgent precision that drive him up rock faces listed as "Hard Very Severe". He equates aggression, physical energy and creative effort in a way that Yeats would have approved. "I have to get fired up," he says, "for everything I do." The fire, the drive, is of his own making: he supplies his own motivation. Nothing runs his life, not even his art. Along with the dignity he acknowledges the danger of pointlessness, of what headmasters used to call "having no inner resources". Lyall in *Running Down*, Clerk in *The Incalling*, Jones in *The Ice Monkey*, are all dying of a kind of resignation, rousing themselves only to petty acts of spite and occasional spasms of abjection. The point is a moral one, naturally, but not a simple one. Lyall "carried his own entropy around with him": there is no escape from that. Entropy is not a character flaw, it's a fact. The narrators of the three stories, all capable, unexceptional chaps, fasten onto their walking disasters with a sort of humanitarian concern that comes close to being unmasked as morbid compulsion. They can't help them, but they can't leave them alone. Lyall, Clerk and Jones represent an obdurate death-wish; the appalled fascination in the eyes of their companions shows that they know that feeling too. The vile places where the victims hang around until the sacrifice are accurately drawn from life at the edge: Lyall's broken bottles and boarded windows; Clerk at the decrepit old clothes shop suffused with the reek of rotting fruit; Jones in the condemned house holding the baby with its dirty nappy. This is what it's like where things have run down. At the same time these scenes are charged with a potent force, malefic, implacable, anti-life. Ramsey Campbell identifies with the genre to conjure supernatural doom from ordinary deprivation. The incidents of squalor and despair clang like omens.

As his work develops Harrison maintains the supernatural aura, but tightens his grip on the ordinary *Running Down* is a real apocalypse, with lightning and mountains rent asunder, but *Egnaro* is elusive, absent, possibly only a state of mind. Lyall is damned and blasted in true Gothic tradition, but Jones is only a minor victim, like us, like everybody else. "God knows why we do these things to ourselves," says Egerton. In the absence of God, M. John Harrison will continue to take the greatest of care to remind us just what it is we are doing.

Editors' Note: Harrison's short stories *Running Down, The Incalling, The Ice Monkey, Egnaro,* and others, are collected together in **The Ice Monkey** (1983)

The Russian Intelligence
(1980)
193mm x 125mm 160pp
ISBN 0 86130 027 0
Cover: Harry Douthwaite

The Bernard Manning Blue Joke Book (1981)
180mm x 108mm 112pp
ISBN 0 450 05346 6

The Legendary Ted Nugent
(1982)
275mm x 178mm 96pp
ISBN 0 7110 0061 2

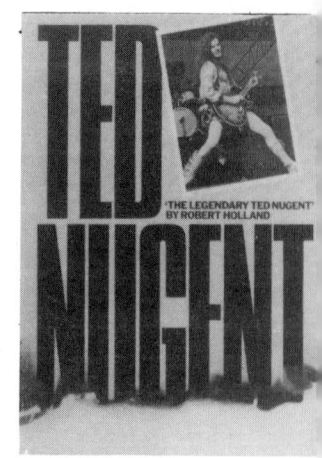

BOOK REVIEWS

Red Queen, White Queen
(1980)
193mm x 125mm 240pp
ISBN 0 86130 020 3
Cover: Michael Heslop

Good Rockin' Tonight
Rough cover artwork for Savoy's proposed printing of Vince Staten's illustrated biography of the King's early years.

Man Pinches Bottom (1980)
193mm x 125mm 184pp
ISBN 0 86130 027 0
Cover: Harry Douthwaite

Chasing Hairy / MICHAEL L. FLEISHER

INTRODUCTION

Michael Fleisher, scriptwriter of the **Sceptre** *and* **Jonah Hex** *comic book series, and author of the definitive reference book on comics, The Encyclopedia of Comic Book Heroes, filed a $2,000,000 lawsuit against* **The Comics Journal**, *the journal's editor, Gary Groth, and Harlan Ellison, for alleged defamatory statements. In an interview with Groth published in the journal (No. 53) in 1980 Ellison actually meant to praise Fleisher's book CHASING HAIRY, but his remarks, ironically perceptive, were held by Fleisher to be damaging.*

At the time of publication of **Savoy Dreams**, *the case remains unresolved, yet it must be said in the favour of both Mr Ellison's party and, in personal terms, of Mr Fleisher himself, that it was on the strength of Mr Ellison's remarks that Chasing Hairy came to the attention of at least one British publisher.*

Sewers, Ayn Rand once wrote, are neither very rich nor very deep. She was speaking of the school of literature that obsesses itelf with human depravity; she preferred to focus on human greatness. Her point was, of course, that depravity is inherently limiting. There is only so much that can be said about the evil men do or the ways in which they ruin their lives. But going in the other direction, the possibilities are limited only by the stars.

The bottom of the sewer, meanwhile, has just been hit. Michael Fleisher, a comic book writer perhaps best known for his disturbingly twisted Spectre stories, has written *Chasing Hairy*, a novel that certainly qualifies for the award of the most repulsive piece of fiction ever written in English.

The cryptic title explains itself once you learn that as used in the book, 'hairy' is a noun and refers to the female genitals. Fleisher also uses every other synonym known to the language — cunt, pussy, all the rest — but a book called *Chasing Cunt* would be difficult to market. And that's what the book is about: the pursuit of the vagina. Where Fleisher's main characters run into trouble is in the fact that hairies aren't available by themselves, but have whole women wrapped around them. Dealing with women as human beings causes his protagonists such difficulty that at the end of the book, as a symbolic protest against "taking shit from one hairy after another," one of the characters pours gasoline on a girl he has picked up somewhere, and sets her on fire. Since she's in a car at the time, the gas tank explodes and literally blows her apart. A book for the entire family, this one.

Chasing Hairy
The third book in Savoy's 'Black Jacket' line.

The story is told from the viewpoint of Simon Weiner, a young Jew from New York City who goes to Chicago to college. It seems quite possible that Simon is largely an autobiographical projection of Fleisher himself, since many of the details in Weiner's life parallel those in Fleisher's. I can only hope that the similarities don't extend beyond relatively minor background material. In other respects, Simon is a latter-day Holden Caulfield and *Chasing Hairy* is *Catcher in the Rye* taken completely over the edge. *Chasing Hairy* follows Simon over a period of years, meandering without any sign of a structured, purposeful plot, and describing the odd people he meets. The story is told in the first person, using a disconcerting run-on sentence pattern that can go for long paragraphs at a time without any periods. It may be Fleisher's attempt to establish the feel, not of formal prose, but of actual conversation or interior monologue. However, a sentence over 350 words long is a little hard to take in one gulp.

In contrast to the other characters, Simon seems relatively sane, but only relatively and it's clear he has a few problems of his own. He is amoral, perfectly willing to lie to get what he wants — though he never seems certain just what it is he does want. He does have aspirations of being a 'serious' writer, and one incident smells strongly to me of being explicitly autobiographical:

> Last semester, I wrote a short story on my own, called *The Dress*, about a teenage boy who has an affair with his mother. I showed it to my adviser, because I was very proud of the story and I hoped that maybe she'd use it to help me get admitted to an advanced creative writing course that freshmen usually aren't allowed to take. And you know what the bitch did? She Xeroxed my story and dropped it in my file in the dean's office, along with a handwritten note to the effect that the content of my story was a clear indication of my urgent need for psychiatric care...

Certainly, many fans were wondering about Fleisher's sanity after his ultraviolent Spectre stories began appearing. Writing is such a personal activity that people often look at a work as a reflection of the writer's state of mind.

Simon's father reads *The Dress* and pronounces it "very, very good. I'm very proud of you. Maybe one day you'll be the writer I always hoped to be but wasn't." Something's wrong here. If you recall your Freudian psychoanalytical theory (not that I believe in it any more than I believe in astrology), males in general supposedly have the Oedipus complex — a frustrated desire to have sex with their mothers. But that's only half of it. The other half is a desire to kill their fathers so they can get at their mothers. For Weiner Senior to read a story like that by his own son and not feel at least a little threatened strikes me as improbable. And for him to *like* it...

The only really sympathetic character in all of *Chasing Hairy* is Simon's Black girlfriend and later wife, Heather (whom he rather crudely describes as a "gorgeous spade chick"). When the marriage breaks up due to Simon's growing indifference to her, not to mention chronic unfaithfulness ("I was onto one strange pussy after another"), Heather is so distraught that she tries to murder him with a steak knife. Failing at that, she commits suicide. It is difficult to make any sense out of Simon's feelings about it.

Simon Weiner is primarily the Watson to the Sherlock of one Ken Pedersen (and something tells me that the phallicism of the names Weiner and Pedersen is not accidental), who is a first class wacko. *Chasing Hairy* is his story, as seen through Simon's eyes. By the time he comes on stage, Pedersen has already been hospitalized for a nervous breakdown sustained after attacking his girlfriend's father with a pair of scissors (though, it must be admitted, not entirely without provocation). Later on in the book he stabs his mother-in-law 28 times with a kitchen knife and as a result spends some time as a guest of the State of Illinois. Much of *Chasing Hairy* is given over to Pedersen's milder but no less crazed antics, his philosophy, his sexual obsessions, and his bizarre humor. Simon is his one friend, whose reaction is usually amusement. Simon regards Pedersen as such an interesting character that he resolves to write a book about him. *Chasing Hairy* seems to be it. (Anyone looking for second-level orders of meaning can take it from there. If Simon is Fleisher, who is Pedersen?) It is Pedersen who sets the girl on fire as his protest against hairies.

Though it's the novel's recurring motif, 'hairy' may not be the right word, since Simon and Pedersen both prefer oral sex. "It's always preferable to stick it in their mouth," Pedersen tells Simon. "Never forget that, because their pussy is filled with corrosive juices that have the chemical power to rot your dick off." Pedersen says it twice: once on page 7, at the beginning, and again on page 239, at the end. It's hard to tell if this is

Pedersen being witty or if Fleisher is actually trying to make a point. It may also be argued that fellatio is a one-way transaction: Simon and Pedersen are so incapable of relating to women as anything else than annoyingly self-willed vessels for their urges that they favour fallatio precisely because it's a quick physical release that requires little effort on their part and they don't have to get personally involved with their partners.

Fleisher is trading on his career as a comic book writer to sell the book through fanzine ads to comics fans. There are some odd references to comics sprinkled through the book, but any comics fan who buys the novel expecting something related to the field is going to be disappointed. The most substantial mention of comics is on page 115, and Fleisher manages to make even his own bread and butter unwholesome:

> I once made friends with a spastic named Carl who worked as a therapist with retarded children and lived in an apartment hotel about two or three blocks from the University of Chicago campus. Inside his room, he had this gigantic collection of comic books, thousands and thousands of them, he kept them all in plastic bags so the dust wouldn't get on them, he had all kinds of comics, every kind you could think of, super-heroes and Donald Duck and even the old scary horror comics. And hung up all around his room, hung up in aluminum picture frames all around the room, were obscene paintings of comic-book heroines, Wonder Woman and Sheena, Queen of the Jungle, he would write letters to his favorite cartoonists commissioning paintings of Batgirl and the Catwoman and dozens more I never heard of, he had one painting of Sheena being fucked by a black panther, and another of Catwoman giving Batman a blowjob.

Chasing Hairy, as I said earlier, is a repulsive novel. It is 240 pages of obscenities, sewer-level sex, and mentally-ill characters. A little of any of that goes a long way, and this is about ten light years worth. But despite its grossness and lack of taste, it is not pornographic if pornography is defined as that which is written to titillate and arouse the reader. The effect is just the opposite: spending a few hours in Fleisher's world is positively numbing. Fleisher isn't writing to pander or push buttons the way a genuine writer of pornography would (although the loving detail lavished on the three-course blowjob at the end — just before the girl's body parts are spattered across the landscape — makes me wonder). God help me, I think he honestly *means it* as a work of serious fiction.

But like his hero who in all ignorance of human feeling wrote a story about incest and couldn't understand why the readers thought he was sick, Fleisher is about to discover that his innermost feelings are 180°

from those of most other people. I don't advocate censorship, but I think I'd feel better about public taste if Fleisher had been forced to publish it himself as a mimeographed booklet and sell it through fanzine ads much as those thin pamphlets about 'catfighting women!' and 'thrill as a beautiful young girl is tortured and beaten to a bloody death!' were marketed through The Buyer's Guide a few years ago.

Chasing Hairy has already acquired a reputation as a psychopathic classic of sorts, chiefly because of the girl's gory death scene. But that's just at the end. For the most part, the book is badly written and stupefyingly dull, a character study of characters who aren't worth studying. If it has a message, it is that the human race is inherently corrupt and driven by irrational and irresistible demonic urges. It is useless to pretend to aspire to anything nobler than the filthy, defecating, copulating anthropoids we are. We are not fit to even try to climb out of the sewer.

One thing bothers me.

Comic books are still read to a great extent by children.

Michael Fleisher writes comic books.

Dwight R. Decker

The Savoy Book / EDS. DAVID BRITTON and MICHAEL BUTTERWORTH

The Savoy Book does not speak about its origins; no editorial or other information is supplied for the reader. It looks like it has arrived from nowhere, an ectoplasm out of the sunset. Such reticence is a pity in some ways because this publication is part of an interesting literary undercurrent.

The Savoy Book is a paperback anthology, professionally made up, of stories, poems, interviews and other unclassifiable texts (boundaries are not important here) interspersed with some intense graphics. Most of this material first came out in Wordworks magazine, a 'new writings quarterly' based in Manchester. (Wordworks itself used to appear under other names — Concentrate, Crucified Toad, Corridor — and can be obtained from the same address as *The Savoy Book*.) This magazine started off during those years in the sixties when *avant garde* writing and science fiction/weird fantasy material came very close together. That was the era of New Worlds magazine, which was a forum for a lot of exciting new writing and exploited science fiction's potential, strangely neglected up until then, for making literary as well as speculative leaps into the dark. After that it was only a step on the time warp from distant suns down into Ladbroke Grove and from the Grove over into 'inner space'.

The Savoy Book (1978)
193mm x 125mm   144pp
ISBN 0 352 33001 5
Cover: Holman Hunt

This books retains some of the flavour of that age back over the hill. It is a mixture of ideas jutting out from reality, explicit sex, and fairly experimental writing that makes use of cut-ups, minimalism and other techniques. The datedness isn't necessarily a bad thing. There is no reason why this tradition should not continue and *The Savoy Book*, despite some over-writing at times, still has more vitality and originality in it than much of today's insipid stuff. This is true of the first piece in the book, a rancid tale by M.J. Harrison, *The Incalling*, which disturbingly evokes a seedy bit of London's dirt-encrusted wen, "the land between Camden and King's Cross Station, with its tottering houses and its old men spitting in corners full of ancient dust each grain of which has begun as dog-dirt or vomit or decayed food...."

Other lively stories include Harlan Ellison's *Eggsucker* (a prequel to his famous story, *A Boy and His Dog*) which takes place in a very nasty near future, and fiction from the disturbed present by Paul Ableman and Heathcote Williams. H. Williams is a fine, natural writer who I sometimes think wastes himself with too much Grand Guignol. The poetry in *The Savoy Book* includes Jay Jeff Jones' often anthologised fierce lament to the San Francisco scene, *Howl Now*, and Richard Kostelanetz's *Milestones in a Life*, which has pretensions to epic minimalism but seems rather slight. *The Savoy Book* also prints an interview with Brian Aldiss. In fact no 'breakthrough fictioneering' collection like this is complete without either Aldiss, Michael Moorcock or J.G. Ballard, that trio of 'new wave' fantasy titans, holding court. All three have travelled on to a greater or lesser extent from the New Worlds landscape but they agitate this book like radioactive fallout. Though Aldiss's interview was done several years ago a lot of his comments still seem valid, as when he talks about science fiction's potential for being subversive.

The graphics in *The Savoy Book* seem closer to mainstream 'weird fantasy' — in both the erotic and speculative senses of the term — than the writing. This may show the influence of David Britton, art editor of Wordworks, who is a pretty weird illustrator himself. The illustrations sometimes are a bit over-indulgent, but as with the text this is often compensated for by their unnerving intensity. James Cawthorn's title illustration for instance is a scene from Moorcock's *The Jewel in the*

Skull. The hero, Dorian Hawkmoon, sails up the river into the city; bridges, ships, buildings are all alive; the evil is literally palpable.

Savoy Books Ltd are a new publisher. This is their second book. (The first was a collection of Moorcock pieces — articles, juvenilia and so on — called *Sojan.*) They have plans to bring out work by other authors, including Harlan Ellison and Henry Treece, as well as more anthologies. Savoy Books are attempting to transfer the approach and layout associated with magazines into the paperback format, which is commercially more viable these days. And *The Savoy Book*, for all its excesses, does work quite successfully presented like this. Opportunities for publishing this kind of experimental borderline writing are getting fewer — witness the troubles Ambit magazine (another publication incubated in the New Worlds hothouse) is now going through, with its Arts Council grant recently cancelled. Such publications are a good breeding ground for new ideas but if starved of funds they too easily become extinct.

Peter Inch

Followers of Michael Moorcock's editorship of the large-size 'new wave' period of New Worlds, which achieved a minor literary revolution and in the process joined Private Eye in being banned by Menzies and W.H. Smith (and copies of which now change hands, I'm told, for £2-£3 apiece) will find the flame still burning in *The Savoy Book* which resembles nothing so much as a book version of that magazine, right down to having many of the same contributors and lacking only Moorcock himself. Fiction, poetry, a long interview with Brian Aldiss (in some ways the most interesting item) together with eighteen pages of absorbingly interesting bizarre artwork (tending to dark erotica and including a simply enthralling two-page frontispiece by James Cawthorn) aroused in me, at any rate, a distinct sense of nostalgia. As with the old New Worlds the content ranges from the solidly professional (as in stories by M.J. Harrison and Harlan Ellison) to the gimmicky and inconsequential, but there's plenty worth reading, particularly *The Incalling*, a breathtaking piece of mood prose in which a dying novelist seeks to save himself by spirit possession in the dingiest parts of north London. Perversely, however, I most of all enjoyed Paul Buck's *The Kiss* and *Kiss Kiss*: what a poetical computer might have turned out if told to produce metaphysical pornography. The images need thinking about, but are rich indeed.

Barrington Bayley

The Golden Strangers, The Great Captains and The Dark Island / HENRY TREECE

The Golden Strangers (1980)
193mm x 125mm   224pp
ISBN 0 86130 018 1
Cover: Michael Heslop

The Great Captains (1980)
193mm x 125mm   256pp
ISBN 0 86130 019 X
Cover: Michael Heslop

The Dark Island (1980)
193mm x 125mm   256pp
ISBN 0 86130 021 1
Cover: Michael Heslop

One of the aims of Manchester's independent paperback imprint Savoy is to give exposure to those neglected British writers who influenced SF's New Wave movement, and here Savoy have acquired the rights to a trinity of Fantasy classics. I read Treece at school, and I suspect Michael Moorcock did too. He writes introductions to each volume, and it is easy to draw parallels between Elric and *The Golden Strangers* set in a 'grey twilight world of the Stone Age when the line between magic and reality was less easily drawn – and more easily crossed than it is today', or to think of Moorcock's Melnibone while reading *Captains* set after the collapse of a great empire – in this instance Rome, or to compare Moorcock's *The Bull and the Spear* with Treece's Celtic mythology in *Island*. Indeed Treece now seems more powerful and relevant than when these books were written, portraying poetry, violence, and the dark undertow of mysticism.

Andrew Darlington

226

Sojan (1977)
193mm x 125mm   160pp
ISBN 0 352 33000 7
Cover: James Cawthorn

Sojan / MICHAEL MOORCOCK

Sojan is a collection whose main feature is a series of stories written while Moorcock was editor of *Tarzan Adventures* in the mid-fifties (when he was in his teens). One or two of them are followed by an apologetic note pointing out that they were initially drafted even earlier. The book is filled out with a few fanzine pieces.

The Sojan stories are quite unreadable, and I think that no one knows this better than Moorcock. Had he not had such a generous and sympathetic editor they might never have reached print. They are prefaced here by a delightful parody of the general tone of Sword and Sorcery fiction called *The Stone Thing*, and this must surely constitute an ironic comment. There are also comments (straightforward ones) on Elric and Jerry Cornelius in the informal non-fiction extracts from fanzines (which appear to be letters rather than articles) and these, for me, were the only items of real interest in the book. Devoted collectors of Moorcockiana will need this book — others beware.

Brian Stableford

The Golden Barge / MICHAEL MOORCOCK

On some timeless morning, Jephraim Tallow — "four feet of wide-mouthed, red-haired, grinning travesty of the human race" — awakens to find that, although his mouth no longer bleeds, he has lost his navel. And as he ponders this transformation, the river on which he lives spawns a beautiful golden barge, coursing steadily onward, apparently without a crew or motive power. It is then that Tallow realizes that "(he) was no longer the integrated and impenetrable thing he had been, for he had not taken the golden barge into account before".

So begins *The Golden Barge*, Michael Moorcock's first novel, completed in 1958 at age 17 and published only now through the auspices of Savoy Books. The manuscript was apparently never submitted to a publisher, and has been printed here with only minor revisions (most evident in the opening chapters). It is recommended reading for historical curiosity

The Golden Barge (1979)
210mm x 148mm   208pp
ISBN 0 86130 002 5

The first full colour 3-D foil cover
Cover Art: Gustave Moreau

value rather than for literary or entertainment merits; yet the novel displays a maturity of thought (if not writing style) sufficient to stand on its own.

The Golden Barge has an allegorical intent more akin to Moorcock's recent work than his early published efforts in the heroic fantasy field. To describe it as a Mervyn Peake version of *Heart of Darkness* would be neither unfair nor unflattering. Jephraim Tallow's story is a quest into the mystery of self, as he leaves his whining, over-protective mother to follow the golden barge down the eternal river, always just out of reach and always leading Tallow into situations of moral ambiguity. It is a journey through landscapes of despair, perhaps even more relevant now than in the 1950s, as Tallow's obsessive pursuit of the barge acts as the catalyst for a wake of emotional and physical destruction — crime, revolution, war, treachery, failures of love, and vindictive rejections of philosophies and ideals. For Jephraim Tallow cannot reconcile his desperate need for individuality with the obligations of humanity; and the golden barge looms ever on the distant horizon.

Those so inclined might have a field day of literary detective work; for example, there is a city named Melibone (sic), a character called Slorm, and several other, less direct references to later novels. And, of course,

Jephraim Tallow has reappeared (if only to meet his end) in *Gloriana*. But as M. John Harrison observes in his adroit introduction, the conclusion of such efforts can only be: "Look here! When he wrote *The Golden Barge*, Moorcock was Moorcock!"

Savoy is to be congratulated for preserving this charming curiosity piece, and its packaging, with Gustave Moreau cover reproductions and James Cawthorn interiors, is superb. Rumour has it, however, that the gold-leaf Moreau reproductions have rendered the book irretrievably unprofitable. I hope not; further scheduled books by Savoy indicate that this publisher is dedicated to preserving some excellent fantasy rarities.

Douglas E. Winter

My Experiences in The Third World War /
MICHAEL MOORCOCK

A character in this book suggests that the Fourth World War was fought in the country of the soul. When asked who won, he replies: "No one. It merely prepared us for this."

If only we were prepared for Michael Moorcock. He is a writer of genius, beholden only to an intensely personal vision that is arresting and original, sometimes enigmatic and often elusive. His name appears on novels that were years in the making — *Gloriana* and the forthcoming *Byzantium Endures* — and those that were written over the space of a week, such as *The Great Rock and Roll Swindle*. In America, he is revered for quickly-written fantasy novels (several of which he despises), while his serious fiction remains misunderstood and undersold. In England, he is gaining recognition as a novelist of major literary importance. His work transcends fantasy and science fiction, and may best be classified as "unclassifiable".

My Experiences in The Third World War is a potpourri of Moorcock's experimentation, spanning the more than twenty years of his writing career. The title refers to an opening trilogy of short stories written in 1978-79: *Going Into Canada, Leaving Pasadena,* and *Crossing Into Cambodia*. They are the compelling eschatological memoirs of a Russian political

My Experiences In The Third World War (1980)
193mm x 125mm   176pp
ISBN 0 86130 037 8
Cover: Michael Heslop

officer as he experiences an "alternative apocalypse" in which America and Russia are allied in a rather ambiguous Armageddon. Moorcock's focus in these stories, however, is not the "Third World War", but the nature of his narrator. The experiment is one of narrative subjectivity, in which the narrator "is revealed not so much by what he says as by what he selects to say to the reader."

The remaining two-thirds of the collection represents vintage Moorcockiana. A previously uncollected Jerry Cornelius story, *The Dodgem Division*, is paired with the rare Cornelius comic strip from International Times (co-authored by Moorcock and M. John Harrison, with graphics by Mal Dean and R. Glyn Jones). *Peace On Earth* is described by Moorcock as his "first adult SF story", originally published in 1958 in a form expanded by Barrington Bayley. It concerns the quest of two spacefarers for an answer to the fathomless ennui caused by their immortality. *The Lovebeast*, written in 1957, is an ironic allegory that bears reading in juxtaposition with Harlan Ellison's *The Beast That Shouted Love at the Heart of the World*. The collection concludes with the 1965 novella, *The Real Life of Mr Newman (Adventures of the Dead Astronaut)*, in which a dead or dying English astronaut returns to an Earth whose cities are changed to reflect the moral subconsciousness of their inhabitants.

All of the stories invoke the moral concern and allegoric intent that has characterized Moorcock's recent novels. To be sure, the earliest works are rough-edged and imbued with a certain naivete, but the collection confirms that time has dimmed neither Moorcock's raging, iconoclastic humanism, nor the continually growing ambition and polish of his prose. Highly recommended.

Douglas E. Winter

Buck Rogers, the comic strip created by Phil Nowlan in 1923, stayed in continuous production until the mid-sixties, around about the time when Jerry Cornelius made his first appearance in New Worlds magazine. Whereas Rogers was a twenty-fifth century adventurer with nineteenth century morals, Cornelius soon showed himself to be an altogether different breed of cartoon character: dissipated, cowardly, and curiously reflective when it came to action. Moorcock encouraged other writers to use Jerry in their stories and placed him at the centre of one of the most important fictional achievements of the seventies: his own *Jerry Cornelius Quartet*.

His new anthology, published by Savoy as an original paperback, contains rare pieces of Corneliana: *The Dodgem Division*, a previously uncollected short story in which Jerry cruises round Brighton pouring vitriolic abuse on the rambling narratives of John Braine and Kingsley

Amis; and *The English Assassin*, one of the most famous Cornelius comic strips with illustrations by Mal Dean.

But the book is something more than just a rehashing of old material. There are three excellent new stories which revolve around the theme of the Third World War. Set against a background of apocalypse, these fictions show Moorcock at his most ironic and most moral, experimenting with the role of the unreliable narrator while questioning the Western stereotype of Soviet aggression.

Richard Rayner

Kiss / ROBERT DUNCAN

This cheap creep-sheet is sold with a back cover anti-female image almost hack and vacuous enough to match the quality of prose inside, where 'biography' of course means all out sycophantic representation of the four, poor, sick Kiss apes. No examination of their dandruff Disneyland. *Ass* is a better title, maybe?

New Musical Express

Kiss (1980)
193mm x 125mm   176pp
ISBN 0 86130 040 8

The Fudge Series / KEN REID

In 1938 a young man called Ken Reid, who lived and still lives in Manchester, approached the Manchester Evening News with a lot of hope, several lay-outs and a rough script for a strip entitled *The Adventures of Fudge the Elf*. To their eternal credit, the Manchester Evening News decided to run it as a regular feature and it was soon to appear every night. With only brief absences, *Fudge the Elf* was to run in the M.E.N. right up to 1962, and even as late as 1974 reprints were still appearing in their pages. Ken Reid's imaginary characters and milieu captured the

Fudge in Bubbleville (1980/81)
335mm x 244mm   136pp +
4pp colour art inserts
ISBN 0 86130 010 6
Cover: Ken Reid

Charles Platt's **Sweet Evil** was
to have been the second book
in Savoy's 'black jacket' erotica
series which commenced with
Samuel Delany's **The Tides of
Lust**.

Fudge and the Dragon
(1980/81)
335mm x 244mm   136pp +
4pp colour art inserts
ISBN 0 86130 007 6
Cover: Ken Reid

hearts of generations of Manchester school-kids, enriching their bleak surroundings with his fantastic and magical images. But a note of caution for Savoy. Tastes change and perhaps *Fudge* and *Speck* will be overlooked in favour of the current *Star Wars* annual or similar dross. Certainly a cover price of £3.50 will weigh heavily against them. I hope not. They are still enchanting books, still as original and fresh today as when they first appeared.

Two books of interest (again from Savoy) are *Tides of Lust* by Samuel R. Delany, and Charles Platt's *The Gas*. Both are highly erotic, some would say pornographic, and are definitely not for the squeamish. *The Gas* has an absorbing, if slightly laboured, introduction by Philip José Farmer who presents a rational argument for the existence of such books and puts the writers intent in context. Some readers may view the dichotomy inherent in publishing books like *Fudge the Elf* and John Warren's *Return from the Wild* alongside *The Gas* and *Tides of Lust* with some puzzlement. Exploitation — if so which? The answer is neither. Britton and Butterworth care deeply about all the books they publish and are quick to defend them, reasonably, against unreasonable attacks. An interesting footnote is that the **Savoy** offices on Deansgate, Manchester, were raided recently by the police, who took away 3000 copies of the *Tides of Lust* and 2000 copies (approx) of *The Gas*. The authorities appear to have made up their minds already; have you?

Jerry Morrell

The Jewel In The Skull 335mm x 244mm (80pp) ISBN 0 86130 006 8 Cover: James Cawthorn

The Jewel in the Skull / _{Adapted by} JAMES CAWTHORN

In the introduction to *Swords of Heaven, Flowers of Hell* Moorcock expresses his distaste for the more baroque American styles of comic book art, and judging by Jim Cawthorn's *Jewel in the Skull,* he may have a point. Cawthorn's book is simultaneously the least elaborate and the most visually effective book discussed here. Instead of focussing on surface decoration, Cawthorn has attempted to give substance to the stone, metal and flesh of this world, and he has succeeded. The problem is, as with Brunner, in the narrative. More than anything else, *Jewel* looks like one of those profusely illustrated 19th century novels with the text removed. This can be traced to inexperience (this being Cawthorn's first extended comic work) or to trying to follow the original story too closely. But when it starts to move, as in the battle scenes, the effect is stunning. Recommended, provided you've read the book first.

Practically all of the artists and writers mentioned here could have pulled it off if given a chance to develop it, and Cawthorn may make it yet. Until that fine day, rest assured that the Champion Eternal shall continue to roam the bookstalls, fighting Chaos, restoring the balance, asking for directions to Tanelorn, and picking up royalty cheques.

Comic's Journal

Jewel in the Skull illustrated by James Cawthorn is truly a really excellent work! Cawthorn has not yet reached his best stride and dimension in his work, but there is a quality here that is most compelling and fascinating. He has gone far beyond any of the existing fantasy interpretations of the cartoon heroics one finds in most book material today. He has reached a point of the unpredictable in his characterisations, his mood, his strange atmosphere and gross, brutal intensity. One almost feels a quality of the bizarre, dark, forbidding quality first shown in certain classic Russian movies (of the war genre) like *Alexander Nevsky* by Eisenstein – the Teutonic Knights, for example, and the battle on the ice. There is something of a crude power here – which disavows the matinee idol posturing in cliché assumptions of most vapid styles of Marvel Comics. I'm impressed by the gargoyle quality of the masks, the helms(?), the garb(?), the uncharacteristic settings. Perhaps if Cawthorn were to experiment with a brush instead of pen work, his drawing would begin to get the *tragic* density his power is searching for. But he has an authentic talent and I'm happy to see this opus – and anticipate the next. He's on the threshold of big things!

Burne Hogarth

No living comic artist has so successfully assimilated the myriad art schools of the 20th Century – German Expressionism, Surrealism, Art Nouveau – and moulded them into a unique composite graphic form, as Burne Hogarth. His **Jungle Tales of Tarzan,** *is THE definitive comic strip. In both this and its prequel,* **Tarzan of the Apes,** *Hogarth proved that the comic form – "the most despised of mediums" – could be transcended. Mr Hogarth, who has always struggled to assert his belief in certain strongly-held values over the cynicism and imaginative poverty to be found in his field (see his essay* **Tarzan: A Myth Man in the Age of the Macromachine,** *elsewhere in this collection), wrote Savoy a long letter, part of which formed the critical review of James Cawthorn's "pictorial fiction" adaptation printed above. His comments are supplied in full.*

Jack Trevor Story Series

Live Now, Pay Later (1980)
193mm x 125mm   144pp
SBN 0 86130 029 7
Cover: Harry Douthwaite

Something For Nothing (1980)
193mm x 125mm   176pp
ISBN 0 86130 031 9
Cover: Harry Douthwaite

The Urban District Lover
(1980)
193mm x 125mm   208pp
ISBN 0 86130 033 5
Cover: Harry Douthwaite

The enterprising Manchester-based publisher, Savoy Books, has embarked on an ambitious plan to bring out in paperback the Collected Edition of Jack Trevor Story's fiction. As his books become available once more (10 are planned at present), it will be possible for a wide audience to appreciate the richness and breadth of Story's writing. Already published are *Man Pinches Bottom*, a comic sixties tale of cartoonist Percy Paynter, caught up in a case of mistaken identity in a murder hunt, and a new book, *Jack On The Box*.

Jack On The Box contains, among many other things, some pertinent comments on the Story style, which one reviewer as long ago as 1955 said was "as difficult to describe as the taste of strawberries." (The book in question was *The Trouble With Harry*, which was filmed by Hitchcock.)

But like many writers whose commercial success is, at best, intermittent, Jack Trevor Story's publishers have been legion and his works are for the most part out of print. Even *Live Now, Pay Later*, the classic tale of the world of the "never-never", of hire purchase debt, has been unavailable for something like a decade.

Albert Argyle is the tallyboy of *Live Now, Pay Later* (1963). Contemporary opinion saw this book and the two which followed − *Something*

For Nothing and *The Urban District Lover* — as part of the Angry Young Man movement.

Like most labels, this one concealed more of the trilogy's qualities than it illuminated, for while Albert's brashness and the verve of Story's writing evoke distant echoes of Joe Lampton and Lucky Jim, both the setting and the author's preoccupation are a long way from John Braine.

Albert Argyle is a sharp lad, educated at secondary modern school and, driven to a kind of frenetic entrepreneurial activity by the shadow of the "Agricultural Tractor Factory (which) was Albert's private salt mine. Physically and spiritually it had loomed over him ever since leaving school."

The Screwrape Lettuce (1980)
193mm x 125mm   176pp
ISBN 0 86130 038 6
Cover: Harry Douthwaite

Jack On The Box (1979)
193mm x 125mm   160pp +
4pp art insert
ISBN 0 86130 025 4

The factory was where his schoolmates clocked in and out, and one of the most powerful moments in *The Urban District Lover* comes when Albert realises that Callender – the ace tallyman and Albert's former employer – has finally succumbed and gone to work there. The personal guile of Callender, and that of Albert, cannot match the power of the clique of local businessmen and councillors that run this Home Counties town, set somewhere between Hertford and Cambridge.

Hitler Needs You
Douthwaite's cover artwork for the first volume in Savoy's proposed printing of the Jack Trevor Story trilogy featuring Horace Spurgeon Fenton.

Albert Argyle dies at the end of *The Urban District Lover* in a perverse tragi-comic accident that is typical of Jack Trevor Story's power of invention. The book also introduces one Horace Spurgeon Fenton, an author who holds hands with Albert's wife Alice behind the shelves in the public library where she works. Horace is the next of Story's central figures, appearing in *I Sit In Hangar Lane*, *One Last Mad Embrace*, and the tender and funny *Hitler Needs You*, set in pre-war Cambridge and the Fens where the author himself grew up.

A comment in *Jack On The Box* provides the appropriate phase for the latest shift in Story's work:

> "Another skin gone, the anonymous third person god-eye re-moved and a disreputable version of the author babbled to his readers. The last door – apart from the trapdoor that's always ahead – opened five years further on in 1970 and 71 and Jack and Maggie came through, first in Paris in the Evening Standard and then on the arts page of The Guardian. Two fictional characters but with skins so thin you could see the blood."

Writing about love – sexual love – is, in the end, the thread that runs through all of Story's work from *Live Now, Pay Later* to *The Screwtape Lettuce*. One of the most powerful scenes in all his novels is the moment when Coral, a new customer, is initiated into the wonders of Callender's H.P. warehouse in *Live Now, Pay Later*.

Undeterred by the smutty jokes of the junior salesmen, her excitement grows as she realises how much she can take away on the never-never. Albert Argyle, apologising for his colleagues, takes her into the office to finalise terms – 33 bob a week. "They laughed together. It was the beginning of a weekly relationship which could last longer than a marriage''. For the customer, Albert's attraction is inseparable from the attraction of the goods he sells.

For all his philandering, Albert too, is given a complex sexual awareness by the author. In *Something For Nothing* (where he gets involved in a trading stamps operation), he is sitting in a pub listening to an all-male group telling dirty jokes:

"They were still schoolboys in a lavatory laughing the fear out of their ignorance of Woman...Soft-seeking, beautiful, heart-rending woman in all her delicate shades of emotion and love and need — and only stinking old man dog for her companion. Somewhere evolution had gone wrong. Woman deserved a special creature for her mate. Albert could well understand Lesbianism; the soft and the softer yet."

A curious paragraph, with its mixture of sentimentality and surprise. The art of Jack Trevor Story lies in such mixtures.

Dave Laing

Up the Boo Aye, Shooting Pookakies /
MIKE HARDING

Popular comedian Mike Harding here offers a delightful gallery of inspired lunacy set firmly in the classic tradition of Edward Lear and Lewis Carroll. A bunch of nonsense poems that will raise many a titter and shudder. The book contains twenty-one poems of varying lengths and scope from the near haiku *Hippoportant Poem*,

"A hippopotamus
Would squash a lot of us
If it sat on us."

to the epic title piece, so titled in memory of the author's Aunty Guy ("Up the Boo Aye..." was her answer following the young Harding's constant "Where are you going?")

Up the Boo Aye, Shooting Pookakies (1980)
228mm x 152mm   64pp
ISBN 0 86130 059 9
Cover: Roger McPhail

There is — as in Lear and Carroll — a macabre surrealism that pervades much of this work especially such pieces as *The Moon, The Grebs* and *Fingummy* and these are generally the better pieces. However, *The Idle Yellow Oozit* which is far from macabre remains my favourite.

McPhail's illustrations are in the main very appropriate, especially

238

those in full colour, of which there are ten. However some of the black and white pieces seem to be almost the work of a different artist.

Still the marriage of picture and poem works extremely well and the book is highly recommended.

Gordon Larkin

Takes a lot to upstage that Mike Harding
(There's many have tried and have flopped)
But a Westhoughton artist called Rodger
McPhail has the cowboy fair topped.
It is all on account of his pictures,
For Rodger's no bodger, you see:
John Hassall, Heath Robbo — you name 'em —
He has the lot off to a tee.
Now his artistry's matched with Mike's poems
And a rare combination they make,
For Harding's a dab hand as wordsmith
(Though he follows in one or two's wake).
Yes, he sometimes has trouble when scansion
Goes off the proverbial rails,
But this book is a treat for all children
And adults, too, will welcome these tales.
They're something to read to their offspring
Without boring themselves, don't you see:
Up the Boo Aye, Shooting Pookakies
(Savoy Books, two pounds fifty pee).

Lancashire Life

The Eye of the Lens / LANGDON JONES

Reading the book, it is not difficult to understand why, as Jones explains in his introduction, publishers have been reluctant to touch it. Nor is it any surprise, considering their eclectic and iconoclastic output, that it is Savoy of Manchester who have finally rectified the omission.

Only one of the stories could be described as instantly likeable, *Symphony no. 6 in C Minor "The Tragic", by Ludwig van Beethoven II.*

Perhaps our musicians would ask why a composer of such talent has remained completely unknown. We can only surmise that his extremely unfortunate name has quite a lot to do with it.

From this understated beginning the piece continues in its recounting of the life and works of a composer who originally preferred law, and used to study at night by candlelight after his hated music lessons. But even in the midst of such hilarity we are in the presence of a writer of very dark vision. The black humour of Beethoven's overshadowed namesake finds its echoes in the black landscapes of *The Garden of Delights*, in which a man visiting his now derelict childhood home slips back in time to make love to his mother, all the while knowing it will be the only full moment of his otherwise empty life. Along similar lines *The Time Machine* describes the final assignation of an adulterous affair through a slowly dislocating sense of time. *The Great*

The Eye Of The Lens (1980)
193mm x 125mm   176pp
ISBN 0 86130 022 X
Cover: Michael Heslop

Clock, the only 'linear' story in the book, portrays a desperately mechanical existence, whilst the title story − in fact three linked pieces − is like a collage of madness, enigma and surrealism.

Even at his most conventional, Jones' aims are not those of more traditional writers. He is quite firmly in the New Worlds 'school', whose only common aim was to extend the possibilities of representing experience, and find more worthy areas of experience to explore. In his introduction he discusses the kind of non-sequential writing which he attempts, making clear that he never intended anything but 'experimental writing', whilst occasionally seeming to display a naive puzzlement that there could be any other way for a serious writer to approach his work.

On the other hand, none of the stories present immense problems of understanding, though they all require work to uncover their depths. *The Great Clock* is laboriously sequential, *Ludwig van Beethoven II* is a pseudo-article, and *The Garden of Delights* employs an old trick of nesting flashbacks, with an ironic twist. *The Time Machine* and *The Eye of the Lens* only present difficulties if viewed in rigidly traditional terms: if approached as something like a collage, or a piece of music, and not made to yield up some kind of 'story', they can reveal a great deal.

Jones' work has a stark power, derived largely from the nature of his themes: sex, madness, and a bleak and isolated view of life and death. *The Eye of the Lens* ought to sell far better than it will, but any reader with more than half a brain will go out now and do his bit to rectify that injustice.

Steve Higgins

240

Who Writes Science Fiction? /
CHARLES PLATT

Who Writes Science Fiction?
(1980)
193mm x 125mm   320pp
ISBN 0 86130 048 3
Cover: Derek Twiss

LORD PLATT

A writer I know told me to read Charles Platt's *Who Writes Science Fiction?* He said to read it with all the lights on. I can afford to care less than this writer, who has a family to support. So I read it with half the lights on. And I was up till 3 a.m. with a depression so total I would have taken my life if it had seemed worth the trouble. I recommend this book to any of you who think you'd like to write. It is horrifying. I wish I hadn't read it. Worse than confirming my darkest thoughts, it told me that my cynical pessimism is as starry-eyed idealism to the reality.

It's a book of interviews, in a chatty tone, with 30 SF writers. A massive polyphonic nightmare on a single theme, the same story over and over, the same structure elaborated with the savage psychotic inventiveness of personal circumstance. One voice: the *genius loci* of science fiction. A litany of pain, loss, defeat, capitulation, futility and silence. Edward Bryant, A.E. van Vogt, Barry Malzberg, E.C. Tubb, Kornbluth, Bradbury, Dick, Aldiss: one voice. One message. This field kills. Soon or late, one way or another, by success, neglect, or both in the wrong seasons, it will break you and leave you in pain so great it cannot be rationalised or repressed.

Some are frank about this; the message is implicit in the rest. What to think of van Vogt's "exhaustion therapy", in which psychic traumas are expunged by mental repetition till the painful groove's worn flat? Or Dick's earnest account of another mind taking him over? (This mind, he says, is with him yet). These are gruesome and vividly real images of the process of survival in SF — and Vogt and Dick do not even realise that they are speaking in metaphor.

241

Stay alive, stay alive, is the message. Not one of these writers says, or can say: I did my work, I enjoyed it, and when it was over I stopped and never looked back. Alfred Bester wants to die with his head in the typewriter. Not all do, but, one way or another, all will. Bryant says he tells students "never to become writers because it will do them no good...discouraging them every chance I get", and it's no joke, friends. No joke to discover that what once seemed the noblest thing in the world is, by any yardstick of reality, about as vital as the marketing of pet rocks.

The situation's not unique to SF; it happens to writers everywhere. But there's an especially grotesque, cloying irony to it here; that men whose stock-in-trade is the future should have their own futures mortgaged so completely. No one's free. The balance of art and commerce is impossible to adjust. These men are professionals. They have all written soullessly, for money only. But they have also, most of them, tried at some time to reach past that. Silverberg believed that "as you grew, and deepened, and enhanced your craft and your art...there would be a reward — and I don't mean a monetary reward." I learned at an earlier age than Silverberg that this is not so; in fact the effort to improve your craft past minimum competence works against you in every way; it is hard work, and no one wants you to do it. I am, perhaps, still a little bitter about this; Silverberg is not. His is the healthier attitude.

How do you deal with this? "Serious" writers sometimes wish they had the audience of science fiction, but the audience is a beast. Ellison: "Who do I think I am? I think I'm the guy who can write a story as good as *Count the Clock That Tells the Time* while sitting on a goddamn pyramid while thousands of people are trying to break my bones." Wilhelm: "People aren't interested in good prose, or beautiful language. I wonder sometimes if it isn't a mistake to nitpick and go after the prose flaws in students, or even in other writers. Maybe it's beside the point." Knight: "They don't want prose that demands close attention....it would actually annoy them if the story were written very carefully, very well, because it would slow them down." Bryant: "Eleven short years, from Clarion to a Nebula. Another overnight success. Oh, Christ."

And after half a dozen interviews, this book, like all the science fiction that sells by the truckload, arouses no feeling at all. It merely stuns by repetition. It numbs. Not even cheery Bradbury can raise a grin. By the time he has praised his own poetry and mentioned his "all new" play of *Fahrenheit 451*, there is no way even to be bitter about what he once had. Nor to feel loss when Silverberg has his "odd moment of guilt" at "walking away" from the gift of *Dying Inside*. Nor upset at Aldiss's "Christ, where else do you go?" Nor anything for Tubb's "I started writing, as most authors do, first through love, and then through money; and I'm afraid, like the majority of authors, the love starts to vanish and the money stays." Nor this, from Malzberg: "I don't think it matters at all, and I think my career in science fiction to have been a mistake at best, a tragedy most likely. But if I had to do it all over again I would do it exactly this way." This is *not* an affirmation.

Confessions, or repressions, cowed or strident, beaten or self-secure, a decade's silence or an awful fetish for productivity....one voice, one story, finally deadening; a bitter, black play for voices all one voice — like the entire literature of SF itself, monstrously, psychotically rich in detail and incident, but every single work a compromise, a failure, a more or less good approximation, each a vantage point from which to view the one imaginary Ideal Science Fiction Book, which itself is unwriteable. Still we strive. One life, one story, refracted through 30 lenses. And mind you, these are the successful authors.

If this is so....if I believe it....then why do *I* write science fiction? Ah, my story is the same. One lucid moment caught my eye. There was a time when the field seemed full of promise. I believe it was on a Wednesday.

Carter Scholz

The Glass Teat /
HARLAN ELLISON

From 1968 to 1970, Ellison was television critic for the Los Angeles Free Press. His columns have been collected in two volumes, *The Glass Teat* and *The Other Glass Teat*.

Most television critics refuse to take the medium too seriously, thereby blunting the force of their own criticism. Ellison, perhaps influenced by his own experience in the medium (as scriptwriter), fully appreciates the importance of television and its effect on the mass culture. For Ellison, television criticism becomes a no-holds-barred war against mediocrity.

The Glass Teat (1978)
210mm x 148mm   224pp
ISBN 0 86130 004 1
Cover: Diane and Leo Dillon

During his two year tenure, Ellison came out in favour of TV violence ("dispensing with violence on TV is tantamount to dropping a Bufferin and thinking it'll cure cancer"), repeatedly supported dissenters, offered some inside info on the hazards of writing for television, and listed the shows providing the best accompaniment for sex on a waterbed. For his efforts, Ellison received the dubious rewards of causing the Free Press building to be bombed and having the original publisher of *The Glass Teat* back out of doing the sequel.

With an ego that knows no bounds, Ellison constantly intrudes into his writings. The reader learns of his career as a writer, his love life, his hatred of cops, the anti-Semitism he encountered as a small boy in Ohio, his involvement in the civil rights and anti-war movement, and just about anything else one might want to know about him. Like most American writers, Ellison is his own favourite character.

Tom McCarthy

David Bowie — Profile / CHRIS CHARLESWORTH

The profuse-photo coffee-table biog doesn't suit all artists, but for Bowie perhaps it's the only way. His career is as much concerned with the shuffling of visuals as it is with sound — a real music for chameleons. He is a whiteness on which images can be layered, no matter from what the source or discipline. So this time-travel of sloughed-off skins and discarded personas is as important as the album sleeves, and perhaps more so than what lies within those sleeves! And although (according to Charlesworth) "the pop process is foreign to his nature — and more importantly, to the nature of his art", Bowie suggests his own alternative strategy: "diversify and become a nuisance everywhere". Such rhetoric, such ambition, is not entirely unprecedented, but the odds against their consummation are prohibitive. The whole shambling turgid beast of Rock is riddled with immovable traditions and sales-enforced inertia; conventions and conservatisms as much related to audience antipathy as to industry structure. It is a mechanism so deeply entrenched, so time-lagged and hide-bound that the smart, fast, sharp ideas (McLaren's cassetisation), or the intelligent subtlety of lyrical/musical innovation are dumped and ignored in favour of the regulation known quantities. Bowie's success is unique in that he's lived his blueprint all ways, through several lives. "As soon as a Rock'n'Roller becomes an archetype" he said in '76, "he's served his purpose."

In this book he's pictured performing with Iggy Pop, and with Bing Crosby — and by shucking off successive archetypes he's been able to cover all the spaces between them, and then go beyond both. Yet he's less the innovator than the catalyst, his use of ideas is as much flirtation as it is thievery and only slightly is it a real distillation of Bowie. Each period

— visual and musical — had its mentors, its alter-ego's, its gurus, and these relationships are as important as the thin white Duke himself. Be it Ronson for the Ziggy phase, be it Fripp or Eno, Lindsay Kemp, De fries, or Lou Reed, be it the intellectually invigorating cultural debris left in the wake of Burroughs, Jean Genet, Brecht, Harlan Ellison, or Andy Warhol, they all played their part, and their roles are all here-in photographically documented. Not that this eclecticism denigrates Bowie. Real artists invent themselves, and none more than this cracked actor! Indeed, insofar as '80s culture is more about mix and match cannibalism than originality then Bowie is the ideal cipher for this planned obsolescence artform. It don't matter if he ever was/is Gay/Bi, it's not important if he ever was/is fascist. The only truth worth recording is that it was the correct gesture/guise for the moment.

David Bowie Profile (1981)
272mm x 206mm   96pp
colour & b/w
ISBN 0 906071 82 8 (h/b)
ISBN 0 906071 67 4 (p/b)

You know Bowie's history of scene-shifting, so it would be tedious to regurgitate it now; suffice it to say that everything you most remember about Bowie is here, in this book — the bio-file from Brixton Mod to the famous 'man's dress' MM cover that launched *Hunky Dory*, then the terminal weirdness of Ziggy/Diamond Dogs, then Bowie kissing Lou Reed, the Nazi salute, the movie stills, the sexually explicit Playboy interview, the Iggy tour, the White Light tour, Berlin, clear through to the *Ashes to Ashes* step by step video. There's also a full appendix of bootlegs and a mass of Bowie trivia for devotees. Charlesworth (former editor of MM as well as Bowie's press officer) writes with authority, despite stating that *Life on Mars* was culled from *Aladdin Sane* (instead of *Hunky Dory*) and that the *Sorrow* original came from the Merseybeats (instead of Rick Derringer's old band the McCoys, although I'd have accepted the U.K. cover by the Merseys). But, nit picking aside, this is the best book on Bowie I've read. And, incidentally, there are publishers' in-references aplenty that the uninformed reader will miss. Why, for example, are so many of Bowie's 'seminal influence' books published by Savoy? And what connection does the Dave Britton cited in the 'Operation Moonbeam' bootleg bust (page 84) have to the manic Savoy Books artist/ director of the same name?

I ain't telling. Buy your own copy....

Hot Press

Gerald Scarfe Review

One major disappointment which accrued from the liquidation of Savoy Books was the failure to follow through and publish the collected work of Gerald Scarfe. Savoy had assembled, with the assistance of Mr Scarfe, 90% of the artwork eventually published in the Thames & Hudson book, **Gerald Scarfe.** *Complications that arose over the exact ownership of Scarfe's work for the Pink Floyd film,* **The Wall,** *at that time precluded use of that cartoon work in the book. This was later resolved and is used in the Thames & Hudson edition. (Editors' note).*

The Gerald Scarfe page from Savoy's 1980 catalogue.

With *Gerald Scarfe* (Thames & Hudson, 1982) we leave these small personal lives for a full-scale attack of the cosmos; even on the front cover the world leaks blood. This is an anthology, a retrospective with many of the most famous images. Wilson returns to lick Johnson's arse, the gorillas stalk the streets of Manhattan, the gossip-column fly settles on the dung heap.

Scarfe was the greatest shocker of the satire boom. Does he still shock? The answer, I think, is sometimes. Many of the monsters he drew are dead or have retired into private life. In some cases his hate and rage seem unproductive, like slapping a corpse. Sometimes his tendency to distort features to the edge of incoherence defeats itself. We have to look to the captions to see who these junk heaps of suppurating spare parts actually represent.

Yet when dealing with universalities — with greed, cruelty, power — he retains his ability to shake us out of complacency. Whenever his brilliant draftsmanship and Swiftian disgust coincide, he approaches genius.

George Melly

Scarfe's 'Aubrey Beardsley' was scheduled to appear in Savoy's proposed collection of Gerald Scarfe's Drawings. It was omitted by Thames & Hudson from their edition.

Charles Platt's **The Gas** is Savoy's most consistently requested title. Despite this fact there have been no reviews for the book. Savoy have found no English distributor bold enough to release the book; no shops, except Savoy's own, have been persuaded to put **The Gas** on their shelves. Potential readers will have to be content with this black-and-white reproduction of Harry Douthwaite's colour cover, and the book's notorious reputation!

Here to Go:
Planet R101 / TERRY WILSON

In the wake of the Final Academy come two oral autobiographies of Burroughs and Gysin, his master-technician and inventor of the 'cut-up'. Both are shaped by the demands, or peculiarities, of the interviewer, and naturally share a common if often divergent history. Cutting between the two (mainly because I got bored by the Bockris book), you'll get versions of the famous Stanley Knife scene — Burroughs finding Gysin improvising new meaning from newspapers he'd inadvertently sliced up, and adapting it to his own work; mirror

Here to Go: Planet R101 (1982, Re/Search Publications. Co-originated by Savoy and the author, **Here to Go: Planet R101** was complete at the time of Savoy Books Ltd's liquidation in 1980. The book was issued subsequently by Re/Search.

staring (the first step in personality-switching); drugs, sex, days in Tangier and Morocco, and brewing up the universe marked out by Control, Hassan i Sabbah, transcendentalism, viruses, the machineries of joy and pain and space travel without rockets.

Thanks to Wilson and, naturally, Gysin, *Here to Go* is worlds apart from Bockris' gatecrashing antics. The style and sensitivity of Wilson's book, aided tremendously by a highly visual design, makes *A Report From the Bunker* look even more like idle tittle-tattle. Burroughs has proclaimed as much loudly, so it's no backlash, but from Wilson's interviews Gysin emerges as the puckish magician to the court at which Burroughs is detained as a rather fractious troubadour. Sly, charming, humorous, arch, dangerous, Gysin is almost a modern-day Rimbaud, alive for the adventure of it all ('Here to Go' being the meaning of it all; mankind is here to go — into space), a volatile force in any media and responsible for more of Burroughs' ideas than just the cut-up. Unlike what one sometimes suspects of the court chronicler, Gysin seems to have lived it, and gloriously so. And where Bockris offers no more than a gossipy gloss, Wilson engages and spars with his subject, has been there and brought back evidence. He may be partisan, but that penetration is necessary. And anyway, isn't the impossibility of ever really knowing the best bit of all, paranoia theory?

John Gill

Led Zeppelin — in the Light /
HOWARD MYLETT & RICHARD BUNTON

Arguably Led Zeppelin took the tired old whore of Rock'n'Roll further, bigger, and grosser than anyone else. After Zep it could only change direction, or descend into parody. By processing the H.M. blueprints laid down by Clapton and Hendrix in the late sixties through the business suss of the early seventies they got so gargantuan that it was impossible to top them; and thus they made punk inevitable.

But behind the platinum albums, the leviathan mega-tours and the dinosaurian demi-god status Plant, Page, Bonham and Jones remain near invisible — or as Mylett prefers, "pure and uncoloured by person-

Led Zeppelin: In The Light
1968-1980 (1981)
272mm x 206mm   96pp
colour & b/w
ISBN 0 906071 65 8

alities". They never *represented* anything like the Stones or Clash. Even Bonham's death, which put the final full stop to their gradual drift into inactivity, was a non-event engendering none of the culture shock of an Ian Curtis, a Sid Vicious, or a Jim Morrison. In fact — once you get past the pre-Zep scuffing period from early session work and failed group projects (Page's first chart role coming as early as the Jet Harris & Tony Meehan No. 1 hit *Diamonds* in '63) to the extinction of the Page-led Yardbirds in '67 — it all comes boringly easy. The album *Led Zeppelin 1* established a pattern of global gross-outs and mass tour schedules that merely got repeated for each subsequent album.

There's probably a lot you could read into the music itself; unlike the real lumpen drones, the Purples and the Sabbaths, Zep never devolved into turgid cliche; they could move better and slicker than any H.M. brand on the market — vis *Whole Lotta Love* or *Rock'n'Roll* — but by incorporating acoustic elements (Sandy Denny, Roy Harper) and electronics (*In The Light*) they were still capable of springing surprises. But Mylett doesn't delve into such esoteric areas as actual critical analysis. He fails to construct any kind of coherent thesis about their development just as he draws no conclusions on their ultimate significance or musical worth. His prose-style is strictly ground-level — vocals are "trance-inducing", drum solos "skull-crushing", gigs are performed "to their fans' delight" — although it must be admitted that he's well-genned on dates, detailed trivia, fax 'n' info, relevant quotes and playing orders.

This lavish large-format coffee table book is essentially hagiographical, a fan's work. The band are always referred to by their first names which is always a dead give-away with its inference of imagined intimacies, and their motivations are never called into question. Evaluation is substituted for sales figures and superlatives. To be a Rock and not to Roll.

But the pictures are regulation flights of streaming matted hair, bare chests, double and triple necked guitars — the stuff of every Rock Tsar legend — reproduced in faithfully clean and glossy print, and the market's staked out in advance. I must confess I never actually *liked* Led Zeppelin, although the Beck/Page sequence in *Blow Up* is one of my favourite movie moments, and the vintage ads in here for New Yardbirds/early Zep playing the Marquee, Klooks Kleek, and Birmingham's Mothers, are vastly collectable. There's probably a good book to be written in here somewhere, but until they get around to writing it this one's not without its moments.

Hot Press

Best known for his informed biographies about Zeppelin, Howard Mylett has turned his hands to a picture book of the band's activities from 1968, to their tragic demise in 1980.

Helped by fellow Zep fanatic Richard Bunton, there's 96 pages of well printed colour and black and white pics of the band together with an authoritative text. I reckon that you won't have seen at least 65 per cent of the material before and they've even managed to beg borrow or steal a rare picture of Plant (love the haircut dear) when he was an unknown singer signed to CBS in 1967.

It's good to see that so far the Zeppelin legend hasn't been exploited by flea bitten hacks, instead it's being written about by people who care.

Record Mirror

The Tides of Lust / SAMUEL DELANY

Fans of science fiction writer Samuel Delany have long been frustrated by the unavailability of his erotic novel *Tides of Lust*, which went out of print soon after its paperback publication in 1973. At last it's obtainable again, for $4.95 from Savoy Books, 279 Deansgate, Manchester, England. The story might be described as a pornographic picaresque; it's a chronicle of various sorts of sex, hetero and homo, but lingering on rather down-&-dirty black/white S/M of a sort what would be automatically labelled racist (among other things) if the author weren't black. The relentless style suggests William Burroughs, or David Meltzer's classic porn trilogy *The Agency*. "Not," as the saying goes, "for the squeamish." OK bedtime reading for the rest of us though.

Ian Young

The Tides Of Lust (1980)
193mm x 125mm   176pp
ISBN 0 86130 016 5

The Brothel in Rosenstrasse /
MICHAEL MOORCOCK

What Michael Moorcock's aged roué Rickhardt von Bek recreates in the lurid account he's compulsively scribbling out against time, pain, the weight of his pen and the chidings of his faithful manservant is a youthful infatuation in fin-de-siécle Mirenburg with under-age Alexandra. Bek's finicky touch for detailed topography matches his energetic particularising of his many rococo sexual bouts — in threes, in groups, homo, hetero and bi, with whips, or drugs, or hat-pins, or whatever else Rosenstrasse Brothel can supply.

The brothel is, Bek fancies, like a nation — hermetic, microcosmic, rampantly selfish. History in Mirenburg comes sexualised, so do European politics: 'Sexuality is the key to personality'. It's a decadent notion that suits old pornopolitans. Is Alexandra, Bek wonders, a mere invention, like the city that's known to no real atlas? Probably. But then Bek can return to woman or city 'whenever I wish', and the more fantasising the encounter, it would appear, the better. Which will make *The Brothel in Rosenstrasse* mightily pleasing to readers with a relish for Moorcock's customarily extravagant courses.

Valentine Cunningham

252

The novel, **The Brothel in Rosenstrasse,** was commissioned originally by Savoy (note the book's dedication) but had to be relinquished to New English Library following the demise of Savoy Books Ltd in 1981.

AC/DC — Hell Ain't No Bad Place to Be / RICHARD BUNTON

Richard Bunton's *AC/DC: Hell Ain't No Bad Place to Be.* is difficult to judge. The author certainly captures the power and ferocity of the band, with plenty of interesting quotes; but he laces his text with obvious admiration for these hard drinkin', livin' and womanisin' men. "The toughest of the tough" is his proud description of the band at one point, and after a couple of chapters all but their most dedicated fans are liable to find his constant glorification of their more unsociable habits rather tedious.

AC/DC's original lead singer, Bon Scott, drank himself to death in 1980; and Bunton does tone down his admiration for this stunt, although the rest of the book makes one think that secretly he regards Scott's 'sordid' death as all part of the attraction of the band's wild image. It might not seem fair to judge the biography of a rock group on their own image of themselves; but when that image is presented as something to be admired, then it's impossible to divorce the subject from its treatment. AC/DC fans will no doubt find what they want here, which is obviously the reason for the book in the first place.

Record Collector

Before Men at Work, Icehouse, and Birth-Party, was AC/DC. Australia's 'revenge of the terrible schoolboys...'. But wait — having a high regard for HOT PRESS readers' intelligence — are they expected to take all this enfant terrible stuff seriously? I ask Bunton (a writer of sound credibility) if his book is on the level, or just to pay the bills? "It started out as a strict commercial commission" he admits, "but the more I got into it, the more I appreciated AC/DC, until now I consider them the logical successors to Led Zeppelin". And persevering on such recommendation, there are bits to sink hooks into memorabilia freaks. Of the six Glasgow born Young brothers who migrated Down-under in 1963, George founded the Easybeats (for the classic 60's pin-up *Friday on my Mind*), John Paul charted some years later with the tedious

AC/DC: Hell Ain't No Bad Place to Be (1982)
275mm x 178mm   96pp
colour & b/w
ISBN 0 7119 0061 2

smoocheroonie *Love is in the Air*, while Malcolm's guitar twinned with Angus' school-uniform, shorts and satchel founded AC/DC. From there it's a short step to conceding that *For those about to Rock* was a ludicrously enjoyable single, and if '1812' cannons are O.K. then why not Angus' juves-drag? 'Dennis the Menace with an electric dildo!' — mini-Pops he ain't! And flicking through this lavish profusely illustrated biog it becomes clear that this is Bunton's argument. The best Rock has always been absurd, irreverent, exaggerated, irresponsible and over-the-top. If it's subversive it's only so in the sense that it uncages lascivious and monstrous energies that polite conformity does its best to screw down tight. "There is a compelling sexual fascination about the absurdity of corrupt innocence" he offers as token psychology. It's a recent journalistic conceit to expect significant sociological messages in Rock. So, I guess, no, we're not expected to take it seriously, because being serious ain't the point. With that compass bearing Bunton dons school-cap and hammerdown prose for some 90 pages of breathless narrative snaring the high-voltage saga to rights; indoctrinates the text with lots of unpretty paedophile pics of gurning, mooning, sweating, guitar-hero, nasty retarded school-kid antics; and then tamps it down with full Discography (including bootlegs). I mean, I'd still take ten minutes of Cabaret Voltaire, Box, or U.V. Pop over every grotesquerie in their Heavy Metal catalogue, but that's probably just a journalistic conceit. And, as a cautionary note, there's still two more Young brothers to go...!

Hot Press

The Legendary Ted Nugent / ROBERT HOLLAND

The first mistake, according to Holland, is to file Nugent Heavy Metal. To see him in context he should be relocated to the more respectable pantheon of Bo Diddley, Little Richard, the Stones, Hendrix, and Iggy Pop. To Holland he is that very special artist, that very rare phenomenon, a true Rock 'n' Roll star. An original, a one-off, a gargantuan elemental force that refuses to be bound by the vagaries of fashion. To hang an academic critique on him is as pointless as trying to "open an umbrella in the face of a 90 mph gale". Holland's vision of Nugent moves into Guy Peelaert's *Rock Dreams* territory where personalities are exaggerations. A screen onto which the collective wills of journalists, publicists, and fans, project their most lurid fantasies. How far or how accurately these fantasies actually reflect any real qualities in the music is open to question. Everything about Nugent is blown up to epic proportions — from his sexual rapaciousness and his appetite for raw meat killed by his own hand, to the raucous decibel-level intensity of his amplification. A volume as huge as his ego. "I am," he boasts, "totally the product of my own desires." As if Rock can only be defined by mock-heroic excess, can only be experienced through the senses, must totally by-pass reason.

"If you can't take a bite out of it — it doesn't exist."

Neither Nugent nor Holland see any possibility of evolution beyond that crude caricature. They see the fault with New Wave as "too many of the Punk Rockers THINK about what they're doing." To declare "No more heroes" is sacrilege. Rock 'n' Roll to Nugent/Holland IS heroes. They allow no place for subtlety, objectivity, analysis, or lyricism. The only permitted language is the no-quarter, over-the-top speed-freak hyperbole. Yet Holland states his case remarkably well, albeit in twelve foot neon lettering. He commandeers allusions from every-which-where.

Nugent represents himself as an all-purpose, larger-than-life traditional electronic frontiersman hero. He owes a debt too, to Edgar Rice Burroughs' Tarzan.

Not that this 'tooth fang and claw' legend is without substance, far from it. Nugent lives wide screen. He's played in bands since age ten, and stories are legion; urinating over a Nun, jacking-off in a prison cell, massacreing elk with bow and arrow, hanging out in the Motor City Madness of the Detroit hard-Rock bands MC5, Stooges, Mitch Ryder and Shadow of Knight. He played support for Beau Brummell's and the Supremes as part of the psychedelic Amboy Dukes (promoting their hit *Journey To The Centre Of The Mind*); and made his come-back solo set with Zappa producing.

"If God played Rock guitar" he brags, "he'd come a poor second to me." In the meantime, Holland (an unlikely-sounding pseudonym that could probably be substituted by the name of any other minor European state) is currently reported to be working on a biography of another bombastic Rock eccentric — P.J. Proby. I can't wait.

Soundmaker

The reader's wife of American mega metal, Caliban with an electric guitar, John the Baptist for an onslaught of saliva, grit and guts.

Well look at the competition — trussed up, padded out bilge like Aerosmith, milksops like Foreigner and Boston or tarty old windbags like Blue Oyster Cult. It's a huge stinking connection of flimsy myth and plain old inert gullibility that makes these bands successful.

In comparison Ted Nugent — where the comic meets the savage — just requires a sense of the ridiculous. Jesus, it's only in such a world that you could even think of calling this collection of growls stabs and snarls healthy!!?

Ted Nugent is the pagan's reply to the cruddy rock process. Pretentious he's not, not for Ted the usual 'if you can't convince them — confuse' psychorama of Moorcock, black magic and bad sex. He plays it straight down the line, a sabre toothed looney from the backwoods whose songs and onstage persona is an exercise in barbaric primitivism.

So if you've heard Ted and you want all his famous opuses on one record — the great *Cat Scratch Fever, Wango Tango, Paralysed* and *Dog Eat Dog et al* then *The Legendary Ted Nugent* is just for you.

If you've heard Ted Nugent and you don't like him then don't buy *Ted Nugent* coz you'll hate it.

And if you've never heard Ted Nugent just consider yourself very lucky.

Gavin Martin

The Legendary Ted Nugent
(1982)
275mm x 178mm   96pp
ISBN 0 7110 0061 2
The published jacket of the Ted Nugent book differs significantly from the original Savoy design (reproduced here). Savoy were informed by Music Sales supremo Bob Wise that the original was too far over the top for wholesale distributors W.H. Smith. The final design, by Omnibus Press, like all their Rock jacket designs, achieved the required condition of muzak.

The published jacket of the Ted Nugent book differs significantly from the original Savoy design (reproduced here). Savoy were informed by music sales supremo Bob Wise that the original was too far over the top for wholesale distributors W.H. Smith. The final design by Omnibus Press, like all their Rock jacket designs, achieved the required condition of muzak.

I am the Greatest says Johnny Angelo / NIK COHN

There are only ten copies of the Savoy edition of *Johnny Angelo* in print. Only ten 'advance printer's' samples survived the company's 'reorganisation' early in 1981. The intended run was printed-up, never jacketed, and was subsequently pulped.

The recipients of this publishing rarity were Savoy themselves, Michael Moorcock, Harlan Ellison, Sonny Mehta (head of Picador Books), Nick Webb (Savoy editor at N.E.L.), Nik Cohn, and, of course, P.J. Proby — more of Proby later.

I am Still the Greatest Says Johnny Angelo (1981)
193mm x 125mm   176pp
ISBN 0 86130 041 6
Cover: David Britton

I purloined Savoy's file copy when I signed contracts with them to write *The Legendary Ted Nugent.* When I finally sat down to structure the book, amidst my amassed Nugentalia and genre Rock bibles by such luminaries as Nick Kent, Greil Marcus, Lester Bangs, Robert Palmer, Nick Tosches, I read and was surprised just how contemporary Cohn's novel remained. In many ways it is still the perfect blueprint Rock novel.

Cohn writes in such a rich, strange prose style that its responses linger long after the book's initial impact. His opulent, staccato sentences add weight to the edginess and near hysteria of Johnny Angelo, the novel's central character. And in Angelo, Rock singer and shaman, we have a genuine archetype. He is no cheap pulp writer's empty creation. He is as genuinely idiosyncratic as P.J. Proby, Angelo's counterpart in real life. Cohn's affection and not misplaced admiration for the disgraced 60s star is amplified throughout the book.

Like Proby, Angelo experiences life as a highly charged fantasy. Certainly immoral, he acts on the premise that his art justifies any excess going down. Large chunks of real Proby monologues scatter hedonistically throughout the novel. The writer leaves no doubt that Angelo is a novel of morals. He approves Angelo's belief that his excessive desires, ultimately sane, should quite rightly take precedence over society's restrictions.

Perhaps, not surprisingly, his unhinged life style leads to his eventual martyrdom. With his death he achieves more than his already secured legendary status — he becomes a true Rock icon. Quite simply, he is

more talented, more driven. He deserves to be regarded as a notch above
— in fact, *far, far* above.

"By the end of the month, there was truly a small army, 10,000 strong, all eager to perish for Johnny Angelo.

"They were hardly what he'd had in mind. Somehow he'd imagined that he would collect an elite, commandos and gurkhas and American marines, men that had fought in five continents. Therefore he was disconcerted to find that the desert was full of mutants, of mongols and morons, of the blind and deaf and dumb, the sexually perverted, the criminally insane, and thousands of midget schoolgirls, hardly past puberty.

"By any standards, these were the scrapings, strictly the flotsam and jetsam of society: 'Human garbage,' said Johnny Angelo. 'I might have known'."

Surely, this was the vinegary stuff of P.J. Proby's dreams? Angelo's righteous arrogance was born of the 60s. His somewhat tongue-in-cheek immoral displays earn the full approval of the young Nik Cohn, who writes the book at an exhausting intensity. In the process Cohn invents the first quintessential electric *fin-de-siècle* Rock novel, and probably the best.

Cohn's fictional hybrid of Elvis, Little Richard and P.J. Proby deserved to be kept in print indefinitely. Interestingly, Savoy were scheduled to publish not one but *two* versions of the novel. The first version, carrying the book's correct title, is a reprinting of the powerful original Secker & Warburg edition. The second version, to have carried the slightly but significantly different title, *I am Still the Greatest Says Johnny Angelo*, and to have appeared on the stands more or less simultaneously, was to have been a reprint of Cohn's *revised*, more formal, less powerful 1970 Penguin edition. This, because Savoy felt that both versions together told the full story of Johnny Angelo.

David Bowie ripped-off 'Angelo' for Ziggy Stardust, and it is a great pity that the book will now be denied the larger audience that Savoy's editions could have brought. Not that Cohn needs the money. *Saturday Night Fever* made him a millionaire.

Robert Holland

To The Gang at Sardy's

All My Jury Best

Post Time!

J. Plossy

Jim